JUDGMENT
THE CHOHISH WARS

JUDGMENT

THE CHOHISH WARS

G.J. MOSES

Copyright © 2023 by G. J. Moses

All rights reserved. No part of this publication may be reproduced, distributed, or transmitted in any form or by any means, including photocopying, recording, or other electronic or mechanical methods, without the prior written permission of the publisher, except in the case of brief quotations embodied in critical reviews and specific other noncommercial uses permitted by copyright law.

ISBN 978-1-7341152-4-6 (Digital)
ISBN 978-1-7341152-5-3 (Paperback)

10 9 8 7 6 5 4 3 2 1
First Edition 2023

Cover image and design by Damonza.com

"The seeds of war are insidious. The desire for power is complex and sometimes hard to recognize. They are not usually understood or seen until after hostile actions start. A robust military can pause even the most ambitious antagonist."

Signed:
General Thalo Daneb
Year 4189

PROLOGUE

THE DESTROYER SLID silently through space. Drifting past a pair of defense batteries, they changed direction to allow passage past another two. Then, passing through the middle, the destroyer identified one directly in their path.

"Helm, take us to port, slowly. Keep as much distance as you can away from that battery. They would have detected us if we had been going faster. Slow and easy."

"Aye, Captain will do."

As the destroyer passed the defense battery, two more were quickly identified. The placement of these batteries forced them away from their goal.

Turning away from the pair of batteries, the destroyer continued cautiously. The Captain searched for some path through the maze; turning around would be a disaster.

"Guard ships Captain, a pair to starboard, one at fifteen degrees, another at fifty-two degrees. Just identified another, one at seventy-four degrees below us."

Continuing forward, the destroyer barely moved as it slowly slid past the guard ships. Then, turning to port, they resumed heading toward the station, even slower than before.

Going a short distance, they had to stop while a battleship flew past.

"Follow that battleship; they are headed in the right direction," ordered the Captain. "Slowly, we do not want to get too close."

They followed the battleship for over an hour before it separated when it turned in the wrong direction. They had only made it a short way before they came upon another defense battery.

"We will never make it in the time required if we keep going around in circles. We will have to up the risk," stated the Captain. "Helm, change direction; head straight for the station slowly. Scanner, see if you can find any drifting rock we can piggyback on."

"Captain, an asteroid is floating in the right direction. It will not get us the whole way, only about half."

"Helm, hide us if you please."

Increasing speed, the destroyer slid close to the identified asteroid. With bated breath, they slipped sideways until they trailed the asteroid. The destroyer rocked from the slight gravity. Occasionally, small debris would impact the ship's hull, ringing throughout. Shields were set low to minimize detection.

The destroyer turned off when the asteroid started heading in the wrong direction.

Their target was in sight. The station loomed large ahead. Just one more set of defense stations to get past. Hope rose just before the alarms sounded.

"Captain, energy readings straight ahead. Four battleships are powering up, shields and energy weapons coming online," reported the sensor technician.

"Damn, where did they come from?" muttered the Captain. "Get us the hell out of here, Helm. Bring up the shields. Let's give them a race for their money. Head for the station at full speed."

The destroyer increased speed to swing past the battleships heading directly towards the station, and the battleships gave chase.

Nearing the station, the destroyer was almost in position to deliver its package when more defense batteries came online simultaneously, along with more guard ships.

"Surrender, or die!" came clearly through the speakers.

Sulking, Captain Meghan Kennedy stared at Captain Zeke Kinsley, who wore a silly smile. They were sitting in a conference room on a Royal Galactic Navy Battlecruiser.

In the room, there were three admirals present. Admiral Katinka Chadsey, Rear Admiral Nkosana Okeke of the RGN, and Admiral Timeti representing the Sorath.

With them were Captain Jeanne de Clisson, Captain Lance Henry, Commander Anne Dieu-Le-Veut, Lieutenant Commander Masson Dieu-Le-Veut, Major Bridgette Okeke, Sergeant Jan de Bouff, Science Officer Hawke, and Lieutenant Commander William Farren.

"Surrender, or die? Really?" asked Anne. "Who came up with that? That was humiliating."

"Don't blame me. Jeanne is your sister. I quit trying to get her to stop that crap. She had too much fun planning and executing it, then laughed about it for weeks afterward. And it's not like your crew did not enjoy it, especially when they knew it was her voice saying it," answered Zeke.

"Was she hiding on one of the guard ships?" queried Meghan.

"No, she passed out a recording to all defense batteries and guard ships as they were built if they detected anything. Told the Kolqux that it would insult the honor of the Chohish. They adore her, so they installed it without question," explained Zeke. "As I said, she's your sister."

"That does not resolve our problem. Captain Kennedy, we appreciate you running a test for us. Still, the station we need to capture intact has many more defenses than the one here," lamented Katinka.

"When did the Kolqux detect me?" asked Meghan. "That may help us determine how to get past the Chohish since they have the same equipment."

The looks she got from Jeanne let her know she would not like the answer.

"Actually, they identified your ship after the second defensive battery. The crew on the third battery notified us. We asked the battery to let you pass to see how many of the batteries would know you were out there."

"You suck. Do you know that?" Meghan angrily retorted.

"Actually, it was good news as the Kolqux are learning fast. The problem is a destroyer is too large to get through," acknowledged Katinka. "But anything much smaller does not have the distance."

"How many of your special units do you need to deliver?" asked Zeke.

"Based on the station size, at least three or four would be optimum. Better add a few more for redundancy," specified Bridgette.

"Any special skills needed for operating the units?" queried Zeke.

"None besides turning them on. The units run by themselves." Holding her hand up to pause the following question from Zeke, Bridgette went on. "But they will only run for three to four hours. If the database cannot be secured by then, the Chohish would have destroyed it manually."

"And the station is expected to have top-of-the-line defenses. If we do not get that database, any navigation database we capture in that system will only take us back to where they came from recently. So we need that database to head straight to their home worlds; otherwise, we could end up going in a large circle," worried Katinka.

"Uh oh, he has that damn smile," stated Jeanne. "He is coming up with some crazy plan again."

"What if we do this? We let the Chohish invite us in..." A smiling Zeke laid out a plan.

UV'EI

THE WIND BLEW softly with a chill in the air, leaves dropping, carpeting the ground. The pink color of the leaves contrasted with the purple trunks and brown bushes. The rustle of a small animal could be heard rustling through the underbrush.

The silence was broken by the sound of a branch breaking as two small figures moved into the area. Wheezing, not accustomed to moving through a forest, Uv'ei paused momentarily to catch his breath. Squatting, waiting for his brother to catch up, Uv'ei wondered if he could complete the task.

Uv'ei, and his brother Uv'ek, were dressed in the new armor provided by Khaleesi. The armor automatically blended with the foliage he stood in. The RGN supply ships had replicators producing new units to meet the Kolqux size specifications.

Stepping over a log that had fallen across his path, Hu'de gripped his rifle tighter, afraid he would lose it. Moving meticulously, he glanced down at his feet to see where to place his foot next. Bending, he kneeled as he moved to the top of the hill. Carefully, he raised his head until he could peep over.

What he saw was what he expected. There was a standard four-lane highway that ran north to south. Further north, he could see a junction with a two-lane road that ran east to west. Small trees lined the street, with bushes more prevalent. There was an old feel to it; parts were in disrepair.

Traffic was sparse, consisting primarily of trucks carrying produce. The three-wheeled electric trucks ran on a hybrid rubber type of wheel that bounced when it hit pits in the road.

But he was not here to sightsee; his goal was to get to the small rundown restaurant near the junction. From there, he was only several miles from reaching his final destination. So far, he had not seen the Marines he was trying to avoid.

Waiting until no truck was visible, Uv'ei crawled until he crested the hill with Uv'ek slightly behind him.

Stopping to remove several small sticks, Uv'ei looked around for a path. Off to the right, he saw what looked like an animal trail. Indicating the track to Uv'ek with his hands, he rose up where he ran swiftly down the path on the balls of his feet, making every effort to keep the noise down.

The trail went off in the wrong direction as it neared the highway. Crouching down, Uv'ei looked around carefully. Not seeing any motor vehicles or foot traffic on the road, he ran across before dropping down.

Uv'ek crouched on the other side and waited for Uv'ei to check for any change. Seeing none, Uv'ei signaled Uv'ek. Getting the wave to come across, Uv'ek jumped up, running as quickly as he could. Dropping down next to Uv'ei, Uv'ek grinned at his brother while sweat ran down his face.

Close to the restaurant, Uv'ei raised up to take a step to the right. Then, using a method Khaleesi taught him, Uv'ei started walking side to side, stepping to the right with his left foot and then to the right with his left foot. They had been instructed this helped with keeping their balance.

Turning to check on Uv'ek, he watched him repeat the same

process of walking. Then, checking his path to the front door, Uv'ei watched where he was going, not at his feet.

Reaching the door, Uv'ei scrutinized the handle. There were no windows; the only option for him to see what was inside was to open the door to see what awaited him and Uv'ek.

Slowly, ever so slowly, Uv'ei started turning the rusty doorknob. He could hear a slight noise but hoped it was not loud enough to alarm anyone inside. The sound from inside indicated children was present.

Pushing the door open just enough to get a peek inside, he saw Khaleesi sitting with several of her officers at a table facing the door. Her finger gesturing for Uv'ei to come inside was disappointing. He had hoped he could avoid detection.

Straightening, he opened the door wide before striding inside. "Come on, Uv'ek, Khaleesi knows we are here." The cursing behind him matched what he felt.

Looking around, he saw several families and individuals sitting alone, scattered around the room. All were watching him and the humans with hero worship. The kids were pointing at them and jabbering excitedly.

Stomping in, Uv'ei sat down at one of the available chairs. His only satisfaction was that the chairs were made for Kolqux, hence small with no sides. So Khaleesi and her officers might as well have skipped the chairs and sat on the floor.

"What are you frowning at, Uv'ei? You did great. You two have only been training for three months," complemented Khaleesi. "And that is when you can get free of your government duties."

Before Uv'ei could answer, a child came up shyly to Khaleesi. "Are you her?" she asked.

The child had great big eyes opened in wonderment, shaking slightly with excitement. The sound of her happiness when

Khaleesi lifted her to put her on her lap made her officers' stoic expressions soften.

"Well, that depends on who '*her*' is, young lady. I am just a marine doing my job," Khaleesi said as she poked the child playfully in the nose. "What is your name?"

"I am Gu'eb. I was named after my grandmother. She died to save my mother," the little girl stated while playing with a small magnetic medal on Khaleesi's armor.

Taking the medal off, Khaleesi asked, "You like this?" At this point, Khaleesi handed it to Gu'eb. "You keep it; I have no use for it."

The look Uv'ei gave was incredulous. "You cannot give her that. That is the medal we gave you; we had a lot of trouble creating that."

Ruffling the girl's head, who laughed as she played with the medal, Khaleesi whispered, "This young lady will have much more use for it than I will."

The little girl leaned in to kiss Khaleesi before she jumped off her lap, before running back to her parents in excitement, showing off the medal.

"So what's the problem, Uv'ei? You seem overly wrought with impatience," said Khaleesi, leaning back in her chair before crossing her feet.

Wringing his hands, he looks at the woman who had been in a medical pod fighting for her life just a short time past, injuries she obtained while fighting to save his people. "I am anxious to go. There are Kolqux suffering," he answered.

"Going in before you or your people are ready will not do them any favors. What we are going to attempt is fraught with pitfalls." Khaleesi raised herself from the chair so quickly that it surprised Uv'ei and Uv'ek.

"We cannot move until the Navy figures out how to recover

that database in that station and your people are trained. Otherwise, lives will be lost, unknown how many." With her officers now beside her, Khaleesi's voice became all stony and professional. "You did commendably until you reached here. Next time, resist the impulse to go into the establishment."

"You set the destination to go past this place on purpose, didn't you?' asked Uv'ek.

The smile answered his question. "We have been here since you started out. Remember, next time, your goal is to reach the target, not stop and explore."

"We were thirsty; we knew the area and had been to this restaurant before. Damn it, you did do it on purpose," complained Uv'ek.

Following the marines, the two joined them in entering the transport that had arrived while they had been inside. The transport arrival so quickly confirmed that Khaleesi knew where they were before they opened the door.

As they flew, Uv'ei looked at Khaleesi sitting across from him. It brought back memories of when she finally emerged from the medical pod.

Working with a nurse, the human doctor stood by as the pod opened. They ran diagnostics on her health, reading the results for several minutes before they started to assist her in getting out.

Seeing her hands rise to grab the sides brought tears of happiness to his eyes. Then, when her head finally rose above the pod, he was about to scream in joy until he saw the pain in her face. When she glanced at him, seeing the blood-filled eyes squinting in pain tore at his heart. Uv'ei could not stop his hand from covering his mouth when she opened her mouth in a silent scream. It had been filled with blood.

Somehow, he had thought when the medical pod said she was good enough to survive on her own, she would come out fully healed. That was far from the truth. The nurse told him they had to revive her early so she did not lose too much muscle mass. That was standard procedure for Marines.

It took another week of the nano's repairing her injuries before they let her out of the infirmary. Yet, she still found a way to exercise against the doctor's orders. And once they did, she wasted no time for a complete workout. On the first day out, Khaleesi started a brutal physical regime to recover muscle loss. The medical staff insisted she put it off until the nano's finished their work, but she scoffed at them. "War doesn't wait because you want it to," was her response to their protests.

Uv'ei would visit for several hours every day, where he would join in her workout. Not that he could mirror her intensity, but she had given him a routine designed for a Kolqux. It was tough initially; he had never worked on building his muscles or endurance. Never even considered it; what for?

Within a week, Uv'ek had joined him. Every time they thought it was too much, seeing the pain on Khaleesi's face, they were guilted into continuing. Now, months later, they looked and felt totally different. And as Uv'ek said, their wives' admiration for their appearance was a nice bonus.

After Khaleesi had been released a month, they told him about the images and data on the world controlled by the Chohish. He was horrified by what he saw. Both Kolqux and Endaens are being treated harshly by other Kolqux and Endaens. He would never have visualized such a situation.

Admiral Chadsey patiently explained that the data obtained suggested the Chohish had engineered this. Those living on this planet had been put there over a thousand years ago. At that time, the Chohish had elevated certain Kolqux and Endaens to rule over their counterparts. The Chohish remained the overall ruler.

The Admiral had Bridgette explain how her people had hacked into their database to get all the information being shared. Several of the shielded probes Zeke's foray had released were hidden in one of the moon's orbits.

The situation on the planet did not improve as time progressed. The Kolqux and Endaen leaders ruled with an iron fist just as harshly as the Chohish had on Sobolara. The images Uv'ei, Uv'ek, and Vopengi were viewing horrified them to know their own race was responsible for the devastation shown.

Uv'ei and Vopengi wanted to attack immediately. The admirals then proceeded to bring them back down to reality. They needed to be able to capture that database so they could shorten the war.

Invading the planet would not be easy; this would require more planning and manpower. The RGN and Sorath could not be used on the ground as that would stiffen resistance. It would require Kolqux.

Hence, why Uv'ei and Uv'ek were out in the forest. While the RGN trained many thousands of Kolqux, Khaleesi trained these two. When Uv'ei heard what it would take, he requested to lead his people. And if he had to go, he wanted the marine he considered the best to train him.

Stepping off the shuttle when it landed, Uv'ei felt the heat as it hit him with a vengeance. The cement tarmac radiated the heat like an oven.

Months ago, he would have staggered under the heat wearing heavy armor; now, he was barely fazed. He followed Khaleesi as they headed for the firing range. Today, they were scheduled to run through another obstacle course with the enemy and civilian 4D popups.

The first time through, Uv'ek had killed more civilians than enemy combatants. Uv'ek had become seriously depressed as he never believed he could differentiate between the two.

Then Khaleesi had one of her officers, Sergeant Emanuele Egnatius, run through the course to show them how to do it. Emanuele ran, rolled, crawled, hid, all types of movement with barely a pause while shooting regularly.

What was different now, some of the enemies were dressed the same as the civilians. Even so, Emanuele did not shoot any civilians. Uv'ek was even more depressed at the time.

It took Khaleesi sitting both down and explaining how any war was not without risk to civilians. Civilians would die; no matter how much they trained, mistakes would happen. Then, turning to point at Emanuele, she explained what he was looking for. A weapon, not what they were wearing. The helmets they would start wearing would assist with that. But first, they needed to learn what to look for and how to make the identification without assistance. You never knew when computer assistance would not be available.

Learning took a lot of practice. Every day, they spent several hours running course after course, which was always different. They still shot civilian targets, but now at a one-digit percentage. Confidence was soaring. Then they were given helmets to wear.

It took a bit to get accustomed to wearing it. It was heavy while looking through a faceplate overlayed with images and information. They went through training on what the helmet could provide and how to use it for several days before they were sent through an obstacle course.

Uv'ek and Uv'ei were sent in as a pair through a course prepared by Khaleesi herself. The first 4D enemy combatants wore women's clothes and carried a baby. The helmet displayed a red circle around a muzzle hidden in the baby blankets. Before the combatants could fire, Uv'ek and Uv'ei took them out.

After eliminating these two, they came next to an apartment building. Uv'ek was about to continue when his helmet put a red circle around a window in shadow. Then, a flashing red 'energy reading' appeared on his screen.

Lining up the window, Uv'ek put a shot through, after which a figure holding a shoulder-fired weapon rushed to the window. With his gun already centered, Uv'ek pulled the trigger to blast the figure.

While Uv'ek had been caring for this assailant, Uv'ei raced on. Sliding underneath a building overhang, Uv'ei came upon half a dozen armed military rushing toward him. Then, pulling a grenade from his vest, Uv'ei threw it toward the group. Uv'ei fired his plasma rifle at the approaching group without waiting for it to reach its destination.

Using the helmet designators, he took out the individual identified as the most immediate danger. Then the grenade exploded, causing mayhem. Uv'ei was able to eliminate the survivors before they could regroup.

This went on without stopping for another hour. When it ended, both were exhausted and collapsed in front of Khaleesi.

Expecting some time to get a rest, Khaleesi had them get up before she sent them through another course. How they finished, neither of them knew nor cared. Instead, they slumped against a wall with their eyes open wide in exhaustion, feeling sweat pours down their faces. The armor strained to cool their bodies but with little success.

They looked in horror as Khaleesi bent at the knees to put her head level with theirs. The evil smile on her face told them she was about to send them through another course. Seeing Khaleesi point to another course entrance, Uv'ei promised himself that he had to revisit his opinion of Khaleesi.

Standing unable to stop the groaning, he thought, '*No sane individual can be this heartless.*'

YAJF'ARD

THE SHUTTLE SLAMMED sideways, only to drop violently next. Standing within armor locked into the marine dropship armor cradles, Uv'ei looked over at two of Khaleesi's officers on the opposite sidewall. How they could be so relaxed while being flung around like this was inconceivable to him.

The sound of Uv'ek barfing into his helmet let Uv'ei know he was not the only that wanted to empty his stomach. They had practiced dropping through the atmosphere in a marine dropship before, but nothing like this. And then, they had done it only once. But, as Khaleesi said, better to spend the time available on how to survive once on the ground where you could affect the outcome. There was nothing the Kolqux could do to help while in the air. They either made it or they didn't.

If they had more time, the humans would have trained them on how to survive if they had to do an emergency ejection before landing. But they did not have months to allow that; what they were doing now had to be done before getting control of the station.

The look on Hu'de's face when informed of the plan to sneak the electromagnetic pulse devices onto the station, was something to see. It almost made him laugh as Uv'ei was flung around in his suit one more time.

EMPs were unknown to Kolqux. Jax, working with the other engineers in the RGN fleet, identified that the Chohish did not protect their equipment against this type of device. In fact, from all reports, he only found it by accident and was shocked when he did.

Before they even reached the stars, this had been everyday protection in all aspects of human and Sorath electronic designs due to potential solar flares. RGN and Sorath military equipment was built to handle weapons using this type of issue without impact.

The only drawback was that the EMPs would not work if they had to go through a shield; they needed to get the devices inside the station before they could be used. This may explain why the Chohish never bothered modifying equipment against solar flares; everything not protected by an atmosphere was behind a shield.

The RGN and Sorath had spent the time while the Kolqux and Endaen soldiers trained to build their special EMP weapons and load them onto Kolqux fighters. The constructed EMPs would be much more potent than a typical eruption of solar electromagnetic radiation.

And the individual who devised such a plan was not surprising to Uv'ei. As he had shown Uv'ei many times, Zeke had a knack for creativity. Zeke had developed a risky solution to the problem of getting the EMPs in undetected where the Chohish themselves brought them in. The RGN would identify the transponders on the Chohish fighters, destroy a few, and replace them with Kolqux units of the same make and design carrying EMPs. The fighters, over a dozen of them, were then to emulate damaged Chohish units and land inside the Chohish station.

This required steel nerves as they would have to fly through a major battle raging all around them. Then, ignoring the Chohish engineers, they all had to land in predetermined areas in the landing bay to maximize EMP effectiveness. To lend credence to support the need for returning for repair, each fighter would be equipped with something to mimic multiple types of damage.

And if that was not enough, others had to park their fighters with the EMP devices outside the station, waiting for the ones inside to take out the shields. Then, once the shields were down, they would turn their units on and sit there like sitting ducks. The RGN would send protection fighters and warships with them, but that would do little to relieve the nerves of the pilots sitting there defenseless.

Once the EMPs went off, they were set to repeat every five seconds until the Marines could take over the station. Khaleesi would lead the majority of her marines in that effort.

But Uv'ei could not worry about that part of the plan. It was something that would occur in the future. They were dropping through an atmosphere hoping the Chohish would buy their transponder as a Chohish shuttle from the station. The Lucky Strikes AI, he still did not know what to make of that thing, notified the ground command the station was landing additional forces in case of invasion. They would station themselves in the countryside and do not attempt to contact any for security reasons. So far, no pushback. That was one good thing about an order from a 'Sovereign.'

From what he had been told, the Marines typically dropped from thousands of feet up and glided down. But they forgo that to stay with the Kolqux army. The marine dropship would be landing hard where the back ramp would drop and, while still moving, disgorge the army inside. When the ramp is down, the cradles would start cycling towards the exit, release them, and finish by pushing them out.

Now, this they did train on. Working with her officers, Khaleesi had them prepare the Kolqux and Endaens for a week on how to start running before hitting the ground so they did not lose balance. Well, that was the plan anyway.

With the shuttle dropping so fast, Uv'ei thought it may have been damaged; he was surprised when the get-ready lights came on. The two officers finally moved. "Ok, all you plebes, it's time for your graduation class. Check your equipment, then do the same for the ones on your right. We will be down shortly," one of the officers announced.

The lights changed to red, indicating ten seconds; five seconds later, it changed to yellow. The whole while, it felt like an eternity. Nervousness threatened to control Uv'ei. When the light turned green, what Khaleesi told him would happen occurred. The anxiety faded, and all the training took over.

The cradles started moving back towards the ramp, which dropped with a bang, hanging just off the ground. The cradle raised Uv'ei, armored unit and all until his feet were above the ramp. Running while still connected seemed odd until he was over the ground, where he was dropped. Around him, dozens of shuttles disgorged their occupants onto a grassy plain just over a dozen miles outside the capital city.

The shuttles roared away, streaking to safety in the skies. Several of the marines tripped, causing a large pileup. It took several minutes to get everyone moving again. Thankfully, the only significant injuries were to their pride besides minor injuries.

Running, he reflected on how this was unthinkable six months ago. Now he was leading thousands of Kolqux soldiers in an effort not to free his own world but another. The capital city was where the main concentration of the Chohish resided. They were backed up by both armed Kolqux and Endaens. So Uv'ei was here to show them the error of their ways.

But everything depended on the resistance movement that Major Okeke's intelligence squad had identified and contacted. The details were limited as the group was paranoid and afraid it was a trap. Only after weeks of contact had they finally agreed to a meeting.

That meeting had occurred a little over a month ago. Bridgette, Jeanne, Hawke, Vopengi, Hu'de, and his daughter Te'ln had made a secret trip to the planet in a unique stealth ship. The stealth ship was smaller than a shuttle and loaded with specialized equipment to avoid detection. From what Uv'ei heard, that small ship cost more than a destroyer to build.

Stepping over a tree trunk that he could surprisingly recognize, Uv'ei paused before putting weight on his right foot. He saw a glint under the leaves where he was about to step down. Raising his hand mid-level, he signaled to those behind him with his fingers facing forward, repeatedly putting his fanned left palm facing the earth down.

The group behind him went prone except one who passed the signal on to others. In a short time, all were prone except for Uv'ei and Marine Sergeant Marcellin César, who was making his way over. Uv'ei watched as Marcellin did that walk where you crossed your feet. The ease with which he took one foot to swing it out from behind and do it repeatedly made Uv'ei realize his training had been for a good reason. Even though the sergeant wore heavy armor and carried some large weapons, the noise was almost nonexistent.

Patting Uv'ei on the back when he reached him, Marcellin whispered for Uv'ei to not move. They were not using their communications to diminish their electronic presence. Then, putting his hands around Uv'ei's chest, Marcellin picked up Uv'ei like a rag doll and placed him back behind the trunk.

Putting one knee on the log, Marcellin carefully brushed the leaves away. Running the length of the tree trunk for several dozen feet was a silver wire. Meticulously walking down the tree trunk until he reached the end, Marcellin leaned down, bending over to look inside the hollow tree trunk.

Uv'ei watched as he reached into the trunk. Seconds later, he pulled his hand out while rotating his head to look around. He did this for several moments before returning to where Uv'ei was crouched down and continued looking around.

"If you had stepped on that wire, it would have set off an audible alarm and notified whoever set it; we were here. I have deactivated it." Then, turning to look at Uv'ei, he signaled they could move out. "Good catch. You will make a good marine if you ever decide that is something you want to do."

Signaling to the other sergeant, he indicated for him to take point. Following behind Marcellin, Uv'ei could not stop the smile from creasing his face at Marcellin's comments.

They continued walking for several more miles, finding more elaborate traps as they got closer to the meeting locality. Coming up to a heavily forested area, Marcellin slid behind a tree and signaled everyone to halt.

Stepping out cautiously onto an animal trail, Marcellin headed towards a hut in the middle of a glade. The glade did not have grass but rocks. The stones were perfect tools to cover any trap of notifying someone they had a guest.

Guessing, Uv'ei figured out this was the meeting place. What concerned him were all the trees around the area. They could be hiding enemies without their knowledge as they had turned off their electronics.

Uv'ei watched as Marcellin slowly walked on the outer edge of his feet, rolling his feet from back to front. No noise, even when Uv'ei is so close to him. Then, looking back at his men, he could see they were nervous but resolute. Everyone here had fought the Chohish with much less than they had now. The men at his back were hand-picked out of the millions that had volunteered for this mission. All had faced death and survived in the just-ended struggle for freedom. Landing on a new world against unknown adversaries was not the time to find out if they had the courage.

As Marcellin neared the door to the hut, it opened. Out stepped two individuals. One was a Kolqux, and the other an Endaen. Both were dressed in camouflage uniforms carrying Chohish weapons that were clearly too large for their more petite build. But if the weaponry were hard to hold, they gave no indication.

"You must be Sergeant César. I am Codri," said the Endaen, "and my partner here is Feekal," indicating the Kolqux. We are your guides. Excuse me if I say it wrong; we are not used to titles. Lady Major Okeke gave us a rundown of the situation. She was hard to understand and too technical for most of my people. The other one, Jeanne, is that correct? Anyway, that one got across what you are here for. The others lent some validity to both their stories, especially the winged man."

"I prefer to be called Marcellin; I hate titles. Next to me are Uv'ei and Uv'ek, civilian leaders on the planet Sobolara. They are here with fellow countrymen to fight with you for your freedom if you want it. We are working on that assumption; still true?"

"We do, but what I see is not going to win our freedom, far from it. The ruling class is many and will not give up without a fight. We are not going to sacrifice ourselves. This is not what was promised," argued Codri swinging his arms to point at the thousands surrounding them.

Feekal spat on the ground. "When you get an army, come back." Then, turning, he started walking away until he heard Uv'ei laughing. Turning back around, he looked at Uv'ei in puzzlement.

"Did you think we were going to land our entire army here? Good thing you are just guides. Otherwise, we might have left until you get some real commanders. These men and women are my personal guard," declared Uv'ei. "The army will land at selected locations all over the planet once the station is under our control."

Startled, Codri and Feekal were about to argue when Uv'ei raised his hand for silence. "Take us to the ones that count."

As the pair started moving towards the trail on the other side of the glade, Uv'ei hand signaled a squad to take point. Ten Kolqux soldiers raced forward and spread out. He could not help but feel proud as Codri and Feekal were startled as the ten moved quickly past them to enter the forest, quieter than they were.

About to enter the forest himself, Cordi stopped with his hand resting on a tree. He watched as several other squads silently entered the forest around them. "Hmm... this may work..." he whispered to Feekal.

"It just might, Cordi, it just might," answered Feekal as he entered the forest.

DATABASE

STANDING ON THE bridge of the control station over the planet Yajf'ard, Eytun wondered what deviltry the humans were planning. He was unsure what his fellow sovereign, Alak, had thought when he took the main guard warships with him to chase after the human probe. No word has been heard from that fleet since.

Most of Alak's fleet were battleships, so he doubted the human warships could be caught. The battleships were just too slow. But Eytun knew the imbecile would try. Well, he could not do anything about that.

What he could do, was continue to build up the defense batteries. He had instructed the Kolqux and Endaens to stop building warships and change the production lines over to defensive batteries. He would saturate the system with them and make it impossible for the humans if they ever attempt to enter this system.

Changing the production was labor-heavy, but he knew it was the right thing to do. The humans could not be ready to move for several more months, consolidating their short-term victory. The significant Chohish fleet that went through earlier should be pushing them back by now, if not eliminating the fleet the humans sent. Although, he was concerned about how a human probe could get around that fleet. It was also puzzling how no status reports were coming back.

He would build more fighters, but he had no spare Chohish pilots. Regrettably, they had sent all their extra pilots with the fleet that would destroy the humans. He still had a decent-sized fighter force, but only because he had refused to turn all of them over when asked.

Eytun had tremendous doubts about what he had been told; he distrusted the reported early human successes. It was inconceivable to him; the Chohish was superior to all. Slipshod tactics were all it was. Those forces had become complacent from not having had a real challenge in many years. Well, they would not say the same about him.

The alarms suddenly went off, and the massive door to the bridge slammed shut with a bang. The sound of the locks engaging could be heard throughout the bridge.

It was getting really irritating to Eytun; enough testing already. This was the fourth time in the last two days. Yelling for the technician to turn the alarm off, he was surprised when he was told it was not a test. Several defensive batteries were coming online, responding to enemy warships transitioning through the slipstream.

"Let me know when the batteries destroy the enemy probe," ordered Eytun.

"Sir, the batteries closest to the enemy have been destroyed. They were still bringing up their systems when they were hit by missiles. The enemy had to know where they were to have had such accuracy. All the other stations have reported in and are ready to fire once the enemy is in range."

"Order all pilots to their fighters, do not deploy until I order. We are short of fuel; that damn fleet took almost everything we have," Eytun lamented.

"Sir, the enemy is continuing to transition through. Over a

hundred, and… crap, we lost the last battery supplying sensor data at the slipstream. We are now blind to what is happening at the slipstream," the Chohish sensor technician reported.

"Send out several destroyers; we need to know what is happening," fretted Eytun. Maybe he was wrong. Such a significant fleet on his doorstep could not spell well for Alak or the previous task force. What was he facing?

"We are continuing to lose more stations. The humans are taking them out before entering our missile range. Update, Sir, the pilots are positioned."

Things were spiraling out of control. He needed to do something, but what? "Send out the fighters; we cannot wait for the destroyers. Send out any ship still stationed here."

Panic, something he could not remember ever feeling, threatened to take control. Not from dying but failing. He had never failed at anything. He grew up knowing being larger and stronger was all that counted. How dare these puny weaklings challenge a Chohish?

Pacing the bridge, he reviewed what his options were. That damn Alak had taken away a significant piece of his defensive strategy. Those ships working with the fighter squadrons were supposed to support the batteries, which were not moveable. But now, due to Alak and the demands of the previous fleet, he was severely short of large warships and fighters.

The display now showed a large enemy fleet slowly heading toward the planet. The number of ships in the fleet was increasing as he watched. But the sensors in the batteries could not determine what ships were taking out his batteries before they came into the range of their weapons.

He had argued for bigger and better defensive batteries, units with twice the range of the current ones. But his superiors voted down his request as that would have required resources they were critically short of. That damn fuel.

Even the new batteries he was building would be short of fuel. His plan called for these to be placed in support of the existing units. They would only be powered up when needed, suitable only for a short time. The empire needed to find new fuel deposits before the whole realm ran out.

The number of his fighter icons made Eytun mad. There used to be thousands of fighters; now, there were only hundreds. Instead of over seventy battleships, he had less than a dozen left. Thankfully he still had over a hundred cruisers and destroyers.

Saying all that, he watched as the old and new batteries were removed. He could not allow that to go on without striking back. "Get Commander Tsaray on the line."

Anger was building as he waited; what was taking so long? Everything depended on moving quickly.

Hearing Tsaray finally reporting in, Eytun had to control his anger. Later would be the time for punishment; if he survived, that is.

"Sovereign, Tsaray reporting. I have been monitoring the incursion. I have sent what remains of your fleet with our remaining fighters to meet the invaders in support of the defensive batteries. They will eliminate our platforms piecemeal if we wait for them near the planet."

Maybe he would not punish Tsaray; he would have to rethink it after they took care of these weaklings. When they won, he could take the credit; if they took massive casualties, the blame would go to Tsaray. Win, win for him. Unless they lost, but of course, that was impossible.

"Go with the fleet. Let me know once the invaders have been eliminated." Eytun had the communications cut before Tsaray could respond.

It would take hours before Tsaray could get into position. It would give him time to get something to eat and wash up. "Do not bother me until I return. I will be back by the time Tsaray has eradicated the enemy." Eytun had to wait while the main door was opened before he left the bridge feeling much better.

That could not be said for his bridge crew. Instead, they watched as one defensive battery after another was destroyed without being able to fire any of its missiles or energy weapons. Fortunately, the further away from the station, the fewer there were. Most were close by. Only one even thought about the lives lost, and that was only because he had been stationed on one of those platforms just a month prior.

Hours later, Eytun returned, wearing a fresh robe, hunger abated, and now relaxed. "Have we heard from Tsaray?"

"The battleship he was on is no longer registering. We have been unable to reach him," reported a concerned technician.

Shocked, the calmness that Eytun had before vanished. "Status of our fleet? Who is in charge?"

"The majority of our ships and batteries have been destroyed. The fighters are fighting against overwhelming odds. We are repairing damaged fighters and warships just enough to get them back into the fighting. No one is in overall charge that we know of."

Roaring his rage, "Why was I not informed?"

"Following your orders, Sovereign."

As Eytun expressed his displeasure, the lights switched to emergency lighting. Emergency power slammed the bridge door shut with a bang. The sound of power shutting down sounded throughout the bridge.

Raised voices in confusion reigned. Before anyone could move, the emergency lighting went out. Eytun felt around, searching for his command chair. His fingers came in contact with the panel on its side; using that as a guide, he slowly made his way to sit in his chair while his eyes slowly adjusted.

Getting upset was not going to help here. Eytun needed to find out what was going on. The room was totally black until one of the techs turned on a handheld light. It lasted just a few seconds before it went dark.

"What is happening? Ideas anyone?" he asked calmly, even though he struggled to keep his cool. Give him someone to fight, and he is ready to go. Figuring out issues like this was not one of his strong points. That is why he had assistants.

He was not going to like what he heard next.

"No idea. Something is affecting anything we try to power up. Whatever it is, I smell burning; something is frying the circuits," responded one of the technicians. Who had responded? Eytun had no idea, even though he was starting to see shadows. Chohish had excellent night vision, but they could not see where there was no light. So, what was allowing him to see shadows?

Looking around, he saw why he could partially see in the pitch black. One of his hobbies was cultivating plants. One of those plants was luminescence.

"Grab that glowing plant and pull it over to the control panel. It won't last long, but it is our only light," Eytun ordered.

One of the technicians dragged the heavy tree to the control panel, where he popped the panel off. Looking inside, he frowned. Snapping two circuit boards out, he held them up, showing them to Eytun. He pointed to an area with black burn marks on the boards. "These circuits were overloaded and burned out. I see other boards that have the same burn marks."

It wasn't like Eytun could see what the technician was trying to show him in this light, but he got the idea.

Grabbing the tree, the technician moved to another panel. Then, ripping the panel off, he yanked out another board with the same burn marks. "Something is burning our circuit boards up. Both our main circuits and our emergency circuits. It must be happening when powered up, as the emergency lights worked for a bit after the main boards failed."

The tree was slowly getting darker. Eytun knew he had to get off the bridge and see what was happening. Ordering the technicians to open the door manually, he was startled when the bridge shook violently. "Hurry, open that door."

Confusion reigned as the shaking was repeated again and again. It was not lost on any that the station must be under attack. Without power, no one on the bridge could tell what was happening. Were the shields up? Were the defenses operating?

Opening the main door to the bridge manually took time. It had many locks that required tools they had not used in ages. It took more time to find the tools than it took to open the door. But finally, they had all the bolts pulled back. All that was needed was to rotate the giant wheel in the center of the door.

Two technicians grabbed the wheel in the diminutive light the tree was still giving off. As they braced themselves, it occurred to them that the shaking had stopped a while ago. The wheel did not require their full strength, but they still had to move a massive weight.

Slowly the door opened with Eytun ready to exit to find out what was happening. As the door finally swung open, Eytun could see prominent figures standing in the darkness on the other side. Elated to see others waiting for him, he was about to leave when the figures strode through the entrance.

Ready to tongue-lash the impertinent soldiers, he was stopped when the fading light reflected off of what the newcomers were wearing. They wore armor and a type he had only seen in reports. Armor that the humans wore.

Angered, humiliated, and enraged all at the same time, Eytun charged the central figure with a tremendous roar. The next thing he knew, he was on the floor in great pain. Something was smoking, and based on the smell, it was skin. And from the pain in his abdomen, he knew it was his skin. He could feel the blood leaking around his hands as they tried to hold his insides together in vain.

Around him, he could hear a battle raging and see weapons blasts. The sound of Chohish's war cries was smothered by death cries. But he could not move. He knew he was dying.

Then, in great pain, he remembered his two main priorities above all else. His first priority was to protect the system and eliminate any rebellion or attempt to free the Kolqux. But his top priority, above all else, was to ensure the coordinates database never fell into enemy hands. Doing so would open the Chohish home worlds to potential attacks before a proper defense could be put together. No Sovereign had ever failed in the history of the empire spanning thousands of years. Until now.

Bending down over him, an armored figure with an insignia on its right shoulder spoke through speakers in Chohish. "I am Major Richards of the RGN Cruiser Lucky Strike. I have been informed, once again, that we have no immediate need for any more Chohish Sovereigns."

The helmet lowered so it was only just inches from Eytun's face. The interior of the helmet's lights turned on so he could see a human female smiling at him through the faceplate.

Eytun saw the humans' lips move as he heard the last words he would ever hear. "You are free to go to whatever hell you believe in."

TIME TO FIND OUT

THE FOUR SHIPS slipped through the slipstream, emerging silently into the system. The two destroyers led the way, with one cruiser and one battleship following in their wake.

"Probes away, Captain," reported Isolde. "Do you think we will find anything in this system? The last four systems were empty."

"No idea; we will have to wait on the probes," responded Zeke. "Unfortunately, our info told us where to go but nothing about the systems we must pass through."

"They were definitely paranoid, weren't they?" stated Jeanne. "I wonder how the battle on Yajf'ard is going?"

"Do you think Uv'ei will succeed?" asked Will.

"It will not be easy; this is not just against the Chohish like they had on the other planets. There you knew your enemy by just looking at them. Now... but Uv'ei has several advantages. First, the Soraths eliminated the air power on the planet in short order; their opponents did not last long. Not only were they no match skill-wise, as Soraths are unsurpassed in the air, but the Chohish and their allies used antiquated equipment. If the ground forces are equipped with the same, I believe Uv'ei will be successful," Zeke answered.

"My uncle told me that they were surprised by the age of the equipment, but he said the air conflicts would not have mattered if they were in the latest models. The enemy's skills spoke of trainees, no battle experience," stated Hawke.

"That supports our theory that the Chohish stripped that system of any resource they could get their hands on," interjected Jeanne. "I doubt they spent the time or resources on updating the equipment on the planet; it had been secure for several millennia."

"Captain Kinsley, I do not understand why their shipbuilding facilities were not building ships," asked Hu'de, who had joined the conversation over the link.

"It made sense, Hu'de. They knew we were about to attack; a few more ships would not have made much difference. They had switched over to building defensive batteries. If they had time, they could have loaded the system with them. They are relatively easy to construct compared to a warship and do not take anywhere near the time or effort. The problem was the quality of the platforms they built; they used antiquated designs. Their missile range was minimal, energy weapons even less. Because of their limitation, we could take them out without getting in their range."

"Captain, we are starting to get results from our probes. We are picking up a lot of energy readings. There looks to be system traffic near one of the asteroid fields. As the readings come in, there seems to be much more than normal," reported Isolde.

"What type of traffic? Can you tell?" asked Will.

"I may be wrong, but it looks to be mining facilities. That is based on all the equipment signatures I am getting on the asteroids. Similar to what we saw on Nocuous. I am not picking up any men at war. Will not know for sure until we get closer or more data," responded Isolde.

"It makes sense; they need something to feed all the shipbuilding facilities. Will, head over there to see what else we can find out.

If we see any military ships, redirect us to the other slipstream. Our main priority is determining if the database we captured was accurate on where the Chohish home system was located," Zeke ordered.

"Is there any way you would go back to the Fox while we have time, Jan?" asked Jeanne.

"Sorry, Captain, not an option; orders are orders," responded Jan. Although his jovial tone did not sound like he was sorry, not at all.

Neither did the expressions on the four Irracan marines. Instead, the chuckles from Michale and Shon drew an intense glare from Jeanne at the two RGN marines who were back in their locations.

The trip to the mining facilities was uneventful until they got much closer. Three Chohish destroyers came from behind the most significant facility to meet them.

"Hold the pilots near their fighters," ordered Zeke to all ships. "Let's not deploy them until needed. We will attempt to do this remotely while we have a missile range advantage with the Lucky Strike and the Freedom. Will, Hu'de, all yours."

The X207B Chohish designated ship, renamed the Freedom after being upgraded with a few RGN defensive weapons and shields, fired first. They were still producing the old Chohish missiles in their system. It was not time to change the production lines; they needed to build as many warships and weapons as possible for their defense. The Kolqux were in the process of creating new ship factories, but this would take months, if not years, to complete.

As their missiles raced away, dozens of large, cumbersome ships came into view. They were accompanied by a pair of destroyers heading out of the system.

"Meghan, Lance, we cannot let these get away. So take your fighters and intercept," ordered Zeke.

"Zeke, this is Hu'de; please, do not destroy the mining facilities. They probably have my people on them. We got our materials from ships that resemble those that are running away. The Kolqux on those ships told us of the horrors working in the smelters. So please, let my marines make an effort to take control."

This was not something Zeke planned on. He was ordered to find the Chohish home systems and relay that information back to the admiralty. But Hu'de's main concern was valid. At the same time, he could not leave the facilities functional in Chohish hands to feed their war machine if possible.

But there was a secondary issue that should be factored in. The Kolqux home systems were running out of material for their factories. If they could capture these ships and the mining facilities, the Kolqux could continue with their work to build home defenses. That was going to take a constant supply of material.

But one thing bothered him. Were the Kolqux Marines any good? Signaling Isolde to mute the connection to Hu'de, he requested her to ask Khaleesi to join them on the bridge.

Meanwhile, Zeke went to the central situation board to look over the layout of the situation. Jeanne, Will, and Hawke joined him.

Several moments passed before Hu'de asked what Zeke had decided.

Getting Isolde to open the link back up, Jeanne announced out loud. "Hu'de, this is Jeanne. Zeke is working it out. Give us a few."

Hand signaling to mute the connection again, Jeanne examined the board and Zeke's updates.

"You're leaning toward going for it, aren't you?" queried Jeanne.

"I am. There are a couple of good reasons to try it. But then again, there are even better, healthier reasons to pass it by," Zeke responded.

Wrapping an arm around his waist, Jeanne leaned her head toward the board he was playing with. "But you were never one to let *'healthier'* dictate to you what is the right thing to do."

Hearing Zeke mutter under his breath, Jeanne popped him on his arm.

"I said, *'Damn woman, she knows me better than my own mother.'* I said that with love, my dear." Zeke defended with a smile.

"Good riposte, you must have been saving that one," a laughing Jeanne exclaimed.

The sound of heavy, loud running footsteps sounded from the hallway outside the bridge. The sound was odd as it also had a squeaking sound mixed in. Not until a fully dressed marine in armor with weapons attached slid around the corner to enter the bridge that everyone knew who it was made by.

"You had to have me on the bridge? Whatever happened to electronic communications?" echoed out of Khaleesi's helmet.

"I needed you here because I like your company?" retorted Zeke.

Pulling her helmet off, the look she gave Zeke told him she was not amused. "I am getting my marines loaded into shuttles. Can we make this short?"

"Well, I guess that answers one of my questions; you want to capture the facilities. Look, it would be great if we could capture these mining facilities, but I am not sure we can do that with the forces we have or, if we did, hold it. So, I need your thoughts on how well-trained Hu'de's marines are. Are they any good? What if we let them lead and your marines be the heavy backup?" questioned Zeke.

The questions make Khaleesi pause in her anger at being pulled away. "I never considered Hu'de's marines being the point of the sword, so to speak. I was planning on our Marines being that, but you make a good point. The miners, what makeup are they made up of? Hu'de's marines are mainly Kolqux, but there are some Endaens."

"Have you seen or been part of their training?" quizzed Will.

"No, we worked with Uv'ei's personal guard; the RGN and Irracan managed training the rest of his army. Volunteers flocked in from all three worlds. Their numbers overwhelmed the RGN and

Irracan resources. The Soraths stepped in and aided with training Kolqux marines, including Hu'de's group," Khaleesi related.

"The problem is that Soraths are larger, yet lighter than the Kolqux. Soraths have a whole different fighting style than the RGN or Irracan. It looks good, but I have just never seen it in action. But this would be a good time to find out, so we know what to expect if we need them if we run into a problem," Khaleesi said, explaining her views.

"My people's marines are good, but not as near good as the RGN's, but that is due to lacking density and physical strength, not because of their training. They are best used in an atmosphere where we can use our wings. If my people signed off on Hu'de's group, though, they are competent," Hawke said.

"How many marines on the Freedom? Do they even have enough to take over such a large facility? Especially since multiple facilities are spread over a large area?" challenged Jeanne.

"The Freedom is twice the size of the Lucky Strike. They redid what they could to maximize space usage since they captured it, mostly to living spaces. They have a force of close to seven hundred and fifty marines, with another fifty in their command group. So yes, with us as backup, they should have enough," speculated Khaleesi.

Zeke gestured Khaleesi and the others over to the situation board. "How would you recommend we deploy Major?"

For the next fifteen minutes, they reviewed different options. Then, when they finished putting together a rough plan, they had Hu'de unmuted.

"Ok, Hu'de, we have decided to go for it," announced Zeke.

They had to wait a moment as the sound of cheering in the background drowned out Hu'de.

"Sorry, Zeke, the marine commanders were here, and they have been anxiously waiting. They are ecstatic they may be freeing more Kolqux and Endaens," apologized Hu'de.

"I hope they are just as ecstatic after we make the attempt. Anyway, we reviewed with Khaleesi what she recommends. She will get with you and your officers and go over what we came up with. Once you've had time to review it, adjust the plans to incorporate suggestions she may find worthwhile," concluded Zeke. "Meanwhile, Will, make sure the backup combat information center (CIC) is manned."

Just over an hour later, they were finally in missile range. As agreed, both battleship and cruiser concentrated on one of the three destroyers. Then, as missiles ejected from the ships, the fighters started showing up.

The fighters from the Kolqux ship came out in several smooth waves, four at a time. Until a dozen was headed outwards. How they grouped to fly around the battleship showed cohesion that wasn't present just six months ago.

Meanwhile, a ship that was initially built to carry six fighters ejected dozens upon dozens, accompanied by a dozen bombers. All raced towards the three Chohish destroyers.

It took a dozen minutes for the missiles to reach the targeted destroyer. Between the three destroyers, they were able to knock off all but one of the missiles. The one missile caused no deaths, but it did destroy a good portion of the defensive array on one side. The destroyers rolled just in time to meet the second wave of missiles.

It did not go as well this time around. Two missiles got through. Once again, a missile removed the defensive array on the destroyer's side. The other missile, which used to be Chohish munitions, took out the bridge. It was vented to space. It spiraled out of control. That is until the next round of missiles arrived, where none were stopped.

By this time, the two Chohish destroyers had reached their own missile range. Their primary deficiency was they could not deliver the same destructive power. As a result, their missiles were smaller and less able to avoid defensive fire.

The Chohish sent out their fighters, which was the same as suicide, against the forces arrayed against them. The fighters met in the middle of the two forces. Less than a minute later, it was over.

The men of war raced towards each other, and Zeke had the fighters hold back as he wanted to reserve them for the battle at the mining facilities.

There was no fancy flying; both sides headed directly at each other. Missiles flew past each other to deliver destruction.

Alarms rang on the Lucky Strike, signaling impact. But then they reached a point he had been waiting for. They entered the energy weapons range. Beams of destructive power connected the Lucky Strike with one of the Chohish destroyers.

The lendolium lasers went in one side of Chohish Destroyer only to come out the other. Debris, flames, and bodies were thrown out. Surprisingly, the warship continued onward, only to shatter into a dozen pieces when four missiles raced in unopposed.

The other destroyer did not fare much better. The Kolqux battleship had its primary weapon rebuilt to use the RGN-processed lendolium, and the ship was filled to the brim with fuel. That weapon burned a lot more fuel than used in an RGN lendolium laser with devastating effects. The RGN did not like it because it was easy to avoid once identified.

The laser smashed into the destroyer along with half a dozen other smaller fusion strikes. The destroyer stopped firing immediately upon impact before drifting away as a smoking wreck.

The cruiser and the battleship headed toward the largest mining platforms.

"Will, get with Jax; I want a damage report asap. Have someone check with doc. Let me know if we took any casualties. Isolde, connect me with Hu'de, then get in touch with security. I want Omaw brought to the bridge, under guard, and restrained."

The last took Isolde by surprise. "Captain, just to confirm. You are talking about the Chohish that is in our brig, correct? You want him brought to the bridge, now?"

"Yes, Isolde, under guard and in restraints."

"Jeanne, if you would, can you ensure our guest is comfortable? And kept secured? No reason not to use those marines you keep complaining about." implored Zeke. Her only response was a smiling, approving nod.

"Captain, Will here; while we have a few minutes, can you explain why we did not destroy the destroyers with missiles, staying remote?"

"I do not want to give the Chohish additional time to harden the facilities against attack. Every minute would mean additional deaths for the Marines and could take success away from us," clarified Zeke. "Will, have Jamie send out the marine shuttles when in range. Fighters and bombers are to provide security for all shuttles. We will provide the heavy punch where required. Isolde, notify Hu'de of the same. They are to stay on our starboard side."

"Helmsman, take us in, half speed," ordered Zeke.

FULL SPEED AHEAD

"WHY AM I here?' demanded Omaw. He was strapped into a chair against the back wall. Arrayed around him were the four Irracan marines, all of whom had their arms on their armor locked so their weapons were pointed straight at his chest. They had warned him that any movement to escape would mean instant death.

"I want you to witness smaller, weaker beings fighting larger, stronger ones. It doesn't always go the '*larger ones*' way." Then, turning to look at him, Zeke continued. "Push hard enough; any size animal can turn deadly. Push them too hard; may force them to do things they would not normally do."

"Such as?" Omaw asked combatively.

"Eliminate the threat totally. Eradicate the threat so it will never be able to threaten again. There is an old saying that humans have that has survived the ages. '*There is always someone bigger, stronger, and meaner than you.*'"

Turning back to the screen, Zeke finished with. "We have met others that are bigger and stronger than us. But we have never met anyone, any race, meaner than us. That includes your race. You have not seen us get down and dirty, not yet. We have only just begun to fight."

"Words are easy; the Chohish will not go down so easily, human," contended Omaw.

"You Chohish have made a huge, deadly, costly mistake. You attacked the one thing that humans nor Soraths cannot abide by. Unites us all onto the same goal: protecting that one item. And if necessary, we will eradicate the offender to protect that item," declared Zeke.

"You like puzzles, human. First, you brought me on this ship instead of leaving me with my men. Then you bring me to your bridge in the middle of a battle against my people. Now you tell me that we made a costly mistake but do not tell me what that mistake was. Well, what is it, human? What was that costly mistake?" yelled Omaw.

"Your people attacked and killed our children, both human, and Sorath, for no fault of their own. The one thing both our races prize above more than everything else. We will go to any length to protect them. Even if we must eradicate the Chohish as a race." Zeke answered with hate and anger in his voice.

Turning to face Omaw, he showed that it was mirrored in his body language, not just his voice. "You are here because I hope you can see the futility of this war and bring some sense to your people. I do not want to kill your children, but if it becomes the last option to protect mine, I will, we will."

Omaw did not respond.

"Captain, we are getting new power readings. Like warships powering up," reported Isolde.

"Put up the locations on the main screen," ordered Zeke.

The screen lit up with a map of the immediate space with all the structures and asteroids. Behind one of the main structures, a growing energy reading was shown. Another more significant power reading was located behind a massive asteroid.

"Isolde, tell Hu'de he is to stay here, protect the shuttles, and support the battle to gain control of the structures. We are going to go take care of a minor problem."

Unbuckling, Zeke walked over to the helmsman to peer over his shoulder. "Tim, can you magnify that area?" he said, pointing at a section of the asteroid field where the second power reading was coming from.

Pointing to an area amidst three large asteroids between the two power readings, "I want you to take us through that gap, maximum speed. Can you do that?"

Taking a moment to play with the image, Tim rotated and expanded it before replying. "Yes, Captain, I can do it; it will be tight. And once through, we may run into an asteroid, especially if we are at full speed."

"Make it fit, turn us sideways if necessary. We will worry about getting through the asteroids beyond when we get there," assured Zeke.

The look on Tim's face made Zeke pause. "Lieutenant, were you a fighter pilot before this?" The grin on Tim's face became more expansive as he answered.

"Four years on the Black Reaver Captain. I wanted to drive something a little larger with more protection. It seemed like a safer bet at the time. How wrong could I be, huh? But you sure make it fun driving this big battlewagon."

If it was any other time, Zeke would have laughed, but now was not the time. He had heard of the Black Reaver; that carrier had been in many nasty scrapes and survived them all. They were good fighter pilots, all of them. Although he heard most flew like madmen and had a feeling from the smile the helmsman had, he now had one of them.

Going next to Hawke and Jeanne, he reviewed what he wanted them to do when he got there. Hawke looked at Zeke like he was crazy, but Jeanne loved what he planned. Both confirmed it would be done.

"Full speed ahead, helmsman, take us in," commanded Zeke.

The Lucky Strike bolted forward, and the engine roar could be heard throughout the ship as the engines passed their safety margins.

The call he was expecting came through as they surged forward to the designated area.

"Do not have time to talk with you, Jax, unless it is an emergency. We are about to engage the enemy who outguns us more than two to one," urged Zeke.

The call ended without the connection being made.

"Captain, the energy signatures have both been identified. They are both Chohish battleships who appear to be converging on us," reported Isolde.

"Acknowledged. Stay on course, helmsman."

The ship barreled through space and rocked, suddenly signaling a missile launch. The shaking ended only to shake again at another launch. This continued briefly before the ship pitched hard to port from a near missile miss.

"We are now taking enemy fire, Captain," reported Isolde.

"Had a feeling that was what pushed us, Lieutenant. I expect we will get a few more of those before we…" only to be cut off when the ship staggered from a shock wave.

Alarms sounded, but the ship hurled on without slowing. The sound of missile launches was now accompanied by the energy weapons going off.

"The two battleships are trying to head us off, Captain."

Watching the battle screen, Zeke could see that for himself, although he was glad Isolde relayed it to the rest of the bridge, who could not watch the battle screen and their own instruments at the same time.

"Keep us on the course, helmsmen, and if you can get more thrust from the engines, make it happen," directed Zeke.

And he did somehow. The ship lurched forward with more speed. "*Damn it,*" Zeke thought. Now he would definitely be getting a ream out from Jax when this was all over. He should know better than to tell a fighter pilot to put on more speed. Tim must be redlining the engines. Zeke could imagine Jax swearing at him in the engine room right about now.

Then they were there. Zeke could not tell what damage they had given the Chohish battleships, but that is not what concerned him. Getting through flying between the gap of the massive asteroids did.

Just as he was about to unstrap to assist Tim if he needed it, the ship suddenly turned sideways, causing many on the bridge to curse. More curses followed as it flipped to come to a new heading.

The ship struggled to make headway in its new direction. At the same time, it continued sideways towards a massive asteroid that had been in front of the vessel just seconds ago. The main screen showed the asteroid as the ship careened towards certain doom.

"What the hell?" came gasping out of several throats. Then when it looked like they would hit, the ship shot forward, and they were beyond the asteroid.

Behind them, the two Chohish battleships had maneuvered to get through the gap without slowing down. As the battleships passed between the asteroids, the asteroids shattered from multiple missiles and energy hits.

The "*Gotcha, you old sea dog*" and "*Stuff that down your throats, you mongrels*" yells told him who was responsible. "When we get through that opening, close it, and use whatever you think you need," he had asked the pair. And they did, in a splendid fashion.

The two Chohish battleships ran right into thousands of rocks loaded with iron ore the size of large houses or larger, going full speed. Their shields buckled and failed, unable to push all the objects away. As a result, the hulls were unable to stop an unstoppable force.

43

With nowhere to go, the boulders breezed through hulls, weapons, storerooms, bodies, and finally, the power plants. Then, having lost control, the two battleships ran into the same asteroid the Lucky Strike barely missed. A nova blossomed behind the Lucky Strike as they jockeyed away.

But their troubles were not over. The Lucky Strike careened around asteroids. Zeke could hear the engines roaring in reverse, trying to slow their speed down. The ship was tossed when it clipped a rock.

Straightening itself out, the ship flew straight for a period before he heard Tim sigh.

"We are out of the asteroids, Captain. And when time permits, Sir, can I be excused for a few moments? I need to change my pants," an exhausted helmsman announced.

Now that was a fighter pilot's comment if he ever heard one. Zeke had heard similar statements before when he was a fighter pilot himself. Anything to lighten the tension, even though it must have been used millions of times. And it worked, as he heard the bridge release their tension to laugh at a helmsman who had only recently joined their crew. Through his actions and words, he integrated himself as being one of them.

"Status? Need a status people, now!" he ordered.

"The two battleships are destroyed; no additional signs of enemy ships," reported Selena.

"Getting damage readings on multiple decks. Most are from an asteroid impact. Engines are reading they overheated but are now lowering into an acceptable range, no indication of any aftereffects," Isolde yelled.

"Captain, this is Will; I have reports of at least a dozen injured, two seriously. Doc is sending personnel to those locations now," before he paused. "A particular engineer has been giving me an earful. If you want me to pass him on, he is still on the line."

"No thanks, Will; I appreciate the thought, though. Give me a damage report when everything settles down. Right now, I want to get back and see how the battle for the factories is going. Captain out."

Turning to look at Omaw, he gave him the evil grin he always gave his brother when he beat him at a game. "Larger is not always better."

"Helmsman, take us back to where we started. You will have to wait for a change of pants break. Besides, I may have another course I need you to run. It will save you from having to take another break. Side note, good steering. You'll have to show me how you did the flip as we went through it. Never saw a cruiser flip like that."

The Lucky Strike had to take a challenging route to return to where they had left the Freedom. It was not like they could retrace the way they came. Their return route was littered with asteroids and debris left over from previous mining.

While on the way, they contacted Lance and Meghan to get a status on their end. They had good luck in that they could destroy the two Chohish destroyers while losing only one pilot and two fighters. The freighters had surrendered immediately afterward, and all of them were now returning to support Hu'de.

Seventy-eight minutes after starting their road back, they finally made it. Thankfully their assistance was not needed. Instead, the Freedom was anchored to the central factory with fighters flying all around in guard mode.

Upon arrival, Hu'de requested a conference call.

"Hi Zeke, it is good to see you back in one piece. We monitored the explosions; we were afraid it was you at one point since we did not hear from you at first. Thankfully, Isolde finally reached out to us to let us know the status and that you were returning," voiced Hu'de.

"We took some injuries and damage, which we are still assessing. How did it go here? Looks like you were able to get control."

"It was rough going for a while. Thankfully, some of the miners opened hatches for us that allowed us to get behind the Chohish. We still lost a lot of good people. Experience, as the Soraths taught us, differs greatly from training. But it was worth it. There are over fifty thousand of my people and Endaens stationed here. I do not want to tell you what their living conditions are like. A good many need medical attention," exclaimed a visibly upset Hu'de.

"We will do what we can, Hu'de, but as bad as it sounds, I doubt we will be able to save them all. Have your medical staff triage all the injured. Instead, concentrate their attention on who you can save. We will send help, but the numbers are overwhelming; I am afraid we may have only one option," replied Zeke. "Let's understand what we have and make plans from there. Zeke out."

ORE

IT WAS OVER a day later that the situation was finally ironed out. Between the miners and the marines, there were more injured than could be handled by the ship's infirmaries. So many would die if they stayed here. Zeke had known there was only one option available when he had talked with Hu'de. The review confirmed it.

When he announced it, it surprised no one. The numbers made it obvious they needed to reach Sobolara to get the treatment they needed. What even made it a possibility, as the number of critical injuries was in the thousands, was the capture of the freighters. They were all over half filled with ore, but that still left vast open areas that could house the injured for a few days.

The freighters, fortunately, had been manned solely by Kolqux and Endaens, as it was considered beneath a Chohish warrior. Since the Chohish manned the warships, they controlled the freighters with the threat of destruction. It was not like the much slower freighters could get away.

The first day was prepping the freighters to be able to hold oxygen. It was easier than Zeke thought. Sergeant Garcia, again, was instrumental. Working with the engineers from the mining facility, they quickly put up barriers using readily available supplies that were crucial when mining. Support beams, metal slats for walls, bolts, sealer foam, and all the needed materials were accessible in large quantities.

The next step was to load supplies to last at least several weeks, if not longer. That was done with a never-ending Kolqux and Endaen chain passing supplies from the main facilities the freighters were docked to.

All the while, the warships made any repairs they could while getting some rest. All that is except for the marines. They were busy setting up charges all throughout the mining facilities. If anyone tried to enter without the proper identification, they would be in for a big surprise. Zeke had no intention of leaving these intact for the Chohish, but he did not want to destroy them outright. They could be valuable to Kolqux and Endaens in the future.

Then they loaded the injured. Unfortunately, many died before all could be loaded. Many more would die during the trip. The Chohish worked the miners with little regard for safety. If a miner was injured severely enough that they could not continue work, they would be killed like a rabid animal. Any that died, well, they would just be replaced with another.

But finally, they were ready to depart. The ships had been on the way for several hours before Isolde raised the alarm.

"Captain, the probes are picking up warships transitioning through the far slipstream. The one we were originally headed towards."

"Can you identify the number and make-up?"

"Waiting on that data now... should have that in several minutes."

Silence reigned while everyone waited on the data to arrive. In the middle of this, communications requests came from the Fox and the Jackal.

With Isolde busy interpreting data from the probes, Selena

handled the requests. Seeing Isolde about to report to the Captain, she held off on what she had discussed with the other two ships.

"The probes are identifying four cruisers and...," and before she could finish, the Captain finished what she was going to say. "And one destroyer."

"I am guessing they are the rest of the protection squadron for the mining facilities. I was wondering where they were hiding," Zeke explained as he looked around the bridge.

While Will had a questioning look, Hawke had a predatory one. The one on Jeanne's face was one of merriment watching Hawke. She already knew Zeke was working out how to attack the oncoming force. No different than herself.

"Isolde, please work out how long it will take them to reach us. Make sure you count on our forward progress. Meanwhile, Selena, before I ask you to organize a conference with all the captains, can you let me know what the two ships wanted?"

The surprised look on Selena's face brought a slight chuckle from Isolde as she worked on Zeke's request. "It takes a bit to get used to; I swear he hears and retains everything," Isolde whispered to Selena.

A little flustered, Selena responded. "The two ships' captains were reporting the same as what we were detecting. They wanted to ensure you were informed, and if so, what were your plans."

"Let them know that is what the meeting is about," he responded while standing. "But now, I need to clean up while I can. Be back in ten."

Looking at Jeanne, he pointed to the exit in a questioning manner. She answered by rising and leading the way out. She flipped her famous hat on to hide her smile when he whistled appreciatively while following her out.

When they reached their room, Jeanne turned and halted him

just as the door closed. "Ok, what's the deal? You did not come here to just clean up."

"I wanted some time alone with you?' seeing the sarcastic smile on her face, he sighed and sat down in one of the chairs.

"Ok, you got me. I wanted to confirm that I am about to make the right decision. What I am going to propose could be disastrous if it does not go as I planned."

Sitting in the chair next to him, Jeanne grabbed Zeke's hand to caress before replying. "Everything about this damn war has been horrific. Every decision we have made since the beginning could have been disastrous, some have been, but it would even be worse if we did nothing. What is the saying? '*Nothing ventured, nothing gained.*'"

If she thought that this would help, she would have been mistaken. But she knew better. Zeke was here not to ask for her ok but to get control of himself before he told the rest of his decision. She was here because her presence gave him someone he could vent to beforehand, knowing she had made the same decisions in the past and could relate.

"Want to tell me what you have decided?" she whispered into his ear as she leaned forward to put her forehead against his.

"Do you remember the Admiral saying she would put together a sizable fleet to follow us once she finished up with Yajf'ard? Just in case we ran into a situation beyond our control and needed to flee?"

What he said gave her a hint for her to understand what he was planning. This hint helped her understand why he was so conflicted. If that fleet was not where he hoped it would be, close to a hundred thousand could perish if his actions failed.

The Admiral wanted to wait on additional forces before she left Sobolara. The fleet needed to be reinforced to allow the Kolqux and Endaens decent protection. Especially now that Yajf'ard has been added into the mix. But the Admiral wanted to send some support in case they needed it. So, it all depended on how the battle for Yajf'ard went.

"I know the admiral some; I believe she will have sent that fleet out as soon as she could," Zeke whispered back. Then, grabbing her head, he pulled her so her ear was next to his mouth. "If it was me, I could accept that risk. But… can I take that risk with the others?"

Kissing the side of his face, she pulled his face back so she could look him eye to eye. "I know what is bothering you. It is who is most at risk with your decision. The men and women on the warships volunteered for this, knowing the risks involved. The miners didn't. But would they be better off if we left them where they were?"

The look he gave made her melt inside. Oh, how she loved this man. He was so bright and handsome, but his compassion for others made her fall in love with him.

Nodding, he slowly stood. "I guess I better clean up, as they might think I have another ulterior motive for dragging you to our bedroom. And my reputation would be ruined, let alone my pride, if they assumed it only took ten minutes."

Her laughter followed him as he made the way to the bathroom. "And my reputation would be ruined if they thought I could not make you happy in less than five minutes."

The 'ouch' sound let Jeanne know he had heard her. Then she watched as his head popped back out, wearing a big grin saying, "well, if you insist," only to duck back in when she threw a pillow at him.

Walking back onto the bridge twenty minutes later did not help nor hurt their reputations. But it did allow Hawke to have some fun asking why so tardy.

Sitting in his command chair, Zeke signaled Isolde he was ready for her report.

"Using our current speed, I estimate it will take eighteen hours

for the Chohish to reach us. One note, though, they are not traveling at the normal max speed. I cannot tell if they are holding back
or why the difference," Isolde reported while putting their current
position up on the main screen. The main screen started running
a simulation of where the Chohish would intercept them in the
system.

"The Chohish is not slowing down, and their direction indi-
cates they will bypass the mining facilities, heading directly after us.
They will not be able to intercept us before we leave the system."

"How many hours after moving into the next system before
they would?" Jeanne asked.

"If there were no changes, about three hours."

Turning to look at Zeke, Jeanne nodded.

"Isolde, track the speed of the Chohish closely. I believe they
are traveling at maximum speed. I noticed the destroyers that we
faced were slower than normal. This group may be using older
model warships as they are basically guards, not front-line units. If
so, we should have an additional speed advantage on them than we
normally would. Selena, please bring on the rest of the captains,"
ordered Zeke.

The three other bridges came onto the side screens with the
Kolqux bridge on one while the other two shared the one screen.
Zeke thought it was appropriate, considering what he was going
to suggest.

"Isolde, send your projections to the three ships so they can
see what I will discuss. Please let me know when you have them
available," Zeke asked while he stood, so he was standing in the
center of the bridge.

Upon notification that all had it displayed, Zeke explained the
simulation before reviewing what Isolde told him. And then, he
went on to explain his plan, how he wanted to deal with the Chohish, and the risks involved.

Looking at Hu'de, he asked if he understood everything he was asking. The answer did not soothe his soul, but it helped to know that Hu'de knew the risks being requested and approved.

"Ok, let's go with this plan. First, I need to confirm several more things before committing. Second, if it's a go, let's start executing in twelve hours; that should give everyone enough time to get prepared and some rest. Let's meet back up twenty minutes prior."

Standing, Zeke signaled Jeanne and Hawke to join him as he walked off the bridge. The marines were going to follow until he stopped. "Really? We are not leaving the ship. So please, stay here; we will be back in fifteen minutes." Then, seeing the marines relax, he continued on.

Walking beside him, Jeanne knew he had apprehension about the plan he had put together. And she was a big part of it, but he was heading toward one of his primary concerns. There were so many ways his plan could go wrong.

Walking into one of the internal fighter bays, he made his way toward Jamie's office. Unsurprisingly, Jamie was standing at her door with Gunner and Roy leaning against the wall on either side.

"Figured you be heading down here when I heard you say you had to confirm some things before going with your plan. Do you want to step into the office?" asked Jamie.

"No, I need to stand to bleed off some of my tension; we can do it here if everyone doesn't mind." Then, seeing their shrugs, he sighed before resuming. "I came down because I need to ensure everyone knows the risks and signs off on them. I will understand anyone who wants to sit this one out. It will not reflect negatively on my high opinion of them. I mean that for all of you!"

Seeing Jamie about to speak up, Zeke waved her off. "I want to be sure everyone understands the risks. You will be sitting ducks if they figure it out before we are ready.'

It was Gunner that stopped Zeke before he could finish. "We

know, Captain. I discussed it with all the fighter crews before you got here. I already talked with the fighter commanders Lieutenant Hayreddin Barbarossa on the Fox and Lieutenant Sudie Bolt on the Jackal. In their opinion, your plan is risky but well worth the risk. Count all the fighter pilots in."

The slow drawl of Roy picked up where Gunner left off. "Cap, before I got here, they used bombers in a limited standard manner. But doing so made it obvious when we would be present. That meant we went against prepared defenses and paid the penalty. Your tactics are unique and refreshing. The bomber crews are glad they are now being used as they should have been. We are a go. And I personally have got to say, exciting."

As Zeke looked at each of these men and women, he tried to get their faces imprinted in his mind. Then, turning, he looked at Jeanne, who started laughing.

"Oh no, you will not give me that guilty look. You do not need me here, so I am going with my crew. I wouldn't miss this if you paid me. If this works, oh, what fun we will have."

"I know; I would never ask you to be anything other than what you are. It is not what I was going to ask. I expect I will be busy, so I will put you in charge of all the fighters and bombers. You will be closer to the action than me, so I will defer to any changes you believe necessary."

Hugging Zeke, Jeanne leaned up to kiss him on the cheek. "Thanks, it means a lot to be with my friends."

"Oh, and one other thing," Zeke asked Jeanne while hugging her close before releasing her. "Please bring yourself back in one piece. I do not have time to break in another woman," at which point he took off running for the exit.

Standing there, Jeanne chuckled before announcing to those around her. "He actually thinks he will get away with that by beating me back to the bridge."

Tapping her communication pod in her ear. "Jan, Jeanne here. Zeke just insulted your Captain in front of others. He is heading to the bridge to avoid my wrath. Can you intercept him before he gets there?"

Seeing her nodding positively in confirmation, the officers around her laughed, knowing Zeke would pay for that comment.

The next twelve hours were busy even though the plan was to get some rest. But there were repairs, ships to be refueled and rearmed, injuries to manage, and finally, deaths to mourn. Then it was time to start, even though engagement would not occur for several more hours.

Sitting back in his command chair, he had Isolde connect him with Hu'de. "Ok, Captain Hu'de, how well can you track the Chohish?"

"Hello, Zeke; I am not sure I will get used to being called Captain. Te'ln is now able to ascertain the Chohish ships clearly. She can track their speed and energy readings."

"Excellent, that is what we have been waiting on. We needed to know when the Chohish can do the same tracking on us. So we are now ready; please start operation Junk Ore."

Slowly, the freighters started moving apart. When they reached a certain distance, large ore blocks began dropping out of their rear. Then, after a freighter dropped a load, their speed picked up a small percentage. This went on for the next forty minutes. After all the ore had been dropped, the freighter's speed had increased close to a quarter speed. The ore trail was long and scattered.

While the ore was being dumped, the three RGN warships followed close behind, weaving around the ore to maintain their position at the rear.

Another twenty minutes later, the RGN cruiser and two destroyers started a wide turn. It took twenty minutes before they were headed back towards the Chohish at full speed.

Each of the three warships started discharging fighters, three fighters from each of the two destroyers and six from the cruiser. The fighters slid in close to their respective warship flying escort.

The Chohish came rushing on, never deviating from their course. Shortly, their fighters appeared, ten from each of the cruisers and four from the destroyer.

"Looks like they added additional fighters to their normal contingent. It's like you said, they would start changing at some time," declared Will.

"It had to happen; they cannot afford to continue losing the number of warships as they have been. I will be busy monitoring the entire battle zone Will, so you will oversee the Lucky Strike. So let's do that as a standard from now on. Same for Selena, as I will probably require Isolde's services. The ship is all yours," ordered Zeke.

Time slowly passed as the two opposing fleets raced toward each other. There was no signal when they entered the missile range other than a slight jolt and missile launch sound.

Zeke looked over at the empty seat Hawke would typically be at. Hawke had decided that Will did not need his assistance in fire control for this action. So now he was sitting anxiously in his fighter, waiting for the signal from Zeke, along with over a hundred others.

The missile launches continued unabated. The Lucky Strike got four salvos off before the Chohish fired their first. The ratio for firing was close to two to one, but since there were four Chohish cruisers, the numbers were in the Chohish favor, except for one factor. The Chohish had one destroyer to provide defensive protection, while the Lucky Strike had two. And the difference made itself known as soon as the first set of missiles arrived.

Will had the pair of fire control technicians slow down the missiles from the first five salvos until they combined into one massive group. They then directed these against one Chohish cruiser farthest away from the destroyer.

It was not obvious what would happen until the missiles, which had been heading for the group's center, suddenly changed direction. The Chohish destroyer was late in changing its focus to intercept the missiles. Three missiles got through the cruiser's defenses and punched through to cause damage.

The cruiser was not put out of action but was leaking air and equipment. The Chohish, in reaction, pulled all their cruisers close together into a diamond formation. The destroyer flew into the center of the diamond to maximize protection for all ships.

The Chohish continued on the same path, and shortly after, they started passing the ore dropped from the freighters.

The Lucky Strike rocked from the near missile hits from the Chohish. The Chohish concentrated all their fire on the Lucky Strike as they understood it was the real danger to their ships, not the destroyers. The fighters from the Chohish shot forward, rushing towards the RGN cruiser.

Watching the distance shorten between the two forces on the side screen, Zeke quietly sat. It was starkly in contrast to the fiery emotions running through his body. When the Chohish fighters reached the position he was waiting on, he nodded to Isolde.

Isolde had been sitting with a finger held over a button waiting for Zeke to give the command. But, as he told her, that was all she needed to do to unleash hell.

When the button was pushed, a predetermined command sent out a signal to all fighters and bombers.

A pair of pilots had been waiting on that signal. They were sitting and sweating as they sat defenseless just a short distance from the Chohish cruisers. Roy and Masson sat motionless in a bomber hidden behind an ore block.

When they got the signal, Roy started the engines and systems on the bomber. "If you do not mind me asking, why did you request to join me on this mad adventure?" Roy asked while checking all the gauges.

The chuckle caused him to pause for a second to look at the man mirroring his actions and checking the gauges on his side.

"I have heard of bombers but never seen them in action. Since the controls are nearly the same as an RGN fighter, it did not take long to brush up on how to fly a bomber. After the 'adventure' you recently had, I had to see what it was like for myself," Masson responded good-naturedly. "Now I can see the appeal. Snug while drifting helplessly, waiting for the enemy to find you and blast you to smithereens."

"Generally, we are sent only after air power superiority has been confirmed. But Captain Kinsley has made it much more challenging. And more deadly," Roy said while tweaking the sensors. "About time someone made use of us properly."

"I must agree with you there; the Captain does seem to get the most of people and equipment, uniquely so. I thought Jeanne was the best at that, but between the two of them, damn. It has been exciting and dangerous, and I expect it will get even more so before this is all over."

With the bomber power now online, Roy brought up the shields and headed away from the ore that had been covering their ship signature.

"Do you remember where the throttle is? We sure are not moving fast. The Chohish may laugh at how slow we are going before they blow us up," exclaimed a worried Masson.

"Now you know, young man, why bombers are not sent in without a fighter escort. Roy said this as he watched the two fighters that had been sitting here with them came barreling past. Their startup sequence was shorter than a bomber.

"Well, it looks like we are ready to start the fun. Do you want to kick it off?" asked Roy.

"It would be my pleasure, my good man. Fire in the hole! Take that, you bilge-sucking scurvy dogs," yelled Masson, at which point he pushed a button that Roy pointed to.

The bomber rocked hard when a pair of huge missiles fired off. As they headed towards the Chohish cruisers, they could see the vast warships from their cockpit window that made their own craft look and feel tiny in comparison. They continued firing even as the bomber went into evasive maneuvers to evade return fire.

Suddenly, the bomber's proximity alarms started blaring just before the bomber flipped over from an explosion nearby. Heads slammed inside the helmets were pounded against the seat padding. Deep pain blossomed in both occupants as their harnesses bit into them. Then, when Roy was getting control again, the warnings repeated their alarm, indicating another pair of missiles headed straight for them.

As Masson braced for impact, their two fighter escorts flew so close he swore they scraped paint off the bomber's hull. But he was not about to complain as he watched them take out the oncoming missiles.

"Shiver me timbers, that was close! Time to batten down the hatches. Those fighter pilots are me matey's Roy, that be me matey's. That is how Irracan pilots do it! Go get 'em me bucko's," proclaimed Masson.

Never taking his eyes off the controls, Roy could not help smiling while listening to Masson. He had heard about the pirate slang the Irracans mimicked. Roy had even listened to a few of their phrases uttered while on the Lucky Strike. This was to be expected as many of the pilots stationed on the Lucky Strike were Irracan. But this was the first time he heard it directed at himself.

They finished unloading all their missiles without any additional close calls and headed away, escorted by their two pilots.

While on the Lucky Strike, when Isolde pushed the button,

nothing happened for several minutes. If you did not know why you would have thought the signal was not received. But then, power readings suddenly appeared intermittently behind some of the most significant pieces of the dumped ore. This was soon followed by missiles fired by hidden bombers.

The bombers had been sitting still behind the tumbling ore, only with enough energy for their shields to stop the dust. No hot engines, no power to their defensive array, all waiting on a signal. When that signal came, all dozen bombers started their power-up sequence.

When Zeke had put this plan together, that was one of his primary concerns. One of many. That the Chohish would detect the bombers and send their fighters to eliminate them before being able to power up to defend themselves.

When the first missiles from the bombers were detected, Zeke could not stop from doing his fist pump or exclamation bursting forth. And as he watched half the icons for the Chohish fighters turn toward the location of the bombers, no one could miss the savage grin he now wore.

It would take several moments for the missiles from the bombers to reach the Chohish. There was no more he could do for the bombers; they were beyond his reach. He would have to rely on someone else for that.

And as the Chohish got closer to the bombers, that someone became known. They, too, had been at minimal power waiting for the bombers to unload. Then, as the bombers raced away, they were accompanied by a pair of fighters for protection.

But these were not the only fighters; another three dozen other fighters came racing from around the ore, flying towards the Chohish fighters headed their way.

Simultaneously, the RGN warships started ejecting the rest of their fighters. Dozens joined those already present until four dozen flew before the warships.

And as the two opposing fighter groups met and dueled by the dumped ore started their deadly dance, the missiles fired by the bombers finally reached their targets. Dozens upon dozens of missiles rained down on one of the cruisers and the lone destroyer.

The destroyer lasted longer than the cruiser, but both were drifting hulks when the missile barrage ended. This helped alleviate the pounding the Lucky Strike had been getting, barely.

But if the Chohish fighters who went after the bombers thought they would have an easy time of it. They couldn't be any more wrong. They met the fighter group led by the now famous black and red fighter, made up solely of Irracan pilots. They demonstrated that mediocre pilots' skill does not cut it in their navy.

The Irracan fighter pilots came in pairs against lone Chohish fighters with no wingman for protection. And dramatically paid the penalty. Within less than thirty minutes, all twenty-some Chohish fighters were eliminated at the cost of two Irracan fighters whose pilots ejected safely in their pods.

The cruisers made no course change; with one still leaking debris, they continued on without letup while their remaining fighters streamed far ahead.

"Hawke, take groups C and D and blast through the Chohish fighters, afterburners all the way. Do not stop to dogfight. We will follow you to engage. Then, sweep around and rejoin the fight when you can join as one group," ordered Gunner.

"Aye, aye, me matey," replied Hawke. The groan from Gunner was heard throughout all the RGN fighters' cockpits.

Hawke led his fighter group straight at the Chohish fighters firing missiles and lasers as they went. The fighters fired their afterburners the entire way through the Chohish position. The Chohish fighters expected them to engage and started turning towards them when they were hit by the group led by Gunner. Now, out of place, the Chohish took massive casualties.

The rest turned to meet the new group only to be attacked from the rear by Hawke's group reengaging. Gunner and Librada joined Hawke and his wingman to chase down the last two Chohish pilots.

The RGN and Irracan pilots raced back to rejoin the RGN warships. When near, the fighters went into a tight loop going to the port side of the three warships, slowing to match their speed.

And then, just as the Chohish cruisers were minutes away from reaching energy firing range, the three RGN warships swung sharply to starboard. At the same time, their fighters went to the port. The Chohish, though, was in the energy range of the Lucky Strike as the RGN warships turned. The two undamaged Chohish cruisers were buffeted by missiles and energy.

Two of the Chohish warships swung to follow the RGN warships even though all three were now trailing debris. One of the cruisers, the first damaged, continued straight following the freighters' path.

The RGN warships suddenly swung back, heading directly towards the remaining pair of Chohish cruisers. The RGN warships got close enough for the Lucky Strike to fire their energy weapons again before turning away. When the RGN warships swung away this time, the Jackal continued its loop to head for the slipstream following the Chohish cruiser.

This went on for an hour, with the Lucky Strike and the Fox staying out of the Chohish energy range. The Chohish cruisers were taking damage but still able to fire missiles.

Then the forgotten group showed up. As the RGN warships swung in one more time, the RGN and Irracan fighters, regrouped over a hundred strong, came in from the rear. Hundreds of missiles ran up the backside of the Chohish cruisers.

The damage to the Chohish cruisers was horrific. Sections separated and floated away, and flames came out of portholes and left a debris field trailing them. But they never deviated from their course until the energy blasts from the Lucky Strike finally tore them apart.

It took nearly an hour to recall all the fighters before the Lucky Strike started making its way to the slipstream where the Freedom and the freighters had traversed hours ago. Captain Kennedy on the Fox had agreed to stay back, finish the recovery process, and rescue any Chohish that desired it.

Racing to the slipstream, thoughts of what could have happened on the other side gave Zeke grave concern as he had not heard back from the Jackal sent to check it out. The arrival of Jeanne did not alleviate any of his worries.

Hours later, they finally transitioned through the slipstream. Coming out, they brought up their shields and armed their weapons, ready to do battle.

"Isolde, Selena, any response from our prior probes?" asked Zeke with apprehension evident in his voice.

"Yes, there is a large debris field off to starboard. It looks like it is by the path taken by the freighters, based on the exhaust signatures. The Chohish cruiser and the Jackal also traveled through the area," reported Selena. "Isolde is reading the history from the probes to see what she can determine what happened here. I am getting the data from the probes further in."

Without looking up from her console, Isolde started to give her report out loud. "Captain, I am going through the history files; a large battle was waged here between the Chohish cruiser and the Kolqux battleship. Still waiting on more data to determine the outcome. Meanwhile, I am picking up the signatures of the...."

"Cap... sley... go.. see you," came through the speakers loudly at Selena's workstation.

"Sir, I have Captain Hu'de for you," a happy Selena reported. "I am working on strengthening the link."

"Put him on the bridge speakers," ordered Will. "Bring him up on the center screen.

The screen showed a proud Hu'de standing tall in the center of the bridge in his new Captain's uniform. Behind him sat his crew sitting in their new chairs, concentrating on their duties. The short glance from Te'ln was so different from the panicky Kolqux woman from just a few months prior. She sat with confidence and pride at her workstation.

"Captain Hu'de, it is good to see you. Can you give me a status of you, the freighters, and the Jackal?" asked Zeke.

"Everyone is good. The Jackal went off to check on a signal they picked up to ensure it was not more Chohish. Sorry, they had reported they were supposed to report back to you. Still, with the Freedom out of position, they were the only warship left to check it out," explained an apologetic Hu'de.

"I understand and agree with Captain Henry's decision. So, what happened here? Unless our data is incorrect, a battle occurred here, " Zeke asked.

"Unless I am mistaken, our newfound Captain Hu'de had his first command victory to celebrate. Is that not so?" asked Jeanne

The glance at Jeanne by Hu'de could not hide his smile when he heard that. "We saw the Chohish cruiser come out from the slip-stream by itself. We thought you were either destroyed or crippled in your fight with the cruisers."

Walking towards the screen so he was closer to the camera, almost like he could talk in private to Zeke. "Zeke, I was scared, terrified. That cruiser could destroy the freighters easily. I remembered what a wise Captain told me once a long time ago. Concentrate on what options you did have and ignore the ones that you did not. I figured I only had one option. Freedom was the only warship present that could stop the Chohish."

Running his right hand through his long stringy hair, Hu'de

glanced around the bridge like he was hoping they were not paying attention. "I turned the ship around and attacked. The Chohish seemed surprised when I fired off the main weapon as they made no move to avoid it. They must have thought we did not have the concentrated lendolium fuel they were short of. The weapon conversion to use RGN fuel is not as powerful as it normally is, but the glancing blow was enough to give us a major edge. The shot eliminated much of the defensive armament on one side. Our missiles were able to hurt the cruiser enough for us to finish it off with our energy weapons."

"Wow, you and your crew did great. Any casualties?" asked Zeke.

"We lost just over half a dozen, many others injured. I lost a few fighter pilots; I did not know the cruiser was damaged, so I sent them in. I could have held them back," replied Hu'de.

"It is hard to lose crew; they are like your family, well, in our case, they are. But it happens in war. I would like to say it will get easier, but it won't. Just something you must get used to living with," stated Jeanne, Zeke nodding his confirmation in the background.

"Captain, you are definitely a Captain now, Hu'de; we must continue our task. You need to escort these freighters back. I will send you a packet of data to give to the RGN fleet command back at Sobolara. It is possible you may meet an RGN support fleet headed this way; give them a copy, too, so they know what they are headed into. One final thing Hu'de, you and your crew did well. You all saved many thousands. Remember that when burying your dead, it is why you are in that warship. Goodbye, my friend."

"Thanks, I needed that reminder. You and all your crews, take care. We expect to see you soon. Hu'de signing off."

While the Lucky Strike was turning, the Jackal showed up on the probes. Zeke and Lance agreed to meet with the Fox in the other system, where they would resume their search for the Chohish home planets.

DISGUST

CROUCHED LOW BEHIND a retaining wall, Uv'ei pressed his plasma rifle tighter against his chest. The coolness supplied by his armor contrasted sharply against the sun's searing heat. It was just before midday, which was forecast to be a scorcher in this immediate area.

They had been slowly infiltrating the cities for weeks now. The Chohish and their counterparts ignored the countryside for the most part. The resistance has been active for generations and was well established.

The resistance had been smuggling people and weapons into the city through tunnels and large trucks almost at will. But the opposition had been severely limited in the past on what they could do as the Kolqux in charge would get the Chohish to step in when they could not handle it. Now, though, they were anxious to right the wrongs done to them.

The group attached to Uv'ei and Uv'ek had been smuggled in throughout the night. Since the Sorath took control of the skies, the Chohish and their allies have hunkered down in their fortresses.

The massive building on the other side of the retaining wall was the capital building for the Kolqux and Endaen overlords. The building had defensive batteries on all four corners. Overlaying it all was a silvery sheen indicating a force field. Other batteries stationed on the roof of the building were removed by the Sorath over a month ago. Shield or no shield, the Sorath would not be denied; instead, they had brought on overwhelming firepower to get through the shields.

The whirl of mechanical gears blared in his ears as two of the batteries tracked the roar of a Kolqux fighter flying overhead. The batteries fired a short burst before the fighter was out of range.

"Uv'ek, when I tap your shoulder, take down the shields. Feekal, upon my signal, your group is to take out the four batteries. Codri put penetrators into both main entrances on both sides of the building once the batteries are destroyed. Remember, Feekal, we must confirm that the shields are down, so you must wait for my signal."

Looking over at his brother, Uv'ei could not hide his fear that this may be the last time he saw him alive. When he made the tap on his brother's shoulder, it would signal to all the armed forces around the world to start the fight for freedom from the Chohish and their lackeys.

They were starting later in the day than Uv'ei would like, but the Chohish main encampment was on another continent. The RGN was going to take the lead attack on that facility. Since no Kolqux nor Endaen is stationed there, using RGN soldiers would not be an issue. The Chohish there had heavier weapons than those he would be pitted against; he agreed that the RGN would make the call on when to attack. The RGN plans called for going just before sunrise on that continent but would allow Uv'ei to give the start signal.

When Uv'ei tapped Uv'ek, the AI in his armor would signal all the commanders worldwide. Knowing he could not delay any longer, he tapped Uv'eks shoulder. Uv'ek and half a dozen others fired the missile they had lugged miles through the city, even though it must have weighed nearly half his weight. Seven missiles raced into the air, swinging around to slam into the building. As the missiles passed overhead, Uv'ei, ignoring everything Khaleesi trained him not to do, raised his head to see over the retaining wall.

The batteries twirled down when it identified the missiles but failed to gain lock before the missiles hit the shields. Uv'ei smiled as he remembered when Marcellin told him to have one of his fighters fly past just before their attack. This repositioned the batteries to point skyward, delaying a lock on the missiles as they would have to move downward.

Uv'ei watched as the shields flickered, then died. "Feekal, fire! Hurry before the shields can regenerate," he yelled into his helmet.

Dozens of missiles and plasma bolts struck each of the batteries. There had been concern about using too much firepower. But Khaleesi had told him better to have too much than not enough. It's not like he could just go back and do it again. Uv'ei had taken that to heart and doubled his original plans. But, as he was local, Uv'ei had to make the call on how much force to use.

The shockwave that rebounded from the batteries forced Uv'ei to the ground. Without the helmet, Uv'ei was sure his eardrums would have been shattered. Still, the sound was tremendous. Thankfully, he had followed Khaleesi's recommendation to only have fully armored soldiers equipped with helmets within several blocks of the blast.

The thumbs up displayed from a shaky Uv'ek, leaning against the retaining wall while bits of metal and concrete rained down around them, almost made Uv'ei laugh. But the sound of the penetrators firing reminded him where he was and why.

These missiles were designed so most of the blast would go forward and not spread out. That was to enable the opening of armored entrances without taking out the surrounding support. It would not bring down the structure, but you did not want to be in front of the blast. Instead, each building entrance had a large explosion forced outward from the opposing penetrator.

Uv'ei jumped over the wall and ran towards the entrance without waiting for the debris to finish settling. Laser fire from the upper floors rained down on him from open windows as he ran towards the door. All the training he had painfully endured came to the forefront. He ran, using the power assist in his armor to propel him faster than he could have ever dreamed of just six months ago. Then, jumping a large piece of masonry from the battery platform, he landed on his feet only to roll forward to enter the building, searching for targets.

Seeing a movement on the floor one level up from the atrium, he saw a rifle barrel peeking over the railing. He fired his plasma rifle as he leveled up onto his knee before running towards the upstairs stairwell. His shot was not at the rifle barrel but midway to the floor below it. It went through the decorative front and punched through the body hidden behind it. Uv'ei did not wait to confirm the shot but continued toward the stairwell. The sound of the rifle falling into the atrium was enough confirmation.

A pair of laser beams to his left did not surprise him, as that was his purpose for being in front. He was the rabbit. Following behind him were the hunters who made short work of the pair of Kolqux soldiers who had exposed themselves to fire at him.

The stairs before him went up, but another set went down. Then, taking three steps at a time, he went up. Uv'ek took a group with him as he went down while more spread out to check all the rooms at this level.

Reaching the second level, he threw the small camera past the three openings on the right. The camera floated past the opening relaying the data back to his helmet. His helmet showed multiple red icons from the first hallway of elevators. Without pausing, he triggered the grenade launcher towards the first opening. The grenade bounced off the opposite wall to sail down into the first hall station. Screams of panic rang out before the thermal grenade went off. The red icons on his helmet display for that section disappeared.

Two red circles on the middle right of his helmet indicated rifles from the second opening. He dropped to the floor and slid past the entrance, spraying plasma without letup. Laser blasts went through the area where he would have been standing in. The helmet enhanced his vision to show the destruction of plasma bolts. Limbs were torn off arms, holes appeared in unarmored bodies, and heads exploded. The thought he was doing this to other Kolqux disgusted him. But not as must as they disgusted him for what they did to innocent Kolqux.

Not stopping to check on the results of his plasma blasts, depending on the group following him, he rolled to his feet and ran on. Now floating over his head, the camera had shown a female Kolqux with a child huddled in fear in the rear of the third hall station.

Past the third opening, he raced forward to a door leading to a stairwell. He had gained intel while waiting in a dirty shack at the city's edge. The Kolqux president and generals were known to reside in sumptuous rooms at the top of this building. He planned to meet them head-on.

Lowering his shoulder, he slung his rifle backward to where it attached to his back magnetically. Then, reaching to draw his pistol from his holster with his right hand, he used his left to pull his marine knife in the other. Seeing his destination just ahead, he lowered his shoulder a little more before slamming into the door. The door burst open, throwing two guards against the far wall. While others were standing on the stairs.

Before they could react, he kneeled while firing on the ones standing startled at his sudden entrance. Then, using his left hand, he knifed the two that had been knocked down. A sudden burn feeling on his left shoulder let him know he had been hit by a laser, but it had not penetrated his armor.

Bracing, he pushed up the stairs against the crowd of soldiers, trying to come down. Using the power supplied by the armor, he stacked up the soldiers against themselves. Firing into the mass of soldiers, he found that Khaleesi was right. The pistol fire was adequate, but the knife, in close quarters, was devastating.

Slashing high, low, and mid-level, he took out soldier after soldier until they started panicking. Screaming as they tried to avoid him, their laser shots went wide. Seeing a sniper at the top of the stairs on this level, he slid sideways to put someone between them. Knifing the soldier standing in front of him in the throat, he lifted the body onto his back. Without the assistance from the powered armor, he would never have been able to lift and hold it.

Putting his pistol back in its holster, he grabbed his second knife behind his neck so he had one in each hand. And then, he went to work. Using the native power provided by months of physical exercise, paid for in pain every night, and the boost from servos in his armor, he waded through the dozens of soldiers in the stairwell.

While they tried to use rifles with long barrels in a crowded stairwell, he used two blades whose blades shone with the sonic laser edges that could slice through solid steel an inch thick. The composite armor worn by these soldiers did little to impede his knives.

Slash, knee, stab, punch, kick, slash again, all occurred without thought. Suddenly, he was standing alone amidst dozens of bodies. Gasping for oxygen, he looked down at three terrified kneeling soldiers who had thrown away their weapons with their hands raised.

Cursing behind him cleared the rage in his mind. Codri, climbing through the bodies with his escort, looked around in wonderment. Not waiting, Uv'ei continued up the stairs leaving the soldiers that surrendered for others to manage.

His helmet indicated multiple areas of his armor that had taken damage. Only the knee on his left side and the shoulder on his right were colored red. Half a dozen others flashed yellow.

But he was still functional; Uv'ei had not come all this way to stop now. Glancing back to ensure his guard was still following, he raced up the currently empty stairs. As he went, he sent a command to the floating camera to race ahead.

The images coming back showed five soldiers planting explosives on the ceiling three levels up. Slipping his knives back into their sheaths, he grabbed his rifle, leaned over in the stairwell, and fired into the explosives they had been planted. Plaster, metal, and dust rained down. Mixed in were body parts and blood.

Reaching the next floor level, the stairs were gone. Uv'ei was forced to grab metal beams hanging from the wall to pull himself onto the next level. Reaching into the pack on his back, he pulled out a thin rope that he quickly tied off to a metal beam and dropped the rest down the opening in the stairwell. Not waiting for the escort to climb up to meet him, Uv'ei continued on.

It was another dozen floor levels before he came to the top. In front of him was a heavy steel door. He knew whoever was on the other side was waiting on him. They would be ready with whatever weapons were at hand. Inspecting the area, Uv'ei saw a small camera blinking red at him. He knew they were watching him. Smiling, he gestured with his finger at the camera, then leaping high, Uv'ei ripped it from the wall.

Pulling his backpack off, he reached in to grab several breaching charges. Removing the cover over the holding paste, he placed one on the door. Following the same procedure, he stuck another on the wall several feet away on both sides of the door. Taking the last one, he put this one on the ceiling.

Crouching under the charge on the ceiling, he switched back to his knives before setting the timer to have all four go off at once. When they went off, several things happened at once. First, the door flew inwards; second, the wall shattered; and third, he jumped.

The five occupants had been expecting the charges and had been hidden behind barriers quickly placed. Couches, bookcases, desks, chairs, and so on. They all fired heavy-duty lasers at the new openings. The firing only paused after a minute when there was no return fire.

The only indication something was wrong was when there was a sudden creaking from the ceiling before a large body dropped through to land behind them. What they saw made them pause in fright. A helmeted figure in futuristic armor stood there, covered in blood and gore.

But where they paused, the figure didn't. It swept forward, sweeping past each of the standing figures until it reached the other end. Turning, Uv'ei watched as the final two joined the other three on the ground. The slit throats pumped blood all over the floor.

Looking at fellow Kolqux who reveled in keeping others downtrodden filled him with rage. The sudden sound from the blown-out doorway had him dropping one knife to grab his pistol without thinking.

Codri peeked around the corner before hesitantly entering the room. Behind Codri, others mirrored his actions. Walking gingerly over to one of the Kolqux lying dead on the floor, Codri removed his helmet to spit on the figure.

Holding his helmet in his hand, Codri looked at Uv'ei with amazement. "I remember when we first met. I was not that impressed."

Running his hand over his sweat-streaked face despite the armor he wore, Cotri sat on his haunches. "I had some grave doubts then and almost pulled out. How wrong could I be? Where did you learn to do what you just did?"

Taking off his helmet so he could look at Codri eye to eye. Calmly, with none of the rage that still ran through his blood showing or in his voice, Uv'ei replied. "I learned from the best of the best. She is known to the humans as a Marines Marine, a rarity. But even more important, she is my friend."

Looking back at the bodies on the floor, Codri asked Uv'ei what they should do with them. He was shocked when he heard the reply.

"That's up to you. This is your world now. You are free to do whatever you want. These scums only disgust me; I want nothing more to do with them."

With that, Uv'ei stopped to retrieve his knife before heading downstairs to meet his brother, who had just finished mopping up the resistance on the bottom floors. It was time to start planning how to take the war to the Chohish.

GUESSING

THE THREE SHIPS entered the slipstream slowly and quietly. A bomber took off from the skin of one ship heading inward. It made no course change or speed adjustment after reaching full speed.

"Enjoyed your last trip so much that you had to do it again? Do you have a death wish?" asked Roy.

"My wife says I am an adrenaline junkie. She should talk. If not for the baby, she would be here instead of me. Our first date was parachute jumping. We had a bet about who would open the chute first," answered Masson.

"I gather she won the bet?"

"By a mile. And by that, I mean she beat me by a mile in distance. Damn woman scared me to death that she was going to hit the ground. As it was, she hit hard enough that even Jeanne yelled at her for being foolish. I knew then I had to marry her. I had never met a woman who matched my love of the thrill."

"From what I heard from the Irracan pilots, Jeanne is worse than her sister. True?" asked Roy.

"You have no idea, I thought Anne was unique, but it seems her whole family is. Jeanne's passion is the fighter, like her father. None is better in the cockpit, although I heard Zeke is. Gunner swears by him. Her brothers like larger toys but just as crazy," answered a thoughtful Masson. "It has been a trip like none I could have dreamed of since I met my wife. How about you?"

"My wife, Carol, is the opposite of me. She is quiet, reserved, average looking, and extremely shy. But has a heart of gold, is solid, dependable, and knows how to make me laugh. I could not imagine life without her. Spencer used to say she is what made me so effective. Someone that forced me to think and not just react."

Quiet reigned in the cockpit for nearly an hour as each contemplated their past life. Habit forced Roy to turn off the timer before it went off. "Are you ready? Never heard of a bomber doing this before, so I have no idea what will happen if we have visitors in the system."

"Puckered up and ready to go! Here, let me do it while you relax," laughed Masson.

From out of the bomber missile tubes came a pair of probes. Both sped away to disappear in the distance. Then with the bomber turning slightly to port, two more flew away. Once more, the bomber turned, now far to starboard. Again, two more probes shot out.

"Now we get to see if anyone has been watching," whispered Roy as he turned the bomber around to head back to where the cruiser should be.

The probes continued on their path unopposed. But they did not go undetected. First, one electronic signature appeared, but it was soon followed by more. One by one, defensive batteries came online and were now visible to detection.

Then what Roy feared most happened. Missile signatures came looking for them.

"Damn, why didn't they go after the probes first? Why us?" demanded Roy.

"Probes are too small to worry about; they would never get

through their shields. But us now, possible," answered Masson. "You would know that if you were a fighter pilot. They go after the men of war first; fighters are secondary targets. All based on size."

"Well, I hope you made peace with the world and your wife because we will never outrun these missiles," exclaimed Roy.

The laughter Roy heard puzzled him, but he did not have time to ask why; he was too busy trying to avoid the missiles and stay alive.

"You need to understand Irracans more. Do you think my wife or sister-in-law would allow us to do this without taking precautions?" asked Roy as he sat relaxed in the co-pilot chair. "Zeke made the same assumption when we first met."

As if in reply to that statement, half a dozen Irracan fighters' signatures came online.

"Masson, my sister, wants to know when will you stop playing with these death machines and get back into the cockpit of a fighter?" It was a voice Roy had heard before but could not place with all the electronic disturbance.

"You should try this sometime, Jeanne. It is a rush, not for someone that is skitterish, that is for sure."

"Masson, if you tell that to Anne, so help me, I will make you regret it. She will demand to go out on the next flight to check it out. She has a baby to worry about now."

"Ha! You're just afraid she will make you watch the baby while she has some fun."

No reply came, nor did Masson expect it; instead, the two bomber pilots watched as the fighters chased after the missiles.

"How did the Captain know there would defensive batteries in this system?" wondered Masson.

"I am not sure he did. Guessed it most likely, or as this Captain seems to do, deduced it. We have gone through six empty systems since the mining facility. We must be getting closer to their home system. It makes sense to have something to slow down anything coming this way," conjectured Roy.

The cruiser and two destroyers appeared shortly on their screens, taking no further steps to remain undetected. Then, as they got closer, the fighters returned to escort them the rest of the way.

Landing and disembarking, Roy was surprised to see Captain Kinsley and Lieutenant Commander Chandler waiting for them.

"Gentlemen, great job. I had a feeling that these things would show up sooner than later. But, because of your actions, we were able to avoid being in the middle of them before detecting them," Zeke stated while putting his arm around their shoulders.

"Oh, crap Roy, he is about to ask us to do something else," exclaimed Masson.

"Now, come on, Masson, aren't you the one that keeps telling Jeanne that he likes to do something different as long as it has a thrill associated with it?" asked Zeke.

"Normally, yes, but with you, I am starting to reconsider that," answered a cautious Masson.

The laughter from Roy had all looking at him. "Ok, Cap, what crazy idea do you want to try? Spencer would have loved to be here, as this is the type of crap he likes. Just spit it out, and we will do it. Don't pay any attention to Masson; he is ready to go no matter what."

The sound of marching alerted everyone to a new presence. When the reason for the sound came into view, it did not surprise the Captain nor the Lieutenant Commander, so they must have been expecting them. When Roy saw them, he rolled his eyes as he suddenly knew the Captain's crazy idea. "Oh hell, you are one crazy Captain; how do you get to keep your stars?" he exclaimed.

"By having the best crew in the entire fleet," Zeke laughed while saying it.

"What, have you figured out what he wants us to do?" asked a puzzled Masson, looking between the Captain and Roy.

"Yeah, unless I am mistaken, the Cap wants us to deliver those technicians and marines to one of the Chohish batteries. What the hell are they going to accomplish? I have no idea."

"Damn Roy, you are good. Where have you been? I could have used you a lot earlier. That is precisely what I need to be done. Smooth believes if we can get the guts of a defensive battery, we can override the code to have them destroy themselves."

Seeing Roy looking at him in puzzlement, Zeke clarified his answer. "You may know Smooth better as Lieutenant Commander Jax Andrews."

"And how are we supposed to get to a defensive battery that works in sync with the other batteries?" asked Masson.

"Oh, that is easy, Masson; the Captain is going to rub his magic lamp and wish all the rest shut down until we can land next to one and steal all its components," answered Jax as he joined the group.

"I would, but Jeanne stole my lamp; she is a pirate, you know. Looks like we have to do it the hard way. We are going to send you all out in a shuttle, and whoever survives lands on the battery," joked Zeke. "Actually, it should be pretty easy if no men of war are present. Find the closest one, and use missiles to remove the supporting batteries. Then hit the battery in question with lasers to remove defenses. See, simple, easier than a lamp."

"We're sending a bomber as it has heavier shields and armament in case we miss something," Jamie clarified.

"And when do you expect to do this? Do we have time to catch a nap?" asked Roy.

The laughter from Jax and Jamie answered Roy's question. "I guess them being all dressed in armor should have given me a hint. But please, give me enough time to go to the bathroom, ok?"

With a sweep of his arm, Zeke pointed to the restrooms next to Jamie's office. "Of course, we would not deprive you of that."

That conversation was on Roy's mind as he piloted the bomber toward the Chohish battery that had been neutralized. Well, that is what they said anyway. As they got closer, the ship rocked from a laser hit. And the laser did not stop. Alarms blared as Roy tried desperately to bring the bomber around the battery, away from the laser.

The proximity alarm now blared along with the damage alarm. Desperate to find out what the hell was coming at them, Roy was surprised when the damage alarm settled down.

"Sorry about that; we thought we had crippled all the weapons," Isolde's voice came through the speakers. "That laser popped up unexpectedly. We took it out with a small defensive missile; anything larger, and well, goodbye you." Her laughter did nothing to soothe Roy's nerves.

"You know Masson, maybe I will try flying a fighter. It cannot be any more dangerous than what this damn Captain has us doing," stated Roy.

"What the hell are you complaining about? I am an engineer on a cruiser; I am not supposed to be sitting in a cramped bomber getting my ass shot off!" yelled Jax.

Roy and Masson looked at each other before saying, "so true," and laughed loudly.

Directing the bomber next to the large battery, Roy used the magnetics to look it down. Ensuring everyone had their helmets on correctly, he opened the door. "Good luck to you all; we'll be here waiting for you."

The look he got from Jax was enough for Roy to respond with a smile.

Carrying his toolkit, Jax stepped onto the skin of the battery. Walking around the area he could reach, he stopped by an access hatch. Then, pulling a small laser from the kit, he cut through what looked like a door lock. About to open the hatch, an armored hand closed over his stopping the action.

"We go first, Sir; that's why we're here. Please move aside." The marine watched him while he moved away. He stopped when he thought he was far enough only to be waved back even further.

The Marine walked around the hatch paying close attention to the piece Jax had cut out. Something must not have looked right as he took a string from a pouch around his waist. Using the line, he tied a weight which he swung around his head before smacking the hatch with the weight.

The hatch exploded outwards. Surprised, Jax dropped to his knees to keep his balance. He watched as the marine threw an object through the hatch, and another minor explosion occurred. And again, another object was thrown in, but nothing happened this time.

"Stay here until I give the go-ahead, Sir." The marine then carefully eased his way inside the battery. Jax stayed kneeling for another ten minutes before hearing the marine tell him he could come in.

Entering, Jax was entranced with the different technology. He had examined many of the Chohish equipment, even a few defensive batteries. But nothing like this. The equipment looked like older versions. What he did notice was the height of the workstations. These must have been made for Endaens.

Having an idea where to start, he settled on the floor under the table at the far workstation. If this matched the others he examined, this was where the database and control codes resided. Getting what they needed was not going to be easy, hence why he was here and not one of his associates. Oh well, this comes with being in charge; time to get busy; he would be here for a while.

Hours passed, and the only thing breaking the boredom in

the bomber was when the marine came to get new oxygen tanks. Masson was surprised and happy when Roy brought out a deck of cards. After more than five hours, Jax emerged from the platform with the marine trailing. Both were lugging multiple pieces of equipment with wires hanging over their shoulders. Several trips were necessary to transfer everything to the bomber.

Finally, they were ready to leave. As Jax sat next to the marine, he finally decided he had time to ask what had happened when they first got there. Then, twisting his body to face the marine, he asked his question.

The marine removed his helmet and leaned his head back against the hull. A large scar ran down the left side of his neck to be hidden under his armor. "I thought you were familiar with these types of installations. The Chohish boobytraps installations that are not manned by personnel. We do the same. Hell, even the Soraths do it. When you cut the lock, you set off a trigger to explode when the hatch is opened. Then again, they had motion sensors as a backup."

"Thinking back on it, I only ever went onto ones that had already been cleared. Thanks, you saved my life," expressed a grateful Jax.

"That is why I'm here, sir. Glad I was useful."

"Do you mind me asking why you wear the scar when you could have it removed?" asked Roy. "You do not have to answer if you are sensitive about it."

"I wear it to remind me that officers can be assholes. At the same time, certain ones are to be admired," the marine answered.

"Where did you get the scar?" Jax asked, working on a hunch.

"Yeplillon" was all he answered, confirming what Jax suspected. This marine was one of the half dozen surviving officers other than Khaleesi.

"It is widely known of your thoughts on the Major. What about for the Captain?" The deep rumble of chortling from the marine let Jax know he was not insulted when asked.

"They are of the same cloth. How many Captains do you know that would risk their lives and career for a fighter lieutenant? Then, hiding being critically injured, he is ready to go alone on a *planned, suicidal desperate one-way trip to attempt, against all odds, to save civilians.* All in an attempt to save people he had only just met. As I said, they are two of the same cloth. A Captain's Captain, a Marine's Marine. Both worthy of my respect."

The rest of the trip was in silence. Not because Jax did not have any more questions, he had lots. But unless he was mistaken, the marine was sleeping.

The rest of the trip was uneventful. Upon returning to the Lucky Strike, Jax was again met by the Captain in the bay talking with Gunner. The prior conversation with the marine came rushing back.

"Well, any idea on how long before you know if it's a go or not?" Zeke asked. "I have held off wasting missiles to take out enough platforms to get through the system. I may have to cancel our trip to rearm."

"I should know within a few hours. I will need assistance from the ship's AI to run some calculations."

"Done. LS1 will be made available." Zeke stated before turning to leave. He paused when they heard, "I am ready when Lieutenant Commander Andrews is," come from the speakers.

"Damn, Cap, I am not sure I will ever get used to that," uttered Jax looking at the ceiling.

"Same here," came a reply from above.

It would have gotten a lot stranger if not for Zeke bending over laughing. "How can you not love that?"

Walking onto the bridge, he saw the questioning look from

83

everyone. "Jax has what he needs, well, what he believes he needs. Your guess is as good as mine if he can do it."

It was a hundred and ninety-some minutes when they would have their answer. Standing on the bridge, Jax explained to Zeke, Will, and Jeanne that he was ready to try it. It was untried with no guarantee. Only when he had been examining Chohish equipment for lack of EMP protection did he notice the exposure he hoped to capitalize on.

The three ships were now stationed back at the slipstream. They did not want to have calculated wrong and initiate a disaster. Everyone looked at Isolde as she prepared the code she had received from Jax for transmission.

"And how is this going to work?" asked Jeanne.

"I am sending out a priority command overriding their original program. I am instructing them that the platform next to them has been compromised, and they are to eliminate them. All platforms are to lower shields, as that is how they were compromised. Since we will be sending it to all of them..." where Jax shrugged. "If it works, I expect we may get a pretty large light show at the minimum."

"Odds?" Zeke asked while watching the main screen.

"No idea; it would only be a guess anyway," Jax answered with a shrug.

With a theatric performance worthy of a major movie star, Isolde gave a dramatic death scene while pushing the send button. At first, nothing happened. Seeing everyone looking at him, Jax said to be patient. It took time to get to all the platforms. So they waited. And waited.

Just as they were ready to give up hope, the system lit up with a big bang, not piecemeal, but all at once. Then slowly, it settled down to individual explosions.

"Well, I guess it worked," Jax said proudly. Only to look up when he heard, "*I guess it did; congrats Lieutenant Commander,*" come from the speakers on the ceiling. "*I approve.*"

A startled Jax stared at the ceiling. "Well, LS1, I guess you deserve some credit too." Blushing, Jax looked around, perplexed, while pointing at the ceiling. "Holy crap, am I actually congratulating an AI?"

"*Yes, I do deserve some credit. And yes, you are. Thanks, Jax.*"

The laughter on the bridge only made Jax blush all the redder. Knowing he could not win, Jax could only sigh in resignation before joining in with the laughter.

MIRACLE

PASSING CAUTIOUSLY THROUGH the system, they were surprised at the number of destroyed Chohish defensive platforms drifting past them. Not all were destroyed; some were damaged, while others looked pristine but showed no power readings.

"Based on the probes, I knew they had placed a lot of platforms here, but what we are seeing surpasses what I expected by the hundreds. We would never have gotten through with the missile supply we had. I hope we do not meet any more systems setups like this," Will said in amazement. "It is a shame, though. Jax does not think the algorithm he created will work again as each system would probably have different versions."

"He said we would have to go through the whole procedure again. Jax will train one of his associates to go next time; something about once was enough for him. Oh, he also said these have been here a long time based on analysis of the material he brought back," updated Hawke. "Masson said he is returning to his fighter; bombers are fun but too damn slow for his taste."

"I would bet some ran out of fuel; that would explain the undamaged ones. No energy; the rest did not target them. I am curious about where they built them and how they got them here. There must be something close by," mused Zeke.

When they entered the next system, Isolde reported that the sensors recorded they had been probed, but the signal disappeared almost immediately afterward.

Moving further into the system, they got an answer to one of Zeke's questions. But one that brought dread and sadness to all. It took hours and double the number of probes typically used to fully understand what they were looking at. But when they did, in anger, Zeke had Omaw brought up to the bridge.

"Are you aware of this?" he yelled at him while pointing to the images rolling across all three screens.

At first, Omaw did not know why he was brought to the bridge. Seeing the faces expressing horror while others looked at him with hate surprised him. Prior visits to the bridge have never shown such animosity towards him. It was not until he looked up where Zeke was pointing, did he understand why. He reeled back against the guards in shock.

Across the screens rolled images of a destroyed world. Modern cities lay in ruins. Tall skyscrapers toppled over the top of transportation thoroughfares. The wind blew debris around in a swirl. As the images moved away from the cities, you could see a long line of ground transportation heading out, destroyed in place. Downed air transports dotted the landscape. In one of the larger cities, a vast factory that never should have resided in an atmosphere had flattened whole city blocks. Blackened tree stumps littered the countryside, with weeds growing everywhere. Rural housing districts were demolished.

The clear indications that this had occurred while populated were the most depressing. Apparent signs of torso remains were everywhere. It could not be definitively determined what race had existed here without landing. Still, from what they could see from the size of the doorways and vehicles, the population had been small in stature. Similar to the size of the Kolqux or Endaen. Zeke could only imagine the outrage this would cause when they saw this.

When this occurred, they could not determine, but it could not have been that far in the past. A rough estimate was this had to have happened within the last hundred years. What was most disturbing was that there was no sign of humanoid life. Wild animals could be seen roaming the landscape but no signs of civilization.

"No, I did not know about this. We traveled in ships sealed from external views. We are soldiers, trained to fight, not enjoy comfort," Omaw replied, never taking his eyes off the screens. "My soldiers would never have condoned or participated in something like this."

"How is this different than what your soldiers did on Niflhel or Nocuous? They destroyed cities of innocents and killed millions? Soldiers killed small helpless children indiscriminately. What you did here was done on a much larger, grander scale. You talked to me before of your people's honor. Where is the honor in this?" No one could not hear the anger in Zeke's voice. "A whole world. Dammit, your people destroyed a whole damn world. How many more like this exist?"

Unable to hold eye contact with Zeke, Omaw lowered his head in shame. "I did not know."

"Will, take us into orbit. We need to land and find out precisely what happened here. If the people that died here are who I think they were, when the Kolqux, Endaens, and Soraths see this, there will be no stopping them from exacting revenge. It is hard enough to hold them back now, but when they see this...." Zeke voiced while looking at Hawke.

There was no mistaking what Hawke was feeling. His feathers were standing on end, and his hands were clenched tight and shaking as he stared at Omaw with hate. "My people have experienced this from these monsters. I love you like a brother Zeke, but if you stand in my people's way in eliminating animals like them, like him, I will fight you. They do not deserve to exist."

No one was shocked at these statements from Hawke, except maybe Omaw. Everyone here knew the atrocities the Chohish had committed against the Soraths. They had seen it committed themselves just recently against their own people. Most held the same feelings.

"Captain, I am picking up a space graveyard. It was obscured by the planet and moon. It looks like a significant battle was held here along with destroyed shipyards," reported Isolde. "Damn, Selena, check probe nine. Was that an electronic signal on the planet?"

All eyes swung over to Selena. "It was momentary, but definitely a signal, almost like it was turned off. It could have been anything. A relic, maybe?"

As they got closer to the planet, more signs of conflict appeared. The moon was littered with debris; smaller debris they took to be warships, fighters, and shuttles still floated in orbit around the planet.

Entering orbit over what looked to be the largest city on the planet, they prepared to descend. Several shuttles of marines would go first to secure a landing site before a select group of officers from each ship would join them.

When Zeke stepped off the shuttle, he was met by two marines. Both had their helmets on, but he knew who one was immediately by the Major insignia on the armor.

Checking the atmosphere readings on his helmet, Zeke saw it matched the reading from probes they had sent down before departure. The atmosphere was in the range safe for humans. No dangerous pathogens could be found. Then, as he took his helmet off, he got a warning from Khaleesi that she recommended he leave it on for security's sake.

89

"I am willing to take the risk, Major. I need to feel the wind on my face and experience the smell of a destroyed world."

The wind blew around them, carrying the smell of pollen from an unknown plant and dust. Then, walking toward what used to be a road, Zeke bent down to pick up an object half hidden in the soil. The half that had been exposed had severely deteriorated. Still, the section that had been buried showed the features of an animal. Zeke did not recognize the animal, but the object was something that would have been owned by a child, a toy.

Kneeling, Zeke opened the hole that had contained the toy broader and more profound. Placing the toy inside the spot, he covered it with reverence. Then, bending his head, he said a small Godspeed to the owner of this toy.

Rising, Zeke waved the marines to lead the way to the city's center. Hawke silently walked next to him. Zeke was not surprised to see he had taken off his helmet too. Jeanne had stayed back to take command of all the ships if something happened to the group on the ground.

The trip through the city was challenging. They had to climb over or through rusting cars, backtrack when the way was blocked by a building lying across their path, or traverse through deteriorating buildings. But all that was minor compared to the most significant impediment. Craters caused by an explosion or melted metal from intense heat were common throughout the city on almost every street.

Sweat running down into his armor, Zeke stared up at the building in front of him. The exterior contained some type of windows at some point; none existed now. Entering the building, he entered a massive atrium with stairwells running up both sides. Inches of dust covered the floor. No sign of disturbance marred the dust, showing that nothing had been here for ages.

"Jax, we're here. Do your thing. Let me know if you or your staff need any assistance. I am going to look around down here."

Jax and several of his staff headed up the stairs, led by a marine escort. Meanwhile, Zeke headed towards what looked like offices. Entering, he saw that it was also covered in dust. A curved desk lay on its side, cracked down the middle. On the floor were two sets of bones huddled against the back wall.

"I cannot imagine the terror these people experienced. This must have been the center of their government. They must have known their world was being systematically destroyed. I wonder how they died? Did they just give up once they knew everything they knew was gone?" asked a somber Hawke.

"Captain, Isolde here. We have received another hit on probe nine. We were able to pinpoint the location. We are sending you that location now. We will let you know if we have anything further. Isolde out."

Turning, Zeke told Khaleesi, who stood in the doorframe, "Gather a team; we are heading to check that signal out. Hawke, notify Jax to bring another tech with him; they are going with us."

"I am having a pair of marine shuttles come to our location. There is a clearance large enough several blocks over," Khaleesi reported while hand-signaling the pair of marines behind her. The two marines went running off.

As they walked out of the building, a squad of marines surrounded them. Two battleoids came stomping around the corner of the building.

"Where the hell did they come from?" asked Zeke.

"I brought a dozen down with us. This is an unknown territory with no idea what we will encounter." Khaleesi responded. If Zeke thought it was overkill, he was not about to mention it. He was sure Khaleesi would have preferred to bring *ALL* the battleoids down but knew Zeke would not have approved.

It still took them over twenty minutes to get to the shuttles, having to climb through all the debris. Jax and his technician were the last to arrive, carried by battleoids that bulldozed their way through the rubble.

The shuttles took off, heading to the location supplied by Isolde and Selena. The shuttles were flying low in silent mode. Shields were up with weapons charged. The site was hundreds of miles away at the base of a mountain range. They should arrive in less than half an hour at the speed the shuttle was making.

"Thoughts on what we will find?" quired Zeke.

"Could be anything. Old sensor or shield left on and running out of fuel. If it is powered up when we get there, we will find it quickly enough, " Jax mused. "It may even have a working computer that could tell us what happened here."

"Khaleesi, have the pilots take us in low and circle the immediate area of the signal. I want to see what the surrounding neighborhood looks like. May give us an idea of what the site was built for," requested Zeke.

Shortly, they were circling the area in smaller and smaller rotations. Zeke had every monitor in the shuttle bay set to a different camera. Then, as the images started displaying, he moved around to look at each camera closely. He would look at one, expand the image, move to another, and back to the prior one. This continued for longer than the others expected; they started looking at each other questionably.

"Ok, let's get this bucket on the ground," ordered Zeke.

The two shuttles came to land on the street inside a small town that did not show the same level of destruction as the large city.

The shuttle with the battleoids landed first. Marines in full armor came running out first, taking up guard positions around the shuttle. Then came the two battleoids. One deployed further down the street while the other kneeled with its weapon sweeping in a half circle.

The shuttle with the Captain landed behind the battleoid up the street, and the ramp dropped where marines ran out, taking up similar positions. No movement occurred for a dozen minutes.

"Hey Hawke, I have a huge favor to request of you," Zeke asked while removing his armor, ignoring Khaleesi's vehement protests.

Puzzled at first, Hawke smiled as he must have guessed why. "I have been cooped up too long. It would be great to feel the air under my wings again."

"Khaleesi, Hawke, and I will go out while the rest stay in the shuttle until I give the ok. You and one other marine will accompany us," ordered Zeke.

He may be an idiot for doing this, but he had seen something while examing the terrain. In fact, he could get Hawke, and himself killed if he was right.

Stopping at the top of the shuttle ramp, he breathed deeply, smelling what he had seen. Growth. His family had been in the cocoa business for his whole life. Some of his fondest memories were running through the cocoa fields with his father and siblings. He loved the smell of plant *growth*. Every plant gave off its own particular scent, but once you discerned one, you perceived them all.

Moving out from the shuttle, he stepped over the edge onto a plot of turf half a foot high. He had no idea what the turf was, but it was better than sitting on a street that had seen better days. Hawke settled in beside him.

"When did you figure it out?" asked Hawke as he snapped a short length of what looked like orange-looking grass before putting it between his two thumbs. Then, blowing between his thumbs, he produced a high whistle shriek. Then, moving his thumbs around while still blowing, Hawke created a sound resembling a bird in his native land.

"Is that the Ruqualash bird on your planet?" asked Zeke.

"I am impressed you would know that. I used to wake up to their singing every morning. A large nest of them lived in the tree in our side yard. My family used to sit in the yard singing with them every spring just before dusk. The birds would fly around the tree, singing, looking for a mate."

They sat there momentarily before Hawke repeated his question that Zeke had not answered.

"You used to play that bird melody when we were in the Academy. I wanted to know more about it, so I looked it up on your planet's database. Regarding your question, when Isolde reported the short signal from the planet, I hoped some survived. We will see," he answered.

"How long will we sit here?" Hawke asked. "Would it be ok for me to take a short flight? I really would like to stretch my wings."

Seeing Zeke smile and swipe his hand upwards, Hawke jumped up before leaping into the sky. Hawke flapped his wings hard and shot upward with speed and agility before coming down to sweep by Zeke, who laughed at his antics. During one of Hawkes' sweeps, a new presence made itself known.

"From your words, you know we exist. We had hoped to stay unknown. So why are you here?" asked a cowled figure squatting on the turf behind Zeke.

Still watching Hawke make patterns in the sky, Zeke replied. "I am always envious when he does that; I sometimes wish I had wings too. Oh, just to ensure we do not get off the wrong foot. If you do not lower that weapon you have pointed at my back, the Major standing behind you will do it for you."

"I am Captain Ezekiel Kinsley of the Royal Galactic Navy. I prefer to go by Zeke. We are here looking for the home worlds of the race we call the Chohish, whom we are at war with." "That" Turning to point behind the cowled figure "is Major Khaleesi

Richards, in charge of the marines and all military land contingents on my cruiser and other warships under my command. As small as my command may be. She is not one you want to piss off like you are currently doing by not lowering your weapon."

Standing, Zeke finished while brushing off his clothes. "If the Major wanted to, she could have taken you out before you came out of your hidey hole back there a couple of klicks. She has been tracking you since we landed."

The figure stood, which did not increase the height much, showing no outward signs of fear. Finally, with precise and swift movements, he pushed the cowl covering his face back to rest on his back. At least Zeke thought it was a he.

The figure was just over four feet tall, broad-shouldered, with a trim waist. The skin was gray-toned with a tough leathery texture. There was no hair on his head, but he wore a goatee on his face. Clothes looked like milled fabric mixed with an animal hide jacket, boots made of a rich dark material Zeke would swear was leather.

The figure kept his gaze locked on Zeke. Then, lowering his weapon, which looked like a small rifle, he turned his eyes upon Khaleesi. Who acknowledged the gun lowering by tipping her rifle a notch before centering it back onto his back.

"I am Elyot, leader for the Fassoin on the planet Drecholea. You are not of the race you call Chohish; what race are you? Now that you know we are here, what do you want from us?"

"I am a human, and the one flying above us is a Sorath. As to what we want, well, for one thing, it would be helpful to know what happened here. Several of our own planets were attacked similarly before we stopped it. So now we want to make sure that it never happens again. We captured a database showing where the enemy's home worlds are. Well, we believe it to be their home location. Still, I am assigned to scout them out before sending our fleets to engage them."

The startlement on Elyot's face was evident even though Zeke could tell he tried to hide it. "*You put a stop to it? How?* In the past year, we watched them send warships that had to be over a thousand strong through our system. No one could stop them. It is impossible," he exclaimed.

"There is always someone, something, bigger and meaner than yourself; the Chohish finally met that someone," Zeke replied. "Now we can sit here all day and talk in this hot sun, or you can invite my friends and me in for a drink or at least let us get out of this hot sun. I tend to burn easily."

Seeing Elyot hesitate, Zeke spoke aloud to Khaleesi even though he had a com in his ear. "Major, where is the nearest entrance?"

"To your left, Sir, about a hundred paces due east. There is a metal covering that I can have one of the battleoids pry off if your friend there would like some assistance. There is another one behind you, further back, around three hundred paces, heavier roof, may require both battleoids to remove that one."

The sigh from Elyot let Zeke know that he had made his point. "Ok, you can follow me in. But no weapons inside."

"My Captain may be so trusting, or foolhardy in my opinion, to go unarmed into a lion's den, but that is not gonna happen. Where he goes, I and my marines go, armed. Captain Kinsley would like to do this peaceably, but he is on an abridged timeline. Millions, potentially billions, of lives, are at stake. I hope you get my point." Khaleesi stated.

Elyot looked at Khaleesi like he was contemplating refusing before nodding his acceptance. "This way."

Walking east, Elyot went the distance as Khaleesi described before tapping on the entrance. Everyone could hear the quiet murmur of gears as it moved the covering before it showed a stairwell heading down.

"One second, Elyot, I want some engineers to join us. They

were not as trusting as I was. Jax, if you would?" at which point the engineers came scampering out of the shuttle wearing their armor.

Watching the additional party members with apprehension, Elyot was jolted when Hawke landed next to him suddenly. "Hello Elyot, they call me Hawke."

"You must be one of the ones they called the winged ones. We have heard of you. We heard you gave the Chohish a good fight, but after a long time with no more mention of you, we thought they had eliminated you."

"Not hardly. They tried, though. We are allied with these humans to teach them the error of their ways." Hawke stated. "Permanently."

Leading the expanded party down the stairs, Elyot took them through a narrow hallway that barely fit the marines in their armor. They only went a short distance before approaching a heavy-looking metal door. Elyot stopped in front, putting his hand on a pad shoulder-high.

The sound of bolts unlocking before the door began slowly swinging open like a spaceship hatch, only twice as thick. Inside was a long hall with a barrier running across at the other end. Behind the barricade were more Fassoins dressed in armor pointing weapons.

As each looked at the other in a standoff, there was a loud banging from the ceiling. Pieces of roof rained down on the two parties below.

"That, Elyot, is one of my marines suited up in a large battleoid. Telling your people that it is time to stop this silly nonsense before someone gets hurt," Khaleesi said as she pushed forward to place herself in front of Zeke.

Waving at the other party to put their weapons down, Elyot guided them past the barricade into a large room. The room resembled a restaurant, except now it was filled with scared but armed Fassoins.

Tension reigned until Hawke spread his wings until he had enough room to fly just off the floor. "Hello all, nice to meet you," he said while bowing. At first, nothing happened until one laughed. Then like a dam, the tension broke, and the weapons lowered.

"I knew I brought you along for some reason Hawke. Major, please have all the Marines point their weapons down? You are making even me nervous," requested Zeke.

"Captain, everyone kept saying you were all in a rush, so let us keep this short. What do you need from us?" asked Elyot.

Waving Jax over, he had him bring up the location identified by the captured database as the home worlds of the Chohish. "Is this correct? And do you have any information of the current revolt we were notified of?"

"Revolt? There is always a revolt going on. It always ends up one way. We revolted, and we paid the price," argued Elyot.

"We were told by the Endaens that a Chohish home world or two has revolted with the Endaen's assistance. We were able to assist the Kolqux in freeing several of their systems and planets just recently. The Kolqux are in the process of freeing another planet of their people and the Endaens. So it is possible," corrected Zeke.

Hearing this, the Fassoins went into a frenzy, talking with each other at a fast clip. At first, Zeke was going to ask what set them off but decided to wait until it quieted before asking.

Meanwhile, Zeke studied Elyot and several others that had come to join him. The others must be either friends or leaders in their own right due to the familiarity they displayed. He could hear the confusion and concerns echoed in their conversations.

At first, Zeke was confused about why he could understand them so quickly. Usually, it would take a hand AI ear unit some time to correctly interpret. Then, as he listened more, he realized their language resembled the Kolqux language. Made sense in a way. They were all in the same proximity space-wise and must have interacted with each other at some time in the past before the Chohish came along. Their languages must have cross-pollinated between the two cultures.

Seeing the conversation between the Fassoins settling down, he stepped in their midst to ask what set them off in such a tizzy.

"The Kolqux, did they look like this?" Elyot asked excitedly, pointing to a tablet one of the other Fassoin was holding. On the screen was an image that could not be anything but a Kolqux.

"Kinda looks like Hu'de, doesn't it? And that image in the background resembles his daughter, Te'ln.' commented Hawke peeking over Zeke's shoulder.

"They do, don't they. To answer your question, yes, those images match the ones we know as the Kolqux. Why?"

They pushed the tablet back in front of his face without responding to Zeke's question and showed him another image. "And this?"

"That is an Endaen. Again, why?" Zeke asked emphatically.

"How do you know them?" Elyot excitedly asked while the others looked at Zeke with undisguised happiness.

Looking for Jax, he saw him deep in a conversation with a Fassoin. He did not want to interrupt a vital exchange, so he signaled Jax's assistant to join him. Then, taking the assistant's tablet, Zeke pulled up the history he knew they all carried.

"I could bring up the battles we shared, the devastation caused by the Chohish on several of the Kolqux cities, but I think the one that will mean the most to you is this one." With that, Zeke searched for and found the parade held in Sobolara's capital.

As the parade streamed across, several had to sit as their legs could no longer hold them up. Tears rolled down the faces of others. When it ended, they asked for more videos. Finally, they asked for the parade to be repeated once again.

The questions were nonstop for the next half hour. How bad were the battles? How many died when the cities were bombed?

What was happening there now? Why were they not with them? Who was the leader leading the parade? What was he walking next to and had his hand on?

When they asked the last question, Zeke turned and pointed to Khaleesi. "That was a medical pod containing a particular marine Major at death's door from that video you saw where she and her marines repelled the Chohish from the Kolqux station."

The look on the Fassoin faces was no different than the Kolqux at the parade. The earbud in Zeke's ear went off. "Really, you needed to tell them that? This is really getting embarrassing."

"I think we are safe enough now for you and your marines to remove your helmets." Then he laughed as the Fassoins mobbed her when she took hers off. Khaleesi was stymied when she kept indicating the other marines around her who had also been there only for those marines to pretend ignorance. Her death stares at her marines did not stop them from laughing at her predicament.

Half a day later, the small task force was on its way again.

"Well, what did you learn?" asked Jeanne leaning against the command chair while twirling a throwing knife. "And if you leave me here again while you go galivanting off meeting a new race, I will test my accuracy with my pigsticker. Get me?"

"Understand; I was sorry you were not there, but with our mixed force, you needed to be here." Zeke was looking at the planet Drecholea receding in the distance. "It is a wonder any survived. They had reached a point they could not take being ground down any longer. The Fassoin spent several generations putting their plan together." Then, grabbing Jeanne's knife out of the air, he flipped it so that the point balanced on the tip of his index finger.

"Quit showing off, Zeke," admonished Hawke, who went on to explain. "Zeke used to win our drinking money in the Academy by betting on his knife skills. Used to sink a bullseye on a dart board at forty paces nine out of ten times. The one he missed was the sucker setup shot."

"Yeah, he ran that damn scam on us pilots on the carriers, too," complained Gunner sitting beside Isolde. "I lost plenty before I figured it out."

"I never did get to thank you for all those drinks, Gunner, so let me do that now," laughed Hawke.

"Anyway, to get back to the Fassoins. The Fassoins built substantial underground living facilities around the planet. At the same time, they secretly constructed shipyards and mining facilities in the far reaches of their system. For centuries they fabricated men of war and fighters. Better ones than what they were forced to build for the Chohish. All of this activity was done in secrete. Many, many died to accomplish all of this."

"What happened?" asked an enthralled Isolde.

"The Chohish caught a shuttle returning from the shipyard as they landed. All but two died during the battle to bring them in. One was killed during interrogation, and the other, the Fassoins, never did learn the fate of what happened to him. The Fassoin leadership, though, could not take the chance that the Chohish knew their plans. They had no choice but to put their plans into motion before they were ready. The Fassoins attacked the Chohish with only half the forces they had hoped to have."

Zeke looked at the planet one more time before finishing. "The Fassoins were able to take out the Chohish station above their planet in a surprise attack. The Chohish guard fleet was beaten off. Things looked defensible for a few months, then the Chohish returned. They overwhelmed the Fassoins fleet in a matter of hours, and the Chohish started the bombardment."

Seeing how hard it was getting for Zeke, Hawke picked it up. "The Fassoins were caught unprepared. They were not ready to lose so quickly. Billions died before they could get to any of the

101

underground facilities. Then crops they counted on were destroyed. Millions more died from hunger. Only a tiny fraction of the population survived. They have been hiding out ever since. They set up probes and sensors near the slipstreams to give them a warning whenever anyone came through so they could go dark. That is what we caught, the slipstream probe and the receiver on the planet."

"Well, don't stop now; tell them the good part," encouraged Zeke with a smile.

Hawke could not help smiling himself. "It seems the Chohish never learned about the shipyards nor mining facilities. They are so far back that you would not see them unless you sent a probe there. The Fassoins manning the facilities slowly returned to the planet, afraid any use would be discovered. They mothballed as much as they could before they left. The Fassoins have repaired the damage caused by age and have been operating them for the last decade. Nothing too much at the moment, shuttles, farming equipment, and supplies for the underground facilities, but now they will be putting more resources into building their own fleet again. Besides the ore needed for fabricating warships, they have been mining lendolium. That is how they have been powering the shelters. The Fassoins discovered a huge quantity of the mineral."

Seeing the startlement on everybody's faces, Zeke shrugged. "Sometimes miracles do happen."

DEATH

THE ENORMOUS SHIPS silently floated into the system with no legible signature except their shields. The energy readings were so minor that the intruders hoped they could not be tracked without being in very close proximity.

An hour passed, yet no indication they had been noticed. Small ships flew off the hull of each to move in front. Tractor beams reached out from the small vessels to connect with the larger ones pulling them into the system. Speed was limited, but progress was being made.

On the bridge of the largest, the Captain turned to his science officer. "Hawke, can you confirm we entered per your calculations?"

"We are at the extreme end of the system. Unless the Chohish has put probes out here, they should not notice our presence," reported Hawke. "But I do not detect anything that they have."

"Isolde, what have you been able to detect?"

"I am picking up transmissions of enormous energy output. It matches the location of what the Fassoin had in their database. It's been over a hundred years since their last update. Still, the Fassoins records said the base has existed for as long as they have any history of the Chohish. They used to have to deliver weapons for Chohish soldiers here. The Fassoins were never allowed to disembark; the base was strictly for Chohish soldiers."

"Then we will go with our plan. We need to get through this system. We will have to power up our systems when we get closer to the slipstream to enable transition through. So, Will, please work with Tim to ensure our ships are pointed in the right direction. Hawke, you are to coordinate all ships to eject their missiles simultaneously. Let's go with eight rounds apiece," ordered Zeke.

"And what do you want me to do?" asked Jeanne.

"You, my dear, will get with the pilots and relay my plans. They are not going to like what I want them to do," Zeke said as he wrung his hands.

"Sink me! What the blimey do you want our fighters to do now? You set us up to be blasted out of the sky without power last time. What can be worse than that?" Jeanne exclaimed, throwing her hands up in the air.

"I would never ask them to do more than that after what they just did," responded Zeke calmly.

"Then what the hell… oh no, you wouldn't dare, not even you would ask that. Tell me that is *NOT* what you are planning… damn…." Jeanne said as she threw her hands up in the air.

"You can tell them that I would not ask them to do something I was unwilling to do myself. And I mean that!" Zeke said while crossing his heart.

The puzzled look Jeanne gave him matched what Will and Hawke also matched her puzzlement. Until Hawke, who must have determined what Zeke meant, started laughing. "Oh, you are a sly one; someday, my friend, it will catch up with you."

"If the data the Fassoins supplied is still accurate, and I have no reason to believe it is not, then we have to take the chance to hurt them severely. According to the Fassoins, the Chohish empire has been in decline for the last five hundred or more years. That is why they started thinking they could rebel against their rule successfully. The Chohish shortage of fuel is just one of the reasons; a big one, mind you, but their treatment and severe retaliation on conquered races are another. They were removing the very populace that kept them in power faster than they were dominating new ones. If we can impact this base, we may give the nearby systems time to build up their defenses." explained Zeke.

"And how do we do that?" asked Will.

"You all know my plan to eject missiles and let them fly towards the base using the push the warships give them. They will not be traveling fast, but that may actually work in our favor. They will not get through the shields and armor on the base; I am pretty sure of that. But with our three ships the only ones visible when the missiles hit, the number of warships present will not add up. So, the Chohish will think there is a much larger force present. Our three ships will swing away from the slipstream allowing the Chohish the opportunity to send whatever ships they have through the slipstream for help. So simple!" he said as a matter of fact like they followed along with his thoughts.

"What if they have a fleet?" asked Will.

"You saw the reports from the Fassoins. In the many centuries that the Fassoins made deliveries there, the Chohish never had a fleet stationed there. They didn't need to; only Chohish resided here. No chance of rebellion. There was no reason to waste ships they could use elsewhere. Not until now, that is! It's worth a shot," assured Zeke.

"I am confused. We force out the Chohish ships to get help, which reinforcement we probably cannot defeat. So what good does all that do us?" asked Hawke.

Seeing Jeanne close her eyes and shake her head, Zeke knew she had guessed what he would suggest. "He never said we would let the ships get through the slipstream, just that we would help the Chohish along to send the ships." Then, leaning against the situation table, she spelled out precisely what Zeke would do. "He plans on destroying any ships they send out with the fighters. He will drop the pilots off in the optimum path from the base to the slipstream and have them lay in wait, powered down. And he will be with them."

"*Bingo*, give the lady a star!" yelled Zeke while clapping his hands.

Now all but Zeke moaned in grief while looking at him like he was crazy. "Oh, come on, people, that is what we do. Poke the bear. I intend to do more than that; I will make them bleed."

"What does all this accomplish, Zeke? We cannot hurt the base much, if at all," asked Will.

"Fear, Will, fear, instill fear where it never existed before. The Chohish have had some disastrous news in the last few months. I do not want them to have time to regroup," he replied. Then, turning to the table, he had Isolde join them, where she brought up a map she had been working on for Zeke.

Taking off his gloves for the fourth time since they were dropped off, he wiped his sweaty palms with a towel he had brought with him. He could see Jeanne's craft on his starboard drifting in the same direction as his. He waved a kiss at her even though he knew she could not see him through the cockpit window. But knowing that he may never see he again, he had to give her one last kiss, even if it was only symbolically.

The waiting was the hardest part. The warships had dropped them off several hours ago and headed back into the system, so they came to the base from a different location. It would not be much longer; the missiles they had released toward the base were almost in position. Soon, they would fire off, and the Lucky Strike and the two destroyers would make themselves known and add their fire to the mix.

That was the plan anyway. Zeke could not stop from laughing when he thought of all the things that could go wrong. There was a good possibility that the fighters would find themselves overwhelmed, and Will would become the cruiser's new Captain. Although, Zeke expected Will to be taking that role soon anyway. When this was over, Jeanne would be returning home. She was related to her planets governing body, so he knew it would be wrong to keep her away. But Zeke is also unwilling to lose her, so he would resign his commission and follow her. Well, they had to survive this war first; best to work out the details later.

The light of the missiles hitting the base shields was the first indication it had started. Soon, they should be able to get some data from the probes the warships sent out along with the missiles. That would allow them to know when, or even if, the Chohish sent ships to get support. The cramp starting in his left leg disappeared when he got the signal he was waiting on.

Leaning forward, he scanned the data, but nothing to indicate any ships had left the base yet. He did not expect it to happen this fast anyway; he was just getting anxious. That is why they had sent eight volleys toward the base; the first was just a warning, and the rest were that they would not leave. Hopefully, the Chohish were getting concerned about additional forces showing up.

The second, third, and fourth volleys hit the base again. The three ships swung around simultaneously, making it look like there were additional ships that the Chohish could not track. Then, just after the fifth volley slammed home, a movement was caught as the RGN ships raced away. Around the back of the base came multiple ships.

Two destroyers with three humongous ships trailing came running toward the slipstream. The destroyers Zeke expected, but the transports took him by surprise. But then again, thinking more about it, it did make sense. They had to be evacuating the soldiers that were in training. They did not want to take the chance the base was destroyed with all those personnel still there. Zeke would bet that more were present, but they did not have enough transports to carry them.

This would change his plans; he would have to take a chance to communicate with the rest of the group. "Captain, to the fighter group, you should have received the data from the probes. So, we have five ships headed our way. Jeanne and I will skedaddle the hell out of here and let you have all the fun."

Waiting for the responses did not take long. *"Oh, you are a funny man!"* *"You aren't going anywhere, dude."* *"If you're not staying, I am not staying; I am outa here!"* And the last one came with a twang they all knew. *"You may want to skedaddle, but I will not miss this turkey shoot!"*

The last one had laughter ringing out. "Ok, looks like Jeanne is going force me to stay. But with the unexpected transports, we need to make some changes. Gunner, Hayreddin, and Hawke, your groups are to take out the troop transports. If they surrender, let them; if they continue running, take them out. If you have to, I recommend you gang up on one, their shields will be formidable, but it is your call. Jeanne and I will take sixty fighters to take on the destroyers. I have sent out notifications on who will be joining our group. Good luck, ladies and gentlemen. May your thrusters burn hot, but your plasma bolts even hotter. Good hunting. Captain out."

They waited for another hour for the warships to get in range. The Lucky Strike and its destroyers' escorts did not change what they had been doing, giving the impression their main task was to take out the base. Finally, there were just out of range. Enough time to get powered up and up to afterburner maximum speed. And, of course, it was no surprise who announced they were on their way before anyone else. "Fire in the hole me bucko's, do not forget, no prey, no pay! Time to feed the fish."

The joystick vibrated with the power it controlled as Zeke took off, following Jeanne by only a few seconds. The sudden push back into his seat took his breath away as the afterburners kicked in. Jeanne was in for a surprise. Jax had installed a new engine in his fighter, giving him a fifteen percent boost. And he felt it as he passed her. The compression on his legs increased to maintain blood flow until it felt like pliers trying to crush his legs. It slowly eased as his blood flow evened out. The pain had been so intense he almost missed her cursing at him; almost, it was worth the pain.

Slowing to allow the group to catch up, he headed towards the destroyer nearest the transports. Then, checking his group's icons, he was glad to see they were sticking with him and Jeanne. They would all go after one before the other. He knew immediately that this would not be a cakewalk as space lit up with defensive fire and missiles.

Twisting and turning to minimize his profile, he headed toward the rear of the destroyer, hoping to damage their engines. Then, suddenly, his head slammed against the side of his cockpit. His fighter was sent spinning from a near hit. Fighting the joystick, his cockpit screamed with warnings. It moved in a random circle refusing his control. Gritting his teeth, he clenched his hands with everything he had trying to stop the wild swings. Slowly, he started to master control of the fighter once more. The warning sounds settled out to minor damage reports, which he shut off.

The taste and smell of copper permeated his helmet and his tongue. Finally, getting possession of the fighter, he realized he was past the destroyer. Wabbling the joystick, his fighter handled a little sluggishly but still seemed flyable. Yellow damage indicators lit the board. Then, pulling the joystick back near his chest, he swung up into a tight circle. Finally, he stopped turning when he was headed back toward the destroyer.

As he headed back, he saw that Jeanne had two Chohish fighters targeting her. Swinging wide, then twisting to port, she did not shake the pair on her tail. Instead, laser fire bounced off her shields. Jeanne did a tight circle, after which she flipped the fighter to head straight at one of the enemy fighters. She peppered it with plasma bolts until they tore through the shield, taking the fighter apart.

But that allowed the second fighter to close up on her rear when Zeke tore him apart. "You need to be more aware, my dear."

"I was; I saw your icon closing and set the fighter up for you, *MY DEAR*!" snarled Jeanne. "Are you ok? I did not have an opportunity to check up on you. The transports released close to a dozen fighters each. That was unexpected."

Checking on what was in the area, he saw one destroyer heading away with the three troop transports. "Did we lose anyone?"

"Yes, they took us by surprise. We lost half a dozen pilots, nine fighters," Jeanne lamented. "Let's go show them the error of their ways."

"But let's not lose any more pilots if we can avoid it. So, let's knock out the engines and let the big boys take care of them," suggested Zeke.

With that, Zeke and Jeanne led a group of fighters at the Destroyer. If only it was as easy as Zeke made it out to be. But to get their missiles through the destroyer's defenses, they would have to get close.

Swinging around to the port side of Jeanne, Zeke's fighter wobbled like the engine missed had a hiccup. Then it was back to full power. Then, firing his two plasma weapons, he saw them flare when they hit the shields on the destroyer, soon joined by those of Jeanne.

As he turned to fire his missiles at the engine, he felt the engine stutter once more. Before he could check to see what was being flagged, the engine died. He heard the sound of metal tearing before he felt something pound into him before the cockpit went black. Pain blossomed over his body like he had fallen from a ten-story building. Sudden acceleration took the pain up several notches until he fought to stay conscious. Running through his mind as he struggled to stay awake. Are Jeanne, Hawke, his crew, his ship, and the fleet safe? His last thought before he passed out was, shouldn't his life be running past his eyes before he died? He never found out as he faded into darkness.

CAT AND MOUSE

HE WAS FLOATING in warm water was his first conscious thought. It was so peaceful. Then he tried to remember who he was. What had happened? Then little by little, it started to come back. Panic flooded through him. Where was he?

The feeling of floating started leaving him. His body was getting colder, like he was rising out of the warm water. He tried unsuccessfully to open his eyes, but they felt crusted over. Then, moving his hands, they stabbed with pain when he flexed his fingers.

A soft pressure rubbed on his eyes. At first, he was ready to panic but realized whoever it was, was not trying to hurt him. He tried once more to open his eyes when the pressure stopped. Painful light flooded in before it eased, and he started seeing some shapes. . The face poised just above his leaned down to softly kiss his lips before pulling back. He would never forget who kissed like that. "Hello, angel, where are we?"

"You are in the medical bay on the Jackal. It was touch and go there for a while. You were pretty banged up. Your fighter ejected your pod but suffered almost catastrophic damage before discharging. Fortunately, the Jackal was able to pick you up in time," replied a visibly upset Jeanne.

Feeling colder by the minute, he realized he was naked. Then, looking past Jeanne, he saw a group staring at him in concern. "Ok folks, peep show is over; if I could have a private moment to get out of this liquid mess, I would like to put some clothes on. That does not mean you, honey; I will probably need your help until my muscles stop complaining."

A cough by a woman in the white medical uniform that has resisted changing over the Millenium interrupted him. She was standing at the bottom of the pod, entering commands. "You are in my ward, Captain; you will get out when I say you can. Dr. Javier Preruet told me you were going to give me trouble. Let me run my tests, and we will see."

As Zeke was about to tell her he was getting out, with or without her ok, when he was stopped by Jeanne putting her hand on his face. "Let Dr. Sisk do her thing. If not for Letitia, we would have lost you. It was a close call."

"Can I at least get a blanket? This is embarrassing laying here naked. And Letitia? You are already on first name basis?" he asked, embarrassed.

"Yes, we bonded over what an inconsiderate partner will do to another, you know, someone like *you!* I will get white hair sooner than I should be worried about you. Your pod informed us of the damage before the last run," Jeanne lamented. "You should have bowed out."

There was no reasonable answer he could give her; she was right. He would have ripped apart any of his pilots if they made the same boneheaded move. Instead of arguing, he simply agreed by nodding his head.

Seeing that he was not going to argue with her, as she had expected, Jeanne sighed and announced. "The great Captain Kinsley is alive, although we are not sure about his mental health. He just said I was right."

Laughter echoed in the small medical bay before the group behind Jeanne broke up until only a pair stayed behind.

"Sorry, Zeke, we have seen you without clothes enough times that the horrible disfigurements you carry no longer bother us," teased Lance stepping up to the medical pod. "How are you doing?"

"I have had better days. Can someone give me a rundown, please? How many did we lose?" Zeke begged.

"The destroyers were a tough nut to crack. They took out over a dozen of our fighters between the two of them. We lost six pilots; the rest we were able to recover in their pods. You being one of them. We lost more pilots from the fighters that came from the soldier transports. That took us by surprise, although, thinking back on it, it shouldn't have. The troop transports were packed with soldiers, and they had to increase their protection somehow. Once our fighters disabled their engines, we pulled back to wait on the big guns. They made short work of them," reported Hawke smiling down at him. "Good thing you survived. I am not sure my uncle would be thrilled having to pay the exorbitant cost of your family's cocoa. He has become used to getting a family discount, that being free."

"How are you doing?" Zeke asked Jeanne, as he knew most of the pilots were Irracan. Many of those lost were probably her friends.

"As best as can be expected, I guess. It seems to get more painful the more we lose. One of the pilots was my childhood friend. I was a bridesmaid for Raye at her wedding. Her husband was killed during a battle against the RGN. Now she is dead fighting for the RGN. I am not sure how to feel," agonized Jeanne.

Holding Jeanne's hand tight, he pulled her in for a tight hug. She may complain about the gel later, but she needed to know he was here for her. Same as she was here for him.

Looking at the doctor with a questioning look, she let him know he was well enough to leave as long as he took it easy. Pulling the towel around him closer, he got out of the soup he had been lying in. He was not sure he would ever get used to that gel feeling once he woke up.

Everyone turned for modesty's sake to allow Zeke to wipe off the excess gel. A shower is definitely near the top of the list of things to do. But getting a status on the fleet was at the very top.

Dressing using the clothes that he was provided, Zeke, along with his companions, made their way to the bridge. Then, stepping onto the bridge behind Lance, the crew stood and pounded their chests over their heart, a sign of love and respect, before resuming their duties.

The primary monitor displayed the system with icons of the known ships, the Chohish base, and the debris field of the recent battle. No indication of any new Chohish warships.

Walking over to the situation table, he had the table bring up what showed on the screen in 3D. Enlarging the database, he only saw minor damage from the pounding they had given it.

"Lance, any thoughts?" he said, pointing to the image of the enormous base as it revolved around. "Can you think of any way to destroy it?"

"Not with what we have here. The base's shields and armor are damned powerful. We could spend the next month firing on them with what we have, and they would just shrug it off," shared Lance. Pointing to the slightly damaged section, he went on. "That was just blind luck. Their shield failed on its own, not because of anything we did."

The look he received from Zeke had Lance wondering if he had said something wrong.

"I wonder. Did the shield generator actually fail or run out of fuel? Everywhere we go, we are reminded of what drove them to the Pandora system in the first place. Not that we can do anything, but we can leave another communications module for any fleet following us," Zeke theorized.

115

"I have a thought… can the RGN missiles be set to sit idle for days, then fire when a nearby probe identifies the shields or a section has powered down? Aim for those particular units?" Jeanne asked as she touched the damaged section on the Chohish base. "My idea is following on your thought, Zeke; if a shield failed because it was short of fuel, the Chohish may not be able or want to keep all of them up constantly. That would burn through a lot of something they are very short of."

Turning to Lance and Hawke, both looked back at them perplexed.

"Don't know, we have never used it in that fashion before. But I don't see why not." Turning to his first officer, Lieutenant Commander Wilma Cross, Lance asked if she knew. Shaking her head, Wilma said she was clueless, too, but she would find out.

Signing to the communications officer, the center screen broke into a split screen with the bridge from the Lucky Strike and the Fox on the other. After brief congrats for Zeke surviving, they got down to what their plans going forward would be.

Leaning against the back of the command chair, Zeke mused on what he thought they should do. "Based on what we learned from the Fassoins, the following system should be empty. The next populated one is not a planet but a pair of moons, two systems past this one. I was hoping our support fleet would have arrived by now, but that does not change our orders."

"What did the Fassoins say who or what was on the moons?" queried Meghan.

"There was a military base on one and mining on the other. The Fassoins used to have to travel there to pick up processed ore," updated Hawke. "They did not know what races were on the moons. Instead, they were directed to the facility loading the ore."

"Ok, let's see about setting up the surprise Jeanne discussed. If anything, it may force them to keep their shields up, wasting their fuel supplies. Once that is done, we will continue following the path found in the database that was confirmed by the Fassoins. The moons, not sure what we can do there until we get there. Hell, it's been over a hundred years; who knows what changes have occurred since then," Zeke stated as he smelled his shirt. "Oh, and I need to take a shower. But I want to get back on the Lucky Strike to do that so I can wear my own clothes."

Three days later, there were entering another system. Unlike the last system entrance with a known Chohish presence, they came blasting through on full power. Probes were deployed immediately. Shields up and weapons online.

The noise on the bridge of the Lucky Strike was muted as everyone went about doing duties already reviewed. Zeke monitored the primary screen for the probes' data updates, watching as the details changed in real-time. It would be hours before he had the whole system, but he should see details on the two moons within an hour or two.

But he would not have time to wait on that before dealing with the Chohish force headed towards them. Zeke did not have to sound battle stations; they had been there before entering. Knowing there was a reasonable probability that Chohish was in the system, he had sent in probes and a pair of fighters to check it out.

Headed towards them were two destroyers and a pair of carriers. When the probes and fighters had entered, a destroyer had been in the neighborhood. It had detected them and taken off towards the interior of the system. The limited probe readings of the system confirmed the destroyer was alone at the time with no support. But Zeke knew that would not be for long.

Everyone who had actual experience flying a fighter was sitting in one, except for Zeke, who was waiting for the signal. With the pilot losses that have occurred since they started on this mission, they were short of pilots. Jax and every spare engineer had spent the last three days putting together every boxed fighter and bomber.

When Zeke told Tim that he would have to fly a fighter again due to a pilot shortage, Zeke was surprised when Tim let him know he was hoping he would get a chance again at some time. Not that he ever expected that chance to be so quick, but Tim had to admit, he missed the thrill of flying that only a fighter could provide. Not that he wanted to go back to it as his primary duty, he loved being at the helm of the Lucky Strike, but he would not mind doing it here and there to stay in practice. Tim said that last part with a smile. Zeke understood, as he felt the same way.

The three ships held a conference once they knew what they would have to deal with and came up with a plan to deal with it. Now all they had to do was make it work. Planning was one thing; putting all the pieces in place was another. Execution rarely ever went the way you hoped.

When the RGN warships reached a certain distance from the approaching Chohish, the Lucky Strike went to port while the two destroyers went to starboard. The two Chohish destroyers followed the RGN destroyers while the carriers started unloading fighters which went after the RGN cruiser. Once the carriers unloaded, they headed back into the system from where they came.

The tension on the bridge was high; as Zeke had told Lance, he was in command of the two destroyers. Zeke would be busy elsewhere. Watching the Chohish destroyers' race after him, he knew his destroyers could outrace the Chohish. Still, he wanted them to follow him for a bit. Both the RGN destroyers were throttled down to be a little slower.

"Meghan, we need to get a little further away from the cruiser before we execute the plan. Hang in there, ok? Lance out."

"We are with you, Jackal; lead us to some booty, Meghan out."

Getting used to how the Irracans talked was challenging at times, as he would have to look up what they said in common more often than not. Lance was afraid the Chohish destroyers would leave them at some point to follow after the Lucky Strike. Still, they had not made any indication of changing direction, not yet anyway.

"Lieutenant Tanner, get me online with the fighter bay, please." Lance watched the primary monitor as it tracked all the ships identified. They would soon be in the position for plan Cat and Mouse. Lance wondered if Zeke had fun naming plans as much as he did. The names Zeke had come up with were funny to say but deadly serious in the details. Plan A was Cat and Mouse, and plan B was Run. If they had to name a plan C, Lance would bet Zeke would have called it Panic.

Upon seeing Tanner nod, confirming the requested parties were available, "Lieutenant Barbarossa, Captain Henry here, are you all set down there?" asked Lance. "And Lieutenant Commander Dean?"

"We are all a go, Captain. Prepped and ready with hot engines waiting for the signal," responded Hayreddin.

They had swapped fighters from the Jackal for the bombers that had been stationed on the Lucky Strike. Meanwhile, the Fox was supplied with the most experienced Irracan fighter pilots and the best fighter craft available. Any Jackal or Fox open bay slot was filled up by more Irracan fighters. The Irracan fighter commander, Lieutenant Hayreddin Barbarossa, was transferred to the Jackal to confer with Roy before the planned action. Commander Barbarossa was going to lead the defensive fighter cover for the bombers, so Lance felt they should get to know each other a little more.

The distance between the two groups had widened considerably; it was time. "Tanner, bring on the Fox."

Meghan and Fox's bridge came up on the port side screen. "Hello Meghan, you ready over there to execute Cat and Mouse?"

Even though tension had to be high going into battle, the laughter on the Fox let Lance know they were an experienced crew. "We are ready, Captain; engines are purring like a kitten and ready to run, waiting on your signal."

"Then let's show these Chohish our tails, execute Mouse," Lance ordered while signaling his helmswoman. The engines sounded loud as they went into overdrive and pulled away from the Chohish. Both the Jackal and the Fox turned to head after the two Carriers.

The Chohish matched their change of direction but fell further and further behind. "Wilma, how long before we intercept the carriers?" asked Lance, calm now that he was in his command zone. It was something they were taught at the Academy, but few could attain. All the fears and doubts vanish once combat is initiated, and you enter a mind zone where you focus on the battle at hand.

"The ship's AI estimates interception in twenty-three minutes and sixteen seconds, Captain."

"Have Tanner notify the flight deck we expect to deploy in twenty-two minutes and thirty seconds. Communicate that with Meghan," ordered Lance.

The next twenty minutes were peaceful; if you considered being chased by two Chohish destroyers and heading toward a pair of Chohish carriers, *peaceful.*

There was nothing he would be able to do for the Lucky Strike; they were too far away now. This plan counted on separating the large number of fighters deployed from the destroyers and the carriers. That had been successful. They had played the mouse perfectly.

Watching the carriers grow huge on his screen, he knew it was time. "Release the bombers and fighters. Notify the Fox."

Around them, bombers started making themselves visible; flying out to meet them were fighters. More fighters began showing up on the screen from the Fox, all now headed away from them, heading toward the carriers.

Now, it was time to become the cat. "Helmsman, I am tired of being chased; turn this ship around; let's show the Chohish our teeth."

Now at maximum speed, the Jackel made a sharp turn to head

back directly toward the Chohish destroyers with the Fox at its side. It would take more than twenty minutes before the Chohish were in the range of their missiles.

While in transit, Lance thought about how he came to be here. He had known Zeke for years and knew he was different than the norm. Because of his personality and presence, the man drew the best to him. When they had flown fighters together on the same carrier, Zeke's squad consistently rated at the top. They trained harder, flew better patterns, and had unparalleled teamwork, yet none ever lorded it over others. They knew that if they did, Zeke would get them transferred out.

That same magnetism is why the Lucky Strike had the crew it did. Lance was proud of his team and wouldn't switch any of them out for anyone else. But he also knew Zeke's had to be near the best in the RGN. He knew Isolde, Will, Gunner, Roy, and many more, could and should have their own commands.

Then look at the recent actions. Zeke defends several planets against immense odds. Freed an enslaved new race and caused untold battle damage to a relentless enemy. All the while leading a group that admired him, substantiating personal injury; hell, he almost died twice.

That is why Lance was here. He had seen that in Zeke early on and knew he had to tag along if he wanted to make a difference. Military service ran long in Lance's family history. His father and two uncles had served, one a pilot, one a marine, and one in medical. All three had told him his career depended on who his commander was. Unfortunately, many top officers got there through who they knew, not by competence. To meet Lance's goal of making a difference in this galaxy, he knew his best bet was to tie it to an officer he respected above all others.

But enough reflecting, now was the time to show the Chohish why they had made a mistake chasing his warship.

"Wilma, let's give the Chohish something to chew on. Fire a spread of fire and forget missiles twenty seconds before they are in the recommended range. Let's see if they do us the favor of running into them or changing course to avoid them," ordered Lance. "Execute dodgeball at your convenience."

"Fire command entered, executing dodgeball in one minute twenty-three seconds," responded Wilma.

The sound of missiles firing permeated the destroyer before the ship gently lurched. Then, the destroyer veered down immediately afterward, going into a spiral. This went on for a few seconds before the destroyer deviated its course one more time. Zigzagging, twisting, weaving, the destroyer never went in a straight line. Yet, it still headed for the pair of Chohish destroyers.

"Incoming missiles detected. ECM's deploying, interceptor missiles are firing, defensive lasers are active," announced Wilma. Due to space restraints in a destroyer, Wilma was stationed in the middle of the firing crew. Lance watched as her eyes roved quickly from one control station to the next.

Sliding upward from a sudden firing of a steering jet, they still felt a violent jerk from a near missile explosion. A few groans sounded from slamming against restraints.

"The Fox is still on our starboard, matching move for move. Their helmsman is good, really…," reported Tanner, who had stopped when the ship violently pushed up.

There was no doubt by anyone on board that they took some damage on that one. Several had blood running down their face from cuts caused by broken loose objects.

When they entered energy firing range, it was known to all when the lights dimmed almost to blackness. The Jackal fired every energy weapon at one time. Only the ship's AI could coordinate the computations to fire so many different weapons. Yet, all through this, Jackal flew around the Chohish in a staggered pattern.

"A Chohish destroyer has gone inert and spewing in a circle. The remaining destroyer is spouting flames but still in motion and firing with only half its armament," voiced Wilma over the tumult of another near miss.

"Disengage dodgeball, head straight at the remaining enemy destroyer, and let's deliver the death knell. Let the Fox know our intentions," commanded Lance.

The jackal stopped its wild fluctuations and ran smoothly. Missiles fired at a steady pace, and energy weapons discharged regularly.

"Explosion on the Chohish destroyer's midsection reported. Thrust forward has stopped, and all offensive activity has stopped. Orders, Sir?" asked Wilma.

"Continue firing until termination confirmation. We cannot have these destroyers make repairs and reengage. We are still in a battle. Once done, let's check on the carrier engagement," commanded Lance leaning forward in his chair, trying to see if any of the enemies was playing possum.

The engagement with the carriers was in full swing. Firing another round of missiles, Roy's ship was propelled downward by an enemy missile that slammed through his shields. If not for the extra thick hull of a bomber, he would be toast right now. Still, he could actually see the dent in the hull above his head. Another one like that, and he would be joining Spencer in the afterlife.

The explosion he saw off on his port let him know that at least the Chohish fighter, who almost got him, would not get another chance. He waved thanks at the unknown Irracan fighter pilot who had saved his bacon. He knew they could not see him, but it made him feel better.

Now, he had to concentrate on his target. The Chohish carrier he was assigned to was in flames but still moving. They expected the carriers to have a protection screen, but the Chohish had deployed twice what they had expected.

The dogfighting had been fierce. The numbers, at first, heavily favored the Chohish; only the Irracan's skills and equipment had kept it even. But as time progressed, more and more Chohish were destroyed, and the RGN started to get the upper hand.

But not quick enough to save a couple of his bomber friends. The Chohish had gone after the bombers when they first deployed. Only the brave actions of the Irracan fighter pilots checked the savage attack, with a few pilots paying the ultimate price.

Slamming the control stick forward as far as it would go, he grinned maniacally. "Die, you bastard, die. I am going to jam these babies down your throat," he yelled.

"Damn, you sure do get ugly when you get pissed, Roy," Lieutenant Camille Santos, his new copilot, stated.

"Ugly? This is my welcome to my world happy face, Camille. You should have seen me after being cooped up in the bomber with Spencer for a full day or two. Now that was my ugly face," Roy responded without taking his gaze off the targeting module.

Holding the stick forward with one hand, he turned the plasma weapons on top of the bomber to point at the carrier in front of him. Roy had no idea if they would damage the carrier, but he sure would feel better. "Keep firing those damn missiles, Camille, until we are empty. And if that does not do the trick, I am gonna ram this damn bomber right up its fat rear end!"

There was no evading, no turning, nothing but running the bomber forward at the Chohish carrier. The missiles were getting through, so the shields must be down, but the carrier was so enormous he was not sure they would be able to destroy it before it got away.

"Camille, how many missiles do we have left?" he asked quickly.

"Four, I am about to fire another set," she responded.

"Hold them; we are going to try something different," Roy instructed.

The way Roy said it did not give Caille any comfort; Roy seemed to be obsessed with one thing, destroying that carrier. Rumor had it that Roy was not averse to doing some crazy stuff to complete the objective. "Missiles held. Waiting on your order before firing the next set."

"Oh, you will know when to fire without me saying a word." Roy laughed.

Apprehension ran through Camille. She had been in some tight situations before, but never with a crazy man, whom she now thought Roy may be.

The bomber flew right up alongside the behemoth. Camille waited to fire with puzzlement. They could not get any closer; what was he waiting on? Within a moment, she found out. And when she did, it was confirmed by Roy's maniacal laughter.

Two missiles raced away from the bomber, the bomber turned a half circle, and Camille fired the last two. The first set exploded just as the bomber flew out of the carrier's flight bay. The crazy-ass bastard had flown into the bay to allow the missiles unimpeded access to the inner workings of the massive warship.

They did not get that far before debris and flames flew out of the bay's opening to engulf the bomber. Then, the bomber flew out of the flames, singed but intact, with Roy laughing the whole time. Camille, at first, was ready to scream in terror, but then she started laughing along with Roy.

The Chohish carrier limped for a distance, then exploded in a giant fireball. Roy looked over at Camille before stating. "Never did anything like that before. I only regret that some of our bomber crews paid the price to allow us to get there."

Another bomber came alongside before two more joined the group. Within ten minutes, all remaining eight bombers flew as one group towards the two destroyers headed to pick them up. The sound of men and women signing a dirge to their lost companions reverberated from every bomber.

The Chohish fighters were slowly gaining on the Lucky Strike. Zeke and Will never remove their gaze from the superimposed target distance overlaying the actual. Once both lines met, the cruiser continuously groaned from the stresses of releasing close to ninety fighters.

"Will, once all the fighters are deployed, get this ship turned around and back in the fight. They will need our assistance before this is over," Zeke ordered, gripping his hands in worry. Many of the pilots he had out there were injured, out of practice, or just plain exhausted. He has been asking a lot of them in the past several weeks. Quite a few of the fighters still bore battle damage that they did not have the time to repair back to a hundred percent.

But there was nothing he could do about that now. The hand had been dealt; now was the time to play it and see who won.

The pressure of being ejected in a fighter from the cruiser pushed Jeanne deep into her seat. Jeanne started to feel the blood pooling in her abdomen and legs. Tensing her muscles, holding her breath, and squeezing her stomach, were all done without thought, as she had done so often. As she entered space, she swung over and behind the Lucky Strike.

"This is the Red Feather; you out there, Hawke and Gunner?" she queried.

"Gunner here, I am on your downside. My group is forming now, eta in two, waiting on your orders, Red Feathers."

"Hawke here, I am on your upside. My group is ready and raring to go. And Jeanne, I love the new call sign; it was about time Zeke gave you a real moniker."

"Ok, it looks like we are outnumbered by a third. The Chohish are still following the Lucky Strike, heading off to port from us. If they stick to the route they're on, let's see if we can't chop them up a little bit. We'll hit the rear and tear through without stopping. Once through, Hawke, bring your group in from the port side;

Gunner, take the top. I will take the bottom. We'll meet in the middle. Good luck, gentlemen, happy hunting."

The three groups spread out and headed toward the Chohish fighter group. As they neared the Chohish, the rear section turned to meet them while the rest continued after the Lucky Strike.

Hawke was in his Sorath fighter; he preferred that to the blockier RGN design. The seats were shaped differently to meet his physical requirements while accommodating the special fighter suit necessary for the feathers on his skin. It may be different, but it had the same firepower as any RGN fighter.

And he used them as he barreled through the Chohish. Hawke saved his missiles for now; with all the others using theirs, he did not want to get a double lock from multiple missiles on a single fighter. The plasma weapons, though, he used with abandon.

Flying in front of his group, he fired while swinging wide. The turn, while firing, caused a wide array of bolts to flash toward the enemy fighters headed his way. The plasma bolts did no damage, but they made the Chohish in front of him turn. The warriors behind him, though, took advantage of their turn. Two Chohish fighters exploded in flames and debris.

Then the rest of the RGN fighters hit and swarmed through the Chohish, firing their missiles and plasma lasers. Enemy fighters lit up the area with their destruction.

As Hawke hit his afterburner, he saw his wingmate start to pass when he exploded from a direct missile impact on his cockpit. Anger tried to take control, but he held it down. Hawke had to lead, not allow his feelings to drive him; others depended on him. But he did have his ships AI mark that enemy fighter, so if an opportunity arose to get payback, he would.

They went through the Chohish fighter group's rear, leaving the enemy fighters in disarray. Coming out the other side of the battle, they went into a tight half-circle. Then, returning to the port side, they again entered the contest.

This time, Hawke made use of his missiles. It seemed there were fighters everywhere. Suddenly, a missile lock warning sounded. Twirling his fighter into a loopy loop, he gritted his teeth as the g's threatened a blackout. The blood rushed from his head as he tried to concentrate on firing the ECM measures. He could not speak it; he was gritting his teeth so hard. Finally, his finger hit the ECM button.

Coming out of the loop, the warning signal turned off. In front of Hawke was the fighter that had fired on him. Hawke returned the favor and sent a missile after him. The enemy fighter attempted to imitate Hawke but was only halfway through the loop when Hawkes missile punched through his exhaust to explode next to the fighter's body. The fighter tumbled away with no power.

Hearing a cry for help, he responded, "Hawke here. What is the situation?"

"Diego here. I have two, no, make those three fighters on my tail," a screaming voice came through Hawkes speakers. Hawkes AI automatically located Diego's fighter.

"On my way, Diego, keep evading. Should be there in... thirteen seconds." Hawke notified Diego as he swung around, heading to intercept. Then, pushing the fighter past the ship's redline, Hawke had to override the ship's Ai warning of violating the safety guidelines.

Hawke was impressed as he watched Diego's ship desperately evade the enemy fighters. Laser flashes missed by the barest margins, but miss they did. But Hawke knew Diego could not last long. Coming up behind one of the enemy fighters, he blasted the fighter away before he fired his plasma weapons at the other two in a warning. One peeled off while the other continued on Diego's tail.

This enemy fighter was good. The fighter stayed on Diego's tail no matter how Diego tried to lose him. Only then did Hawke see that the icon on his panel indicated this fighter was the one that had taken out his wingmate.

"Diego, this is Hawke. I want you to peel up for three seconds, slam on your brakes, then go down and out. I will get the fighter off your tail," Hawke ordered Diego as his fighter started heating up. Heat permeated his fighter and suit. Sweat dripped down inside his flight suit and tickled his feathers. If he did not take his foot off the pedal soon, his engine would overheat and melt down. Warning lights flared over his console.

Gripping the joystick tightly, he sped after the enemy fighter. Hawke watched Diego do the peel-up, then slammed on his brakes after three more seconds. The sudden braking by Diego surprised the Chohish enemy fighter, who followed suit and braked. That was when Hawke let loose his last missile and fired his plasma weapons into the fighter, basically sitting there. The fighter exploded dramatically. Hawke watched as Diego raced away. Ready to take his foot off the pedal, his fighter let him know he was too late. The engines died.

Drifting with a dead engine, Hawke, with nothing else he could do, checked on the status of the fighters assigned to him. The number no longer responding depressed him. Seven out of the original twenty-six were marked as destroyed. How many pilots were able to eject, he did not know.

As he watched, the battle continued on around him. Figuring it was an excellent time to see how the enemy fought, Hawke noticed mistakes that the Chohish made. Again and again, he saw situations that experienced pilots would not have made. And he then had a thought.

The mistakes he saw were what a pilot would make if they only had simulation training vs. actual training in a physical fighter. Could that be because the Chohish were so short of fuel? That would make sense. And which would explain their battle tactics. Overwhelming with massive force, not using a strategy requiring enormous training and fuel supplies.

He would have to run this by Zeke when he got back, if he got back, that is.

RELIEF

THE SOUND OF exhaustion and pain echoed throughout the room. Zeke hesitated as he made his way through the cafeteria. Usually, they would hear light banter and laughter when he walked through with Jeanne. That was absent on this trip around.

The hand from Jeanne pulled him along while glancing at him and shaking her head. What he saw was the same as how he felt: tired, deep down, bone tired. A good many were pilots. They were easy to pick out as bruises were evident on their arms and faces. He would surely see bruises covering their torsos if they were not wearing shirts.

They had lost a lot of fighters and pilots this time around. Zeke did not know how much further they could go without relief or replacements to fill holes. They were running short of almost everything, especially missiles. They had hoped when he started this that there would not be a lot of Chohish to fight through. So instead of just running past any Chohish presence as planned, they've had to stop and fight. They could not keep this up.

They found an empty table off to the side of the entrance. As they put their trays down, several others came up looking for a place to sit, only to stop when they saw them. "Please sit; we are all hungry. I promise I will not steal your food," beseeched Zeke. "Although I cannot guarantee that for Jeanne here, she is a pirate, you know."

"Hmm... they do seem to have a better selection than we do...." Jeanne stated as she rose while raising her fork like she would spear something off the closest plate.

The group laughed before sitting down. "Thanks. We will watch our food closely."

Slicing the processed food that simulated a steak, Jeanne raised to sniff before hesitantly nibbling on it. "This is supposed to be steak, isn't it? Not sure what animal it's supposed to come from, but it is definitely not a steer."

"It is supposed to be a steak from an animal called a Whamouni from the planet Soria Q4. That was the crossbreed they created from an earth steer embryo. They are not quite the same, but they are the favorite of the individual who programmed our processors. But, of course, being he is from Soria Q4, that may have something to do with it."

"You seem concerned; what is bothering you?" inquired Jeanne as she pushed her plate away.

"Look around; they are tired; I am pushing too hard. For what? What we were sent out to do, we are failing at. Instead, we are fighting battles that should be done at a much more significant fleet level. I am asking too much of these people," agonized Zeke. "They are dying, by my command, and we are not much closer to verifying the Chohish home planet's location."

Leaning over to put her hand in Zeke's, Jeanne remained quiet. She knew that anything she said at this point would not help much. So, she was surmised when they were interrupted by one in the group at the end of the table.

"Err... Captain... is it ok if I speak?" one in the group asked. He was dressed in an engineer's uniform. The insignia on his collar indicated he worked in Jamie's group.

132

"Sure, what's on your mind?" Zeke responded with a questioning look at Jeanne.

Passing a questioning look at the rest of his group, he turned back to look at Zeke when the others signaled to go ahead.

"Sorry, Captain, we overheard what you said. Kinda hard not to. It may seem like we are tired, but that is true after any engagement. What is weighing on our minds is the devastation that we are seeing. The miners were treated no better than animals. Their living conditions were horrible, with no fundamental sanitation, and they were poorly fed. I helped carry some miners to the freighters. They were skin and bones with bruises and sores all over them. And they were sent to the mines by others of their own kind, all for power. Anyone sent there never made it home."

The man paused as he was apparently reflecting on the horror he saw. "And if that was not bad enough, we came onto a world that was destroyed, and billions were killed because they did not want to live under another's rule. What kind of animals would do something like that?" he almost yelled at Zeke. "Because of our actions, we have saved close to seventy-five thousand Kolqux and Endaens. Gave hope to hundreds of millions of Fassoins on a planet that thought they would never be free to live out in the open again."

"And do not forget what they did at Niflhel and Nocuous. So do not take our fatigue and malaise as a sign that we do not want to continue." Rising so he was leaning over towards the two Captains, he finished with passion in his voice and expression. "We all signed on to stop senseless crap like this. You two have led us with courage, daring, and compassion. Do not stop now. We are here for the duration; let's finish this, now, together."

All in the group stood up, shaking their heads affirmatively. Another of the group added. "What Rickie said is what we hear from everyone on the ship. We are disgusted, saddened, and angry, Captain; we want to end this one way or the other. And there is no one better to make this happen than you two." With that, the group sat down, looking at Zeke and Jeanne with determination.

Taken by surprise, Zeke looked at Jeanne, who reflected the same. Then, turning back to the group, he thanked them for speaking out, letting them know that sometimes, those leading needed to be reminded why. Zeke told them they were always available. And he would sweeten the deal with cocoa.

The two Captains finished up and left the cafeteria. Leading the way, Zeke made his way to the brig. Coming to stand in front of the half dozen Chohish, Zeke just stood there contemplating with Jeanne leaning into his arm.

"Have to come to gloat, human?" asked one of the Chohish.

If Zeke heard the question, he gave no sign; instead, he remained motionless, standing there.

Getting no response, the rest of Chohish, except for Omaw, started making derogatory remarks about both trying to provoke them.

Still, Zeke stood with Jeanne for over fifteen minutes, not indicating what he wanted until Omaw walked up to the force field. Only then did Zeke move a few steps closer to stand in front of where Omaw stood. Both stood there looking at each other without stirring, the only change was Jeanne sitting on the bench across from the cell.

The cell was not massive; this brig section had been deliberately made for the Chohish. Bunks for a dozen Chohish with enough room to support showers and bathroom functions. The bars were extra thick to accommodate the strength of multiple Chohish. Of course, they would have to get past the force field first.

Omaw was the first to move. "What is it you want now, Captain?" he said with no animosity. Ever since seeing the images from the destroyed planet, he had been reserved.

"Contemplating. I am trying to justify my morals against what we find as we make our way. Your people's cruelty knows no bounds. No matter what I decide, I doubt I can convince any of my allies to spare the Chohish." Seeing no reaction, Zeke asked Omaw why.

"That is life. You are born, then you die. Everything in between is for the betterment of the Chohish's survival. You either succeed or fail; the Chohish have not lost yet. We will resist with everything we have. That is the Chohish way." Omaw stated as a matter of fact.

Shaking his head in confusion at the concept that an individual could be so implacable in the possibility of their total race elimination. "You are losing even though we have not yet brought our full complement of warships against you. What you have experienced is just a small fraction of what the RGN can bring to bear. They are still gathering their forces over long distances."

The voice of Jeanne from her seat interrupted Omaw before he could respond. "And if the RGN was not enough, you are facing a second invasion path from the Soraths, who will not rest until you are eliminated."

The facial features of Omaw slipped briefly before slipping back into a bland expression. But his eyes reflected doubt.

"I had hoped there was some hope for the Chohish; now, I am not so sure. I am beginning to be sorry I brought you with us." With that, Zeke walked away.

Following, Jeanne stopped at the brigs entrance, "That man may be the only hope your people have. If Zeke decides there is no chance for the Chohish's redemption, there will be no one else to stop the forces that are determined to finish you. Permanently," she told Omaw before walking out.

Two of the half dozen battleoids stationed as guards moved to stand in front of the one exit out of the brig. Their weapons remained trained on the Chohish wherever they moved around in the cell.

The two Captains padded quietly through the hallways as they returned to the bridge, each lost in their thoughts.

135

Upon arriving on the bridge, Zeke had Will continue toward the slipstream that should lead them to the Chohish home worlds. They could do nothing about the two Chohish facilities on the moons; they were already running short of missiles and fighters. This system had multiple slipstreams, but they followed a set path and did not have time to explore others.

They were three-quarters of the way across the system when alerts signaled ships' entry at the slipstream they had entered from.

"What have we got?" asked Will.

"Multiple ships have entered the system from where we came in. We are still getting details, but it looks like a small fleet of at least ten ships. Several are very large. I am getting particulars on one; it is a warship.... an RGN battlecruiser, oh yeah! Another one," exclaimed Selena joyously.

"Will, you may want to have Tim turn us around. Isolde, can you let the Fox and Jackal know? Selena, can you contact whoever is in charge of that fleet?" suggested Zeke, rubbing his hands in glee. "About time something went right."

"Captain, the probe reports the fleet is a mixture of RGN and Sorath ships. Several Battlecruisers, battleships, four destroyers, a carrier, and several tenders," announced Selena.

Upon a signal from Selena, Zeke had her direct the communication to the main screen. Then, standing, he moved closer to the screen.

An image of a tall, dark-haired woman sitting in her command chair appeared. "Admiral Tomeka Condon of the battlecruiser RGN Annihilator here. I am in charge of the fleet you must now be aware of. I take it you are Captain Kinsley of the Lucky Strike, whose exploits I have heard so much about. Our fleet was much larger, but it seems you and your crew have been very busy. We had to leave some to escort some freighters. And then there was the communication pod telling us about the Fassoins. So, we left some more ships there."

The Admiral was not one Zeke had never met in person, but he had heard good things about her. "Guilty as charged. But it was my crew that has been doing all the heavy lifting. Many of whom paid with their lives, not counting all those that have been injured. Without them, we would not be here when you arrived."

"I am sorry to hear of their loss; isn't that always the way. Heap praise on an officer when he has little to do with the battle itself. What can you tell me about this system? From the data you left at the slipstream, there are two moons occupied by the Chohish. Still true?" Tomeka inquired.

Zeke explained the situation, after which they agreed to meet to start resupplying the three ships. Then, signing off, Zeke asked Isolde to have all the officers meet in the conference room in thirty minutes and request the other two ships to a conference.

He headed off the bridge, indicating for Jeanne, Hawke, and Will to join him. "Isolde, you are in charge until our return. Please, no taking the cruiser around for joy rides, ok?"

"No promises, Captain, no promises." Was the reply Zeke heard from Isolde and loud laughter on his way off the bridge. The smile that lit his face was overdue.

Walking ahead of the other two, Zeke, with Jeanne at his side, headed towards the medical ward. No words were spoken; Jeanne and Hawke have made this walk before for the same reason. Zeke and Will were going to decide who stayed and who would be returning with the tenders. The injured would not like it, but it was for everyone's benefit. Jeanne had already asked Meghan to do the same. Lance would be doing it already on the Jackal as it was routine RGN procedures.

The tenders would leave after refreshing the three ships. They were a liability if they continued on with them. Zeke was reasonably sure the Admiral would be going with the tenders as they would require an escort home. But thinking about it, which brought his crazy smile back, maybe there was something the Admiral could do before they left.

Walking through the infirmary, he was close to tears. So many were injured with grievous wounds. As he passed each one with Doc, they marked which ones would have to leave. And not one of them was happy about it. They knew it had to be done, but that did not mean they wanted to go.

Close to an hour later, the three walked into engineering. Zeke had to notify Isolde to push the meeting forward several hours. It had taken longer than expected in the medical section as each person assigned to go back wanted to thank Zeke and Will and wish them luck. And, of course, they had to hug Jeanne and fist-bump Hawke. So, there wasn't a dry eye when they finally left.

Knowing why the group was here, Jax joined them with several other engineers. Each engineer touched pads, with one being carried by Will, sending over several lists. One, a list of what supplies they desperately needed. Two, another of what they expected to need. Third, what they wanted but could live without. Each explained why they wanted what. Once that was done, Jax dismissed the other engineers.

"Engines are looking good, Cap; these new engines are much better than our last ones. But they burn a bit more fuel, so I am glad to see the tenders. It would be nice to top off the fuel. Our missile count is lower than I like; again, it will be nice to get them refilled. So glad the tenders do have what we need." Seeing the eye roll from Zeke, Jax exclaimed while waving his hands. "They do have what we need? Right? Captain?"

Getting no quick response, Jax swore for a few moments before he made a simple statement. "You don't know, do you? You never asked. You realize that our ship has the latest hardware and software available in this quadrant, don't you? What if they did not bring the right replacement parts?"

138

Turning to Will, he raised his hands in the air hoping Will would sympathize with him; he saw he would not be getting any. Jeanne and Hawke's hands over their mouths, trying to hold in their laughter, let him know not to waste the effort in their direction.

"Relax, Jax, that is not something I can control. We will make use of whatever they have somehow. I know this fantastic engineer who can repurpose older versions to make them fit our needs. We will find out soon enough. See you at the meeting." At which point, Zeke was about to head out when a voice spoke overhead.

"I have checked the lists Will was supplied, along with the one Jamie prepared, against what is available in the two tenders. The tenders have everything we need and more. Same for the lists Lance and Meghan put together."

That update brought a long sigh of relief and a slight jig of happiness from Jax. "You know, I am really starting to like you, LS1."

"Same here, Jax, same here. It would be much easier to like you, though, if you could stop snoring so loud at night. My programming does not allow me to ignore it. It is very distracting. Maybe you could recode my programming, so I could not hear it? Please?"

Where Zeke thought LS1's comments would start another round of cursing from Jax, he was surprised when he saw Jax do the opposite. Zeke watched as Jax leaned against the wall to assist with holding himself up. Jax was laughing so hard he had trouble catching his breath. When he finally did, he squeaked out. "Damn, now that was funny. I will see what I can do LS1; you never know, it may be possible."

Leaving Jax still laughing and propped against the wall, the small group made their way to the marine section. They entered to see the one they wanted to talk to going to a sparring session. The sounds of the impacts of flesh on flesh were loud and echoed in the room.

No one was about to interrupt Khaleesi as she twirled to the side, sidestepped the fist that would have connected with her head, to slam her palm on her opponent on his chest. Grunting in pain, her opponent stepped back to recover. As he was about to step back in, another marine who was watching whistled. Looking at the marine who whistled, Khaleesi saw him point to the group.

A look of disgust crossed Khaleesi's face as she made her way to where the group waited. A marine tossed her a towel just as she reached the Captain. "Isolde told me the meeting was postponed for a few hours. Now you're here. Make up your mind, Captain. I have work to do."

The thought of giving Khaleesi a flippant remark died on his lips as he watched the major wipe the sweat and blood off her torso. The muscles rippled on her biceps as she used the towel. "I wanted to check with you on your staffing needs. Before our meeting, I thought I would pass that on to the Admiral to check on our options."

"Captain, I have already talked with Major Reinaldo Gladden of the RGN Annihilator. They brought several extra marine squads for the Lucky Strike and the Jackal. If the Fox needs any marines, we can accommodate them. Although Jan has not notified me of any such need. Now, if you do not mind, I want to return to my training if we are done here." Then, without waiting for a reply, Khaleesi walked away, signaling the marine she had been sparring with to rejoin her on the fighting mat.

"I should have known; the major is top-notch. I was so lucky to get her assigned to this ship. Ok, that saves us some time. One more stop to go." The group left to the sound of grunts and blows nonstop.

Finding Jamie, Gunner, and Roy were more intensive than they thought. They had to go through several landing bays to learn that all three they were looking for were not there. It seems all three had gone to the cafeteria to get something to eat before the scheduled meeting. All except Will, who was returning to the bridge to relieve Isolde, decided to join them.

The three grabbed a quick sandwich and found the party they were searching for at one of the corner tables. Just as Hawke was about to sit next to Gunner, he was surprised when a figure dashed in to grab the seat right from under him. Isolde looked up at Hawke laughingly while Gunner put his arm around her to pull her close. Taking the seat next to her, Hawke playfully tweaked her nose. "My bad, I should have known. Wherever that big lug goes, you show up." The smile on Isolde's face snuggled up against Gunner's chest was all the answer he got.

Hawke turned to Jeanne, who had sat across from him, where he first pointed at Isolde, then waved his finger at her and Zeke while simulating hugging. The hand gesture he got back from Jeanne had the group laughing before they settled back to eat and reviewed the fighter and bomber requirements.

What Zeke listened to brought home how bad the fighters and bombers had suffered during the last action. Nearly forty percent of the fighters needed replacing; they were too damaged to be fully functional in the time available. A quarter of the pilots had injuries that required more intensive care than the cruiser could handle without compromising future medical needs. Similar needs for the bombers.

Gathering their trays after finishing, they were startled to hear the alarm sound along with the announcement, "Captain to the bridge, repeat, Captain to the bridge."

While the three flight officers raced for the fighter bays, the rest ran to the elevators to the bridge. Running through the entrance, they saw Will standing over Selena, looking down at something she was pointing to. All three viewers showed an area near the slipstream from which the relief force arrived.

Moving to stand next to Will, Zeke waited patiently for an

explanation of what was happening. But he knew better than to interrupt while Will was in an intense conversation, who was more than likely in the process of getting detailed information on what the emergency was about.

Patting Selena on the shoulder, Will complimented her before turning to Zeke. "Our probes reported a slipstream transition. Selena was just giving me an updated analysis. Four Chohish battleships, three cruisers, six destroyers, and a pair of carriers have transitioned through and headed our way."

"They must have come from one of the side slipstreams we did not have time to explore. How long before they reach missile range?" asked Zeke.

"Selena estimates it will be around three hours, give or take ten minutes. It all depends on the speed they make. The carriers may slow them down a bit," Will reported. "We should meet up with the relief task force in less than an hour. Still, that will not give us time to do any resupply or injured transfers."

"Nothing we can do about that; let's get the Admiral on the line so we can start putting a defense strategy together. Unfortunately, we cannot run with the slower tenders present,' requested Zeke.

The Admiral must have been thinking the same as she was calling in. Within short order, all the allies' Captains were on a conference bridge call. After reviewing their limited options, the Admiral decided Zeke would take the lead in a battle plan. The Admiral based her decision on Zeke having the most experience fighting the Chohish.

The first order Zeke gave was to merge the two RGN fleets into one. By the time that was completed, he would have a detailed battle plan put together and sent to all ship captains to review.

The size of a battlecruiser was something to behold. The power they projected was magnitudes above what a cruiser could do. With the firepower the RGN had, they should, and that was the rub;

they should be able to handle the oncoming Chohish force. But at what cost?

Settling in his command chair with Jeanne, Will, and Hawke standing around him, they went over different options with Lance and Meghan on a conference call. The Admiral and the rest of the Captains listened in and offered updates when requested.

"Communication request coming in. Do you want to accept it?" asked Selena

"From who? We have everyone on the line, don't we?" asked Will.

"It appears to be coming from the Chohish warships," announced Isolde.

"Bring them on, but do not let them know the other Captains are on," ordered Zeke.

On the side screen came the bridge he was very familiar with. "Hello, Captain Kinsley, Hu'de here. I found a Kolqux fleet roaming out here and tagged along," the image of a laughing Hu'de appeared standing next to his command chair with a large group behind him.

"Hu'de, it is so good to hear from you. You had us going there for a while. We thought a Chohish fleet had come in from a slipstream we did not have time to explore. So where are the freighters?" asked Zeke.

"I passed them onto the fleet you mentioned I might meet. Several of their ships took over, escorting them back. We were going back with them when we met some of our own warships. They were on their way to find you. Their commander could be someone you know," Zeke was told as Hu'de stepped aside. Standing there, smiling at the screen, were Uv'ei and Uv'ek, dressed in full battle armor.

"Hello Zeke, we thought you may like to have some company out here. So we brought a few of our friends along with us."

"That is an understatement, my friend; we would love to have you join us. But who is running the planets?" asked an astonished Zeke.

"Oh, we gave that to our cousin and the council to handle. They are better at administrative things, so much better than us. We were just figureheads anyway. Besides, the war is not over, and we want to ensure our freedom is permanent," a Uv'ei that Zeke could barely recognize stated.

Upon closer examination, Zeke saw the changes that had occurred in his friends. It was not just the postures and the sound of their voice; it was the whole package. The two, Uv'ei and Uv'ek, stood there tall and confident. Dressed in their armor like it was second nature, their bodies were now lean and muscular with close-cropped hair, and scars were present on their face and arms. They were smaller versions of Khaleesi's marines.

"Well, since you are here, there is something you can help us with. Do you happen to have any marines with you? A mining facility on one of the moons needs to be checked out. They may or may not have forced labor," asked Zeke with his wicked smile crossing his face.

All three Kolqux moved closer to the monitor with their own smiles crossing their faces. "Oh, we can give you all the marines you need, and they are screaming for action."

TRICKERY

THE COMBINED FLEET rested several hours from the moons as they resupplied and transferred personnel. While that was happening, there was a meeting in the situation room on the RGN Annihilator.

Admiral Condon sat on the edge of the enormous round table as they discussed immobilizing the Chohish base and mining facility. The attendance was limited to Zeke, Jeanne, Hawke, Jamie, Gunner, Hu'de, Uv'ei, Uv'ek, and Khaleesi, with three of her officers. The rest of the Captains and whoever they felt should be part of the conversation were on the wall-size screen.

"I have not been involved in fighting the Chohish up to this point, so I have no actual experience with how the Chohish reacts. But I have read and viewed all the data I could get in the last several months. I will defer to you on being an expert in that regard, but what you are telling me sounds kinda crazy," said the Admiral. "And please, call me Tomeka. I always felt that the title causes hesitation in ideas being voiced."

"If you hang around long enough with Captain Kinsley, you will find that having crazy ideas is his norm," declared Khaleesi nonchalantly. "That is a major reason why we are still alive."

The look Khaleesi received from Tomeka at her remark was interesting. Watching the interface between the two, Jeanne thought she saw a slight nod. "Are you two familiar with each other?"

"The Major used to report to me for several years before her demotion. When I heard of what was happening to her, I tried to intervene, but the marine board told me to stay out of it. I was glad to learn Zeke had rectified the injustice shortly afterward," said Tomeka.

"What is this injustice you speak of?" asked Uv'ei and Uv'ek as one.

"Later, they will explain later. We do not have time to go over that now. But I will not be a part of it a second time," said Khaleesi irritably. Apparently, this conversation thread was not something she wanted to continue.

"Back to the subject matter. Are you telling me you intend to capture the mining facilities on one moon while destroying the military base on the other? And do both with minimal casualties?" asked Tomeka.

"We do. Now, this is what Jeanne and I envisioned, with a lot of assistance from Khaleesi, of course. We ran this by Uv'ei and Uv'ek first to get their ok. We believe this is what we should....," Zeke responded.

After listening and watching a simulation that Isolde had created for Zeke and Jeanne, silence reigned for a few minutes until a yell from the Fox came through the speakers. "I love it! I want to go with Uv'ei and Khaleesi," yelled Jan.

The clamoring from the Fox on wanting to join reached its crescendo when Masson demanded to join Jan. The RGN and Sorath ship captains looked around their bridges like the personnel on the Fox were mad.

Hours later, Zeke and Jeanne stood on the flight deck of one of the Kolqux carriers. With the Admiral here to watch over the fleets, there was no reason that Zeke could not go. Besides, he wanted to be on hand if something with his plan did not pan out. Then, of course, Jeanne was coming. Not even Anne could stop Masson from going since Jan was.

Slowly, the group gathered. When Jan saw Uv'ei and Uv'ek, he had to go and check them out. They were not sure what Jan wanted until he explained. They looked nothing like Jan remembered them. Jan had to see the changes up close. But if he was surprised by those two, his jaw dropped when he saw the Kolqux marines arriving to enter the waiting shuttles.

The Kolqux marines marched in fours, all dressed in heavy armor explicitly made for Kolqux. Helmets hung from their right front shoulder; a pair of plasma pistols held by a holster around their waist. A plasma rifle connected to their back with magnets, grenades, and other assorted equipment hung from their chest and abdomen. One odd thing Jan noticed was that each carried a pair of sonic knives, a sheathed knife on their right thigh and another in a scabbard on the back of their neck.

"You and your men look deadly, my friend. It will be an honor to fight alongside you," said Jan as he watched the shuttles be loaded.

The whistle from Masson informed him he needed to get in his assigned shuttle as they were about to leave. Then, as he ran to his shuttle, Jan saw Khaleesi and a couple of marines enter the one he was going to be in. Several dozen more entered four other shuttles next to his. But what caught his attention was how Khaleesi was dressed. Except for Khaleesi's helmet being connected at hip level, she was the spitting image of how the Kolqux were equipped and armored. Or should he say the Kolqux mirrored Khaleesi? The knives were the giveaway. Most human marines only carried one on their thigh. He only knew of Khaleesi having one behind her neck. Damn it, the Kolqux marines was honoring her.

As he maneuvered around the marines, who were stepping into

their battleoids, he located Khaleesi midway in. She was doing her final checkout before she entered. Seeing him, she scowled at him for being late.

"Sorry, I was delayed looking at hundreds of miniature Khaleesi's entering their shuttles. Took me by surprise," said Jan as he started his precheck.

"Standard gear for an RGN marine," she replied. "But no time for that; you need to get ready."

Backing into his battleoid, different than Khaleesi's as it was Irracan-made, he saw Masson smiling at him directly across from him. The Irracan battleoids may be a bit smaller. Still, they had an advantage over RGN varieties, in his viewpoint anyway, speed. Many an argument he had with Khaleesi on which was better. She believed armor and punch were the reason you were in one. While he thought the loss of some of that was made up for being able to get where you wanted to be faster.

The sealing of the units came with the dark before the unit turned on the optics. It was one thing that Jan hated. The loss of sound at the same time as he went sightless, even for so short of time, quickened his heart rate like nothing else.

His battleoid showed green on all systems. Jan had the unit AI put those signals aside and ran com checks. Everything was looking good. Pinging Khaleesi in private mode, he waited for her response.

"Something up? Everything checks out?" came her reply.

"All good here. Had a personal question for you since we will be sitting here for a few hours before the action starts. What are your plans after this war is over? If the database was correct, we should be getting close to the Chohish home words."

"I do not know. It all depends on what the Captain does. I owe him. And respect him. If he stays in the RGN, I will probably ask to stay assigned to him. You?" answered Khaleesi.

"Before the Chohish, my priority was to protect Jeanne. Her

father gave me that task, and he was like a brother to me. But now, with Zeke in the picture, she no longer needs me. I have been able to make my own plans for once. And as silly as it sounds, I want to go wherever you decide to go." Jan replied.

There was no response immediately. Jan knew he may have gone too far, too fast, for one that knew every day might be her last. Finally, she replied. "I would like that. You know what marines' life is like. I have grown quite fond of you and would like to take it to another level if that is what you were trying to imply. Let's discuss more after this engagement. Right now, I need to concentrate on the upcoming activity."

The shuttle lifted off and flew out to loiter, waiting on the rest. The two Kolqux carriers were not used the same as the Chohish or humans. Each carrier had a fighter contingent, but it was only half the usual number. The rest of the space was used to house the shuttles for the thousands of marines it carried. Being much smaller than a Chohish and used to cramped quarters, they could fit several in the space one Chohish took.

While they waited, they got to see the light show. The battlecruisers were pounding the military base and the mining station with missiles from maximum distance. The destroyers and cruisers were given protection detail by any enemy response. One addition to the firepower being directed against the base was from the Kolqux battleships. They used their primary weapon as they had plenty of specially processed lendolium fuel.

As expected, both Chohish sites had excellent shields. The military base responded to the attack with missiles of its own. It was a matter of which was overpowered first. The only difference was the base on the moon could not move out of range if needed.

The warships began a staggered move in and out of range to allow their shields to regenerate. All the while, they continued firing missiles. The further they moved out, the less effective the missiles were, so the warships had to return to within enemy weapons range.

It was over an hour of sitting idle before the shuttles started moving again. They flew around in circles, then they flew over both moons. Then they flew around the moons. Then, after the third pass around the moon with the mining facility, they landed behind what had to be a mountain on the backside.

The shuttle landed hard, and the ramp dropped. Out of dozens of shuttles ran marines of all races with battleoids leading the way. The dust rose from their feet, but no sound in the airless moon. Once the marines were clear, the shuttles took off. Once back in the sky, they resumed their crazy dance behind the warships and around the moons.

Reaching the mountain slope, the marines could see the sparkling shield reflection from the mining facility on top of the mountain running down its sides. They waited while a particular group of marines searched the area. Finding what they were looking for, they notified the battleoids where to begin digging.

When Jan had first been told what they were going to do, he laughed. He thought they were pulling a joke on him. That was until they showed him the shovels. Every RGN warship that carried battleoids had a few of these special shovels with sonic cutting edges. That was to allow for digging trenches and such, quickly and deep. Now they were going to be used for something different. They were now being used to dig into a mountain under a shield to attempt an entrance.

Who the hell came up with this crazy idea, Jan wondered? Zeke or Jeanne. It sounded like something Jeanne would think of. Or, as he dug, then again, this was typical of Zeke. Six battleoids were excavating as fast as they could straight forward. The plan called for each group to dig for half an hour and switch out with another group while the first group would recharge.

From what he heard; Zeke had probes check this side of the moon until they had found what he was looking for. The Chohish had built their main processing facility using this mountain as a backstop. If the battleoids could dig far enough, they would go under the facility's protective shields and through the back wall. The battle engaged above was to cover any noise or vibration the digging may cause in the facility since it did have an atmosphere.

It took over four hours, but they finally reached the back wall. Every muscle ached in Jan's body, and sweat soaked his clothes. Even though the battleoid enhanced his strength over a hundred-fold, it still required him to do the activity physically. The more effort he put in, the battleoid would match it. An excavator could have done the job quickly, but they had none in the warships. No one ever thought they would need one, and since they took up a lot of space, they would not carry one just in case.

The marine engineers gathered around the exposed wall. When the diggers had neared the wall, they had been careful not to hit or scape their shovels against the wall. Instead, another group of marines, not in a battleoid, had carefully scooped away the dirt and rocks with their powered armored hands or small spades.

As the engineers worked on getting access through the wall, the vibrations from the battle above ceased. The pause was to allow all the warships to recharge their shields. The game plan had called for the warships to use only a portion of their destructive power, hoping the enemy concentrated all their efforts on securing against a frontal assault.

That is why the assault shuttles flew over the two moons out of missile range. The Chohish did not know that the shuttles were not carrying ground forces. Instead, the marines they would typically have carried were already on the moon's surface and about to enter from the processing facilities' rear.

What the Chohish probably did not realize, was that there were no plans in place to capture the military base. Once the marines made their presence known, the total weight of the combined fleets would attempt to destroy the base in total, not leaving anywhere for the Chohish to survive. They did not want to leave an enemy force in their rear if they had to retreat later. Only a single cruiser would lash out at the mining facility to signal the marines to proceed.

Air tanks were replaced, weapons were checked, and groups were reorganized into their proper locations. Jan now stood in front of the command group with another half dozen battleoids acting as a guard against whatever was waiting for them on the other side.

Several dozen battleoids, one being Khaleesi, waited behind the engineers to give the signal. Once the breach charges went off, they would be the first through, then the Kolqux marines would rush in to secure the immediate area. At the same time, additional Kolqux marines would attempt to capture the facility and find out who manned it. They would withdraw and destroy it from above if it was manned by Chohish and the resistance was fierce enough.

What surprised Jan was how they entered. Instead of explosive wire, the engineers determined the depth and strength of the wall material. Then they used sonic-bladed saber saws to cut into the wall just shy of the full depth around the entire perimeter. Next, they sliced sections that could be pulled inward. Finally, they attached pulling cables to each section.

Once they completed their work, they stepped back to the wall to see if there was an increase in noise on the other side. Only after they signaled the go-ahead the battleoids grabbed the cables.

The Admiral was notified that their preparations to enter had been completed. They were now waiting for the fleets signal to proceed.

The voice of Khaleesi came through lightly in their helmets. "On my signal, pull the wall down. Be ready; they may be waiting for us. Uv'ei, once we are in, your marines are to secure the area before following us. Ready everyone? Here we go, on the count of two. Two, one."

The wall tumbled inward on a cloud of dust. No sooner than it reached the ground, then a dozen battleoids raced forward, only to pause as they saw what was in front of them. Thousands upon thousands of Fassoin and Kolqux cadavers lay frozen in death, stacked upon each other like wood blocks.

No armed force met them, although many wished they had rather than stumble on what they did. The battleoids had to step on the bodies as they made their way to the sizeable sealed hatchway in front of them. The Kolqux marines had a more difficult time following. Many times, Uv'ei and Uv'ek found it necessary to order quiet as curses of revenge punctuated the com frequently.

Treading carefully through the pile of bodies, Jan could not stop the bile rising from his stomach into his throat. What he saw sickened him. The bodies showed signs of burns, fractures, disease, and so much more, which had to have occurred for years before their death. The Chohish must have used this colossal storage area as a cheap burial disposal site. As he got close to the midpoint of the way across, he saw the bodies were now mainly Kolqux with a few Endaens mixed in.

With Masson at his side, he felt his rage growing. Only when Masson put his hand on his battleoids arm did he realize he had started to press the trigger of the plasma rifle he was carrying. Then, relaxing his trigger finger, he breathed deeply, trying to push the anger down. He would let it loose once he came upon the Chohish.

Unfortunately, he would not get the chance immediately. As soon as the engineers opened the sealed hatchway, the Kolqux marines raced forward, not waiting for the battleoids to clear the way. Revenge was on their minds, and they were not to be denied or delayed.

The sound and pull of air rushing past him raised concerns that decompression in the area might hurt any innocent miners. He was sure there were emergency barriers that would lower or swing into place in case of holes caused by a stray meteorite getting through the shields. But before he had gone much further, he felt the wind die down, yet oxygen remained. So good; the engineers must have sealed the breach temporarily somehow.

But that was their concern; Jan had some anger to bleed off. And his speakers were telling him where he could do that. The sound of a raging battle coming from nearby. With Masson still by his side, he showed anyone watching why the Irracans preferred their slimmer and smaller battleoids over the RGN version. The pair of battleoids may not be able to fly, but they sure came close as they raced forward.

Turning a corner, they saw a barricade with armored Chohish soldiers set up at the end of the hallway. Dead Kolqux marines were piled in front of it. Letting part of the anger in a scream, Jan rushed headlong without any concern for his safety at the barricade. Then, firing his plasma rifle nonstop, he slammed in and through the barrier.

Swinging his rifle butt up through the jaw of one Chohish soldier, he whipped the closed fist of his other hand against the chest of another. The Chohish, with his chest crushed, went flying backward into a group of his fellow soldiers, toppling half their number. Into this group, Jan and Masson waded into with abandon. Still firing at anything that moved, Jan, with his sonic blade now gripped in his hand, tore through Chohish after Chohish.

A laser blast hit his back, throwing him against the nearest wall. Pain blossomed up his spine, and he knew he was injured. Ignoring the pain as best as he could, he tried to get up, but his battleoid was not responding. It had shut down and was in the process of rebooting. If it had enough time, which he doubted.

The backup power allowed him to see what was headed toward

him. A dozen Chohish armored worriers led by the largest Sovereign he had ever seen came striding at him with purpose, and he knew what that purpose was. The readings indicated he was seconds away from complete system initiation.

Then he saw what Uv'ei once saw. Hell on wheels in a battleoid. A huge battleoid roared into the picture with both shoulder guns firing, the plasma rifle spitting flames, and a sonic sword gutting one Chohish before beheading another. In seconds, Chohish soldiers lay around her in death like a funeral pyre.

The Sovereign screamed his rage before slashing at the battleoid with his own giant sword. The pair faced each other while other battleoids and Kolqux marines cut down the remaining Chohish warriors. Jan saw Masson lying beside him face down, his battleoid giving off smoke.

Khaleesi had her left foot back with her sword in her left hand behind her. Even though Khaleesi could have used her guns to take out the Sovereign, she wanted to make a statement to the Kolqux. Khaleesi lunged forward, which was easily blocked. The return strike was met by Khaleesi with a swing upward before she cut down that left a cut on the Sovereign's right cheek.

Enraged, the Sovereign grabbed his sword with both hands and swung it overhead, bringing it straight down toward Khaleesi's shoulder. Then, turning sideways, with a speed that belied Jan's earlier thought that Irracan armor was faster, Khaleesi let the blade flow by her. While the enemy's blade sliced into the ground, she used her sword to cut the Sovereign's other unprotected cheek.

The surprise on the Sovereign's face was seen by all. With blood dripping down his cheeks, there could be no doubt he knew he was outmatched. With resignation, the Sovereign lifted up his sword parallel to his chest, after which he tapped his chest before nodding at Khaleesi. Grabbing a knife at his belt, the Sovereign sliced his own throat.

As the Sovereign lay dying, Khaleesi helped a functioning Jan to his feet. "I know you like your Irracan units, but I sure wish you would swallow your pride and get an RGN unit. There is a reason we use these over models like yours. Those units may be somewhat faster, which is a matter of opinion; they cannot stand up to heavy weapons fire. Isn't that why you are in one? Help me get Masson out of his. His readings say he is alive and well, but his unit is finished."

After releasing Masson from his prison inside the battleoid, Jan followed Khaleesi as she trailed behind the Kolqux marines. There was no staying ahead of them. They were out for blood, and they were getting it. They passed groups of Chohish soldiers torn apart with a scattering of dead Kolqux around them.

"I will have to talk with Uv'ei; he is losing his men because he cannot control them. They need to be able to control their anger," said Khaleesi as she followed the trail of dead bodies.

"There are relatively new at fighting but not new to living or dying from torture. I am not sure if we had lived as the Kolqux had to, we would be able to control our emotions either if we came upon something similar." Jan stated as he stepped over a dead Kolqux locked in a deadly embrace with a Chohish.

Soon, after going through an ore smelter, they encountered some live workers. Close to several dozen Kolqux were being guarded and attended to by Kolqux marines. The workers were emancipated with burn marks over a good portion of their bodies. When they passed, the stunned workers looked at them with indifference.

It took another several hours to finally reach the front of the facility. They had passed thousands of Kolqux workers. Seeing Uv'ei and Uv'ek sitting on the floor collapsed against a pillar, they headed over. The two were covered in blood and gore. Uv'ek wore bloody bandages around his leg and his arm.

"Ah, Khaleesi and Jan, it is good to see you. We are checking the lower levels, but we believe there are no more Chohish to deal with.

We are finding more and more of our people who hid everywhere when the battle started," said an exhausted Uv'ei.

"How bad, Uv'ei?" asked Jan.

"Over a hundred dead and even more wounded. All reason left my men and women when they had to walk over the dead. Too often, we dealt with that ourselves," Uv'ei lamented.

"And you?" asked a sympathetic Khaleesi.

"My brother and I were no better than the rest. By the time we got our reasoning back, the battle was over. Now, time to heal."

The sound of a struggle reached them. From a stairwell, four Kolqux pushed an injured Sovereign down the steps. The rescued workers reacted in fear and huddled together. Then, throwing the Chohish down to lie prone on the floor, one of the Kolqux marines notified them they found him hiding in a closet.

Looking at Uv'ei, Khaleesi asked Uv'ei if he had any use for the Chohish Sovereign. The question echoed through the massive atrium from the large battleoid standing over Uv'ei as Khaleesi had turned up the volume in the battleoid to the maximum.

Taking a moment to regard the prone Chohish, who looked at him with hatred, he calmly told Khaleesi he did not.

"Jan, I think it is time we left. Will you join me?" Khaleesi asked as she headed toward the destroyed entrance. On the way, her eight-ton battleoid foot pads stepped on the Chohish sovereign's head. "We don't either."

The room erupted in cheers.

AGONIZING AMAZEMENT

PUTTING ANOTHER BODY on the pile-stacked on the hovering sled had to be the most demanding work Masson ever had to do. The battle had ended the day before, but they still found bodies of dead Kolqux marines. The destruction of the Chohish military base was accomplished painlessly once they could use the combined fleet's full force. They used the same process Lance had suggested when they took out the gigantic station. Start on one section, and work your way in. As expected, the base had excellent shields but could not withstand the barrage for long. That was the problem with stationary facilities; they could not move out of the way. Battlecruisers carried some awesome firepower that you wanted to be able to avoid if possible. All believed that, typically, a fleet would have been stationed here as part of its protection.

Feeling guilty for not being able to contribute much during the fight, Masson has been assisting with gathering bodies that would be sent home. The Kolqux, Endaen, and Fassoin corpses would be left where they were. There were too many to remove within the short timeframe they had. The Chohish dead could stay where they died. Masson's back ached as he had been at this for hours.

Going down a long hallway, he thought he heard a sound.

Pulling his pistol, he quietly made his way from door to door until the audible sounds of someone moving around could be heard from within.

"Jan, Jeanne, you may want to join me here. I have located some movement. Use your tracker to find me. Do not respond; I do not want them to hear me. Masson out," he whispered into his com unit.

Deciding against going into the room without backup, he laid down against the far wall with his pistol centered on the door. The sound went quiet, like whoever was there may have heard him when he positioned himself on the floor.

Hearing a slight noise at the end of the hall, Masson turned to see Jeanne and Jan with a dozen marines behind them. Motioning towards the door opposite, he indicated quiet. The group crept their way down with nary any sound. Two marines in full armor continued until they stood on each side of the door. Have you ever seen a marine in their armor move to limit the noise? If it was not a profound moment, Masson would have laughed. Reminded him of a man imitating a duck.

Rising off the floor, Masson stole his way to the door. There were no handles nor locks, just a wooden door resting on hinges. Then, pushing the door slowly open with the barrel of his pistol, he peeked inside. A quick movement inside caught his attention. Jumping into the room and rolling to a prone position, he aimed his weapon where he perceived the motion.

From outside, two balls of light came flying in to light up a portion of the room. Seeing a slight figure crouching underneath a table, Masson was less than a second from firing his weapon when his brain finally recognized what he saw. It was a little human girl. Two boys no older than two or three years old held her hands.

Startled, he lowered his weapon. When it was pointed down, a more prominent figure came running from the dark. Then, with no time to raise his pistol, he dropped it. Catching the figure close, he realized it was a Kolqux woman. Stopping her hand as it swung a piece of sharp jagged glass at him, he urged her to calm down. Her hand holding the glass was bleeding profusely.

Pushing her away, he held his hands out in a gesture of peace. The female stood shivering, looking at him in fear. "I mean you no harm. Can you understand me?" he asked. He got no reaction that she understood his words. But she also did not attack or run away.

"Maybe she would respond better to me," Jeanne said as she moved into the room. The Kolqux looked at Jeanne, where she raised the piece of broken glass threateningly. Stooping to place her weapon on the floor, Jeanne raised both hands over her head.

"Jan, ask Uv'ei or Uv'ek to send one of their people here. Maybe she understands their language. Our implants will not help us without her saying something," whispered Jeanne. Slowly, she lowered herself to sit on the floor in a lotus fashion. "Masson, put your weapon away using your fingertips. We want her to realize we mean them no harm."

The Kolqux female moved back to stand before the three children who had not moved. The two boys clutched the young girl's hands as they whimpered in fear, with one of them wiping snot from his nose.

Footpads sounded, running down the hallway after a few moments. Uv'ei entered the room cautiously. Seeing Jeanne and Masson on the ground, he followed their gaze to the table. His breath caught in amazement.

Speaking in his standard Kolqux language, they heard him ask who she was. When he got no response, Uv'ei spoke in a language they had not heard before. At this, the female jerked back and covered her mouth before responding with the same vocabulary. Then, dropping the bloody piece of glass, the female fell to the ground and began crying.

Rushing to hold the woman, Uv'ei rocked with her in his arms, speaking to her in the strange tongue. Soon Jeanne's AI interpreter started translating. Uv'ei was soothing her, confirming that no one would harm her or the children.

Walking into the room next to Khaleesi and a squad of her marines, Zeke took in the situation. Tapping Khaleesi on her arm, he nodded toward the back of the room, which was still covered in blackness.

Moving away just as Jeanne reached under the table to coax the children out, the marines armed their weapons before rolling light balls further into the room. What they saw was that the room ended in another several dozen feet. But on the left side, a larger-than-normal metal door was closed with a bar that ran across to keep it from opening.

Sliding up to the door, a marine carefully lifted the bar before he pulled the door open with the tip of his rifle. Then, getting no response, he threw some light balls inside. Screams and crying sounded from inside the room. Sending in a floating viewer, the images that came back had the marines cursing.

Moving next to the marine, Zeke viewed the images before peeking around the corner. Seeing no Chohish, he made to move inside when Khaleesi grabbed his arm and shook her head. "We have been through this once before, Captain; my marines will go first to ensure it is safe."

As a pair of marines cautiously entered, the crying increased in volume from more throats. Several more viewers were released and showed an enormous room, more extensive than a carrier landing bay.

"Jeanne, please, I could use your assistance here, " Zeke begged.

The sound of Zeke's voice was something she rarely heard. It matched what she heard when they saw the devastated planet of the Fassoins and when he held the dead child on Niflhel. Handing off the children who had crawled into her outstretched arms to Masson, she scurried over to join Zeke. What she saw shocked her to the core.

In front of her were several thousand human children of both sexes dressed in rags yet surprisingly clean. They were all sitting or lying on sleeping blankets. Mixed in were women of human, Endaen, and Kolqux origins. All looked scared, with most of the children crying with their hands over their mouths to keep quiet.

"What the hell? Were the Chohish doing experiments on them?" snarled Khaleesi.

Running his glance around the rest of the room, Zeke responded in a whisper. "No, they would not have kept them at the mines. I think the Chohish was saving them for a future labor force. They no longer had the Fassoins to draw upon and needed a new source of labor. They were going to see how well humans could be trained. My opinion, but I cannot think of another reason."

As word spread, more people of all races showed up. They spread through the room, calming the children and women. Meanwhile, Zeke and a squad of marines headed further into the room, where they located more doors. One led to showers, and another led to a huge kitchen. Hundreds more children were hiding in both chambers.

Reentering the first room with the children, Zeke pulled Uv'ei aside. "Why did these rooms go unsearched? There could have been a brigade of Chohish in here and wreaked havoc on us."

"It is a massive mining operation, Zeke. I have dozens of teams out searching, but checking every location and room will take time. I cannot send out more teams as each team must be at least a squadron size in case they run into a Chohish force," Uv'ei responded.

Exhaling, Zeke closed his eyes for a few seconds. "Sorry, Uv'ei, I apologize. I know you are doing everything you can. Finding the children shook me pretty hard. Any estimate of how many of your people were found alive?"

"I understand. The past couple of days has been rough for all of us. We are still finding some workers, but if I had to guess now, I would say between a hundred and ten thousand and a hundred and twenty thousand. As I said, it is a large facility. Much more prominent than the last one we were at. We found a few freighters that we are converting now to accommodate them. There should be enough. What are you going to do with the children?" asked Uv'ei.

"First thing is to try and figure out where they came from. I am guessing they are from the Pandora System. I will ask the Admiral to take them home; he has the capacity. Knowing his reputation, he will have his staff sleep on the floors and give the kids the beds. He was going back with the tenders anyway," said Zeke. "What about the Kolqux and Endaen women that have been taking care of the babies? They could be from any number of places."

"That can be decided once they are on the way. The longer we stay here, the riskier it is for them." Answered Uv'ei. "Well, I have to run, my friend; there is so much to do."

As Uv'ei passed a Kolqux female, she timidly whispered, "Uv'ei, is that you?"

Pausing to look at the female, Uv'ei walked closer to get a better look. As he did, the female reached up to touch Uv'ei's face. "It is you; you look so different. Don't you remember me? Have I changed that much?" She started crying but never stopped touching his face.

Putting his hand on her cheek, he turned her face upwards. "Uv'em? Is that you? It cannot be. We were told you were dead over two years ago. Oh, wait until Uv'ek hears you are alive. We have missed you so very much."

Without saying another word, Uv'ei crushed Uv'em in a bear hug, a cousin he once thought lost, back from the dead.

Leaving them to their family reunion, Zeke walked on until he was standing next to Jeanne. She was mobbed by the children who were hanging all over her. The children looked undernourished but, otherwise, looked to be in decent shape. But even with all that had been going on, they laughed easily. Maybe it had something to do with knowing life might be getting better. Then again, perhaps that is what a child is? Joy.

Leaving the area, Zeke was joined by Masson. "How could they be so cruel? Do they now have any compassion?"

"That is the question I have been asking myself this whole trip, Masson. But right now, we need to get them the hell out of here and on the way back home before any Chohish shows up. Only then can we decide what to do about the Chohish when the time comes." Zeke stated as he glanced back at the Children. "For once, my father may have been wrong."

It took several more days to get the freighters set up and packed with food, water, and air canisters. Once that had been completed, they could start loading the miners.

While the Kolqux got everything set up for the miners, the Admiral did as Zeke thought he would. Although he did not have to do much, the crew was only too happy to give their beds to the children. The problem that arose was how to keep the children safe in a battle. The delay in leaving waiting on the Kolqux allowed the RGN engineers to devise and install harnesses on the beds. Unfortunately, the Kolqux would not have that option.

Finally, the ships were ready to depart more than a week past the day of the battle. During that time, the crews on the RGN had been unloading the boxed fighters and putting them together. On the day when most would return home, the Lucky Strike, Fox, and Jackal had finished replenishing their lost equipment and reinforced their crew with replacements.

Meeting at the mining facility atrium for the last time, Zeke stood with Jeanne, Hu'de, and Uv'ei. Khaleesi and half a dozen marines stood in a protective circle. "I will not be sorry to see this place destroyed. It is a place of death. The admiral is going to cleanse the entire facility with hellfire missiles; he is going to burn it down to the ground. The missiles will provide their own agent to allow them to burn at extreme temperatures in the void of space. The untold dead deserve to have their ashes free to roam this system in peace."

"When do we leave, Zeke?" asked Uv'ei.

"We?" asked Jeanne with surprise.

"The freighters do not need us to escort them home; the Admiral said he would ensure they get there as he will be going that way anyway. Hu'de's battleship and one carrier under my command with my marines will join you." Uv'ei said as he moved over to spit on a Chohish warrior's corpse. "I am not done yet."

Looking around the atrium, Uv'ei stared at Khaleesi. "It seems you have a talent for attracting Chohish. Saves us the trouble of looking for them ourselves."

"Uv'ei, in all seriousness, our odds are not good. Our job is not to engage but to leave communication pods on our status and if what we find matches what was found in the database. Our ships are faster than yours, which will be an issue."

The laughter from Uv'ei and Hu'de surprised the rest of the group. "That is why I am only taking one carrier. It has your upgraded engines; the other one does not. Hu'des battleship has had RGN engineers working on his engines since he left Sobolara. They finished three days ago and passed all the testing."

Knowing there was talking them out of it, Zeke relented. Besides, it would be nice to have more firepower if the past several weeks indicated what they would find. He had no idea how they could have updated the engines as it was under power, but he was no engineer. And he did not really care. It would be good to have them along.

Putting his arms around their shoulders, "Welcome aboard to the Last Hope Fleet."

"When did you come up with that name?" asked Jeanne.

"Just now. It fits. All of us have survived when we shouldn't have. Now we are heading into an unknown territory under strength. What else would we call it?" Getting no reply, he started singing a tune as they left the facility for the last time.

Within hours, the facility was burning with fires that melted metal and burned corpses to ashes. Saying goodbye to the combined RGN and Kolqux fleet heading home, the now newly named fleet headed toward the slipstream, not knowing if they were going to their death.

LOSS

QUIETLY SLIPPING INTO the system was impossible, as the Kolqux ships did not have the equipment for silent protocol. But Zeke considered the extra firepower worth the risk. Besides, it was hard to tell new friends and allies they were not wanted, even if the reason had validity.

The probes sent in before the warships entered indicated a Cho-hish presence identified by low power readings somewhere in the system. More data would be needed before they could determine what that entailed. More probes were deployed, but it would take a while until they understood what they faced.

One item identified that gave grave concerns to Zeke was all the large asteroids that populated the system. They were everywhere. The ships should be able to work around them, but what could be hidden in them?

Meanwhile, while the warships cautiously made their way through, Jamie and her crew were working overtime to check out the new fighters. A good many had been put together in haste. Jamie would be damned if she was going to send any pilots out in a compromised fighter.

One disadvantage to the multiple bays was the need for

additional support to accommodate them. It made Jamie's job more problematic, but she was not complaining. The number of fighters the cruiser could now deploy, not counting the new addition of having bombers in the mix, blew her mind.

Going from half a dozen to over a hundred fighters increased her workload to a point she thought she would not be able to manage it properly. Primarily when first implemented as she was learning the new processes. But to her amazement, the hypothetical arrangement she proposed when they put this whole crazy idea together worked much better than she thought it would.

Wiping the sweat off her brow with greasy hands was getting to be expected. There just weren't enough technicians, even with the support Jax lent from his group. Jax was in the same situation as she was. Thankfully, she and Jax got along tremendously and supported each other whenever possible.

In fact, Jax was on the other end of the plasma gun she was working on, checking on the connections to the fighter. "Connections look good from here, Jamie. Can you run a check from the cockpit controls?" came Jax's muffled request, whose head was inside the unit.

Levering herself onto the wing, Jamie walked gingerly around the open cockpit to slip inside. Initiating systems check, she watched as the lights changed as they progressed through the process. One light flickered from red to orange before stopping. Then, going through the report, she confirmed with the fighter's AI that it matched what she saw as the problem. "Jax, it looks like there is a blockage on the fuel feed."

"One sec... how does it read now?"

"That solved it." Entering a few commands, Jamie cleared the error message. "I am rerunning a full checkout now."

Jumping out, she saw Jax whipping his greasy hands on a towel.

"I don't know who packed that unit, but it had three times the packing material than usual. A piece got into the intake valve."

"We are almost done, Jax. Less than a dozen fighters left need refitting or being checked. The dozen new bombers are completed. I know my crew is exhausted. We have been working eighteen-hour shifts since we got them. Without your engineer's assistance, it would have taken us another week." Jamie said as she took the rag from her back pocket to wipe a glob off Jax's face.

Taking a deep breath, Jamie could feel the aches from the constant bending and lifting run through her body. Her shoulders had a dull pain that refused to go away. When she got time, she would have to visit Doc even though he would chastise her once more for overdoing it.

Glancing at the next fighter they would have to check out, she staggered when the ship suddenly shifted. Jax's hand grabbed her arm in support. Before either could get settled back on their feet, the ship rocked again. Then, pulling Jamie to the fighter, both grabbed a handhold.

Eeeoooeeeooo bip bip eeeoooeeeooo, eeeoooeeeooo bip bip eeeoooeeeooo, eeeoooeeeooo bip bip eeeoooeeeooo, eeeoooeeeooo bip bip eeeoooeeeooo

Without a word, Jamie and Jax took off running, Jamie to her office in this fighter bay, and Jax to engineering. Unfortunately, they had not gone more than a few steps when the speakers blasted out the warning.

"*Battle stations, battle stations. We are under attack; repeat, we are under attack. All personnel report to your stations immediately. All pilots to their fighters and bombers, repeat, all pilots to their fighters and bombers. Battle stations, battle stations. We are under attack...*" the warning kept repeating.

They took off running. As the two ran others ran past them to prep the fighters. "Do not let anyone get in a fighter that has not been cleared," Jamie yelled as she ran.

Jamie ran into her office and brought up the half dozen monitors to display the area around the cruiser. What she saw shocked her. The area around the cruiser was swarming with Chohish fighters. How did they get near without being detected?

"Jamie, this is Zeke. Are you there?" The sound from the bridge in the background sounded hectic. Jamie could hear Will yelling commands with Isolde screaming her own. Only Zeke's seemed relaxed and collected. She knew it was just on the surface, but it helped to know he was in control.

"Yes, Captain, I just returned to the office to get an idea of what we are facing. It looks bad. We have most of the fighters ready to go, but sending them out with all the Chohish fighters waiting for any that came out would be suicide." Pulling up the stats on what fighters had been cleared, Jamie started marking any not signed-off unavailable. Until she removed the lock, the cockpit controls were locked closed for those units.

"I agree. Have all pilots ready in their cockpits, but do not send them out until I give you the signal. Make sure the pilots do not get anxious. Wait for my notification, Zeke out."

The next shock to the warship surprised her; it was so violent. Jamie was lifted off her feet, where she flailed her hands in vain as she was thrown across the room. The corner walls of her office slammed into her. She rolled down over her desk to end up on the floor. Severe pain, unlike any she had ever experienced before, threatened to overtake her.

Gripping the top of her desk, Jamie made to stand, only to collapse as her left leg would not hold her. Looking down at her leg, she could tell it was broken as it was bent at an awkward angle. But she knew she could not surrender to the pain; she had to keep her pilots from taking off.

Using her hands to the edges of her desk, she made her way around to the front of it. Something was not right beside her leg, but she could not concentrate enough to figure it out. She tried to brush away whatever was touching her face, but all she felt was her hair getting into her face. Her leg swinging as she maneuvered using just one leg brought tears to her eyes. The pain was so excruciating. But she had to notify the pilots not to leave. It seemed like hours, but only several minutes before she finally reached the master control, where she locked down all the fighters.

Punching the communications button, she yelled for her backup before she dropped to the ground. The pain flared anew. Groaning, she tried to rise but failed. Then, as she was afraid she would black out from the pain, someone grabbed her to lift her into a chair.

"Here, Commander, sit still. I am calling for medical help," Jamie heard from someone through the haze.

"Gunner? Is that you? You have to ensure no pilots take off until the Captain gives the ok," she pleaded through the pain. The sounds of other voices let her know Gunner was not alone.

"Ok, we are passing the word around. I will get with the Captain and let him know. Commander, you need to settle down." Gunner did not know how to tell her that a part of her scalp was flapping in her face. But he was soon absolved from that duty as she passed out.

Contacting Zeke to let him know that Jeanne had been seriously hurt and was waiting on Jamies's backup, Lieutenant Tod Clevenger, to arrive. Zeke repeated the order that all fighters were to wait for his order before deployment. The bombers were to hang back until he had a target for them. He asked Gunner to ensure there were some fighters to ask as an escort.

Gunner never got a chance to ask the questions he had, as the cruiser rolled again violently before he even got a chance. The communication ended with a shriek during the roll. Then, holding onto a wall handle strategically placed several places around the room, he centered his weight while looking at the control board. Even with all the violent shaking, over half the fighters had pilots onboard but could not lift off due to the lock Jamie had placed on them.

What was puzzling Gunner was where the hell Tod was? Damn it, he should have been here now. Moving to stand outside the office, Gunner had to step aside as an engineer and pilot raced past. He was not used to being on the other side of this; he would usually be the one running past Jamie to get to his fighter. Now though… until Tod arrived, Gunner knew he would have to step up and take control. But he knew he would need help. Fortunately, he knew someone that may be able to help.

Returning inside the office, he located the communicator to talk with the pilots. "Librada Hindman, please report to Jamie's office in bay four; you are needed there ASAP," Gunner repeated the message several times to ensure she understood the severity of the page. Although, with everything that was going on, she already knew that.

As he worked through the unfamiliar controls to release the fighters and bombers, Librada rushed in dressed in her pilot suit with her helmet tightly gripped in her hand. "I thought that sounded like you. What are you doing? We need to get in our fighters."

"Put that helmet down and help me figure out this damn control unit. Jamie was severely injured during one of the near misses when the ship rolled. I had hoped Tod would show up, but he never appeared."

Sliding up next to Gunner, Librada stopped Gunner from pressing a selection he had brought up. "You can forget about Tod; he was crushed by a pallet that broke loose of its mooring. And stop what you are doing before you do some real damage. See the markings placed on those fighters; the Commander had those locked down for some reason. One second… woooah ok, here we go. She had these marked as not ready for use. So, let's keep these out of available fighters. Now, as far as the rest.…"

Watching her flip through the screens, he had no idea how she knew what to do. "The Captain said we are not to send out the fighters until he notifies us. But when he does, they need to do it quickly. The bombers we are to hold back as they will have a specific target for them. They will need fighter protection, so plan accordingly."

Flipping through the screens, she finally found the one she sought. "Ok, we can set this up to release specific fighters when the Captain tells us." Which she did quickly. "Now for the bombers and their escort. While I am doing this, Gunner, get on the horn and pass the word about what we are doing."

And that he did. While talking with the different group leaders, he was amazed at how knowledgeable Librada was on the programs used by Jamie and her department. Pilots usually spend any free time boning up their flying skills or learning more about the weapons available to their fighters.

As he finished with the last of the group leaders, Gunner spent a few moments looking at the dozen screens reflecting the action outside the cruiser. The Chohish fighters were not as numerous as he had feared at first. Then, suddenly, a pair of fighters disintegrated right before the Jackal came flying through the debris. It was not long before he thought he saw a pattern. "Librada, get ready. I think we will hear from the Captain shortly.'

Standing next to Gunner, he pointed out what he was seeing. "See, he is pushing all the Chohish fighters away from the Kolqux warships, using the two destroyers. Our cruiser, see there… is pushing any back that sneaks by them. The Captain will send out the fighters once there is enough separation for safe ejection. And look at how he is swinging us around. He is prepping the cruiser to attack that asteroid where the Chohish came from using our port side, so give Roy a heads up."

"I see it, but only because you pointed it out. Ok, I will let the pilots know." With that, Librada sent out a general broadcast to all the pilots.

The cruiser went into a spin, forcing the pair to grab the handholds and plant their feet with their magnetic boots against the walls. Pressure built as the spin increased. Flattening against the wall, the two pilots looked at the chairs with their harnesses with envy. As the pressure increased, their weight threatened to throw them from their holds. Librada slowly slid down the wall, but the tension never ended as the ship kept twirling.

Screaming, Librada's handhold slipped. She was flung away from the wall only to be jerked to a halt. Gunner had grabbed her around the waist using his legs. Holding both their weight just using his hands was excruciating. Gunner was not sure how long he would be able to hold on. So, what was going on with the inertia and gravity generators? This was the second time they had failed in the last half hour. That must have been what impacted Jamie and Tod.

Seeing red through his vision as he fought with everything he had to hold on, he was taken by surprise when the gravity returned. Then, dropping to the floor, he gasped, trying to catch his breath. "What the hell is going on?"

They were both still on the floor when an engineer ran in. "You two, ok?" Seeing them nod, he ran out before explaining what was happening. They looked at each other in exasperation before climbing to their feet, weariness running through their bodies. And, of course, that was Zeke pinged them.

"Gunner, you still there? Heard they had power issues in your area." Getting confirmation, Zeke continued. "I am making my final turn. Once I complete it, send out the fighters. Do not wait on a signal from me. You make the call. Captain out."

The background noise let Gunner know the bridge was running on all cylinders. He could hear Will, Hawke, and Isolde yelling commands. The continuous sound and motion of missiles firing let them know the cruiser was in the mix of it. "Well, I guess we will not get any rest, Librada. So go ahead and release the fighter and bomber locks. You will not have time to play with that as I will need you on the com to the pilots. I will let you know when to release the *Gorgons.*"

Releasing the locks, Librada laughed. "The *Gorgons?* You now call our fellow pilots the *Gorgons?* I am not sure they would like that. You and your mythology."

"Oh, come on, they will love it. And the Captain is making his run. Release the *Gorgons!!*" Gunner said without taking his eyes off the monitors.

Through their boots magnetically locked to the floor, as they were not taking any chances after what they had just experienced, both could feel the vibrations of the fighters as they left the ship. Then they waited while they watched the pilots, they should be with going to war against the Chohish. Over a dozen minutes later, they saw an update come through one of the monitors.

On one of them came a marker pointing to an asteroid. Gunner knew the tag came from Isolde. It came with a tiny heart. From the asteroid, he saw an opening where a Chohish fighter roared out.

Excited now, he pointed to the asteroid image to Librada. "We have our bomber's target. Send the target coordinates to Roy. Tell him it is time to release the *Krakens!*" Hearing Librada laugh was good for his soul at a time like this. He knew it would be in pain shortly at the loss of brave men and women he considered family.

The ship rocked again when the bombers took off. There was a difference between fighters leaving and bombers. The bombers were much more significant and heavier. With the bombers leaving, eighteen fighters went along as an escort.

The two pilots then did what Jamie and her crew always did for them when in a fighter.

"*Hey Pixie, you got a bird coming at you at six o'clock.*"

"*Toodles, Gunner here. Your wingman has a bogie coming up on his ten o'clock. Recommend you do the Dragoncraze in support.*"

"*Cricket, Grumpy at two o'clock needs your assistance.*"

"*Attention Gumdrop and Thumper, you have three baddies coming up on your seven o'clock. I recommend you execute Ballet Smash.*"

"*Einstein, disengage. Get your bird back to base. Your fuel line has been compromised.*"

And on and on. Then, of course, there was the part they hated, whether they were sitting in a fighter, or standing here. An icon going red. And they saw that occur again and again. It was not long before the fighter action settled down to the cleanup of the few Chohish fighters still present.

What surprised them was the Kolqux. The two warships had remained at a reasonable distance from the RGN warships. When the Chohish attacked these two warships, they were met by dozens of Kolqux fighters that flew out of the carrier. More than typically carried in a Chohish carrier. This additional firepower and the excellent defensive projection of force from both warships helped tremendously in the battle against the Chohish fighters. At first, the pair were confused about why the Kolqux had stayed away. It took a few minutes before they understood why. The Kolqux did not want the RGN fighters to confuse the two since both forces had the same physical footprint, even though the transponder would tell who was who.

But one item they were excited to watch was the destruction of the Chohish asteroid fighter base. The probes showed a closeup view as the Lucky Strike streaked by the asteroid, firing everything it could at it, whose return fire was just as intense. The opening where the fighters had come out of was now sealed. They had watched as a colossal piece of asteroid had been lowered and slid into the slot. That explained why they had not detected the Chohish presence earlier. But that did little to stop its destruction.

With the two Destroyers running protection alongside, the Cruiser released a massive wall of destruction toward the sealed opening. It was not intended to break through but to reduce the strength of the shields. What had been waiting for the RGN warships to complete their run were the bombers.

Waves after waves of massive missiles slammed into the asteroid. The first salvos finished what the warships started and finished bringing down the shields. Second, third, and fourth salvos broke apart the asteroid covering. The rest of the missiles entered the new opening before exploding in a massive display. Asteroid and structure debris was all that remained within half an hour.

They were giving each other a high five when news reached them that dampened their excitement. Jamie had died from her wounds.

REASSIGNMENT

THE NEXT SEVERAL hours were spent regrouping for recovery, repair, and assessment. And when that was complete, mourning the dead. Several dozen fighter pilots had perished. Just over half of those were Kolqux. Eight personnel on the Lucky Strike died when the power was lost in several of the fighter bays, with many others injured.

Commodore Jamie Chandler had been loved and admired by all the pilots on both the Lucky Strike and the Fox since they rotated pilots between the two ships. Jamie had been one of the first personnel Zeke had recruited, as her management style and performance had been recognized fleet-wide. The officers knew her personally and considered her a close friend and were walloped upon hearing of her death.

But Tod's death, at the same time, complicated matters. Who could replace them? That had to be done before they could continue onward.

Sitting in Zeke's room, enjoying a cup of his cocoa, Gunner and Librada were unsure if they should sit at attention or relax. Why were they ordered, not asked, to be here? Did they do something wrong when they covered for Jamie? Were any of the pilot's deaths their fault? That was in their mind as they sipped the cocoa in trepidation. The severe expression worn by Zeke as he worked on his computer was not encouraging.

They stiffened as he finally looked at each of them before addressing them. "First, since you two seem somewhat nervous, this is not a rebuke. Your performance while stepping into a critical situation was exceptional. We, myself, along with all the pilots, cannot say thanks enough. You saved lives because of your actions. Many would have been sent out in fighters that were not fully operational, let alone the guidance and warnings throughout the engagement."

Gunner relaxed a little before seeing Zeke's expression had not changed. Something was not right here. And then he found out.

"Jamie and Tod will be sorely missed. They were a unique team that worked seamlessly. Learning all the systems they used would take many months of training. Unfortunately, there are no handy replacements. Because of that, I will have to make a difficult decision."

When they heard that, they knew what he was going to ask. No, make that order them to do. They could not help but glance at each other before turning back to look at Zeke.

"I am not sure where or how you learned the systems Librada, but it sure came in handy," said Zeke.

"I did not have a romantic pastime like someone I know, and I was always interested in learning new applications. Something to play with. Jamie and Tod made it fun. They worked together in tandem so efficiently. I will miss them," Librada explained sadly.

"We all will. But they are no longer here, and we have a need that cannot be ignored. I am reassigning both of you. As of now, you are both grounded and in charge of all the bays, equipment, and people. I am sorry to have to do this, as I know how much Gunner loves to fly, but I am very limited in what options are open to me." Then, opening a drawer on his desk, Zeke pulled out several small boxes. Pushing these towards the pair, he indicated for them to open them. When they did, they were surprised to see Commodore pins and stripes.

"Effective immediately, I am awarding a wartime promotion to Commodore for both of you. I have no doubt that this will be approved by Naval Command." Standing, Zeke reached over to shake each of their hands. "Congratulations, you deserve it."

"Captain, I know Librada will do the position admirably, but I do not have any knowledge of those systems. I would just be a burden to her," said Gunner.

"Really, that is not what I heard from the pilots. They said your recommendations on their situations were spot on. There is more to the job than knowing the control system. It is something Librada will have to teach you, but together, you will make an awesome team, no less than when in your fighters." Standing, Zeke walked around the desk until he was beside the two pilots. "Between the two of you, it will allow us to continue our mission. Without it, I would have to consider going back. I would not be comfortable getting an equivalent individual from a destroyer. They would not have the experience needed."

Knowing he would not be one to force the fleet to head back before completing their mission, Gunner capitulated. "Well, this will make one other person happy. Maybe I can work this to my advantage." This brought smiles all around. They knew how much Isolde worried when Gunner was in his fighter.

Having concluded the meeting, the two pilots got up to leave. Opening the door, Gunner was confronted with Isolde leaning against the wall. "Well, it took you long enough."

"Damn it, you son of a...," Gunner started to turn back to Zeke before Isolde stopped him and warned him he was talking to a Captain. "You had her waiting here in case I declined."

Putting his arm over Gunner's shoulder, Zeke shrugged. "I was ninety percent sure you would not decline the new job. Isolde was insurance for me on the ten percent."

This set off Librada and Isolde laughing. "Oh, I was more than your ten percent insurance, Captain. You counted on me to persuade him even if it was ninety-nine percent," stated Isolde.

Turning to look at Zeke, Gunner saw him shrug at him with a great big smile. "Well, you have to use what tools you got, no? Isn't that what our old flight coordinator used to tell us, Gunner?" At which, they all laughed.

Stopping Gunner and Librada from walking away, Zeke requested they hand over the boxes he gave them. Then, having them both face him, he gave Gunner's box to Isolde while he stood in front of Librada. Unpinning Librada's lieutenant pins, Zeke opened the box where he removed the commodore pins. Then, looking over at Isolde, who had not moved, he waved his hand, indicating she should do the same for Gunner.

Holding the right collar tab on Librada's uniform, he lined up the pin before applying. "Now, we can't have you both walking around out of uniform, can we?" Once he completed the task, Zeke stepped back to review. "They look good on you. Congrats again, Commodore," where he checked and verified Isolde had completed the same on Gunner. Stepping back, he saluted the newly promoted pair and announced, "Officers in the room."

At Zeke's announcement, Isolde, startled, jumped back and saluted the pair. Zeke stepped up next to her, where he whispered. "I think Gunner would prefer something more personal. But, of course, I may be wrong," at which Isolde jumped into Gunner's arms for a long kiss.

The group, minus Zeke, made their way to the office Jamie usually worked from. It was the largest and centrally located with the other landing bays. Entering the hatch into the bay, the two newly promoted officers were startled to see technicians and pilots standing to attention in front of them. Without a word, they all saluted. It took the pair a moment to realize the group would not lower their hands until they returned the salute.

Once done, the group rushed up to congratulate them. They then led the commodores to a cleared section where tables were set up with a congratulations cake and drinks. The pair were at first puzzled before Gunner figured it out. Rounding on Isolde, "How long have you known? You set this all up, didn't you?"

"I did, but it was not me that ordered it set up. The Captain told me his intentions before he had me set this up. Oh, Gunner, Zeke was hard hit when notified about Jamie and Tod. But he knew Jamie would not want him to stop the mission because of her. And Jamie had already documented that you and Librada would be her choice to replace her and Tod if something happened to them. This needed to be resolved before we could go on. After you get a piece of cake, we need to leave and join a meeting to determine our next step."

And that is where they were half an hour later, sitting around a table of officers looking at a hovering four-dimensional image of the system. Asteroids of all sizes dotted the entire system.

"We are starting to get close to their home system if the data we have is accurate. So it is not surprising they would have traps like this setup. The question is, how many and how do we detect them?" asked Will.

"What if we sent a remote shuttle impersonating a larger warship?" asked Hawke.

"I doubt that would work; not enough mass. And not sure we could identify any tracking signal back to the origin," responded Isolde. "There is just too much interference with the asteroid's mineral makeup. Now I understand why they did not mine this system, excellent defensive location. I was puzzled about that when we first arrived."

Ideas came and went. The last few were made in frustration as they were pretty far out there. Just as Zeke was about to call for a break, the soft voice he heard before interrupted the meeting.

"From what I understand, the problem is we cannot detect the Chohish installations until we are in the range of their fighters. Anything we send out to trigger a response will fail as you do not believe it would not have the body and mass of a large warship as we are too close to fooling them. Have I summarized it correctly?" asked Roy.

"That sums it up pretty nicely," answered Zeke. "You have a thought on how we can get past them realizing it is not a warship?"

"Nope, I think everyone is correct in their assumption," Roy replied while sitting there calmly looking around the room.

As it looked like no further update was coming from Roy, Will was about to dismiss everyone when Zeke shook his head no. Zeke placidly waited while the rest of the room became anxious to leave.

It was five minutes later that Roy spoke again. "We could turn the tables on them."

If the situation was not so serious, Zeke would have laughed at how quiet the room got. The open mouths in startlement at the suggestion also did not help him in holding it in. "And how could we do that, Roy?"

"You have had enough time to get a complete picture of the system and have determined your preferred course. Correct?" Seeing Zeke nod positively, Roy continued. "Send out the bombers, all of them, pretending to be shuttles. If what you say should happen, they will ignore us. Once the big boys get close enough to trigger them, they will have to lift up the door to their base, which takes time. Before they can send out their fighters, you will have detected their location. Send it to the bombers, and we will close it."

The casual look of disappointment he gave everyone, like they should all have figured out the same thing, collapsed Zeke's hold on his laughter. He was soon joined by half the group while the others lowered their heads in embarrassment.

"I think we have a plan. Roy, please get with Librada and Gunner for review, and let me know when you are ready to execute. Make sure your plan accounts for a fighter escort. They, nor we, would ever send out shuttles without an escort. Damn, I sure hope this works," ordered Zeke.

"I need to keep my mouth shut," thought Roy out loud as he led half a dozen bombers through the path laid out by Zeke.

"What did you say?" asked Camille. "Quit whispering. Damn it, why do I always get the whisperers?"

Moving the bomber to port to avoid an object he would swear was manmade debris, he asked Camille, "where were you before jumping into this bucket of bolts?"

"I was a shuttle pilot for most of my career out of the Horus Colony before enrolling in bomber school. I got tired of shuttling command officers around. I wanted to do more than be a taxi driver to a bunch of prima donnas. Then spent just over a year sitting idly by, waiting on an assignment. When the call went out for this action, I jumped on it." Sighing, she checked the instrument panels for any indication of a remote scan for the thousandth time. "The images shown on the news were bad enough, but what I saw on Niflhel was ten times worse. Even after all these months, they were still recovering dead bodies."

"I know; Spencer and I came out with the cruiser after being rebuilt. When we landed on Vro, they were just doing the finishing touches on it. But they had images of what it had looked like being displayed all over the shipyard. How the Captain survived, I will never know. The cruiser was totaled. Next to them were videos of the destruction and death in the Pandora system. I was told it was an incentive for the workers," turning to look at her. "It worked. The engineers and technicians there put in ungodly hours to get the cruiser redone in the new configuration. They had a special dedication for the warship when completed. When we got to Pandora, we spent some time on the planet. It will take a long time before they can resume a normal life."

Listening to Roy, Camille could hear the sadness in his voice whenever he mentioned Spencer by name. "About Spencer, I know you two were close; I hope I can measure up to him."

"You are doing just fine. No one will be able to measure up to Spencer. Just as no one will be able to measure up to you. Everyone has their plus and minuses. Spencer was like my brother; he had been with me for years, and we went through some tough times. Crews in a bomber usually stick together until one is either promoted or killed. It would be nice to have a sister. Never had one before."

Surprised, Camille was about to respond when a ping came across from the Lucky Strike. "Isolde here; our probes have picked up scanning originating from the asteroid at the following location."

The screen lit up with an icon indicating an asteroid off to starboard at four o'clock. Turning the bomber to the new heading, they presently saw the asteroid appear in their viewscreen. As they neared, the center of the asteroid started moving.

"Get ready, Camille; we must wait until the Chohish fully raise the door before we can fire. Their fighters will be prepped to fly out, so it will get a bit hairy. Our fighter escort will help, but it all depends on how well we do. So get the missiles lined up for that opening asap," drawled Roy. "We may only have one chance."

Two RGN fighters came flying past to put themselves before the bombers. Suddenly, dozens of new icons appeared on the main screen, flying toward them. Per the bombers' AI, the objects flying towards them were fighters, batching the Chohish configuration.

"Damn, there must have been another Chohish asteroid we missed. Camille, get Librada or Gunner on the line. They need to know about this asap," ordered Roy.

"I am trying. But I cannot reach them… wait, one sec… something is starting to come through… ok, I got them on now," Camille said while playing with the controls. "Putting them on our helmet headsets."

"…is home base, can you read us? "Librada's voice came through, interlaced with heavy static. "Bomber One…"

"Home base, this is Bomber One; we can read you. We have dozens of Chohish fighters headed our way. They are going to run up our ass in a moment. So, you need to redirect our fighter protection. Do you copy?" yelled Roy. The bombers couldn't turn now; if they did, they would lose their lock on the Chohish base opening. And he was seconds away from telling them to fire. But that would mean they would have the weakest part of the ship facing the oncoming enemy fighters.

"Bomber One, this is Gunner at home base. The fighters headed your way are Kolqux fighters. The Captain is sending them to confuse the Chohish fighters. Their transponders will be sending out both RGN and Chohish signals. The Lucky Strike's AI broke the Chohish code captured from the battle at the other asteroid. Do you read? Over."

Seeing the Chohish door finally pull in enough to let their fighters start deploying, Roy knew they did not have the time to respond. Librada and Gunner would know they got the message when they heard the following. "Fire Camille, give them everything we got!"

The first pair of missiles rushed away. They were joined by missiles from the other bombers and fighters. Roy fumed as he waited for the second pair to get loaded for firing. Finally, it fired. Again, they joined up with others.

The first group reached its destination, but not before dozens of Chohish fighters could be deployed. And most of these were destroyed by lasers and interceptors. But a few got past. These, although few in number, slammed into fighters. Explosions lit up the area. The next set of missiles, even though reduced by over half, raced through the opening to explode when it hit the far end or any obstructions.

The problem with allowing egress simultaneously as taking fire is that you had to lower the shields in that section between each fighter. Doing it for an individual vessel was manageable when done by an AI. But you had to keep the shields down when allowing an uninterrupted flow, which the Chohish foolishly did. Although they could not be wholly blamed, that is why the bombers were masquerading as shuttles. The Chohish, though, knew there were fighters present who did have missiles, although they did not compare with what the bombers carried. So maybe they thought their own fighters could stop the RGNs from firing?

The third set of missiles flew in through debris and flames erupting from the door. What confused Roy was the Chohish still kept their shields down. They should know by now there were no shuttles. But soon, he had more important concerns. Several Chohish fighters were coming right at him.

Looking around, he saw his escort was already engaged. Jerking the bomber to port, he knew they could not get away; the bomber was just too damn slow. "Camille, hang on. Looks like our escort has been pulled off. Up to you now. The defense is all yours. The AI is good, but take over if you believe you got a shot. The AI will still help you zero in but allow you to prioritize."

Gripping the firing mechanisms for one of the repeating plasma cannons tightly, Camille snidely remarked. "Thanks, old timer, they never trained us on that at bomber school. Instead, they instructed us to sit back and listen to the experienced pilots tell us what to do. You don't mind if I go to the bathroom now, do you? I would hate to crap in my pants before I get blasted into smithereens."

The bomber shook from laser hits. Roy was not overly worried about laser hits; the bomber was built to shrug most of those off. But, of course, that would only last so long. Missiles now, that was a whole different issue. Bombers had heavy shields and thick armor but paid for that in speed. They were not good at evading missiles. The plasma cannons were their primary defense. The little ECM they had only lasted a few minutes. Bombers were usually used only after obtaining air or space dominance.

Whomp… whomp… whomp… explosions occurred right next to the bomber before the impact smashed into the bomber. It flipped end over end. Loose objects went flying throughout the bomber. The harness bit into the shoulders of the two occupants as they were thrown forward.

"*Aaargh*" yelled Camille before all Roy heard was her gagging. The bomber straightened, but he sent it on a wild, twisting route. Several Chohish fighters were still on his tail.

The sound of "*bllgh… blllgggh…. blllllgggghh….*" could barely be heard through his helmet before he felt the joystick starting to respond sluggishly. "Damn it, somethings leaking." If that wasn't bad enough, the bomber started slowing down.

Looking through the cockpit window, Roy could see the two Chohish fighters on their tail were now making a loop. He knew there was not much he could do. The Bomber was barely responding to his commands. They still had full power, but something must have damaged the engines and their controls.

Suddenly, one of the enemy fighters blew up. "Ha, got one of those bastards," Camille said through tight lips grimacing in pain. Roy saw Camille had her right shoulder tucked down like it was bruised or broken.

Looking at the remaining fighter, he watched as the plasma bolts from the Bomber raced after it. From the belly of the enemy fighter, two plumes of fire jetted away. The bomber had no more ECM to send out. There was nothing else they could do. Roy sighed; he knew that he had survived longer than most. By all statistics, he should have died in battle years ago. "*Hope you are still waiting for me, Spencer. It sure looks like I will be joining you real soon.*" He whispered to himself as he watched the missiles tails head for them in slow motion.

Abruptly, another Chohish fighter flew in front of them, intercepting the enemy missiles before they blew up in a ball of flame. Another fighter came flying past, taking out the remaining Chohish fighter. "*What the hell was going on?*" he thought before it suddenly came to him. Not Chohish, Kolqux. They were Kolqux fighters. And one had thrown themselves in front of the missile to save them. "*Why?*"

He would not get an answer for that right now as he watched the asteroid disintegrate in a massive explosion. It was always weird for him how an explosion occurred in space. There would be flames only for a short time until all the stored oxygen was gone, but the debris would shoot away like the old-time bullets. The rubble, some of the pieces very significant in size, would shoot away without impediments found in an atmosphere. Things like air and gravity. Which meant that he needed to get the bomber out of the way before they became another insignificant part of the debris heading towards them.

The only problem was he was losing control of the bomber. No matter what he did, he could not get it to turn away from the onrushing debris. Shortly, the bomber started giving proximity warnings.

After notifying Librada and Gunner, he waited for the end. The bomber had stopped responding to any attempt at flight control. "Well, Camille, it seems we will have to eject. You ready?"

The indicator flashed red when Roy pushed the button to open the hatch to his ejection pod. Then when he instructed the ship's AI to open the hatch, he was informed that it could not be done due to mechanical damage. The AI recommended they prepare for collision. Seeing Camille looking at him forebodingly through her helmet, Roy shrugged. Not much they could do except strap in and wait.

What surprised him was when Camille started singing, Roy did not recognize the song, but her voice was soft yet engaging. As she sang, Roy began to tap his foot in encouragement. Seeing Roy tapping, Camille gave him a thumbs-up while increasing the volume of her voice. Laughing, knowing the odds of avoiding all the pieces of debris headed their way was minuscule, he decided that he would show the Lucky Strike and all who followed him how to go out in style. Connecting to the Lucky Strike and the rest of his bomber squad, he shared Camille's singing.

Surprisingly, knowing what was happening, others in his group started to join in with Camille. Within moments, there was a full-fledged collective signing. Only the constant proximity alarms marred the mood. The sudden impact against the hull startled both.

Thinking it was debris smashing into the hull, they were surprised when a voice came over the suddenly silenced network.

"You still there, Roy? Masson here, I and my buddy Jan are here to get you moving out of here. Hang on, it takes a bit to get an old clunker like yours moving without crushing it."

"How in hell....??" Both Roy and Camille exclaimed. Then looking outside, they saw what looked like a shuttle with an attachment on the front that looked like a heavy metal wall.

"We call it the pusher. We use it to move heavy objects without having to attach anything. During one of his visits, Gunner saw it in our landing bay. He saw your bomber was having issues, so he asked if we could push you home. Good thing we had just returned and the Fox was nearby. So hang on, you two; you are going to be shaken like a good martini."

And with that, both settled back when Camille started singing again. And that was what all the warships heard as the bomber was pushed out of danger, all the way back to the Lucky Strike.

Several things Roy needed to do when he got back. One… find out why the Kolqux pilot did what he did. And thank the Kolqux in person. Two… buy Gunner a drink. This was the second time he had saved his life. Maybe it should be two drinks, one for each life. Then again, perhaps a night of drinks with him and his new shipmate, with whom he was curious to find out how her signing sounded when she was half drunk.

REFLECTION AND INNOVATION

IT WAS HARD getting through what they had decided to call the asteroid system. No one had seen so many asteroids, some as large as a small moon, in one system. They had to clear out three more asteroids. They could not use the bombers again; Zeke was sure the enemy in the asteroids talked with each other. To get around this problem, Zeke had a destroyer race past with the fighters and bombers following. The cruiser with the Kolqux battleship would fly in to give it the final knockout blow. The second destroyer escorted the Kolqux carrier, which was kept out of the action except for their fighters.

But get through; they did with minimal losses. Jeanne and Zeke were initially surprised that the Chohish had not upgraded the asteroid bases with updated defensive armament. But then figured the Chohish had never had any other hostile forces get this close to their home planets before. With that in mind, the Chohish possibly concentrated their resources on the more remote installations to stop any enemy advance. So, the Chohish left the asteroid platforms as a backup, just in case. One additional item supported this hypothesis. The Chohish fighters were several versions back from what they had encountered, and the pilots did not show any experience.

Why the Chohish did not have mining operations in the

Attack Chohish War

asteroid system puzzled many. That was until they got back a result of their scans. Rock and dirt aplenty, useable minerals, barely present. That could explain why no planets had been formed even though the material to do so was.

In fact, since they started on their trip, no significant deposits of lendolium were detected. Maybe that explained why the Chohish started out in the direction of the Sorath those millennia ago. The Kolqux had been conquered after the Chohish and Sorath war had ended. So, the Chohish must have decided it was better to try another direction.

Entering the next system had to be done very cautiously, as they now should be within half a dozen systems of the Chohish home planets. This system was the opposite of the asteroid system. Where that system was filled with asteroids and debris, this one was almost entirely bare.

"System is empty of any Chohish presence, Captain, none we can detect at this time," reported Selena.

"It looks like this system is empty of everything. We will be in this system for a good amount of time. While we transition to the exit, this will give us time to relax and get some rest. Isolde, please contact the different departments and have them meet us in the conference room in two hours. Selena, ask for representation from the Jackal, Fox, and the two Kolqux ships," requested Zeke. "That should be enough for everyone to assign any projects and get cleaned up."

Standing, Zeke stretched to loosen tight muscles. "I have been sitting too much. After our meeting, want to join me in the gym?" he asked Jeanne.

"That sounds great," Jeanne replied. Staring nastily at Jan, who was standing behind her with four other Irracan marines. "Ever since a certain damn Seargent has been restricting my movement, I have been sitting on my butt here instead of where I belong."

193

And Jan responded as any good Seargent does when someone tries to intimate them; he ignored her. And some might say he was insubordinate when he yawned. But then again, standing there so long was enough to make anyone yawn. Although rolling your eyes simultaneously may be hard to explain satisfactorily.

Before heading to their room, Zeked checked with everyone to ensure they had some type of plan to supply coverage while allowing everyone to get some time for themselves. Behind closed doors, they both collapsed onto the bed.

"I know time is of the essence here, Zeke, but I do not think the Admiral ever expected us to get this far without running into something that would stop us cold. Admiral Condon gave me that impression when we chatted. I believe Admiral Chadsey expected us to get so far, then come back to tell them what the next roadblock would be."

With eyes closed, Zeke reached over the pull Jeanne close. "To be honest, I never thought we would get this far. I have some ideas on what may be contributing to that. Nothing to support it except for the lack of resistance. Interested in hearing it?"

Leaning over until she was on top of him, Jeanne kissed Zeke. "Thrill me with your incredible insight, my love."

Laughing, Zeke pulled Jeanne down until her head rested on his shoulder. Running his fingers through her length of hair, he thought for a moment about how best to explain his ideas. "Did I tell you how much I love to run my fingers through your hair? When your hair falls on my face like this, it feels like angel wings brushing against me."

Caressing his cheek, Jeanne whispered, "I love you too, now tell me this idea of yours."

"Ok, but you have to promise not to laugh, well, not too hard anyway. Oh well, here I go. Several concurrent events have allowed us to get this far. And it all started with the war against the Soraths.

I…" Zeke was not allowed to continue as Jeanne had lifted up to look at him in puzzlement.

"The Sorath war? How did something so long ago have an impact on us being able to get as far as we have?"

"Because I think the Chohish burned up a lot of resources they could not afford. Not just in lendolium but mostly in ships and personnel. Remember what Vopengi told us? The Chohish had changed how they raised their children, the new warriors. All because of shortages of personnel. Because of that, several home worlds have revolted and want to change how they are governed and raise their children. Something like that would not occur over-night. It would take many generations before the mothers would rebel against something ingrained as normal."

Jeanne could tell when Zeke paused that he was watching a video in his head on how this all occurred. He had once explained to her that it is one of his tools when planning. Others did the same, Jeanne being one, but Zeke's tended to be exceptionally highly detailed, so the images took longer to view.

The video must have ended because he continued explaining. "The losses that occurred during that war must have been atrocious. From everything I could pull from the Sorath archives, who kept thorough records, the Chohish lost twice, if not more than, the number of warships that the Sorath did. And the Sorath lost over three thousand, closer to four, over the entire course of the war. The losses in personnel were horrendous. Some of the ground battles spoke of huge losses on both sides. The Sorath lost more only if you counted all the civilians. The strain on the Chohish war machine must have been enormous. They left because they could not absorb any more losses. Otherwise, why leave multiple systems with known heavy lendolium deposits when on the cusp of victory?"

"That explains then, but how does that relate to now, more than two thousand years later?" she asked.

"Look at how they attacked us. They sent in a small fleet to explore and, if possible, capture the locations that were mining lendolium. When that force was pushed out or destroyed, as in our case, they sent in a much more significant fleet. That fleet was also destroyed. Vopengi told us we had eliminated their reserve fleets. But I think we did more than that. They stripped everything they could from the Kolqux system to attack us again with what they considered an overwhelming force. I believe they stripped everything they could from everywhere they had resources. Now think what that means if they did the same during the Sorath war?"

Sitting up in startlement, Jeanne softly drawled, "The Chohish would need to replenish everything before they went on the warpath again. But that takes time, a lot of time. A warship takes many months to build from scratch, and they had to build thousands upon thousands of them. The Chohish must have pulled all the experienced soldiers, including their trainers, off the home worlds. It would require many generations to replenish all the lost soldiers with experience and sovereigns. And all during that time, they would be facing unrest."

Nodding in agreement, Zeke resumed. "But you did not even mention the most important item. What it would take to restock their lendolium. I am not sure they have been able to. Their primary weapon on the battleship uses a heavily concentrated lendolium. And yet, we encounter many Chohish warships that have not used them against us, even when outmatched. The ones we captured showed they had no fuel for those devasting weapons. Then, on top of everything else comes the revolts. And the last few battles, I believe we have been facing Chohish leftovers; these are definitely not their prime. Ships are much older models and pilots with no real experience. The asteroid system should have had a large fleet in support. Can you imagine if it had? If we had attacked, they could have sent fighters behind us, on the sides, and in the center. It would have been disastrous for us. With so many asteroids present, it would have negated most of our better technology. That system should stop any invader in their tracks if it was properly manned."

Sitting up, Jeanne stretched. "If I stay snuggled to you much longer, I will fall asleep. But tell me, what do you think we will find in the next system, my love?"

Groaning as he pushed himself up and off the bed, Zeke replied. "No idea; every system so far has been unique. But we are getting close, so I expect the defensive posture to be much more substantial."

Taking a side glance at Jeanne, Zeke started tip-toeing to the bathroom. "Last one in the bathroom gets the cold shower." And then took off running only to trip on a pillow thrown between his legs. Untangling himself, he finally rose only to see Jeanne enter the bathroom laughing at him. "*I should have known better and waited until I was in the bathroom before saying anything.*"

Meanwhile, Roy and Camille entered the office that used to be Jamie's. A small group surrounded a planning table in the middle of the room. The conversation between two of the group was a bit heated, one being Gunner.

"Maybe we should come back later, Camille. Looks like they are occupied," Roy said, turning around.

"Roy, hold up there. You came at the perfect time. We could use your help here," shouted Gunner. "Join us here, won't you?"

Moving with Camille to stand by Librada and Gunner, he looked at what was displayed on the planning table. A 3D halo image of a fighter and bomber was displayed next to each other.

Squeezing past his way through the group, Gunner sidled up next to Roy. "Librada and I are working on an issue that you may be able to shed some light on." Pointing out the two others around the table. "This is Senior Engineer Ronald Estrada, and the lady over there is Senior Engineer Shannon Willis."

"I am not sure what we can help you with. We came here to thank you for your timely assistance once more," stammered Camile.

"And having to do that is what Librada and I are attempting if we can get the engineers here on board with us." Moving closer to the table, Gunner leaned over. "Here, let me show you what we want to do."

Twirling the bomber, so it was showing the rear engines, he replicated the action with the fighter. "Bombers were not made to be used the way our Captain would like them to be. Hell, I should say the way he is. Let's look at our large warships. They are all different sizes with all kinds of specialties. But they all have one thing in common. They are close in speed. All except the dreadnaughts. Some are faster, but not drastically. But when they developed a bomber, they did not build it to be deployed in an active forward engagement. It was to free up a large warship in a space superiority environment. So they concentrated on a much larger shuttle frame with heavy armor carrying huge missiles. So our aim here is to fix that."

Surprised, Roy looked at the two images floating above the table. Tapping the bomber, he put it in a slow rotation. "How do you plan to do that? Has the Captain approved this?"

Stopping the rotation of the bomber, Gunner expanded the view displaying the engine section. Then, zeroing in on the engine mounts, he snipped a section and brought it up as a separate image. "When the Captain heard what I wanted to do, he thought it was a great idea. Zeke had Isolde contact engineering and ask that this be given top priority."

Huffing in indignation, Senior Engineer Estrada snarled. "Ask my ass. It was an explicit order from the Captain that unless the cruiser's engines were about to explode, this situation with the bombers would be resolved before we worked on anything else.

Threatened to send us out on the next bomber mission, which he expected would be required soon, so we could understand what it felt like to be in a slow death trap."

Senior Engineer Willis tsk'd before she leaned over the other end of the board. "My friend and colleague, Ronald here, was exaggerating the orders we were given just a little bit. The Captain never threatened us. Isolde informed us that was something the Captain was muttering under his breath he would do. Still, he never actually said he would do that. Besides, after Jax went out on the mission with Roy, he agrees with the Captain."

"Shannon, you know he would. We have enough work to maintain our department and the added task of putting together fighters. Now, the Captain and Gunner want us to install the engines Gunner got from the relief convoy. So, when are we supposed to get the time?"

"What engines?" a surprised Roy asked, turning to look at Gunner. "You have been working on this since the resupply?"

Another 3D image of a sizeable lendolium powered engine popped next to the engine mounts. "Thanks, Librada, for bringing that up. The engines you see here are typically used in a frigate. When we were moving supplies, I saw a dozen crates or so of these lying behind the fighters we were getting. I asked about them and was told they were older engine models that were no longer used. They had been in storage for over a year and would stay there until they junked them at some time in the future."

"So, you just grabbed them?" asked Camille, who had expanded the 3D images to twice their size.

Shrugging, Gunner pointed to the bomber. "I wish it was that easy. I had to get authorization from Jamie, which she approved, by the way. But, of course, I had to explain to her why and prove it was even feasible before we took up so much-needed space. That was the tricky part: I had to quickly brush up on bomber engine mounts and fuel system feeds. After getting the approval, the relief fleet was only too happy to offload what they considered junk."

Looking at the engine size, Roy and Camille were getting excited. "That engine looks huge. Will it even fit?"

"It should," responded Ronald, who had calmed down. "Your bombers, and yes, I know who you are even though Gunner did not introduce you two. I have seen you both around while working on the fighters and bombers. Anyway, bombers have two decent-sized engines. What Gunner is proposing is to replace both with one that is normally in a frigate. That should increase the bombers' speed to just shy of fighters, maybe more."

"What? You have got to be kidding? Do it!" Roy exclaimed.

"Whoah, hold on there for a moment. There is a downside. The reason bombers have two engines is for redundancy. If your engine gets damaged… you know how bad that can be. In the middle of a battle, that could be the end. Then there is the range. The new engine would reduce range by a third," Shannon explained with concern written all over her face.

"Most of the time, bombers are destroyed because they are just too damn slow. I would take my chances gladly on getting away with one engine. It's not like we would be dogfighting. We deliver our bombs and scoot the hell out of there," Camille stated to the surprise of Roy.

"I am liking you more and more, little sis. And for the range problem, we can drift, if necessary," Roy said while fist-bumping her. "So how do you plan to make this happen, and more importantly, how long will it take?"

Stepping around Shannon, Gunner pointed to the large wall screen monitor, where he had Librada bring up an image of the engines on the back of a bomber. "It may be easier to show you here what we have discussed so far. Librada, without the engines, please."

The following image showed two large cavities and the mounts that had supported the engines. The picture changed to show the space now without the engine braces.

"Now, the section between the two engines and their supports is additional bracing. So let's remove that," which Librada did by rolling to the following image.

A massive cavity in the back of the bomber was now being displayed on the monitor. Librada slowly scrolled through the following half dozen images without words to explain what was happening. First, it showed the support bracing being added in the center rear. The new bracing required a circular reshaping of the bomber's rear frame. Then the engine was installed.

Gasps erupted from the two bomber pilots at the image of the new engine in its mounts. It looked huge compared to a typical setup. But they then became puzzled when they saw additional work on each side of the new engine.

"I do not recognize that. What was installed there?" asked Roy.

Getting no reply immediately, Roy looked around, where he saw Gunner staring at the screen's images. Nudging Librada, he repeated his question.

"That, my friend, are additional shield generators. Jamie, God bless her, said she was not sending her crew out with just one engine without additional shielding. Even as large as that engine is, there was enough space on the sides of it for extra shielding equipment to protect your rear. That engine, being so much more powerful than the older ones, will boost the level of shielding on your entire bomber."

"Damn it, I love it. How long would it take to upgrade one for testing?" a now enraptured Roy asked, staring at the finished product like a teenager in love.

The sound of chuckling from both Gunner and Librada grabbed his attention. "That was the argument you heard when you entered.

Ronald and Shannon have been working on this project since we got the engines. Not alone, mind you; they had support from many others. You walked in just after they told us they had one ready for testing. They disagreed with our suggestions on who should test it out."

"Who did you suggest?" asked Camille, although she thought she already knew.

"Why Librada and myself, of course," responded Gunner with a tone and look like he had been insulted. "Who else? Librada and I deserve it after all the work we put into it."

"Oh, hell no, no way in hell is you taking it out without a bomber crew. Bombers fall under my jurisdiction," Roy declared. "And yes, I know, I fall under yours. You two can sit in the back; there is no way my sis and I will not be on that bomber as pilots."

Seeing they were not going to win, Gunner and Librada accepted that decision with grace. They knew they still had to get the Captain to agree to them going out on an experimental bomber.

However, all noticed how Camille looked at Roy when he called her his sis again. They could see her pride and happiness from finally becoming a full team member. But, of course, that may be only temporary if the bomber blew up in testing.

CLOSER AND CLOSER

THE MAIN CONFERENCE room on the Lucky Strike was packed. Representatives from all the ships were in attendance. Some had been here for over an hour, reconnecting with family and friends.

Being last wasn't wrong when being early would mean everyone would question you on the same thing as what the meeting was being held for, although Jeanne would not say the same. She had been here for over an hour with her sister and a large group from the Fox.

What Zeke was glad to see as he entered was the Kolqux mixing in with the humans. And not just standing there but laughing and jostling each other like the friends they were. Uv'ei, Uv'ek, Vopengi, Hu'de, and his daughter Te'ln were all present with some of their command staff.

Moving to stand next to Uv'ei, who was in a serious conversation with Librada, he was surprised to see Roy and Camille saunter up. They were talking with each other while pointing out Uv'ei. Zeke was unaware that these two had ever met or spoken with Hu'de personally.

When they did arrive, they tapped Uv'ei to get his attention. It

203

was apparent Uv'ei had never met either of them personally as he looked at them with a puzzled look.

"Excuse me, sir, we are sorry to interrupt, but we have an essential question that we hope you can answer," asked Roy. What surprised Zeke was how close these two pilots were after such a short time. Most paired pilots took months to be comfortable with each other. But Camille was standing less than an inch behind Roy with her right hand resting on his shoulder. And Roy did not seem to mind. The whole picture showed the two had become close friends.

And Zeke couldn't be any happier. When Spencer died, it had hit Roy really hard. Rarely did two pilots stay together for as long as they had. Some withdrew into themselves and never fully recovered. These individuals could still function in a cockpit but pulled away from making close friends with anyone.

Putting up his hand to pause Librada from continuing their conversation, Uv'ei glanced at Zeke, hoping he would give him some idea of what they wanted. "I am sorry, have we met before? What can I do for you two?"

"I am Lieutenant Commander Roy Dean, and this is Lieutenant Camille Santos. We are part of the bomber contingent assigned to the Lucky Strike. In the last engagement, one of your fighters flew into a pair of missiles that would have hit our bomber. We would be dead right now if not for their sacrifice. So, we are confused why he or she did that?"

Puzzled, Uv'ei looked at the two before he replied. "You will have to excuse me, but I do not understand your question. Did the pilot do something wrong?"

With sudden concern that Roy's question had been insulting, Camille interjected. "On no sir, please, we did not mean any disrespect. We just want to know why the pilot did that. Why did he sacrifice his life for ours?"

Turning to Zeke, Uv'ei put his hands up? "My friend, I am not sure I understand their question. Can you help me understand?"

Instead of answering Uv'ei, Zeke turned to the pilots. "Camille, you were not with us when we first met Uv'ei and his people. Just a short time ago, life for them was trying to survive one more day. Then we came upon the scene. And they watched as we died to free them even though we could have left. Now you ask why they would do the same for us."

Eyeing Uv'ei, Zeke asked. "Did I explain it correctly?"

"Yes, my friend, you did. I think I understand what they are asking now," said Uv'ei as he nodded in agreement before stepping in front of Roy. Looking at Camille, he went on to explain. "I ordered my pilots to protect the bombers at all costs. The pilot in question was following my orders. Unfortunately, not all my pilots have the training yours do. The pilot in question more than likely figured that using his fighter to intercept the missiles was the only way he could be sure of success. Have you not risked your own life at some time for others?"

"Thank you. It is just that it is rare to have something like that happen, and we wanted, no, we needed to know why. We...." Camille stopped to look at Roy as if lost on how to complete her sentence.

"What she is trying to say is that we wanted to thank whoever their family is. We are eternally grateful," finished Roy.

"That would be hard to do. All my pilots and marines have no families waiting for them. Their families were all killed by the Chohish, and they are here to get revenge. Millions have lost everyone they loved to these animals, and these are here to ensure it never happens again. They do not expect to return home. We did not accept any who still had a family. The families that survived need everyone that still lives to help rebuild our world. But I will pass on your thanks to the rest of the pilots. Will that suffice?" Uv'ei asked.

Putting her hand on Uv'ei's arm, Camille replied. "Would it be possible for us to stop over and thank them in person?"

A smile appeared on Uv'ei's face before he nodded his approval. "That would be very acceptable. The pilots would be honored."

"One last question, if you do not mind. From what I know, you still have family alive. So why are you here?" asked Roy.

The change in Uv'ei's expression went through several countenances while they watched. From friendly to sad to determined. "Because my brother and I were the ones to start this. We will be the ones to end it."

As the two walked away, Uv'ei sighed. It was apparent he was near tears. Zeke threw his arm across Uv'ei's shoulder, pulling him into a quick hug. "Come on, buddy, let's you and me get this meeting started."

Standing in front of the group, Zeke waited for quiet before proceeding. "Thanks for everyone coming. Since it will take over a day to go through this system, I thought it would be an excellent time to get together to plan our next stage. We are getting closer and closer to the Chohish home systems. So I expect the enemy defenses to stiffen tremendously from here on out."

Signaling Isolde, Zeke had Isolde bring up a list of what resources were available. "We are in good shape resource-wise, but I doubt we will get anything additional until we rejoin the main fleet. So what we do now, while we can, will decide how far we can go. I am open to suggestions."

What Zeke never expected was the silence. Everyone looked around to see if anyone was going to offer an idea, but none came forth. He would have laughed; except he did not think this group would appreciate him laughing at them. Finally, one did speak out.

"Captain, each system we have explored has been unique. Everything we have done now has been reactionary based on what usually attacked us. It would be nice to know what is in front of us before we get in too deep. Maybe we should turn it around," offered Isolde.

"You have me interested. How would we do that?" asked Zeke.

"We enter as normal using silent emergent security protocols. But once in, we send out a series of probes. Two of those probes, when halfway through the system, will flood the system with sonic bursts. We see what pops up and decide if we go forward or backward."

"Great idea. Does anyone have anything to add to it?" queried Zeke. But, as he expected, once one idea was suggested, it opened the floodgates for more.

Working on Isolde's suggestion, Will thought it might be good to send the probes in before they entered with the warships and execute per Isolde's suggestion. Then bring that data back for review before their warships may be compromised in the system.

Then one from Anne that he had been considering already. Do a mixture of both. Send in the probes and the destroyers at random locations. The destroyers would enable gathering more detail by sending out additional probes where required.

Several had to be dismissed outright. Both of the Kolqux leaders, Uv'ei and Hu'de, suggested sending in their ships first and deploying all Kolqux fighters ready to meet whatever was in the system.

Some were comical. And, of course, these suggestions came from the Irracans, who could not resist having some fun. One is to use Isolde's guidance but paint the probes with pirate flags. See if that confuses the Chohish.

When no more proposals were being made, the group waited to see what Zeke would suggest. Scratching an itch on the back of his hand, he looked around the room. Zeke wanted to get a feel of the temperature in the room first. As far as he could tell, they were in a good mood and ready for suggestions. It would be interesting to see if they felt the same after what he was going to propose.

"Some were great recommendations and will be incorporated into what I think should be done. Others…" and here Zeke glancing pointedly at the large group of Irracans, "I do not think we can use. My final decision depends on some tests that are planned for shortly after this meeting."

The attendees looked around to see if they could identify anyone who knew what tests he was talking about. Several noticed that the engineering department was awfully quiet and wearing smiles.

"I was going to hold off this meeting until after this test but wanted everyone here to start thinking about what we will meet in the next system and the ones after. We have been lucky so far. Let's not get complacent. With that, the meeting is postponed for six hours. See everyone back then. Anyone interested in the test can watch it here in two hours." With that, Zeke walked out with Jeanne.

When Zeke did not head to the bridge, Jeanne whistled for him to stop. "Ok, me bucko, where are you rushing off to?"

"You don't think I am not going to be on that bomber when it tests those engines do you?" he laughed.

Pushing past Zeke, Jeanne started jogging. "I knew there was a reason I loved you. And it is not I; it is we. And we better hurry, as I am sure Gunner will not wait for us."

They went racing past crew members weaving in and out, laughing all the way. They did not stop until they ran into the landing bay, where they stopped panting before Roy and Gunner.

"Damn, that felt good. We need to do that more often," a sweaty Zeke said as he pulled a laughing Jeanne into a quick hug. It was only then that the pair noticed that all action had halted. "What?" they said together before they leaned against each other and laughed.

"Captain, can we help you? What are you here for?" asked Gunner. To say he was concerned was an understatement. "Are we being attacked?"

It was Jeanne who pointed to the bomber behind Gunner. "We are going with you. Did you think we would miss out on that? You should know us better than that, Gunner."

Turning to Roy, Gunner held out his hand. Camille, who had been standing behind Roy, started laughing.

Cursing, Roy slapped Gunner's hand away. "I'll pay later."

Seeing the puzzled look on Zeke, Camille replied. "Gunner bet Roy that when the engineers told us they had a ship ready, you two would be tagging along. Roy told Gunner captains stayed on the bridge where it was safe."

"Sorry, Captain, I am still getting used to Captains that don't mind getting their hands dirty," said Roy. "But I am not sure how we can fit you in. There is not much room in a bomber. We barely have enough room for Gunner and Librada."

"Oh, do not worry about that; we plan to be strapped down next to the pilots. I assume that will be you and Camille. Gunner and Librada can take the spare seats in the midsection," replied Zeke. "Ron, Shannon, you did complete my request, correct?"

"Yes, Sir. It is going to be tight, but we were able to install two additional seats in the cockpit. It is definitely not something I would recommend as a standard feature," Shannon responded.

"Ha, I would sit on Roy's lap if that is what it took. Zeke is redefining how bombers are configured and used. If it works as expected, it will be an incredible achievement. Besides, Zeke's plan requires he knows exactly how the bomber responds after the upgrades," explained Jeanne. "And enough gabbing, let's get this bomber off the ground and see how fast it can go."

Letting the four passengers go first so the engineers could ensure they were securely strapped in before they took their seats, Roy and Camille commiserated outside the bomber.

With a hanging head, Roy spoke to Camille. "You are lucky, sis, your first engagement, and you got a real Captain. My first four deployment Captains were total buffoons. They did not know the inside of a bomber from a restroom. Fighters, yes; bombers, no. Now you only have to worry about not killing him."

"I am not worried, bro; I am just the copilot. You are one in the hot seat," a sympathetic Camille stated. "Besides, if anything goes wrong, you won't have anything to worry about. More than likely, we will all be dead."

Raising his head, Roy smiled and laughed. "You know, sis, your right. Thanks, that takes the pressure off me."

As she made her way into the bomber, Camille murmured to herself, "*the man is nuts.*" A few hours later, shrugging to shake off the effects of high-speed acceleration and deceleration, Camille revised her opinion. "*They are all friggin nuts; they are just plain crazy. They were all whooping and hollering like they were on a joy ride, even though multiple alarms were blaring. And then, they all had to take a turn in the pilot's seat. I thought for sure we were going to hit something or explode from overheating. Although I have to admit, by the end, it was a lot of fun, especially when they let me in the pilot's seat. Damn, I cannot wait until we get to use this in action. Hahaha, maybe I am going crazy like everyone else on this damn ship?*"

SCRINQAK

TAPPING HIS FOOT as he watched the monitor as the fleet moved through the system was the only indication that he was nervous. The effects of the transition had passed minutes ago, but what he planned could all go wrong very quickly. It all depended on how the Chohish reacted.

"Stop it, Zeke, you are making everyone more nervous," whispered Jeanne. Standing behind the command chair, Jeanne had leaned in where she could rest her hands on the back neck pad. She was watching the same monitor as Zeke with rapt attention. "Come on, you pieces of .... take the bait .... "

The screen showed the Jackal flying past the large Chohish station. "Captain Henry, one more pass, please," ordered Zeke. "We need to get those cruisers out beyond the station shields."

All of a sudden, Zeke turned to look wide-eyed in startlement at Jeanne before he unclipped his harness and raced over to Isolde. "I want you to send several probes here," pointing to a location on her screen. "Get them as close as possible. I want a close-up image of this area."

Even though it took a while for the probes to reach the area, Zeke never moved. He stood there behind Isolde, waiting on the data. Finally, minutes later, the information started arriving on her screen. "Blow that section there up, will you? Put it on the main screen."

Moving back a few steps, Zeke watched as the image flickered to life. Then, flicking his hand at Isolde to keep enlarging, he finally had her pause when half a dozen Chohish cruisers and four battleships were presented. "Isolde, I want you to zero in on the one to the far right."

The screen zoomed in to show a battleship that had seen better days. As Isolde improved the image, more details became available. A jagged hole was visible running down one side.

"What are you looking at?" asked Will, who started unbuckling his harness. Then, moving to stand next to Zeke, he shifted to the other side to make room for Hawke, who joined them.

"Isolde, next one over." The image shifted to another battleship. This battleship showed even more damage, with a portion of the top pressed inward like someone had punched it. Squatting, Zeke rubbed his chin in thought.

"LS1, run a scan on all the warships visible and tell me how many look functional?" requested Zeke.

Draping her arm over Zeke's shoulder, Jeanne moved up behind him, playfully pushing Hawke forward with her foot until she could stand by his side. "Are they pieces of junk?"

Before he could answer, LS1 gave his report. "Captain, indications are that those ships have been docked there for an extended period of time. I do not believe any are operable."

Looking around at Will before turning to smile at Jeanne. "What do we do with ships that are too damaged to repair?"

"*Ahh ha ha*" The laughter from Hawke drew their attention. "Lance has been trying to draw out warships used for spare parts? *Ha ha ha.* Can I tell him, Zeke, please?"

"That does not mean they do not have fighters available," stated

Will. "What are we going to do about that station? We can't leave it behind us. Destroying it would take a lot of resources. It is as big as the first supply station we encountered."

"Oh damn, he has that look again," warned Jeanne. "What now, my love?"

Standing, Zeke gave Jeanne his hand. "Care to go for a walk with me? Will, you are in command until I return."

With Will lowering himself into the Captain's chair, Zeke, Jeanne, and Hawke walked out of the bridge.

Walking in front, Zeke had to make room for the marine guard detail as four moved ahead of them. The RGN and Irracan marines must have devised a plan for when Zeke and Jeanne moved, as he could not detect any hesitation when deploying.

It did not take long for Jeanne to know where Zeke was heading. They had been here several times already in the past several weeks. She had no idea what he hoped to accomplish, but she could see Hawke had figured out where they were going. His posture changed from jovial to now; his feathers were bristling in anger, or maybe, it was hatred.

Entering the Chohish containment area, Zeke was surprised to see that the number of battleoids had increased by two. Walking to the bars, he noticed that the Chohish was not berating them as they usually did. He saw Omaw eyeing him with concern from a squatting position at the back of the room.

Standing slowly, Omaw made his way to stand in front of Zeke. "Why are you here? Why did you bring the feathered one? He would like nothing more than to kill us like an animal," he questioned as he turned to look at Hawke.

"Oh, you couldn't be any more wrong; I would treat an animal with respect; you and yours deserve none," a trembling Hawke said. "I would cut you down where you stand without thought."

If it bothered Omaw, he gave no outward sign, turning back to

Zeke, who had remained motionless and quiet. Remaining still even as the rest of the Chohish rushed to the bars to growl at Hawke.

It remained that way for several moments before Zeke spoke. "I came to give you a chance to save some of your people. We have encountered a large station that, at one time, must have been essential but is no longer maintained very well. It shows signs of age and damage. It also has close to a dozen warships that are inoperable."

Hearing the description, Zeke could tell that Omaw knew what he was talking about. "They have not put up any defense, and their shields would not take much to punch through. I can destroy them, or you can talk them into surrendering. I am leaving the choice to you."

Snorting, Omaw "Why would I help you?"

Spinning, Zeke started walking away. "You are not helping me. They mean nothing to me. I thought you … but it seems I am mistaken." Just as he was walking through the exit, Omaw stopped him.

"Wait. The station you speak of is the Scrinqak," Omaw said sadly with emotion. "It was built when we took to the stars. Now, it only reminds us how far we have forgotten our proud heritage." Then, turning to look at his fellow Chohish, he sighed before lowering his head. "I will see no more of my people die for no reason. Tell me what you want to do."

"Speak to them, see if they will surrender. They will not listen to me, but maybe they would you," Zeke said without turning back. "Depending on how many are there will determine where they be sequestered."

"I want your word, Captain; you must give me your promise they will not be treated like animals," demanded Omaw.

"The RGN does not treat prisoners that way," responded Zeke turning around again. "The RGN…"

"That is NOT good enough. I want your word. This RGN, I

do not know nor trust. You have treated us with honor. You, I will take a chance with."

Looking at Jeanne and Hawke, Zeke was about to respond when Hawke warned him not to trust the Chohish. Putting his hand on Hawke's arm, "you have my word, Omaw." Indicating to the marines to bring Omaw with them, Zeke walked out with a heavy heart. Could he trust Omaw? If there were thousands of Chohish, where would he put them? Were there other races stationed there?

Returning to the bridge took longer than expected. The word must have spread that a Chohish was free to walk the halls. Several were curious, while most expressed hatred. Entering the bridge, Zeke was pleased to see no one displayed any surprise or hostility.

If Omaw thought he could walk in unescorted, he was sadly mistaken. Entering the bridge at a run was Khaleesi. She must have been notified by her marines of what was transpiring. Then, walking up behind Omaw, she slapped a device onto his back.

Turning in a rage, Omaw raised his hands to strike Khaleesi, who calmly stood there with a plasma pistol pointed at his chest. In her other hand was a small handheld device with a small red button that her finger hovered over. "My Captain wants you here, but that does not mean I trust you. That explosive device on your back is keyed to this device and the ship's AI. You make a move I think is threatening; I will blow you into tiny little pieces. If you think to take me out, the AI is quicker than you."

"You do not scare me, little one," asserted Omaw.

"She should. That little one trained me in just a few months how to fight a Chohish. Even though I am aware you did not give me your best warrior," said Zeke, now seated in the command chair. "The Major there makes me look like a child. But enough, what is the best way to contact the station?"

"Send a request telling them Omaw, leader of the Ostraron,

demands to speak with them," instructed Omaw. "If they refuse, tell them the Ostraron will take that as a personal offense, and blood will be the only recourse open."

It went as Omaw had first predicted; the station refused any connection until the threat was made. When the connection request was accepted, Zeke had Isolde put it on the main screen.

Surprisingly, it was not a Sovereign; but a regular soldier that appeared on the screen sitting in the command chair. The Chohish wore a military dress that showed wear and tear. Scars were visible on his face and arms.

"Humans, I am Dhirot. Where is this Omaw that... there you are... what do you want? From what I can see, you are nothing more than a prisoner."

"Do not insult me; you do so at your own peril," roared Omaw. "These humans have destroyed all the forces we have sent against them. The fleet before you is just a scouting force. I have seen one of their main fleets; it is very formidable. And it is only one of many."

"What do you suggest? That we cower in fear?" retorted Dhirot. "Death is a better alternative than living as a slave."

"Yet that is something we do to others. I have seen what the Chohish have done in the name of conquest. I do not want to be a part of that brutality anymore," Omaw said bitterly. "We have become monsters."

Zeke did not miss the expression fleetingly displayed on Dhirot before he responded. "We are what we are; the strong are to rule."

"That is what I also thought. Yet, here I am, but enough of that. I have been asked to speak with you before this fleet destroys the station with all in it. They are giving you a chance to surrender."

Before Dhirot could answer, several young Chohish came running into the picture. Another Chohish, who must have been a female, came into view, trying to usher the children away. Then, the children jumped onto Dhirot, laughing before the female could grab them. The look Dhirot gave Omaw was panic-stricken. The soldiers in the background mirrored the look.

The two Chohish stared at each other in silence for several minutes. "Whatever happened to the Sovereign that should be managing the station?" asked Omaw.

Growling, Dhirot rose from the chair, holding one of the children in his arms while the other rolled to the floor laughing. "He wanted our children spaced. Said they did not belong on a station. So we spaced him instead."

"How did the children get on the station?" asked a puzzled Omaw. "I have never heard of children being allowed with soldiers."

"We have been on this station for close to ten years. They sent our wives to keep morale up. They had to do something as this station is falling apart," complained Dhirot. "But that does not change things; why should we surrender?"

Jumping into the conversation, Zeke answered the question. "To save your wives and children. We can tell from your shields energy output you have failures in several sections. The warships are pieces of junk. We will not treat you or your families harshly or without honor as long as there are no attempts to harm us or escape."

The child, still on Dhirot's arm, jumped up to wrap his arms around Dhirot's neck. The image of the smiling child staring at the monitor contrasted with everything Zeke knew about the Chohish. But the child being there may have finally caused Dhirot to utter, "We will not surrender to a human; we will only submit to Omaw."

All eyes shifted to Omaw, who nodded his acceptance. "I will accept your submission. But I cannot guarantee your treatment since I am also a prisoner. I can only speak of how we have been treated. We have not been tortured nor housed in filth." Hanging his head, Omaw admitted, "We are treated better than we treat our prisoners."

The hands of Dhirot tightened along with a slight growl that escaped. "I accept. We submit."

Moving to stand by Omaw quickly, Zeke asked how many personnel were residing at the station. The response shocked not only Zeke but also Omaw. There were only twenty-eight soldiers. All except three had wives with forty-two children between them all.

How to house them all would be a problem. At first, Zeke was going to ask Hu'de and Uv'ei to put them in sealed sections of their fighter's bay as he had expected thousands. Then, after setting charges throughout the station, he would send the Kolqux's two ships back home while the rest of the fleet continued with its mission.

But now, with so few, he decided on taking another route. Contacting Khaleesi, he asked her to join him and Jeanne in his suite for a cup of hot chocolate. Needless to say, Khaleesi knew something was up when hot chocolate was offered so freely. And after hearing Zeke's request, she swore off accepting cocoa offers from the Captain before knowing what he wanted. Well, then again, she did get a case of his cocoa for her marines, and it wasn't like she wouldn't have done what the Captain wished anyway.

So leading a team of marines in full combat gear and several battleoids, Khaleesi, with Omaw in tow, left the Lucky Strike in a marine shuttle. Entering the Chohish station landing bay, the battleoids secured the landing area to make room for additional shuttles. Meanwhile, Khaleesi and Omaw, escorted by a squad of marines, went to the bridge to meet Dhirot. Others went to critical locations LS1 identified for possible sabotage.

While Khaleesi was coordinating the removal of the Chohish from the station, Zeke was working with engineering and construction on remodeling one of the food stations. Force field generators were installed to stop individuals from leaving a specific space in the seating area. Within that space, cots and blankets replaced the tables and chairs.

Not everyone was in agreement with what Zeke was doing. The Kolqux wanted to attack and destroy the station, regardless of the children. Vopengi stood with Zeke; a group of Endaens lived on the station. The Irracans were conflicted, while Lance would abide by whatever Zeke decided.

Hours later, the new arrivals started arriving. Zeke had the rest of Omaw's team brought to the landing bay to assist. Dhirot was the first to step off onto the RGN cruiser. His first view was dozens of battleoids deployed around the landing bay supported by other marines dressed in full battle armor. What Dhirot didn't know was that Zeke had the battleoids amplify the sound of their movements through speakers hidden in the battleoid. The speakers were usually used for intimidation, such as loud-sounding music. When Dhirot moved, he heard the guns tracking him; when he stopped, the sounds stopped.

Another day passed before the fleet was ready to continue. But all the time was not wasted. A lot of helpful information has been gained. Why were there so few staff on the station? Seems the Chohish had never needed to use the station in all the time it existed for the very reason it was built, a defense platform. No enemy ever made it this far. With severe manpower shortages for many generations, this station was left to atrophy.

Another Chohish database was recovered from the station that collaborated with what they had. It also contained additional information. They found out that the more significant portion of the Chohish empire was on the opposite end of the path they were following. But the most crucial detail identified was that one of the home planets was just a few systems away. This being the home of both Omaw and Dhirot, planet Certh, in the system they called Vion.

CERTH

FINALLY, THEY WERE viewing one of the Chohish home planets. Certh was huge, twice the size of a normal planet. And it paid for it with wild weather that raged across the globe. Massive stations hung in orbit with many factories alongside. Hundreds of warships circled the planet, and traffic between the earth below and the orbiting stations was incessant.

It was a mystery why the RGN fleet had not been attacked as soon as they entered the system. The fleet stayed near the slipstream, ready to run at the first sign of aggression. Long-range communication pods had been sent back through the systems to relay the message that a Chohish home planet had been confirmed. They would update each of the stealth communication pods left behind in every system they had traversed. Any following fleet would get the message, should anyway. In Zeke's opinion, sending a single ship back was too risky and would dramatically weaken an already small fleet.

But they could proceed no further. They could not bypass the existing Chohish forces with any certainty of success. So, they waited and analyzed what they could. It went on this way for several hours before they were unexpectedly hailed from the planet.

"Captain, we are getting a communique request from the planet. The originator is Queen Ktissi, ruler of all on Certh. She is asking for the commanding officer of this fleet. Do you want to take it?" asked Isolde. Everyone paused in what they were doing to look at Zeke. Here they were, finally, in the heart of their enemies territory. And now, a Queen of their enemy was requesting to talk. What could she want? Was it to threaten them?

Knowing all eyes were on him, Zeke took a few seconds to think about how to respond to this surprise event. "Inform the Queen I am indisposed at the moment but will be available in fifteen of their minutes."

Turning to Shon, "Corporal Dennison, let the Major know I want Omaw, Dhirot with his wife and kids, on the bridge in ten minutes. I also want a show of force; maybe even a few battleoids would be nice. And tell the Major I want her in the most intimidating gaudy armor she has."

"Hawke, I want you to dress in your family military uniform. Jeanne, the same. Same for the rest of you here on the bridge. I want you all back here in ten minutes. Doesn't have to be perfect people. Remember the saying that first impressions are the best and never go away. Now away with you all; LS1 can watch the systems for now." No sooner said than everyone took off at a run to bunch up at the exit to the bridge.

"LS1, contact the other ships and have them do the same; the best military uniforms they have on hand. If it includes armor of some sort, that would even be better. I want all the officers standing at attention on their bridge. When I give the signal, I want you to patch us all into the connection to the planet. I want to show them strength," ordered Zeke.

"*Understood, orders are being sent. I am waiting on their acknowledgment. Captain Kinsley, I would like to play chess with you sometime. I have real doubts that I could win,*" replied LS1.

Zeke could not miss the amusement in the tone of the reply. *"LS1 must think that this is a game of some sort. And thinking about it, it is. I am sure the Queen will be doing her best at this also. Why else would there have been a delay before contacting us? Who can games- manship the best? We will see; we will soon find out."* Then seeing he was the only one on the bridge, he ran off the bridge laughing. Now, this is what he thrived on.

It was closer to twenty minutes later, but that could not be helped. When Zeke had Isolde initiate the connection, the bridge was packed. Two battleoids stood on each side of the bridge entrance. Khaleesi stood at attention in her battered battle armor, her helmet attached to her thigh and her hand resting on her plasma pistol. A plasma rifle was visibly connected to her back. Behind her stood six of her officers spread out in a small half-circle dressed the same.

The crew was all in dress uniforms, sitting at their workstations, their chairs turned towards the main screen. Hawke stood behind Zeke's command chair in his family's leather dress uniform, wings spread out like he was going to take off.

Standing at attention with arms crossed in the back, Will was to Zeke's left. He was dressed in his dark black dress uniform, while Zeke was in his white. But both were outshone by Jeanne, who stood at Zeke's right with her left hand resting on the commands chair arm. The purple uniform, mixed with white and red, shone with metallic thread laced through. And she topped it off with a hat of the same design and material, fluttering a sizeable red feather.

A section of the side screens showed Gunner and Librada with Isolde in the middle, with their pilots lined up behind them. Zeke almost laughed aloud when he saw Isolde, so small in comparison, between the two. On the other ships, they were dressed the same. Maybe not as opulent, but Zeke thought Uv'ei wearing his battle armor, still with blood stains on it, was best of all. Behind him were dozens of other Kolqux wearing their bloody battle-damaged armor. Hu'de stood proudly next to his daughter in front of their crew. The only one not in a uniform was Vopengi, who lounged nonchalantly in a workstation chair dressed in his everyday clothes.

And the Fox and the Jackal were not to be outdone. Anne dressed just as elegantly as Jeanne, while Meghan and the rest were dressed in gaudy pirate-themed outfits. Irracan marines in armor are situated around the bridge. Irracan battleoids are obtrusively positioned as if they were in hiding. On the Jackal, Lance wore the same uniform as Zeke, with marines standing tall behind him. While the officers on the bridge looked like a mirror image of the Lucky Strike.

When the connection opened, Zeke knew he was correct. The Queen had been doing the same as himself. But she had more time, more space, and definitely more soldiers. The main screen showed a Chohish with a regal air, smaller than a Sovereign, dressed in striking gold and black layered garments sitting on a large stone throne. In front, on the sides, and immediately behind her stood the biggest Chohish Zeke had seen to date. Behind this group stood thousands of Chohish soldiers in orderly lines. The sound of their heavy breathing could be heard through the monitor.

"Captain Kinsley, I see you have finally made it here. I expected you yesterday at the latest," the Queen announced, almost like she was disappointed in Zeke being tardy.

Even though he should have known the Queen would know who he was, he was still surprised. But he let none of that show through. "Queen Ktissi, sorry, but we had to handle some pesky issues."

At that time, Omaw, along with Dhirot and his family, was brought onto the bridge. Zeke had changed the plans when to have them brought onto the bridge at the last minute. The shock on the Queen's face let him know he had scored his own surprise. But when one of Dhirot's children ran to jump into Jeanne's arms, not even the Queen could hide her shock. That even shocked Zeke.

The stiff posture of the Queen softened when she saw the children. "What are you going to do with the children?" Zeke could not miss the pleading in her tone. But then she gasped when she recognized Omaw. "Omaw, it cannot be. They told me you all died fighting."

The RGN marines stepped forward when Omaw took a step toward the monitor. In his powered armor, Shon stepped in front of Omaw to block his way.

The Queen had raised her hand as if to shield Omaw. "Captain, that is my son. I am sure you already know that. I am guessing that is how you knew who I was and why he was on your vessel. So I ask again, what do you plan to do with the Chohish on your ship?"

Pausing a moment to look at the Chohish child playing with the feather in Jeanne's hat, Zeke responded, "I will give them all to you. Unlike the Chohish, we do not make war on children. We do not take pleasure in torturing children either." All could see the impact on the Queen when Zeke said this. "If Omaw and all adult Chohish prisoners agree not to take up arms against any RGN forces and their allies, they can go with them."

"Why would you do this? What is it you expect in return?" Queen Ktissi asked, puzzled as to why he would do that.

"We will never attack your planet with troops. It would cost too many lives. And we would not sit over the planet monitoring you to the end of time. Unless things change, there won't be a need to. The war will end one way or the other. The RGN and their allies cannot, will not, allow the atrocities done to them to happen again. Like you, we treasure our children and freedom."

The Queen lowered her head, acknowledging what Zeke was implying. No need to land troops on a planet if it held no life. "I am not proud of what my people have done. The old ruler's cruelty and arrogance are why we have revolted against them. We were tired of sending our husbands and children to die in useless wars. Although many will die, maybe all, when they attack next."

"Let me consider how best we can return your people if they make the commitments I ask. Queen Ktissi, I do not have the authority to make agreements for the RGN or any of our allies. I can only speak for my own force. With that in mind, is there anything you wish me to take back to my commanders?" asked Zeke.

Lifting her head high, Queen Ktissi stepped off the throne. "Let them know that the Chohish of Certh are willing to end this war and relinquish any and all systems, planets, and people besides this one. We cannot undo what occurred before, but we will try and make what amends where we can. That is the best I can do. I ask..." The Queen stuttered before finishing. "That is all I can ask at this time. Goodbye."

Everyone was still spellbound by what they saw and heard. Muted conversations started as the crew turned back to their stations. As Zeke was about to rise, Isolde, who had her hand cupped over her right ear listening intently to something, signaled Zeke to wait. Then, when Isolde finally uncupped her ear and turned around to look at Zeke, he knew something significant was taking place.

Rising, Isolde made her way over to Zeke. Glancing first at the Chohish, who was still present, Isolde turned her back to them before whispering to Zeke. "Selena and I intercepted an encrypted message just after our communique started with Queen Ktissi. The message came from the planet sent to a battleship which replied. That ship then sent an encrypted message to a destroyer on the other side of the system. It started its engines and is currently headed towards the remote slipstream."

Waiting, Zeke saw Isolde look at Chohish once more. "And what about the message was so important?"

"The messages' unique encryption that was used is what caught our attention. It was a higher level of encryption than anything we saw the Chohish use up to now." Glancing around like she was afraid someone was listening, Isolde whispered. "Sir, I am not sure

I should say anything with the Chohish present." Isolde nervously looked towards the ground when she saw the Chohish had realized something was happening and were watching them.

Rising, he indicated Isolde to follow him. Jeanne, Will, and Hawke seeing what was going on, followed them to a far corner.

Making sure her back was to the Chohish, Isolde told how they had been monitoring the Chohish messages since entering the system. Their security software had broken the Chohish encryption shortly upon their arrival. It had all been unremarkable, pretty standard stuff. Supplies, staffing, and so on. Until they got one on a different wavelength that they could not crack. They had kept their programs running while the meeting was in progress. The program, unable to interpret the message, followed its standard protocol. It relayed the message to the ship's AI, which was able to decrypt it. Isolde and Selena only got to review it just now.

Pulling out her message pad, she showed Zeke the message. It was not long, and it only took a few moments for Zeke to read it thoroughly. Once done, he passed it to Will, who was on his right. Zeke took back the pad after it had made the rounds. He reread it once more before tapping the message pad against his other hand. He looked at Jeanne before nodding at her.

Jeanne seeing the look on Zeke's face, put her hand in panic on Hawke's arm. "Oh, hell no, here we go again. What is running through that crazy head of yours now?"

Still tapping the message pad, Zeke proceeded to make his way over to the Chohish group. Glancing first at Dhirot before he settled his gaze on Omaw. "Do you know who Qilqer is?"

Startled, Omaw gave Zeke a searching look. "How do you know him? He is the commander of the Imperial guards for my mother."

"And Sovereign Norkra?" Zeke asked without answering Omaw's question.

The last question was answered by Dhirot angrily. "Sovereign

Norkra was once in command of the Force of Midnight fleet. They stopped by to resupply us several years ago. He forbade any of his crew to step onto the station. So, they dumped the supplies from the shuttles onto our landing bay. Said he did not want to contaminate his ships with our crud. They all laughed and ridiculed us the whole time."

Hearing this, Omaw growled in anger before asking Zeke. "Why all the questions?"

Tapping the message pad one more time, Zeke looked at Omaw before passing the pad over. "These are messages we intercepted from the planet. It is between Qilqer and Sovereign Norkra. I had the device change it to your language so you can read it."

Taking the pad, Omaw read the message. As he read, Zeke watched Omaw's unoccupied first curl in anger. "How did you get this? When?" was all he asked.

"We were monitoring the systems message traffic, no less than you do. This one stuck out differently than the rest. It took a few moments, but we were able to crack the code. The time stamp is on the top right." Zeke replied.

Looking at it again, Omaw saw that the message had been sent just after the meeting started. "How do I know this is not a trick?"

"What would I have to gain? I do not have to do anything but wait for my fleet to arrive. Or leave and come back with them. Either will not make much of a difference. Meanwhile, it looks like your mother is about to get a visit from a much more powerful opposing Chohish fleet. So again, I ask, what would I have to gain from this?" asked Zeke taking the pad away from Omaw and passing it to Dhirot.

When Dhirot had read it, he passed it to his wife to read. But he looked at Omaw to see what he was going to do. The anger that Omaw had expressed was not mirrored in Dhirot. Strangely, Dhirot was wearing a sly smile like he was not surprised.

"I must warn my mother," snarled Omaw. He reached out to grab Zeke when his hand was caught by Shon. "You cannot let them ambush her."

Pointing to the message pad in Dhirot's wife's hands, "per this Qilqer, they are not going to do that until you land and join her. They do not want the rebellion to rally around you with your mother now a martyr. The message was not sent until after they saw you on our bridge. They probably had planned to assassinate her when their fleet arrived to throw confusion in the resistance command. The question you should ask yourself is, can you count on your soldiers to back you up?"

Shon and Khaleesi had to push Omaw back when he became enraged. "We grew up, trained, fought, bled, and died together, human. They are my brothers; they will fight and die for me as I would for them. Do not insult them or me." But then Omaw suddenly calmed down as if realizing something. "That was an odd question that you should ask me. Not if I trust them, but if they would back me up. Explain."

For the next few moments, Zeke went over why it was critical. The amazement at what he planned was not limited to the Chohish but to everyone there.

Stepping back, Omaw spent a few minutes thinking about what Zeke suggested. Asking a few more questions, he finally nodded acceptance. "If this works, I will understand why we have had so much trouble fighting you. If we survive, that is, which I have grave doubts about. But I have no better idea, so I will agree to do as you suggest."

Turning to Dhirot, Zeke asked where he stood.

"I have sat on a crappy station for many years, abandoned by my people, left to rot, with my family no less. I cannot say what Queen Ktissi wants to do is any better, but what choice do I have if we want a change? My soldiers nor I want to return to that station, but that will not be an option if we do not take a stand. I will talk with my fellow soldiers from the station, but I predict they will all support Omaw and Queen Ktissi," answered Dhirot.

"Well then, both of you talk with your soldiers, and I will speak with mine. Although I expect mine will be a lot more challenging than yours," said Zeke looking around at a primarily stunned crowd. "If everyone is on board, let's plan to meet in four hours."

Walking with his officers waiting for the snide comments and questions, was like walking on eggs. He was surprised when the only commentary he heard was, "The man has gone psychotic. But honestly, he is crazy. Good thing for him that I love him and have to accept his condition, but as to the rest of you? You are just plain mental!"

The full-throated laughter from Jeanne after making her commentary was met by nervous chuckles.

QUEEN KTISSI

THE FOUR RGN marine shuttles landed in the courtyard in front of a vast palace made of many meters thick gray with steaks of white stone blocks. Each of the blocks had to be hundreds of tons. The architecture was brutish but graceful at the same time. With the severity of the weather patterns, they saw on other parts of the planet, Zeke was not surprised at the seriousness of the buildings. Thankfully, they were landing in calm weather.

The trip down had been intriguing, with Hawke, for the tenth time, asking if he would be able to kill Chohish. All the while in the presence of Omaw, who glared and growled at Hawke in anger.

Zeke and Jeanne were still dressed in the outfits worn during the video meeting. The only outward difference was the swords and knives strapped around their waists. What could not be seen was that they had donned their Irracan armor suits under their uniforms.

Standing several dozen yards from where the shuttles touched down, the Queen was surrounded by her Imperial guard. More Chohish soldiers were lined up behind them.

As the ramp was being lowered, Zeke paused Omar with a hand on his chest. "You understand what has to be done, right? You and your men are to surround and protect the queen. You are not to leave her side for any reason. Do not let your anger control your actions."

As Omaw was about to growl and argue, Zeke got in his face and yelled. "DO YOU UNDERSTAND?" Only after getting a sullen "I understand" from Omaw did Zeke turn around to address the other occupants in the shuttle. "Remember, slow and easy. We will lead the way. Omaw is going out last. Once he is seen, I expect they will wait for him to join his mother before attacking."

Walking out first, Zeke moved slowly toward the queen, with Jeanne and Hawke marching behind him. Next came half a dozen marines in full armor and plasma weapons. Zeke waved to the Queen, who was surprised to see him. The Imperial Guard was no less surprised to see the marines marching toward them.

"Hello, Queen Ktissi. I thought I would return your subjects personally. I hope you do not mind." Zeke stopped as one of the Imperial Guards stood in his way. Looking up at the brute, he motioned for him to get out of his way. "Move. Can't you see the Queen is waiting on me?"

Seeing the Chohish guard was not going to move, Zeke just turned sideways and scooted inside the ring. Sidling up to the Queen, Zeke bowed to the waist with his arms out. "Your Highness, it is good to see you in person. May I introduce my companions?" indicated Jeanne and Hawke, who used Zeke's maneuver to stand next to him.

Indicating Jeanne on his right, "This is Captain Jeanne de Clisson of the Irracan Navy." Using his left hand, he then pointed out Hawke on his left. "And this is Hawke; he is on loan to the RGN from the Sorath high command."

"You are full of surprises, Captain. Remarkable that you would risk coming here," the Queen stated. "But I am glad you did. Where are my son and the rest of my people?"

Laughing, Zeke pointed back to the shuttle he came out of and the others that had landed. "They are getting ready. They did not want to meet you without being appropriately dressed as a Chohish soldier should. And there was no way I would allow them to do that with us in there with them."

Turning back toward the shuttle, he glanced at the marines standing at attention before nodding. "Omaw, are you ready?" Zeke yelled.

A growl answered him. Omar sauntered out dressed in full armor, wearing a holster with two giant laser pistols and carrying a laser rifle in the crook of his arm. He looked intimidating. As he walked, other Chohish soldiers dressed in the same gear as Omaw walked out of the second shuttle. They paused to look around before lifting the rifles high and slamming the butt on the ground. Then, raising the weapons to cross their chest, they started singing a Chohish song before marching four abreast to meet up with Omaw. The growls from the Imperial Guard let Zeke know they did not like what they saw.

The Imperial guard tried to stop Omaw and the Chohish soldiers, but they were not to be denied. They pushed past until they surrounded the Queen. The Queen looked confused as she could tell something significant was happening. Reaching his mother, Omaw hugged his mother before passing her a message pad. She was still reading when Zeke asked her who Qilqer was.

A Chohish, standing behind the Imperial Guard ring, who looked to be over nine feet and more than four hundred pounds, answered in a roar before Queen Ktissi could. "I am human. And now it is time for the traitor queen to die." Raising his weapon, he was about to fire on the Queen when his head exploded.

That triggered the Imperial Guard to charge the Queen. Pushing the Queen to the ground, Omaw stood over her, swung his smoking rifle, and fired on the charging Chohish.

From the other two shuttles, battleoids came storming out. But

Zeke had no time for that. Instead, he pulled out his sonic sword and knife. A roar sounded to his side. Raising the sword to block the massive blade, he was pushed to one knee from the blow. Pain blossomed in his hand and arm. If it wasn't for the suit's augmentation, that stroke would have taken off his arm, but it didn't. And that surprised the Chohish long enough for Zeke to slash out with his knife. Then, slicing through the Chohish's ankle, he finished him off as he crashed to the ground with a stroke through the throat with his sword.

Rising, he had to jump aside as a sword slashed through where he had been kneeling. Then, moving toward his attacker, he blocked the downward swing of a blade by crossing his sword and knife. Twirling to the left, his sword bit heavily into Chohish's thigh. This had no visible effect, and he had to turn quickly to avoid getting cut in half. He slipped on the blood leaking from the Chohish but recovered just in time to deflect a backswing. Pushing forward, he swung the sword downward, feinting toward the injured leg. Once the Chohish committed to blocking it, he pivoted and sliced through the Chohish's arm.

Turning back to the fight, he was about to get stabbed when a feathered figure swopped overhead and fired a plasma blast into the Chohish Guard's chest. The Chohish went down, but he was not out of action; his armor had stopped most of the blow. As the Chohish rose, a slim figure pirouetted over him, slicing through his head.

Smiling, the two returned to the fight, and the pair went into their war dance. As Zeke charged to meet the attacks, Jeanne danced and dodged, slicing and dicing, taking the enemy down, and supporting each other.

Suddenly, Jeanne was hit from the side and went flying. Turning, Zeke was confronted by a roaring Chohish wading toward him, swinging a pair of gigantic axes. There was no room to evade.

Ducking under one axe, blocking the other, Zeke was thrown backward several feet by the axe's weight. His arm felt like it had been wrenched out of the socket. Ignoring the pain, he pushed himself back into the fight.

The Chohish did not give Zeke any rest. Blow after blow rained down on him, and Zeke was forced to retreat time after time. Slipping, Zeke fell to the ground, and the Chohish roared before leaping to bring his axe down for the killing stroke. Just as Zeke watched the axe descend on him, what he thought would be his last seconds alive, two plasma blasts smashed into Chohish.

Helping Zeke up from under the large carcass that had fallen on him, Shon chastised him. "How often have we told you not to leave my presence?"

In a panic, Zeke staggered toward where he last saw Jeanne, only to see her leaning against Michale. But there was no more time to check further on Jeanne; the battle was still raging. He looked around quickly to get a status on the struggle.

Most of the Imperial Guard was down, but a handful still fought on. These concentrated on getting to the Queen, who huddled behind Omaw and his soldiers. Rushing over to help, Zeke and Shon tore into the Chohish from behind.

Meanwhile, Hawke using the battleoids as shields, popped up in the air every now and then to take a shot. Then, having finished off the leading group of Guards, the battleoids plowed into the remainder of the Imperial Guard, careful not to step on Zeke and Shon.

Within a few moments, no more of the Guard remained. Several of Omar's and Dhirot's soldiers were down. Zeke had a nasty slice on his arm. Jeanne had a concussion, at least, possibly broken ribs. Hawk had a deep burn on his back from a grazing plasma blast. Two battleoids were blackened by laser fire but unhurt.

They were lucky. The Imperial Guards had refrained from using their laser weapons. Why? Maybe they thought they could walk over the humans and wanted to show the rest of the Chohish the power of their race. Who knows? But Omaw and the other soldiers had taken them by surprise. It was not over yet, though. Still arrayed against them were hundreds of Chohish soldiers. No one knew why they had held back until now, but their commanders were now moving forward.

It was Queen Ktissi stepping forward that paused the Chohish soldiers. "Halt! It was the Imperial Guard who betrayed us." Then, grabbing Omaw's hand, she raised it high. "My son, who returned to us from the dead, stopped this atrocity." Then turning to Zeke, she gestured to the RGN warriors, "even our enemies could not abide such treasonous activity."

The Chohish soldiers stood there for a few moments while they digested what had just happened, then one, then two, then more until all knelt in honor of the queen.

Addressing Zeke, the Queen asked him to select a group to join her and her new Imperial Guard. Then, when Omaw asked who the new guard was, she patted his left arm. "Gather my new Guard, Commander, and bring them along with their wives and kids."

"Excuse me, Queen Ktissi, but you are forgetting something," interrupted Zeke. Pointing to the sky, "You have an unresolved issue."

Fury showed on her face after being reminded. She waved to one of her army commanders and asked him to bring her a communicator to contact the ships above. It took a few moments before a lumbering soldier came carrying a large box-shaped electronic gismo. The soldier was flanked by several others who glared at the Zeke and crew with distrust.

Now accompanied by their commander, the soldiers were about to barge their way past Zeke and Shon when Omaw stepped in to block them. "They saved the Queen. Give them the respect that is due." The looks they gave toward Zeke were anything but friendly. But after a growl from the Queen, the soldiers finally tapped their shoulders. They may have recognized the humans, but their scowls remained.

Before the Queen could trigger the communicator, Zeke raised his hand. Indicating for Zeke to advance, he made his way until he stood next to the queen. Omaw and several of his group stood next to him, and he had no doubt they would crush him if he made any sudden movements.

"I am not aware of your command structure, but what forces does this Sovereign Norkra control?' asked Zeke. Before she could answer, Michale arrived with Jeanne. The paleness of Jeanne concerned Zeke, especially with how she leaned against Michale. Then, whispering to Shon, he told him to get a medic over to Jeanne immediately.

Seeing Jeanne, Queen Ktissi showed concern. At one point, Zeke thought she was going to go to her. Surprisingly, Omaw and several of his soldiers demonstrated the same. The Queen, he could understand, but the soldiers? Now that was interesting.

The Queen did take some steps toward Jeanne before she saw Zeke watching her. Stopping, she looked at the communication device in her hand. Confusion and concern were evident. "Captain, I am not sure what should be done. My officers stationed here do not have any experience in space matters. Those officers are all in the fleets you came through to bring my people home. Sovereign Norkra commands four of our squads. I am reluctant to order them all destroyed. Or if the other officers would even obey such a command."

"If you tried that, Sovereign Norkra would just say that confirms you are not fit to rule," agreed Zeke.

It was Omaw who spoke up. "What would you do?" He put up his hand to pause the growls from several soldiers. Then, turning to them, he asked, "And what would you suggest? Wait here for bombs to fall on us? Go back to the way we lived and died before? Animals to be thrown into wars we do not believe in? What about the honor we owe those who gave up their lives to get us to this point?"

The soldiers, once ready to fight, now looked humbled. Kneeling, they bowed their heads. One of the soldiers spoke up for the rest. "We once swore our allegiance to the Queen. We failed that. Forgive us. We will not fail her again."

"Stand, my friend, all of you. I have my own issues understanding what to do next. Everything is changing. You have seen what has become acceptable to our once proud people." Walking until he stood in front of Zeke, looking down at his upturned face. "I do not know if we will succeed, but I would like the Chohish to revert back to the honorable race our history tells us we once were."

Having such a large mass looking down at you could be intimidating. But Zeke had been training with Khaleesi and her marines in their armor to mimic Chohish; he almost smiled in Omaw's face. But he knew that would be considered an insult.

"Just to make sure I understand your warships breakout correctly. One of your squads consists of one battleship, three cruisers, and six destroyers. Am I correct?" asked Zeke without breaking eye contact with Omaw.

Surprise shook the Queen. Then she shocked everyone by laughing. "I should have known you would know. Yes, you are correct. Any thoughts on what I should do?"

"What Sovereign do you trust implicitly? Contact that one, use any encryption that cannot be broken, make sure no one can overhear, and explain what happened here. Then what you learned, including where it came from. I recommend you tell him Omaw was present when the message was intercepted," Zeke answered. Then, finally breaking eye contact with Omaw, he faced the Queen. "Ask him if he has any other Sovereigns he can trust. Then tell them to all target and fire on Sovereign Norkra's battleship, only his, without warning."

The Queen moved away before activating her communicator. Omaw, however, stayed by Zeke's side. "Why are you helping us?"

Moving over to Jeanne, Zeke swung Jeanne's left arm over his shoulder. Then, he whispered, "lean on me, honey. I am so sorry. You were hurt because of me." Raising his voice so Omaw could hear it, "I told you I would treat you honorably. Knowingly letting your mother be killed by a traitor as you sat locked up on my ship while I did nothing would break my word."

Snorting, Omaw glanced at his mother. "You would risk your crew to keep your word?"

The answer came from behind Omaw. The voice rang across the courtyard from the speakers in a battleoid. "The Captain's word and honor are not to be trifled with. Every one of us volunteered, knowing the risks involved. We would, and have, go wherever he would lead us. We do not give our loyalty out easily. The Captain has earned that loyalty from us many times over."

Watching as a medic worked on Jeanne and others were having their wounds addressed, Zeke stated it was time for them to leave. Seeing the Queen busy in deep conversation, he notified Omaw they needed to get the wounded back to the ship for medical attention. "Please give your mother our goodbyes."

Seeing everyone ready to leave, Omaw was startled to see Zeke pick up Jeanne to cradle her in his arms. "You are the Captain, their leader. Why would you demean yourself doing menial work when there are others available to do the work?"

Looking down at Jeanne, who had wrapped her arms around his neck, "Being a Captain means I have a different job and responsibility than others." Turning to indicate the others of his force. "It does not mean that they are any less critical than me. What good is a starship without engineers or a crew? A fighter without pilots? Marines? Each and every one of them is important."

The battleoid that had spoken before now stood behind Zeke with several others. "And that is why we followed him here into the heart of the enemy."

Instead of being angry as Zeke expected, Omaw looked around in contemplation. Surprisingly, the Chohish soldiers' stares surrounding them were no longer hostile. In fact, several pounded their shoulders in a sign of respect.

Sitting next to Jeanne in the marine shuttle blasting through the atmosphere, Zeke looked around at battleoids stacked against the wall. A sweaty Khalessi leaned against the bulkhead with her eyes closed. Zeke could not tell if she was asleep or not. Hawke sat across from them, staring at Zeke. Several times, Hawke started to speak and then stopped. It was apparent Hawke wanted to ask a question.

"What is it, Hawke? Spit it out," asked Khaleesi without opening her eyes.

"How the hell do you do that? I swear she can see through her eyelids," murmured Hawke. "I wanted to know the real reason why we had to return the Chohish. I got to kill some of the bastards, so I am not complaining."

Seeing no response would be coming from Zeke, who was snuggled in close with Jeanne, Hawke snorted in frustration.

"Please, can't you see I am trying to sleep? It was pretty obvious why he did what he did. Do I need to spell it out for you?" Raising her head before opening her eyes, Khaleesi looked at Hawke. "The main reason he gave is valid. But that does not mean there cannot be secondary reasons."

The pause by Khaleesi has Hawke stamping his left foot and fluffing his feathers agitatedly.

"Relax, Hawke. Khaleesi is pulling your feathers. She will finish in a few," whispered Jeanne. The effort caused her to curl up tighter against Zeke in pain.

Sighing, Khaleesi continued. "If the Queen was killed or deposed, then the planet, but more importantly, their fleet and the army, would probably rejoin the ones we are fighting against. Best to have the two groups fight each other, reducing what would be left to fight us."

That seemed to hit the mark as Hawke relaxed. "Thanks, that make a lot of sense. Did I tell you I got to kill a few? Well, actually, more than a few. Today was a good day." Whistling a Sorath tune, he murmured, "and maybe I will have a better day tomorrow. I can only wish," in between bars.

CLASH

IT HAD BEEN several days since the trip to the Chohish planet. They had watched as a battleship was savagely destroyed as they flew back to their own ships. The whole return trip had been tense for most, concerned that the Chohish would not honor the agreement that had been reached.

Now that they had confirmed where one of the Chohish home planets resided, what action should they take now? That is why Zeke was holding a conference call from the bridge.

Standing next to his command chair, Zeke viewed the Captains of the fleet on the main screen. "Ladies and gentlemen, I do not think staying here is safe nor advances our orders. We need to return and confirm the location information captured as being valid. Does anyone see a reason why we should not return?" The silence let him know that no one objected.

Heading back, Zeke had several probes sent through the slipstream, even though it would take another hour or so before they reached it. What came back just before they entered was not encouraging. Five Chohish battleships were heading toward the slipstream. No cruisers or destroyers, just battleships.

Staying was not an option. It was unknown if these were Queen

Ktissi's ships or not. But no matter, they needed to report back. After Zeke gave each of the different Captain's orders on what to do, the small fleet prepared to enter the slipstream.

Exiting the slipstream, the two destroyers led the cruiser, with the cruiser leaking smoke and trailing fuel. The three ships went hard to port to try and evade the oncoming Chohish battleships.

The bridge on the Lucky Strike was a flurry of activity. Sitting in the captain's chair, Will monitored the Chohish as they changed direction to cut them off. "Easy folks, easy does it. Lieutenant Gaspar, keep our speed down until necessary. Remember, do not let us get in range of their missiles. Hawke, fire on them as soon as we are in our own missile range. Isolde, confirm that the Jackal and the Fox will mirror our course and actions. They will be at the maximum range of their missiles, so they must make their own call if they want to use them."

"Why am I here and not with the Captain?" complained Hawke. "While he and Jeanne are off having fun, I am stuck here?"

"What? You do not like our company?" chided Isolde. "I am starting to get a complex with everyone wanting off the bridge."

The chuckles from the rest of the crew did nothing to relieve the scowl on Hawke's face.

"You know why the Captain is there. He has some bomber flying experience. He flew a couple of bomber missions when we flew together. Said he was petrified the whole time. It took a particular type of courage to pilot a flying bomb, and he said he did not have it. Most bombers at the time were destroyed by aiming at the missiles they carried versus the bomber itself. Kinda funny actually, he is in one again when he doesn't have to be."

"I know, I know. I heard all the reasons. There were not enough experienced bomber pilots available to fly the additional bombers put together with the new engines. Jamie, bless her, recommended not to affect the current bomber deployment but to use the spare crated bombers for the engine test and rebuilds. I heard it all. I should still be allowed to fly one," Hawke whined.

"Oh, come on, you're just mad because you could not try out a bomber with one of the new engines," chastised Will.

The looks Hawke gave to Isolde and Will had everyone laughing, and the side comment from Tim did nothing to improve his mood.

"I do not know why you are complaining so much. I have more bomber flying experience than both of you, but the Captain would not let me go either."

"Parking bombers is not considered actual flying experience," Hawke retorted.

"Still, it was more than yours," Tim said nonchalantly.

"Isolde, update on the Chohish, please," asked Will.

"They are continuing toward us in an intercept course."

The sharp intake of breath by Selena caught Will's attention. "Ensign?"

"The primary weapon at the front of the Chohish battleships is starting to show a power increase," she exclaimed in concern.

"Damn, the Captain was right again. He predicted they would start to use it again when they became desperate, which he thought they would do soon. Isolde, make sure the other ships are aware. LS1, are you ready to show the Chohish why we did not use this type of weapon even though we had it for a short period?" asked Will.

"*I am, Lieutenant Commander Farren. I will take over active control of steering and propulsion when fired upon. Program evade Mean and Nasty beam activated. I do have a request, Commander. Can we rename the program? I am not sure the Admiralty has the same sense of humor as the Captain.*"

"Not my call, LS1. Isolde, check with Gunner and Librada and make sure they are ready with their part of the plan."

The RGN ships continued onward, with the leaking smoke and

trailing fuel gradually disappearing. The Chohish battleships followed, the distance slowly closing. Suddenly, out of the slipstream came the two Kolqux ships. They spent several moments orienting themselves before turning hard to port, racing after the RGN ships.

This went on for another hour, with the RGN ships being chased by the two different forces. The Kolqux were marginally closer, gaining ground faster than the Chohish due to their angle. As the distance closed, dozens of fighters flew out of the Kolqux carrier. In response, a dozen fighters made their appearance from the RGN cruiser and destroyers.

The tip of the Kolqux battleship lit up before it fired on the RGN fleet. A minute later, the lendolium laser flashed through space. It missed the warships, barely, going past the cruiser in a flare of light as the shields lit up, deflecting the energy. But on the way, it destroyed several RGN fighters in a huge fireball.

The chase dragged on. The Chohish warships came at one angle, the Kolqux at another. Within an hour, they had merged into one force, the battleships in front with the carrier trailing.

Suddenly, the RGN cruiser belched smoke and flame, and their speed diminished noticeably. Swinging to starboard, the three RGN warships oriented in the direction of an asteroid field. The RGN cruiser started firing its missiles at the enemy fleet that had entered within firing range. Before the enemy ships could return fire, the RGN fleet entered the thickest part of the asteroid field. Not willing to enter, the fleet slowed down while it debated on what to do.

Shortly, fighters came flying out of all the enemy warships. Ten from each of the battleships and twenty from the carriers. The fighters headed into the asteroid field to try and chase the RGN warships out. Moments dragged by before explosions could be seen between the enormous tumbling rocks. The dramatic light shows of missile and laser detonations continued for an extended period before slowly fading until only blackness remained.

"Is it time yet?" whispered Jeanne.

"Not yet. Will has to do his part yet. We need them to turn around and get a bit closer. Patience, my dear, patience," advised Zeke. He understood her impatience. Sitting here with the bomber idling while waiting on asteroids they had no control over to move to positions they desired to meet his plan… well… it was never easy.

As minutes passed, even Zeke was starting to get concerned. Radio silence was required so no leakage would get back to the Chohish, so he had no idea what the delay was. But the longer the delay, the further the Chohish was out of position.

Finally, they were able to detect the movement they expected. A lone RGN fighter came limping out of the asteroid fields blaring mayday repeatedly. The erratic maneuvers showed that the pilot did not have complete control.

The enemy fleet went wide to turn around. As they neared the fighter, one of the battleships destroyed it with one of its side lasers. The shredding of the fighter acted like a signal as the three RGN warships came flying out of the asteroid field along the enemy's flank. Missiles, plasma, and laser shots erupted from all three warships. The Chohish responded with their own barrage.

Watching the battle unfold, Zeke tested the flight control joystick one more time. Moving it back and forth, front and back, the bomber rocked. "Definitely a lot stiffer than a fighter. Are you ready, my dear? They are almost past us. Will is doing his part. Now it is time for us to do ours."

One thing Zeke loved was the change in Jeanne's voice when she became excited, as she was now. It was so damn sexy. "Been ready. I want to see what these new engines do."

Then it was time for Zeke to wait on someone else. Zeke may be Captain of the fleet, but he also understood he was no expert with a bomber. That was Roy's department. So after having told Roy what had to be done, he had to sit tight until Roy gave the signal. Then he had to accept directions from Roy on where to deploy. Even with that, Zeke could feel the unique excitement he got when sitting in a fighter arrive. When he became visibly animated, the look from Jeanne would have been funny, except it morphed into something else. Something evil.

His expression matched Jeanne's when she pulled out a small box device and attached it magnetically to the hull. He knew what the device was when it first appeared. Soon both were pounding on the hull, the exhilarating beat radiating loudly from the music box. Zeke was not concerned with the music interfering with any communications. Instead, the box was geared to shut off immediately when the radio was triggered. If any could see inside the cockpit, they would have been surprised to see two gyrating Captains pounding the hull and singing loudly.

In fact, one was watching them and frowning. A certain someone who had turned over his firing solutions to the ship's AI had Zeke's cockpit video displayed in the corner of his screen. "*Damn it, that should be me,*" thought Hawke. "*I will be on the next one, or you will have to lock me up, brother.*"

Finally, what Zeke and Jeanne had been waiting for came. The signal from Roy arrived, cutting off the music. Energizing the engines to full throttle, the bomber shook with the power waiting to be unleashed. Then, releasing some of that energy, the bomber shot forward.

Flying around an asteroid that had to be a dozen times more significant than his cruiser, Roy led half a dozen other converted bombers. Around them were more than a hundred fighters with a dozen standard bombers trailing.

Heading towards the rear of the Chohish battleship that Roy had designated for his and two other upgraded bombers, it was apparent that the fighters retained their speed superiority. Dozens raced past him to try and deflect or eliminate any anti-ship missiles fired by the battleship.

Explosions rocked around him, and energy blasts slammed against the shields. Remembrances of why he did not like bombers came back in a rush. "*This thing moves like it is swimming in mud. It definitely does not have the maneuverability of a fighter. Hell, even the cruiser moves better than this piece of* ...." He lost his train of thought as he had to concentrate on staying in his seat as the bomber thrashed violently from an explosion nearby. "*Then again, something like that would have taken apart a fighter.*"

Whipping the bomber back on course, he neared the target. But as he got closer, he could see other missiles being eliminated before they could get through the shields. "Hang on, Jeanne, I am going to try something...."

Maneuvering around debris and defensive fire, Zeke swung the bomber to point to the battleship's rear section. Hitting full thrust, the bomber rocketed forward. "Damn, Roy must be loving the new engines," Zeke yelled over the noise. "But they need to work on the inertia dampers. I think my spine just broke. And the steering sucks big time."

They flew past several fighters who were surprised by their increased speed. Then, getting directly behind the battleship, they encountered the engines' exhaust-spewing intense heat at them. Alarms blared, indicating their sensor and hull integrity was being degraded.

Inside the bomber, both felt like they were being baked alive the heat was so intense. The ship was tossed around violently in the turbulence being created. "Zeke, we need to get out of here. It is just too much. The ship cannot handle it."

"Just a little more. Have to get far enough that the missiles can make it through the heat. Just a little more," Zeke said in gasps as he struggled to maintain control of the joystick.

Just when Jeanne thought the bomber would break apart from the turbulence, let alone the heat, she fired the missiles at Zeke's order. Then, thinking he would now retreat, she was horrified to learn she was mistaken. Even as the first two missiles exploded inside the engine compartment of the engines, Zeke held their position until the bomber had another two ready.

The battleship fiercely jerked and vibrated when the missiles hit. The noise of debris smashing into their hull had to be lowered by the helmet AI to avoid ear damage; it was so loud. The noise, though, was nothing compared to how the bomber reacted. The bomber bounced around like a ball on a wave during a storm.

Gritting his teeth to keep from biting his tongue, Zeke fought the control stick to keep the bomber in position. Once the green light came on that missiles were ready to fire, Jeanne fired without waiting on his order.

Stopping his forward thrust, the bomber was thrust backward to fall out of control when a large piece of an engine part slammed into the side hull. Both Zeke and Jeanne were flung around violently against their harness.

Gasping, trying to catch her breath, she swung her seat around to check on Zeke as he had been unusually too quiet. His head flopping around indicated he had lost consciousness. Switching the flight controls to her station, Jeanne fought against the wild gyrations of the bomber.

As the bomber finally started flying smoothly once more, a voice in her ear replaced the fear in her heart. "Well, I sure as hell am not going to do that again."

What the pair viewed outside was bedlam. The five Chohish battleships were drifting wrecks, several still firing weapons. Around them flew the RGN warships and the Kolqux battleship. The fighters and bombers had withdrawn to a safe distance.

The crackling in his ear clarified after banging on the

communications hub enough to understand the raspy voice that came through. "Captains, are you still there?"

"Hi, Isolde. We are still here and alive. No thanks to your dumb Captain, I would like to add," responded Jeanne leaning back in her seat. She raised her hands before her helmet, watching them tremble with fatigue and fear.

"Isolde, have the warships retreat out of missile range and finish off the Chohish with either the Kolqux battleships primary weapon or RGN missiles. Change that. Use both. We need to move on quickly in case more are on the way," ordered an exhausted Zeke. "Get Will, if he is not working on it already, started on search and rescue immediately. Gunner and Librada need to recover our fighters and bombers, us included, and get them patched up and resupplied. That is a priority."

"Will has already started the SAR, and so have the other Captains. I will make sure the rest of your orders are passed on. How are you two?"

"We are good for now, but I cannot stress the importance of accomplishing this as quickly as possible. Something tells me we do not have much time. We will be heading back to the Lucky Strike. Zeke out"

"You are concerned about their missing support ships, aren't you?" asked Jeanne.

"Yes, I think it is likely they are supposed to rendezvous with the battleships here in this system. So, we need to leave before they show up," Zeke said with deep concern as Jeanne headed the ship back to the cruiser. "If we are not already too late."

PLANS

REVIEWING WHERE THE fleet was in recovery and rearming, Zeke was taken back by the number of personnel losses. The Chohish battleships were built to give and take a lot of punishment. And they lived up to their task.

The Kolqux battleship was the least impacted of the warships as they had taken the Chohish by surprise. The Chohish had not even realized what was occurring until Hu'de fired their primary weapon at one of the Chohish battleships causing severe damage. By then, the Chohish were already heavily engaged with the RGN forces. Yet, even here, Hu'de lost dozens of personnel.

The Lucky Strike was the most heavily impacted. It was the key to keeping the attention of the Chohish battleships away from the Kolqux Freedom. The warship had taken severe damage along with loss of life. Fourteen personnel perished on the warship, with another eight pilots who never made it back. Several dozen were injured. The two destroyers had run next to the cruiser and suffered similar damage, though not as many deaths. Even though the Lucky Strike was damaged more severely than the Freedom, safety gear, procedures, and medical staff made a massive difference in reducing the numbers of the RGN warships.

But everyone knew that mourning the departed would have to wait until they were not in danger. Every warship worked feverishly to get all personnel back on their ships. Injured were sent to overwhelmed medical wards. Equipment was being sorted between salvageable and repairable. Repairs on all warships were ongoing and expected to continue for weeks.

But Zeke was concerned it would not be enough. A standard Chohish squad makeup dictated that fifteen cruisers and thirty destroyers should have accompanied the five battleships. Where were they? Were the battleships built in one side system while the cruisers and destroyers were made in others? How long before they showed up? And from where?

After ensuring everything was being addressed, he allowed the medical technician to look at his arm. When they went spinning around uncontrolled, an object broke loose. It had impacted his arm before ending its travel against the hull. The flight suit he wore did not puncture but did hide the cut it caused. Everything was so hectic for so long that he did not take the suit off immediately upon his return. It was not until he reached the bridge that he and Jeanne took the time to remove them. When he took off his suit, blood that had pooled in his glove dripped onto the floor.

Only after several of the crew squeaked in startlement, Will noticed what they were looking at. He had medical summoned to look at Zeke's bloody arm and Jeanne's bloody scalp before chastising them for flying the bomber.

"Oh, come on, you have seen us a lot worse than this," Zeke admonished Will. When he faced Jeanne, he suggested maybe she should get medical care. Once she heard that, Jeanne looked at him with indignation before she laughed, telling everyone that this was coming from someone who had been knocked unconscious.

But while medical looked them over, they were able to get a full report on how the battle had progressed. The remote-controlled junk fighters had done what they had hoped, convinced the Cho-hish leaders that the Kolqux warships were manned by Chohish. The Chohish never realized that none of those initial fighters had never fired a weapon at them. They did not have any. LS1 had installed a program in Freedom to simulate Sovereign Norkra for communication between the vessels. Zeke thought using Sovereign Norkra's identity would work for either the rebels or the loyalists.

The battle in the asteroid field was difficult due to the debris floating around. A third of all the deaths the allies encountered were due to this. Removing the entire Chohish fighter contingent before engaging the warships was an added bonus Zeke never expected but one Will took advantage of. Sending the remainder of the remote-controlled fighters out of the asteroid field positioned the Chohish where the RGN warships could emerge to their best advantage.

The RGN warships exit positioned the Chohish warships so that when attacked by the fighters and bombers, they only paid sec-ondary attention to them. With their increased speed, the bombers smacked them so hard that they could not recover. The regular bombers were only effective after a battleship was immobilized.

When the fighters and bombers emerged, Hu'de waited until they started firing on the Chohish before he made his move. And the extra thirty fighters Uv'ei's carrier, the New Hope, only added to the odds against the Chohish.

When the commanding officers gathered remotely, as everyone was too busy to do it any other way, this was the main conversa-tion brought up while waiting for Zeke to join. The many stages involved in the plan. If any had failed, the whole thing could have collapsed in disaster. So when Zeke joined from the bridge of the Lucky Strike, the applause was rampant.

Closing his eyes, Zeke put his hands up for quiet. "Ladies and gentlemen, please, the applause should go to the ones that deserve it. The ones that gave their ultimate for this endeavor. And we will do that once we are out of danger." Opening his eyes, he waited for quiet before continuing. "Now, we must ensure their lives were not in vain. I believe other enemy forces are headed this way. More than we can handle."

"Isolde here, let's take this ship by ship. We have to keep this limited for expediency's sake. High-level overview only. Report on the extent of damage, engine status, fuel status, and length of time before ready to leave."

After all the Captains had given a summary, Zeke was nervous. It was too long. "We need to shorten our leave time by half. Use everyone you have; no rest for anyone except those injured. They can rest later. I will not leave anyone behind, so if you have engineers, anyone, to spare, send them to those who require them. We send them back where they belong when we can."

Disconnecting, Zeke made his way over to Isolde. "Can you and Selena track back where the Chohish battleships came from? I doubt the cruisers and destroyers will appear from the same slipstream, or they would have waited for them. There are multiple slipstreams in this system. Somehow, I believe they feed each other. The slipstream we are headed towards had no unexplored slipstreams, planets, or Chohish facilities. I think it would have if it was a gathering or throughway for their non squad warships. If we had an idea of where they may appear, it would let us know if they can cut us off from reaching the slipstream when they do appear."

Their response was to turn back to their workstations and enter commands. Scratching his arm bandage, Zeke signaled Jeanne to join him at the exit to the bridge. When she arrived, he asked her if she wanted to join him on an unpleasant mission. This piqued her curiosity but also raised her concern. What could be worse than what they just went through?

She still had no idea what Zeke was planning when they entered the office for Librada and Gunner. The pair of Commodores looked like hell. Sweaty, covered in oil and grease, red-rimmed eyes and hair stuck out in all directions. When Jeanne and Zeke entered, the look of "*oh hell no, what did we do wrong now?*" crossed both of their faces. The hand signal from Zeke to alleviate that only lasted for a second. They relaxed for a moment only to stiffen up again with an "*oh hell no, what does he want from us now?*" Jeanne would laugh if the situation was not so serious.

"Commodores, sorry to bother you, but I need to speak with Roy. Is he around?" asked Zeke. "And you got any coffee made? If not, mind if I make some?"

While Gunner put out a page for Roy to come to the office, Librada pointed to the coffee maker in the corner. Her eyes were wide open like the devil was here for her soul. That was too much for Jeanne, who burst into laughter. The look from Zeke only made her laugh harder. "Zeke, you're scaring her. They are exhausted and overwhelmed. Then the Captain walks in here without notice. That usually does not portend well for them. Gunner may be used to your…" pausing to indicate quotes, "*style,*" but she probably isn't. Stop it."

If she was laughing hard before, she went ballistic when Gunner spoke up in his dry mannerism. "I am not used to his" pausing to indicate quotes, "*style.*"

And that is what Roy and Caille walked into. Jeanne laughing hysterically, Zeke looking at her like she was crazy, with Librada and Gunner wide-eyed, looking like ghouls that just rose from an oil pit. "Am I interrupting something?" Roy quirked his eyebrows questioningly when Jeanne collapsed onto a chair from laughing so hard when she heard his question.

"You will have to excuse Jeanne; she was not privy on why I needed to talk with you. I have a request that I am hesitant to ask but see no other way," answered Zeke. "Please sit while I gather my thoughts. All of you, please. Your standing is making me nervous."

The seriousness hit Jeanne like a brick, and all her laughter stopped immediately. The other three sat down while Zeke walked around, rubbing his hands together in nervousness. Then, stopping, he looked at Roy for a minute before speaking.

"I believe we are running out of time. I expect the rest of the Chohish warships to appear before we are out of this system. If my theory is correct, there are four other slipstreams they could arrive from." Zeke stopped here.

"Captain, you did not call me here for no reason. Spit it out. What do you want from my crew and me?" Roy asked.

Sighing, Zeke hung his head a moment before straightening up to look at Roy with compassion evident throughout his expression. At that moment, Roy saw what he never thought he would ever see. "*Finally, a capital ship Captain who is reluctant to give a command because he is concerned for those he is giving them to. An individual who knows his orders more than likely means the death of those following them. This is a Captain I could and would follow to the pits of hell. Damn, it was about time.*"

"If this force appears and is as large as I think it will be, I need to be able to slow it down. We need to get to and through that slipstream before they do. The Kolqux ships cannot match our speed, even though they think they can. And I will not abandon them. I need a distraction, which you and some of your group may be able to provide," Zeke explained.

"You only mentioned some of my group, so I take it that you plan to use the modified bombers only. I have been anxious to give them a real workout to see how good they are. How can we assist?"

"When, and there is a possibility they will not, it will take the Chohish forces of that size a moment to regroup into a cohesive force. They will detect that a battle took place, and I expect they will realize what occurred. They will know we are still here as they cannot miss our energy trail. The Kolqux engines cannot mask their

255

signatures. If I were the Chohish, I would position the destroyers out front with the cruisers behind since there are no battleships that require their protection. Working with that hypothesis, I would send out all our fighters, including the Kolqux's, since there is no hiding the fact those two warships are part of our fleet."

Stopping, Zeke said he needed some caffeine and took a moment to get himself a cup of coffee. Then, as Zeke returned from the coffee pot, Roy indicated he would like one himself.

Tapping Camille on her shoulder, he indicated the coffee pot. Roy and Camille excused themselves before making their way to the coffee pot. As they were preparing their cups, Ray whispered to Camille. "Well, what do you say? Are you up for it? Or should I pass on it?"

Confused, Camille peeked behind them before whispering back. "Up for what? He has not told us yet what he wants from us?"

Chuckling, Roy replied as quietly as he could. "You weren't listening. And do not be fooled by the coffee thing. He did that to give us time to consider his plan, and if we think it is too risky, bow out gracefully. And if you haven't noticed, Gunner and Librada are not getting coffee even though they look like they could use one badly. They know this coffee break gives us time to discuss the plan among ourselves. There is not enough time for formalities."

"Damn it, what plan? He never got to it."

"The fighters are our escort. The modified bombers are being sent out to attack a destroyer. Not enough bombers to take out more than one, maybe two. And it has to be sudden-like, hence using the bombers vs. the fighters. Something dramatic. The destruction of one of the Chohish warships so quickly and unexpectedly will cause them to pause. Hopefully, long enough for the rest of the ships to get through the slipstream."

Looking at Roy like he had grown horns, Camille stuttered. "What if we do not have enough fuel? That is a major problem with those bombers. We will be stuck helpless."

A small chuckle preceded his answer. "Hence the coffee break; he will not order a potential suicide mission, not this Captain. I expect he would let us drift and use most of our remaining fuel to hopefully escape through the slipstream. Smart, I agree with him. There is not much else he could do. Going head-to-head with the Chohish would be futile and only destroy the fleet in total. This way, risk a few, save a lot. I like it. So what do you say, sis? Is it a go?"

Looking at Roy, who smiled like he did not have a care in the world even after hearing their death sentence, Camille shrugged her shoulders. "Where you go, I go, bro." Then, suddenly, she looked at Roy in amazement. "Oh hell, I just realized something."

Surprised at her sudden reaction, Roy asked what she realized.

"I am crazy! I do belong on this ship full of nutty people." At which both started laughing as they made their way back to join the Captain and the Commodores.

Sitting back down with coffee in hand, Roy told those assembled there. "You can count us in, Captain; we are a go."

Camille did not miss the fact that the Captain had not touched his coffee as he thanked Roy and Camille before he left the office with Jeanne in tow without another word. Her face must have shown her surprise as Roy tipped his coffee at her in acknowledgment. Nor did she miss the whisper from Roy talking to himself before he took a sip. "*Yoh Spencer, you would have liked this Captain; you most surely would have. I may see you soon, brother; save me a spot up there, ok? Oh! You better make that two spots; we have a sister now.*"

Just months ago, listening to this from her bomber partner would have terrified her. Now? Even though she may die within the next day or two, she could not imagine anyone else to fly with. But, of course, surviving the next few days would be lovely too.

257

CHANGE OF PLANS

THEY HAD BEEN on the way for half a day when Selena notified Zeke that she was tracking slipstream transitions into the system. Zeke had swamped the system with probes anticipating this would occur, and he wanted to know the minute any Chohish showed up. Now they were here at one of the two locations Isolde had identified as probable. At least now, they knew if they could reach the slipstream heading back home before they arrived. They couldn't.

"Isolde, have Selena update Gunner and Librada on the location. Tell her to get the pilots in the fighters and bombers. Once we know the number, we can decide if we need to execute '*Delay the Sons of a Bitches.*' I need you to get in touch with Hu'de and Uv'ei. Tell them to deploy their fighters once we do. Then they are to go full speed to the slipstream. We will be right behind them. We will pick up the fighters before we transition, if possible. Otherwise, we will do it on the other side."

"A dozen destroyers have transitioned through, add three cruisers, and indications are more will be arriving," reported Selena. "Getting with the flight crew now."

"Will, the ship is yours. Jeanne, Isolde, and I will jump into the small conference room off the bridge and keep a conference call going between the warships. If you need me at any time, let me know." Not waiting on a reply, Zeke gestured to Isolde and Jeanne to join him as he made his way across the bridge.

In the bowels of the cruiser, two pilots sat in their bomber, nervously running system status checks. "In case I do not get a chance, Camille, it has been a pleasure having you as a copilot. Don't get me wrong, I intend to get out of this, but ...."

He never got the chance to finish. Camille put her hand on his arm to stop him. "No need, I feel the same. Thanks for taking me under your wing and making me feel like family."

Putting his hand over Camille's, he let her know he felt the same. It was then that Librada's voice came over through the speakers. "We have been notified that the Chohish transitions have stopped. The numbers are thirteen cruisers and twenty-five destroyers. Lieutenant Commander Farren believes they sent what was available, hence the lower number. Prepare for ejection. Librada out."

"Well, here we go, Kido. Let's see what this baby can do." Roy said, settling back in his seat. Tugging on his seat harness, he ensured it was snug before picking up his helmet off his knees. Raising it over his head, he lowered it and let the suits AI seal it tight. *"Seal competed successfully, systems reading in the green, Commander. Good luck, and if you can, Gunner asked that you please bring me home safely. In one piece."*

The two pilots looked at each in surprise before laughing. "Did you get that too?" Roy asked Camille, who nodded positively.

The bomber shook as it was moved into the rail for ejection. Roy was still having issues adjusting to the new method of leaving the cruiser. He understood the reason for the change but still preferred the old way.

"Five, four, three, two, ejection."

The bomber shot down the rail like a bullet. The pressure pushed both back deeply into their seats. While flying down the rail, Roy concentrated on his breathing to use his belly until he felt his lungs opening up. Then they were out. Firing up the engines, he turned towards the Chohish fleet. Around him, others mirrored his actions.

A fighter came alongside on both sides of his bomber. He had to do a double take on the one to starboard, as the model and markings were unique. He knew those, as did everyone in the fleet. But what the hell was she doing here? The rumor was she had been banned from flying. As he was musing on this development, another pair showed up. One on top and one on the bottom. Both were so close he swore he could touch them if he opened the cockpit.

As soon as the bombers reached maximum speed, they stopped all thrust and drifted. They would have to do this quite a few times before they came upon the Chohish fleet. Hopefully, and it was a long shot, they would have enough fuel to retreat through the slipstream.

Drifting, he found, had its plus and minuses. He did not expect any external communications for hours until they reached their designated kickoff point. So his mind went into overdrive on how everything could go wrong. They were bound to meet lots of fighters. What if they were in overwhelming numbers? What if the destroyers all dispersed before they arrived? What if.... It never stopped running through his mind until a noise caught his attention.

It was Camille humming a tune he had heard before. "Is that a lullaby?"

"Yes. My mother used to sing one version of it to me when I was a baby and upset. As I got older, she would sing a different version that was more appropriate for my age. The same melody but was made up of other words. I never could remember the words, only the theme. It always put me at ease. Music does that for me. It takes my fear away while keeping me focused at the same time," she responded in a soft voice.

"Well, if there is a time to have something that will keep you focused, now is that time. Hum away. You are in charge of the missile and plasma blasters. I will manage the steering." Then, looking out the cockpit window, he saw an additional six fighters pull up in front of the bomber. "Oh, that is not good."

"What? The fighters? Isn't it good to have fighter protection?"

"Yes, but it means they expect us to run into many enemy fighters. And before you ask, I know because of experience. We are the surprise package, and they have to make sure we get there to deliver it. If we were not going to run into a lot of fighter resistance, they would group themselves differently. More out front, on the sides, less around the bombers." Roy stopped explaining to reach down on the side of his seat to pull out a beat-up bobblehead animal that looked like a dog. Then, attaching it to the cockpit panel magnetically, he made the head wobble.

Seeing Camille look at him questioningly, he smiled as he told her it was something his children gave him as a remembrance and good luck piece. Then his voice dropped, and anguish could be heard. "I brought it on every mission Spencer, and I had been on, all except one. You can guess which one. I was going to throw it away, but habits are hard to break."

Flicking the bobblehead with her finger, she got the head swinging once again. "I like it, and as you said, now is the time to have anything that can help."

Getting the notification, it was time for another burst of speed; Roy kicked in the engines. Turning to look at Camille, who was humming again, he smiled. Pointing to the communications panel, he looked to port. "Whatcha think? If what they say about her is true, this may liven things up. Not like they can lock us up or anything right now."

Flicking a switch, Camile's humming was broadcast over the com. At first, nothing happened. Then a lone female voice joined in singing words to the lullaby. Then a male baritone. Unexpectedly, a soft beat of the drums merged in with Camille's humming.

Silence reigned for several moments when the song ended until a different female singer started a soft love song. She was joined by a male with a resounding tenor. And this is how over a hundred fighters and bombers spent several hours heading for what may be their last moments alive.

But it could not last forever. Nearing the kickoff point, the singing had stopped a while ago. Ship system checks were performed, including space suit checks, harnesses, weapons, and finally, fuel. Roy was not happy with what he saw. They were just over half full, but it would not last long if they were being chased.

Their instrument panel blinked and refreshed with new data from the Lucky Strike. The Lucky Strike received data from all the probes in the system, where they parsed it into usable data before repackaging it for the fighters and bombers.

What the bomber displays now showed was updated enemy formations. Heading towards them were several hundred Chohish fighters. There did not seem to be any particular formation like groups broken into 'V' formations or 'the hammer and anvil.' Just a mass of fighters in a haphazard grouping.

That could not be said for their own forces. Instead, they were moving forward with twenty fighters across three levels in height, looking like a wall. The bombers were spread evenly in the middle level of this formation.

The half-dozen bombers were each surrounded by ten fighters, matching what Roy was experiencing. Off to the side behind them came the cruiser and two destroyers. The Kolqux warships were farther behind them, heading directly toward the slipstream.

When the two opposing forces met, Roy almost laughed. In the last action movie he viewed with his family, he had to explain it was nothing like this in real life. The film had fighters firing an unlimited number of missiles, with fighters evading dozens of rockets with superb flying.

What was not shown in film usually were all the ECMs deployed before the forces met. What Roy heard in the trenches where the pilots rested between engagements was revealed to be accurate here. The Chohish fired their missiles as soon as each fighter was in range rather than in solid volleys. Experience and battle tactics were almost nonexistent. That lack would make the ECMs vastly more effective.

Even though the RGN and Irracan fighter missiles had more extended range than the Chohish's, the fighters around him held off firing their missiles until reaching an optimum range for all. Then all fired their two missiles before approaching for a close dogfight.

The RGN and Irracan forces' front wall broke into individual dogfights with the Chohish. At the same time, the bombers, with their escorts, barreled on through.

After the initial missile barrage, energy weapons discharged all around.

The Chohish must have realized that the bombers were a particular threat as a large group started targeting them. Rocking and reeling from hits, Roy thanked Jamie repeatedly each time the bomber rocked for the extra shields she had insisted on. But in the distance, he could see his target getting rapidly closer. The destroyers were still lined up in a row, heading to cut off the Kolqux from the slipstream. The cruisers, far behind, were angling toward them.

"Almost there, sis. Run a final systems check on your weapons. They are going to be getting a workout very soon. If we can get past these pesky Chohish fighters, that is," he stated through gritted teeth while gripping the joystick with a death grip.

Their escort had left them to engage any enemy fighter that got close except for the original two. And then he saw why as a group of seven Chohish fighters approached them from all directions.

"Lieutenant Commander, this is Red Feather. My sister and I have to leave to have our unique kind of fun. You will have to have little sis man the weapons until our return. It should not take long. Red feather out."

Before she had even completed her notification, the two fighters raced off. Roy and Camille had front-row seats to watch as the pair went into a tight spiraling routine swirling around the bomber. Then, as each enemy fighter came at the bomber, one or the other of the Irracans would head to cut them off, with the other coming around their side or underneath. The acrobatic displays by the two machines were beautiful to watch, but as the Chohish found out, very deadly.

Yet, they could not be everywhere, even as good as the two were. A pair of enemy fighters headed for them from the eight and the three. The alarm of imminent shield failures sounded after several laser blasts slammed into the bomber.

As the two enemy fighters made a tight turn to make another pass, one exploded in flight. "Take that, you son of a b… " yelled Camille. The bomber guns rapidly turned to face the fighter that had completed its turn, but Roy had grave doubts it would be in time. Then, as the fighter fired a burst into the hull of the bomber, it exploded just before an Irracan fighter flew past.

The two fighters flew in to resume their positions on either side. "You two good in there?" asked Jeanne.

"Yes, thanks for the assist. The hull may be melted a bit, though. Another hit might have finished us, answered Roy.

"Sorry, another pair of Chohish showed up, and we were a bit busy taking out the trash. How long before your shields regenerate to the maximum?"

"Another four to five minutes. These engines are a godsend. The old ones would have taken twice as long," replied Roy. "Our long-range communications system is currently rebooting. The last laser took it down. What is the status of the enemy fighters? Destroyers?"

"Their fighters have been pushed back with minimal losses on our side. Forty-some enemy fighters withdrew. Escape pods are being retrieved by our warships as they follow behind us. The Chohish destroyers are about fourteen minutes out. How are you doing on fuel?"

"Less than half. The new engines are great for getting us to the target, but the bombers are lousy to maneuver with. That needs to be addressed at some time if they are continued to be used in this fashion. Oh, and thanks for the coverage. Please pass on our thanks to your partner."

"You are more than welcome, my friend. It has been too long since I got to have fun with my sister,' said a soft voice. "She is always hogging all the fun with her boyfriend or my husband."

Suddenly he remembered something. Since there was not much they could do until their shields were back up, he might as well ask. "The rumor floating around was that you were grounded, Captain de Clisson. You had marines making sure you did not jump in a fighter again. Was the rumor wrong?"

The laughter that came through the speakers was from both women. "Never send a man to guard a woman. In their defense, they tried their best. The first mistake they made was being in full marine armor. My sister excused herself, saying she had to go to the lady's room. Once off the bridge, she ran laughing all the way to her fighter. Have you ever seen Marines run in full armor chasing a woman in a warship through multiple hatchways? Watch it on your return. Funny as all hell. Anyway, you have to remember there are many of her Irracan family on the Lucky Strike. They had her fighter prepped, ready, and standing by. Her flight suit was all laid out, waiting on her. My sister is a pistol."

"You are here, so you must have known. How did you?" asked Camille.

"I was in my fighter waiting on her before she even left the

Lucky Strike bridge. I grew up with her. I knew those idiots, love them, I ready do, couldn't stop her when I sent Jan over there with his squad. Did it more to piss her off than for actual protection. Jeanne, miss out on this? Ain't happening. I guess I could have nipped it in the bud. But, then, I would have to fly with the next best pilot. My husband is good but not quite the same caliber as Sis. And there ain't no way I'm sitting on my butt doing nothing this time around," Anne replied.

"Speaking of Mason, where is he?" asked Roy. "He did ok when he flew with me."

"Ok? Just, ok? Damn, I can't get a break. First, my wife flies off without me, then I get stuck with Jan, who is pissed to hell after he had to chase Jeanne. And by the way, both of us are just pulling up," a chuckling Mason stated.

A fighter flew to a position above the bomber while another flew underneath. "Jerks, all of you. You would not be happy if you had to sit in a heavy flight suit, sticky with sweat, from chasing someone in armor for hours on end. Your all jerks."

"Well, enough reminiscing. It's time to lay down some hurt. Remember, Roy, make it painful but do not prolong it. Just enough to make them pause so we can bug out of here. We will run interference," advised Jeanne.

Getting on a link to the rest of the bombers, Roy reminded his crew why they were there. "Follow me in, boys and girls. The Chohish are still lined up in a line. I doubt they will stay that way once we get there. Shoot, and scoot is the order of the day. Lock your missile control to my bomber. If we become disabled, it will pass on down the line. Don't forget, the last one back buys the drinks." He finished none too soon. Missiles from the Destroyers had arrived.

The fighters started thinning out the missiles while the bombers dropped chaff and fired off ECMs. The anti-missile weapons let loose whenever one got too close, which was getting more often the closer they came to the destroyers. The scene outside was chaotic. Fighters were evading missiles while at the same time trying to destroy them.

The six bombers were surrounded by a fighter screen, but they could not stop all the missiles. Camille shrieked in terror when the bomber jumped from a hit to the hull underneath. The joystick jumped out of Roy's grasp. Once free, the bomber twirled out of control. He grabbed the jumping joystick and fought the gyrations until his arm and shoulder muscles felt like they were on fire. Then, slowly, ever so slowly, he started to get the bomber back on course.

"You ok, sis?" Getting a positive confirmation that she was, he asked her to turn off the alarms. "Arm the missiles. Be ready to fire on my command." Then, aiming the bomber at the closest Chohish destroyer, Ray pushed the bomber to the maximum. This would burn much-needed fuel, but he did not feel they had much of an option. Enemy missiles were becoming thick again. The sound of the plasma weapons turning and firing was nonstop.

Long seconds later, Roy yelled at Camille. "Fire, and continue firing until time to leave. I have the target pinpointed for the missiles." With the bomber shaking from releasing the first two missiles, both watched as they were joined by the missiles from the other bombers. They streaked with a tail of fire double the length of the giant rocket itself.

Evading missiles was not an option for a bomber. They did not have the maneuverability like a fighter to make sharp enough turns in avoidance. But thankfully, bombers were made with heavy armor because the bomber bounced around like a pinball.

Barely hearing Camilla over the alarms and the pounding against the hull, he knew what she was saying from the feel of two more missiles firing. "*Come on, get through… come on, babies, show Papa what you can do. Do not fail me now,*" he whispered as he watched the track from the first twelve missiles.

267

Four of the missiles were taken out before they were even nearby. Another three exploded before reaching the targeted destroyer, and two more were drawn off by their version of ECMs. But three exploded on target. Missiles meant to get through a heavily shielded large warship pulverized the destroyer. The front quarter section disappeared, with the rest buckling like a cracked egg. It blasted away, tumbling end over end.

Readjusting the targeting pointer for the next volley, he felt the ship lurch again from another release. Then, turning the bomber slightly toward the next destroyer, he saw that the Chohish destroyers were lining up an inward curve. Seeing this, a smile came to his lips. "*I wonder... this may actually work ...* "

Adjusting in his seat from the last bounce, he directed Camille to not stop firing until they were empty. Then he set about setting up his targets for the missiles just released and the ones still left in their cradles. While he did this, his cackling caused Camille to look up from her tasks. The crazy look did not help any.

And the ship continued on its way. When the engine started overheating, Roy resolved it by overriding the alarm to shut it off. He doubted it had been adjusted to the new one anyway. At least, that was the excuse he gave Camille.

"What the hell are you doing? I thought you said the Captain only wanted us to destroy one destroyer dramatically to get the Chohish to pause in concern? We did that." she yelled at him through the smoke swirling around the cockpit.

Roy shrugged, although he doubted Camille could see it. "Well, he didn't actually say anything. I kinda interpreted what he wanted from his gestures."

The sputtering from Camille preceded her question. "What? Making a cup of coffee that he didn't even drink?"

With swirling smoke around him, he worked the joystick while working on finishing the missile guidance. He was about to respond to Camille when the bomber was flung sideways. Then, after it straightened out, he tapped in the last code. "We are here because the fleet needs us to get the Chohish concerned about what the hell knocked out a destroyer so quickly. Especially since there were no warships present. One destroyer could be a fluke, but multiples? Not so easy to explain. Look at how the Chohish lined up. It's just like target practice back at the Academy. The Captain understands something you will learn. Trust your officers."

At least he hoped the Captain had a reason to trust him. The odds of what he devised had to be a longshot, with very little chance of success. But hope blossomed when he saw the second destroyer meet the same fate as the first. And again with the third. The fourth survived but was knocked out of action. By the fifth, his voice was raspy from yelling so loud.

Everything has to come to an end, though. The eighth destroyer survived as it had turned and fled back from where it came from, with the rest following. "Camille, stop firing. It is time to get the hell out of here."

Guiding the bomber toward the slipstream, he radioed the other bombers. Miraculously, they had all survived. Beat up pretty severely, but they still flew. Surprisingly, the fighters still surrounded them, following in the same direction. Checking his monitors, he saw the latest update from the Lucky Strike showed the Chohish cruisers had slowed down. The remaining destroyers were in the process of circling around. It wouldn't be too long before they joined forces. Would they start chasing them again? Reading the data, he didn't think it would matter. They should be able to make it through the slipstream. Hopefully, they would not follow.

Just as he was about to celebrate, the engines stuttered. Panicking, he looked at the fuel gauge. "Fumes, we are running on fumes."

"Crap, they are following us," exclaimed Camille.

Sure enough, the Chohish cruisers had turned in their direction.

From what he could see, the destroyers would join them shortly. The remaining Chohish fighters flew in front of the cruisers. What else could go wrong? He got his answer when the bomber stuttered again.

Looking at Camille, he could see she also recognized they would not make it. They would be sitting ducks for the Chohish when they arrived.

They were looking at each when Roy caught something out of the corner of his eyes. Suddenly, a large object filled the view from the cockpit.

"Lieutenant Commander Dean, this is Lieutenant Commander Cross of the Jackal; please enable remote command of your bomber. Once done, I recommend ensuring your safety harness is on and locked. I recommend you bend over as far as possible, grab your legs around your knees, and keep your head down."

Engaging the remote operations, he felt the bomber change direction. What the hell were they going to do?

The bomber did not slow down but slewed to the side. Unable to see, Roy felt a moment of panic when he felt the bomber slam down hard while hearing loud metal grating. Before he could think another thought, the bomber smacked into something unmovable. Roy lurched forward and backward violently. He would have snapped his neck if he had not been warned to get in a position for a crash.

Groaning, he rose in alarm when he saw Camille slumped over. Slapping his harness release, he was trying to get his legs to respond when the rear access hatch opened. Two prominent figures ran in where he was grabbed and dragged out of the bomber. Two others ran past him to grab Camille.

Seeing they were in a hanger bay, he tried to stand. But the two dragging him resisted his efforts. Not until he was a safe distance away was he let down to rest on the floor. Camille was dropped next to him. Thankfully, he could see she was awake and alert.

Standing, he yanked off his helmet. He was going to say something about the rough handling when he saw why. A dozen battleoids surrounded his bomber. Then, grabbing a handhold, they lifted it where they flipped it onto its side. With sounds of metal straining and bending, they walked, dragging and pushing side to side back to the far wall. Half a dozen men in exoskeletons strapped it in metal bands to the wall. The battleoids thundered back out of the way.

"Commander Dean, Lieutenant Santos, I am Lieutenant Commander Wilma Cross, the first officer on the Jackal," said a statuesque young woman who stood behind them. "If you would move back, it would be greatly appreciated."

Moving further back, they watched as another bomber came slamming in. "Jackal? What is going on?" asked Roy.

Signaling to four men waiting for the bomber to settle down, Wilma explained while directing the activity. "We are recovering the bombers. We have the largest landing bay of the three warships. Captain Kinsley asked us to devise a plan on how to retrieve six bombers that would be running low on fuel. We started with you since you had the least. You would have run out in a few minutes more."

"Hey, you need to move faster there. We have four more bombers to go," Wilma yelled at the men dragging the pilots out. "The Lucky Strike is boarding the fighters while the Fox retrieves escape pods."

The battleoids repeated the manhandling of the bomber. In short order, it was pushed and strapped against Roy's bomber.

Stammering, Camille looked around her. "I thought..." but stopped when she saw Wilma looking at her in puzzlement. Comprehension flashed in Wilma when another bomber dropped in violently and came to rest against restraining cables.

"Did you actually think we would leave you here to be butchered by the Chohish? You don't know our Captains very well, do you? And I believe Captain Kennedy would refuse any order to abandon anyone."

Seeing something she did not like, Wilma excused herself. Before leaving, she said the other pilots would be sent to the medical ward for a medical checkup. They could go there or meet Captain Henry on the bridge. "If you get lost, just speak out loud. The ship's AI will direct you.'

They stayed to watch the rest of the bombers land. Three pilots were seriously injured and had to be loaded into medical pods standing by.

Placing his hand on the back of Camile's arm, Roy directed her toward the exit. "Ok, sis, let's meet this Captain Henry to whom we owe our lives."

Walking through the hallways was easier said than done. Men and women were running from one location to another. It was organized chaos. Finally, they reached the bridge after only asking the ship's AI once. RGN warships were all configured close to the same layout. This helped eliminate confusion when transferring from one vessel to the next.

When they entered, the controlled chaos they saw before was magnified by ten. The Captain, standing behind the scanning workstations, was whispering in the man's ear while pointing at a location on the monitor.

Walking back to his command chair, the Captain looked at the primary monitor that showed the Chohish warship's progress. He stopped to yell at the ceiling, "Wilma, do we have all the bombers? Are they locked down?"

A quick response that she needed another minute. The last bomber was so damaged they were having issues getting it strapped in.

Seeing the two pilots standing there, he waved them over.

"Please, take a seat and strap in. It is going to get hectic in a few."
Signaling to one of the crew, warnings blared through the warship.

"Captain, we are good to go. Bombers strapped and battleoids stored away" reported Wilma.

Suddenly, the ship rocked, and the lights flickered before changing to red.

"People, seems we have someone knocking on the door. It is time we showed the Chohish our heals. Engine room, full speed, take off the restrictors," ordered the Captain.

The warship rocketed forward before leaning to port.

Captain Henry pushed the button for ship-wide communication. "The Chohish are on our heels. But we have been here before. Let's show these dogs that the Jackal is not to be messed with. What do you say?"

Unexpectedly, the crew howled. "*Bark! Bark! Grrrrrrr. Owooooooooooooo*" howled throughout the ship. Even the Captain howled. "Who are we?" he yelled, getting a full-throated response from the entire Jackals crew. "*We are the Jackal. Bark! Bark! Grrrrrrr. Owooooooooooooo.*"

Roy and Camile looked at each other in shock as they had never seen the like on an RGN warship.

"Fire control, please drop Captain Kinsley's little surprise," ordered the Captain. Shortly, the ship jerked repeatedly as missiles were fired.

"Captain, five missiles are heading for us off the port side. ECM and chaff are being deployed along with anti-missile defensive arrays," reported Wilma.

Without warning, the proximity alarm sounded.

"Avast ye me hearties, Captain Kennedy here. We are crossing the Jackals aft. Yo ho ho, we will take care of those pesky missiles tracking you."

"Appreciate the assistance, Fox. Let us know what we can do to assist," responded Wilma.

"Fire in the hole," was the response she got. A barrage of defensive fire erupted from the Fox, which headed directly at the oncoming missiles before swinging away.

The missiles changed direction to follow the Fox. Three fighters suddenly flew out from within the destroyer, heading for the missiles.

The connection between the Fox and the Jackal allowed both ships' bridge crews to hear the fighter cockpits. "Heave ho me bucko's, let's send these bogeys to the briny deep."

There was silence for a few seconds before a lively tune came across. "Forwards, backwards, over the Sea, a bottle of rum to fill my tum, a Pirate's life for me. We're going this way, that way, forwards backwards...."

"Mason, you are to quit playing around. We have more missiles incoming," ordered Meghan.

The sound of multiple missiles firing preceded Mason's response to Meghan. "Ok, me lassie, your wish is my command."

The sound of heavy breathing and groans echoed from the speakers. "Away me hearties, time to go home."

"What the hell did they fire?" exclaimed Wilma. "All five missiles have been destroyed."

"Captain Henry, time for us to leave. Meet you on the other side, Meghan out".

"Ok, helmsman, head for the rally point before transitioning," ordered Wilma. "Captain, any additional orders?"

"None, Lieutenant Commander, the ship is yours. Good job, everyone. But we are not done yet. Let's get through the slipstream first before relaxing." Unbuckling, the Captain walked over to sit by Roy and Camila in a chair. "Well, you two, and your buddies, sure caused a ruckus back there. That sure took the Chohish by surprise.

I have to admit, so was I. I doubt the Chohish will do that again. In case you do not remember me, I am Captain Lance Henry."

"Thanks. That was not our original plan, but when the Chohish lined up like they did…. I took a gamble. But I am puzzled about one thing. Why do I get the feeling that the Captain, or should I say all the Captains, think we will be safe once we get through the slipstream? Why wouldn't the Chohish chase us through?" Roy asked. The nodding from Camille showed she was just as puzzled.

Chuckling, Lance leaned back where he rubbed the arms in the chair. Then, before he could answer, Wilma yelled out. "*bwahaha!* Take that, you sons of a bitch!"

"I take it they got our little present?" asked Lance.

"One cruiser split in half, and another two look crippled. Damn, I wish we had more of those suckers," declared Wilma.

"Really? They take up a lot of space. We had three sitting in the middle of the main cafeteria. Needless to say, there was a lot of nervous personnel when eating," mocked Lance.

Turning back to Roy and Camila, "In case you are wondering what the surprise was, when we met the tenders last time, they had a couple dozen of the new specialty mines. Zeke figured we could use them. So he asked for them if they could confirm the mines would work with any of our ships. Only the Jackal had the missile tubes that could handle the extra clearance needed. The mines piggyback on a missile and drop at preselected coordinates programmed into it. Then it waits for an enemy ship to enter within its range."

Looking back at Wilma, who was standing behind the fire control station. "I was so lucky when she requested to sign on to this ship. But where was I? Oh, that's right, getting through the slipstream. Zeke doesn't think they will. He believes they are part of a force being put together to quell the rebellion on Certh. But if they did follow us, they would be in for a nasty surprise. Zeke was always concerned about Chohish forces sneaking up on us from behind as we had passed many slipstreams that were not explored. So he had the Jackal, or the Fox, take peeks regularly. Yesterday, we detected a large RGN fleet inbound here. Per his instructions, I asked them to wait on the other side of the slipstream and not make their presence known. They agreed. Roy, I believe you know the Admiral who is in charge. Rear Admiral Okeke?"

Seeing the startled expression on Roy's face, Lance leaned in to whisper in confidence to both. "Now, if only we had a way to get the Chohish to follow us through." Putting his hands on his knees, Lance levered himself up to his feet. "But enough of that for now. Do you two want to tag along with me to get a cup of coffee?"

Both Roy and Camila looked at each other in horror.

DISSOLUTION

PARKED BETWEEN A mobile repair vessel and a tender, the Lucky Strike was covered with repair droids. Damage was evident over most of the skin. Most of the sensor arrays had to be replaced, and whole sections of the hull had lost integrity, with some missing altogether.

Loud echoes sounded as two individuals walked the empty hallways. "We really need to stop doing this. I am starting to get a complex."

"Oh, Zeke, war has a tendency to be hard on weapons of war. And it is not like you have been playing it safe. You should be glad that this beautiful ship brought its people home," conveyed Jeanne as she walked snuggled up against his arm. "But that is not what is really bothering you, is it?"

"Harumph, can't get anything past you anymore, can I?" questioned Zeke as he walked into the ship's observatory. "I cannot do what they seemed bent on. They have endured unspeakable horrors for so long that their hearts are hardened against any compassion for the Chohish. And I am having a hard time blaming them, yet, it goes against everything I was taught growing up. It is like telling my parents they were wrong even though I agree with them. There has to be another way."

There was nothing she could say that would ease his angst. This was something he needed to work through himself. The only thing she could do was be here for him. So for the next several hours, they viewed the stars in all their glory.

A cough broke their contemplation. Without looking, they recognized who it was. The sounds of more than one let them know his brother was with him. "Hi, Uv'ei and Uv'ek. What can we do for you?" asked Zeke.

The pair, dressed in their beat-up armor, sidled next to Zeke. Gazing at the spectacular view, Uv'ei spoke sympathetically. "We saw you leave the meeting and guessed you would be coming here. Your views were not widely shared. We are very concerned as the meeting became heated. What does it all mean?"

Taking a deep breath, Zeke let it out slowly before replying. "The Soraths have threatened to withdraw their forces from this theatre of operations if the RGN takes the stance I proposed. Instead, they would redeploy them with their other fleets fighting the Chohish on the other approach. Without the Soraths, the Irracans do not feel the necessary resources are currently available to take on a Chohish home world and would stay out of the upcoming action."

"And then there are my people. That is why I was delayed until now to hunt you down. The ruling council running the planets while I am gone is adamant about what must happen. You will not get any additional resources from them if the RGN follows your approach." Placing his hand on Zeke's arm, he squeezed it in reassurance. "I could override them, but then my people would demand my return. And I vowed I would not until this has been settled. We will stick by your side no matter what is decided. That includes Hu'de and his battleship."

Patting Uv'ei's hand, Zeke smiled. "Thank you, my friend.

You may be the only ones. But it may all be for naught. I am not sure I will even have a warship to command if they vote against my recommendations."

A voice at his side spoke up. "The Fox is yours to command, no matter what they decide. Meghan and Anne informed me that before we arrived here. I did not put any pressure on them. They said pretty much said what Uv'ei said. They wanted in until this is settled."

"I thank you, my friends, I really do. But I do not see what three warships will be able to do," he lamented. "If they take the Lucky Strike away from me, the Jackal would surely be reassigned."

"I think you will have more than that."

Turning quickly, he looked around for who said that. A pair of shadows near the entrance moved into the light. "Admiral Chadsey and Rear Admiral Okeke, it is good to see you."

The two Admirals walked over, where they nodded to the Kolqux. "Uv'ei, Uv'ek, it is good to see you again. Glad you are here. It will save me from having to review this with you later. And please, just Katinka will do. We have been through too much together to bother with titles when in private. Same for Nkosana." Pointing to a sectional near the back of the room. "Would it be possible for us to get to more comfortable settings?"

After they had grabbed some drinks from the self-service machines at the rear of the observatory, they all made themselves comfortable around a pair of crescent sofas.

Blowing on the hot espresso, Katinka breathed in the rich aroma. "Ahhh, I have missed this. Your ship is the only one I can find that carries this flavor. You would think my staff would make sure it was available in more places after I made it known it was one of my favorites."

The feminine laughter from behind them caught them all by surprise. Then, turning, they saw Hawke standing there with

Bridgette, Nkosana's wife, leaning on his shoulder. "Good thing we were not assassins, Hawke. Are you sure these are the ones feared throughout the Chohish empire? And Katinka, your staff cannot get that flavor because of the minimal availability. Only one planet has the soil to produce it. You have to know the family to be able to get any."

Looking back at her expresso, she laughed. "Now that I think about it ...., it was on this ship that I first had it and," turning to look at Zeke, "you were kind enough to scrounge up a case for me somewhere."

Shrugging, Zeke raised his hot chocolate in salute. "My parent's company does not export that flavor. The soil needed to grow the beans only exists on one island. Distribution is limited to the planet only. It is a close favorite behind the cocoa."

Waiting for the two new guests to grab their own drink and grab a seat, they all looked at each other to see who would break the silence.

Jeanne slammed her cup down on the table, breaking the silence. "Oh, come on, really? Admir… Katinka, you cannot tell me that all the main individuals showed up here by accident. You, or that sneaky one over there, Bridgette, arranged this. I would bet on Bridgette, who also probably told you where Zeke was. She is part of intelligence, the sneaky type, isn't she?" The look of innocence from Bridgette only got a glare from Jeanne in response.

That brought a snicker from Katinka. "Looks like she has you figured out, Bridgette. Yes, I did arrange this impromptu meeting. The meeting we just came from went as Nkosana and I predicted. The RGN is in disagreement with the majority. Maybe it has to do with our own complicated history. But we do not intend to start wiping out races as a solution to a problem. There has to be another way."

The stiffing of the feathers on Hawke was not lost to anyone there. But where Zeke saw no reaction from the Kolqux, he was surprised.

Seeing the intense scrutiny from Zeke, Uv'ei smiled. "I am in agreement with Katinka. I will not become what I have hated all my life. There has to be another way."

Now it was Zeke who became suspicious. Glaring back and forth between the Kolqux and the two Admirals, then around at all present. "You all met before coming here, didn't you?"

Now it was Katinka's turn to raise her cup in salute. "See, I told you he would figure it out."

"I think we are being played here, Jeanne," stated Zeke, grabbing her hand in his, "I am afraid to hear what they want from us."

"Nothing more than what you have been doing. Well, maybe a little more," answered Nkosana. "As you heard, a large allied fleet is parked over Drecholea. We have entered into a mutual defense and trade agreement with the Fassoin. There are no plans to move that fleet."

Looking at his wife, Nkosana asked his wife to continue. "Chicken. Anyway, he was saying that the fleet in that system would not be used for offensive actions. We believe it is large enough to stop anything that may be sent against it. There is another fleet entirely made up of RGN ships on its way. That fleet will be tasked with continuing the action against the Chohish. All we are missing is someone with knowledge of the Chohish tactics to lead it."

It was not lost on Zeke, whom she was talking about, not with all three looking at him with smiles. "Are you talking about assisting with the planning or actually leading it?"

All three answered it at the same time. "Both." Then all, except Zeke, laughed when Zeke looked bug-eyed at the Admirals like they were crazy.

"When is this other fleet supposed to arrive?" asked Jeanne.

Pulling a data pad out from a side pocket, Katinka handed it to

Zeke. "Tomorrow. It is in the system next to this one right now. I expect the fleet will require several days to regroup and resupply."

Moving closer to Zeke so she could see and read what was on the data pad, Jeanne whistled at the size and makeup of the fleet. "Do these numbers include the fleet that is already in this system?"

Shaking his head negatively, Nkosana explained. "No, just the fleet that will be arriving. The tenders and support ships will stay here. They will be tasked with building defensive platforms for the planet since they have decided to come out of hiding."

Running his finger down on the data pad to scroll through the personnel listing, Zeke stopped when he reached the end. "I am familiar with some of the officers here. There are quite a few that I would be glad to serve under. Would I have to leave my ship?"

"Yes, you would have to transfer to a command ship. Most likely a battlecruiser," responded Katinka looking at Zeke closely.

Zeke's response was instant after he heard that. "You honor me with the command offer, but I will have to decline." Looking up at the Admirals, he handed the data pad back to Katinka. "I will be glad to assist with any planning, but I would like to stay with my crew if allowed. We started this together, and I would like to end it with them."

"We understand and respect your decision. I believe I would have done the same if in your position," said Nkosana. "We would appreciate you being part of the planning going forward. Speaking of that, with your latest exploits, did you get any idea of the numbers in the Chohish forces we may face?"

Shrugging, Zeke explained that the forces he saw were a few hundred warships but was sure many more were on the way. Jeanne added that even then, were they part of the rebellion or to put the uprising down?

What surprised them most was the question from Uv'ei. "Esteemed Admirals, you do not seem too concerned about the withdrawal of the Soraths. I understand why you wouldn't be for my people. What they can contribute would be minimal anyway. But the Soraths are a different matter entirely."

It was Katinka who answered. "You misinterpret our reaction, my dear Uv'ei. The loss of the Soraths will affect us dramatically. Many more will die because the Soraths will not be there to supplement our forces. The war may drag on for additional months or even years without their assistance. But, like Zeke, the RGN will not be part of race extermination. Especially not now that we know that not all Chohish agrees with how their people have been acting."

Bridgette picked up when Katinka stopped. "We learned a long time ago allies may not always agree with you, so plan accordingly. What is the saying? Hope for the best, and plan for the worst. So we did, from the very beginning. The approaching fleet started to be put together when word of the first attack from the Chohish reached us. We had no idea what we were facing. Still don't, not fully. Every ship is new, fresh out of the shipyards with the latest hardware and software. But where the hardware may be brand new, every crew member has several years of experience."

"Since you will not accept command, Katinka will be taking command once it arrives with my assistance. Meetings will be started while resupplying to look at our options. Any thoughts running through that head of yours on how you would handle it? I would find it surprising if you have not thought about it," asked Nkosana.

Grabbing Jeanne's hand, he squeezed it before moving it to rest on his thigh. "Actually, we have. Nothing concrete, as we did not know the size of the fleet or makeup. But let me ask you a question first. Have you ever played three-dimensional chess?"

The two Admirals looked at each other in puzzlement. "Yes, we have. Why?" asked Katinka.

"If you look at all the battles up to this point, they have been two-dimensional until after actual engagement. Only after contact does it change," answered Zeke.

"I am confused. The plan you set up for the first significant engagement was two-dimensional. Not sure what you are asking," a puzzled Nkosana.

"That was because there was no reason not to. It was better for our plan to execute it that way. But I think you are missing the point. Every battle has been two-dimensional," Zeke replied, taking a sip of his cocoa.

The two Kolqux whispered to each other heatedly. It was Hawke laughing at what he heard that grabbed everyone's attention. "Uv'ei, what is the problem?"

Uv'ei smacked his brother on the head before responding. "My brother asked what the hell chess was? I told him I had no idea but thought maybe it was a game. He then asked why are you all discussing a game? Is the meeting over? I told him he was a knucklehead."

Chuckling, Zeke walked over to Uv'ek. "You are right. It is a game, a strategy game. It is one player battling against another with seventeen pieces of six types on a board marked in squares. Many strategists use it as a reference when putting together a battle plan. Do you have anything similar?"

Thinking about it, Uv'ek took a moment before replying. "I doubt it. We do not have many games. No time for games, spend most of the time working."

"Well, my friend, that is something that we will have to correct. Once we get a break, let me show you what chess is. In fact, let me have a suite of games you can play online sent to your ship. But for now, let me finish with the Admirals."

Moving back to stand by Jeanne, he put his hand on her

shoulder before continuing. "Forget thinking about what we did. What did the Chohish do? How did they position their fleet?"

The startlement on Nkosana was evident. "Two-dimensional. Every time, their initial setup was two-dimensional. They may never have fought against or used a three-dimensional setup."

"Not that I can tell. I tested my theory several times, allowing them to have an advantage over us if they did. They never did," Zeke answered.

"How long have you had that figured out?" asked Katinka.

"He guessed it from the beginning and has been testing it since," Jeanne answered for him. "He did not want to use it until we needed to."

Excited, Nkosana slapped his hands. "Setup two-dimensional and change to three before contact. Throw them for a loop trying to figure out what we are doing while we will know their formation."

That settled, the group broke up to make their own preparations for the arrival of the RGN fleet. All that is except for the two Admirals and Bridgette, who stayed behind. Katinka made the excuse she wanted another cup of that fantastic coffee.

When they were finally alone, Bridgette turned to Katinka. "You were never going to give him command of the fleet. You were testing him, weren't you?"

"Was I that obvious?" Katinka asked. "Handing him control over so many superior officers would have been detrimental to the cohesiveness of the fleet. We could not afford that since most of the fleet had not worked with each other before. But I wanted to check out your theory about him refusing to leave his crew. Seems you are right. His loyalty is something to be admired. I knew he was special when I first saw his record. Have you seen it? His commanders could not say enough about how impressed they were. And his copilots, they loved him."

"We did. After the plan Zeke put together in the Pandora

system, I had Bridgette send me his files. I agree. It is impressive. And after seeing him operate in person, I know why you were so hot on him. He had no issue with relinquishing control if that gave a better chance to mission success. I like him," answered Nkosana.

Putting her hands on her knees, Katinka pushed her way up to stand, looking around her. "Well, let's hope he survives the next stage. We are going to send him back to see if he can get us a meeting with this Queen Ktissi. And before you ask, yes, on one of our ships. I am not sure how the Chohish will react to that. But I have doubts it will be easy or safe. Hate to lose this group now before this is all finished."

TRAP

"I THOUGHT YOU were joking with us when you first brought it up. This has to be one of the nuttiest things we have ever done," whined Hawke.

"Oh, come on, you have got to be kidding? You can say that after the last year that we have been through? This is nothing," retorted Will.

"I guess you have a point there. Oh well, here we go back in the pits of hell," laughed Hawke.

Talk stopped as they started transitioning back into the Vion System. The feeling of your stomach being flipped, and your eyes twirling to the back of your head, happened once again. The usual buffoonery by Hawke was nonexistent. This was not the time for theatrics.

Exiting the slipstream, Isolde checked on the status of the probes that had been left in the system. Meanwhile, the Jackal and the Fox split off to either side of the Lucky Strike. Fighters flew out to lead the way in the system.

"Probes are still in place. We are not detecting any changes, pretty much the same as we left it," reported Isolde.

"Put out the request for contact to the Queen. Pass on our

request," ordered Zeke. "Well, we will find out quickly how this will go."

Some say the most stressful time was not being in a battle but the time while waiting idly by on something you had no control over. Especially when in enemy territory with enemies gathered all around.

When Isolde signaled Zeke, he linked in to hear the Queen talking to someone in the background. When she came on, she was all business. The conversation lasted only minutes between the two agreeing to meet in the middle of the two forces in two days' time. The Queen would arrive in a battleship backed up by two cruisers.

The following eight hours of traveling to the meeting location were spent in preparation. The fighters and bombers had a system and weapons checks run, and fuel was topped off. Battleoids were manned and strategically positioned around the three ships. Marines and army personnel locked and loaded in support of the battleoids. A special contingent of marines dressed in their armor with weapons joined Zeke and Jeanne, who would be traveling to meet with Queen Ktissi on the Chohish battleship.

The two opposing fleets slowed to a stop at the agreed-upon location, and within minutes, five shuttles left the Lucky Strike.

"Well, looks like my escort is back in play again," Jeanne snarled, looking at Jan and the other four Irracan marines. Looking at Shon and Michale, Zeke was about to tell Jeanne that he was happy to see them but stopped short when he saw Khaleesi glaring at him. The argument they had earlier resonated in his mind. The Major was angry with his refusal to stay on the Lucky Strike. But he knew he had no option. The Queen was unequivocal in that she would only talk with him in person on her warship.

The flight to the Chohish battleship was short in duration, and upon landing on the vast landing pad, Zeke and Jeanne led a group of marines off. Seeing Queen and Omaw walking toward them with their own guard following, they met them halfway. The Queen's guards and officers were dressed in gold and silver ornamental armor that Zeke doubted could stop a laser blast, let alone a plasma weapon. Their weapon was their standard laser weapon with a giant sword in a scabbard.

While Queen Ktissi and Omaw walked right up to Zeke and Jeanne, the Chohish guards and the RGN marines stood back, glaring at each other in distrust.

"Queen Ktissi, Omaw, I appreciate you …." Before Zeke could finish, a loud blaring sounded. Omaw swung around, yelling for someone to tell him what the alarm was for. The Chohish guards growled and looked at the humans in suspicion.

A lone Endaen came running out to squeeze through the Chohish guard. Whispering to the Queen and Omaw, the Endaen glanced at Zeke with a smile. This Endaen was the first Zeke had seen from the planet Certh. Checking the Endaen out as he walked with the Queen and Omaw, he did not see any marks nor display fear as he would have expected if he was being mistreated.

Before the Endaen finished discussing what he came to report, Zeke was beeped from the Lucky Strike. "Captain, we have a large group of Chohish fighters and shuttles heading toward your location. Orders?"

Stepping away from the Queen, Zeke pulled Jeanne with him. "Unless I am wrong, they are trying to break up this meeting or capture the Queen. If they wanted to kill her, they would have sent larger warships. I am guessing they want to take her alive so they can have her surrender in public, torture her, and use her as an example of what happens if you dare rebel. Isolde, have Will follow what we reviewed. He is to protect this ship. The same goes for the destroyers. We need to keep the Queen alive."

Glancing at Jeanne, Zeke nodded toward Khaleesi. "It is as we suspected when we picked up those energy transmissions. Isolde and Selena were right, carriers, a lot of them. Let the Major know to get ready. We have some time. We just need to get the Chohish here onboard."

Omaw stomped on over to where they were standing. "It looks like we will have to leave before we can have our discussion. We are being attacked by our own people. Best if you go back to your ships and leave."

Resting his hand on the butt of his plasma pistol as he listened to Omaw, Zeke tapped it with his fingers. "I know. It looks like a trap was laid. My ship just finished updating me on what they are detecting headed toward us. We have another option we would like to discuss with you." As Omaw did not leave but stood there waiting, Zeke took that as a yes. "I do not believe the forces headed our way expect us, the RGN, to sit here and wait for them. Their objective, it is my conjecture, mind you, they wanted to force a meeting cancellation. But they had to make it large enough so you would not stand and fight. Stop and think about how many ways they can win."

Zeke could see he had captured Omaw's attention. He waited while Omaw thought it over. Queen Ktissi, upon seeing Omaw still talking with Zeke, headed that way with several of her officers and guards.

Acknowledging the arrival of the Queen, Zeke picked up where he had left off. "As I was saying, if we leave before our meeting, they win. If you and the Queen are arrested or killed, they win. So they probably expect you to run and not risk it. They would not expect my forces to stay and fight with our enemies. Our staying and being destroyed would be a win in itself. But if we fight together and defeat them, they lose. Not just the attacking force, but...."

"Whoever sent them will look like weaklings. And that would mean a loss of prestige in our society. Arrgghhh.... But can we beat them? I have been informed that many hundreds of shuttles, protected by even more fighters, are headed our way."

Seeing concern but mostly anger, Zeke knew if he could give Omaw some hope, Omaw would be all in. Omaw did not strike him as one to be afraid of a challenge. "It will be difficult, but I brought a few surprises with me to help out. Before I bring them out, your soldiers must be made aware they are here to help. I do not want my people to be attacked. And we need some way to identify your people from theirs. Maybe spray their armor with a red pigment? And your fighters have to stay grounded. No way we would be able to tell the difference."

The response he got took Zeke by surprise. It was not Omar that responded, but Queen Ktissi. She very politely turned to Omaw and said, "We fight. I will be damned if I am running from this rabble. Do as he spoke. Mark the armor in red. Keep the fighters grounded."

Turning to her guard, she snarled at them. "Get me my armor and weapons. If they make it to the bridge, we will show them they made a mistake. Go, get it now." Her guard growled their approval before running off.

The low growl from Omaw spoke of his approval too. "Looks like we will be fighting together, human."

Instead of asking Omaw a question he was concerned with, he directed it to the Queen since she was still here. "Your Highness, I have a question for you. How many knew of this meeting? Someone in your entourage is probably working against you. This scheme is so large that it must have started when you agreed to the meeting. It takes time to put something like this together without being detected."

"Were they undetected?" asked Omaw looking at him. "You came prepared for something like this."

The size and quick temper of Omaw would make most think he was simple-minded. But Zeke knew that was far from the truth in the time he had to observe him. Omaw had a shrewd mind.

"Yes, we suspected. Our scanners picked up large energy signatures, carriers, we believe, in the location where the shuttles and fighters originated after you told us where to meet. That led us to suspect something like this might happen. We were not too concerned as we could evade any force that far away before they arrived. Same for you. But as I said, I do not think an actual attack is their goal. They just want to stop any meeting between us."

"Then let us surprise them. Mother, as we have discussed, this human… "and he stopped where he directed his gaze at Jeanne. "These two know their way around commanding fleets. Our people do not know the human warship's full capabilities, yet they know ours." When he said the last, he glanced back to Zeke, who shrugged noncommittally. "The small ones fly ours, which you would have studied." Then, turning his gaze back to his mother, Omaw continued. "It would make sense that we give him command over our forces to fight this threat. His leadership skill cannot be denied."

The chuckle from Zeke took Omaw by surprise. "You might be willing to let me take command, but your ship Captains would resent it. May even outright refuse. Just tell them to head right at the shuttles and blow right through. Destroy as many shuttles as possible, do not worry about the fighters. Concentrate on the shuttles. My fighters will take care of theirs. Once the warships get past the shuttles, they should look for the carriers. We will supply the coordinates they are in. Make them pay for daring to attack."

The Queen interrupted, asking what did he recommend.

Smiling, Zeke looked at Jeanne before replying. "With your permission, I will lead the military defense of this ship. There are just too many shuttles headed our way to destroy them all. They will not bother with the cruisers. There is no value there. You are what they are after. With that in mind, I expect this vessel to be breached in many places."

Moving to stand directly in front of Zeke, the Queen took

several moments to look into his eyes. Reaching out her hand, she placed it on his chin to move his head back and forth. "So much has happened in the last several years. But who would have thought I would be asking my enemy to protect my people and me." Releasing his chin, she looked at Jeanne before turning back to face Omaw.

Twirling, the Queen marched several feet to stand in front of her officers, where her posture stiffened before she spoke in a voice that dripped with command. "So be it. You all followed me so we could end our malignant path and return to the honor our proud race once held. I now ask that you obey this human and show our people we can change."

Close to a dozen Chohish officers bowed, pledging their allegiance to the queen, except one who growled angrily and raised his pistol. Before he could get a shot off, he was flung back in a bloody burnt mess by a plasma blast to the chest.

Alarmed, Omar pushed the Queen to the floor and stood over her. Everyone else pulled weapons turning to the one casually holding the smoking plasma pistol in her hand. "I guess we know now who the traitor was."

Rising from the floor with a dignity few could have accomplished, Queen Ktissi glided over to Jeanne. "You must be Jeanne. I have heard much about you. My son says you are the Captain's mate. I am in your debt. I would like to get to know you better if we survive this."

Reaching over to push the cool part of the plasma pistol down, Zeke pointed to the Chohish officers and soldiers, all of whom still had their weapons aimed at Jeanne. Seeing this, Jeanne put away her gun while laughing. "*Oops.*"

Waiting until the weapon was fully back in its holster, Zeke sighed in relief. "Ok, now that we have that settled, we have much to do. Omaw, tell your soldiers that they are to follow commands my Marines gave. I cannot have them doing their own thing. Oh, and Omaw, get your soldiers out of this landing bay. Since I will manage the defense, Khaleesi will require some readjustments. And if you are going to stay with me, keep a few of your officers with you."

Turning to Khaleesi, who was standing off to the side. "You ready?"

Signaling to several of his officers, Omaw gave them their orders. Once done, he said goodbye to the Queen, who left, heading to the bridge. While her guard left, Omaw stayed behind with his officers while a few others went about clearing out the soldiers.

A sharp, piercing whistle sounded, and the ramps on the five RGN shuttles dropped with a clang. Half a dozen battleoids came marching out of each shuttle carrying heavy weaponry. Behind each grouping of battleoids came a dozen RGN marines in armor, followed by dozens of Kolqux army personnel. Each of the latter carried large squares of some material over their shoulder, while the former hauled large, heavy bags.

Once they gathered around, Khaleesi was handed a 3D projector she placed on the ground. Then, turning it on, a blueprint of a Chohish battleship appeared three feet above the floor. A dozen locations were highlighted in red.

Pointing to one of the locations, Khaleesi assigned a group of RGN marines and Kolqux army personnel. "Omaw, send one of your officers to escort this group to the location identified. If you have any available soldiers, have them join each group as assigned."

"Why these locations?" Omaw asked, pushing to stand next to the 3D image.

"Access points to life support, engineering, fuel, engines, and the bridge. We will leave the protection of the bridge to your soldiers. I recommend you seal all the hatches, not just lock them, but weld them shut."

Pointing to another location, Khaleesi assigned the two Captains with another group of marines and army personnel, only to have the two Captains shake their heads no. Jeanne pointed to a different icon. Knowing where she indicated, Khaleesi was ready to argue but relented, aware that they would go there no matter what she said. Bobbing her head in acceptance, she delegated the group to go with them, making sure that the protection details for the Captains knew their assignments had not changed.

Following marine Sargeant Alonzo Holmes, who gave Jeanne an evil stare when she started a lively song, the group passed others, setting up choke points. Once, they had to climb over cabinets thrown on the floor, still full of whatever they held. During his scramble over the blockage, Omaw saw a marine putting devices under and around the cabinets.

Finally, the group reached their destination. It was in the vast junction of three hallways, one connecting to the massive hatchway into the engine room and another leading to the bridge. The squad of marines and army personnel went to work immediately. One of the Kolqux dropped the large composite square he had been carrying to the floor, then, grabbing one end, the Kolqux lifted it up until it was perpendicular to the floor. Another Kolqux dropped a square next to his and repeated the process. This went on across all three hallways.

Once all were in position, another Kolqux pulled out a device from a pocket on his leg. Inserting this in the first square, a hum started. It rose in volume while all of them began shaking. A laser shot out from the ones positioned near the walls to burn multiple holes before being filled by rods pushed out by the composite squares. Next, the rest connected to each other with a solid clang, forming a three-foot high wall across all three hallways.

As the barrier solidified, the marines dropped the overlarge, heavy bags they had been carrying behind the barricade, and started pulling equipment out. As one marine opened a bag to pull out a large plasma rifle, another marine handed him a tripod to put it on. A third started placing power packs next to the tripod. Others pulled a more petite bag out and started walking down the halls. As they went, they placed devices randomly on the walls and ceilings.

When one marine pulled a cabinet out of a storage room, dragging it toward the end of the hallway, Omaw looked at Zeke in puzzlement. Looking at what Omaw was puzzled about, Zeke shrugged. "No idea, but I am sure it will be fun to watch. The marines are great at surprises. Very ingenious sappers they are."

The sound of a weapon powering up grabbed Omaw's attention. A plasma rifle had been connected to the tripod and was now being synced with the unit's AI. Moving the barrel in a half circle, the marine ran his fingers under it to ensure it had the proper clearance. The last thing the marine did before moving off was connect the rifle to a pair of large power packs.

What surprised Omaw most was that Zeke and Jeanne did not just sit and wait while their underlings did the work. Zeke was helping set up the second plasma rifle like he knew what he was doing. Meanwhile, Jeanne was deploying the devices down another hallway. It was amazing. Everything these humans did was different and exciting. Even the soldiers he had brought with him were amazed. They kept asking him for instructions, but he had no idea what the humans were doing. Chohish battle tactics were universal in their empire. Being so large, their size was usually all the intimidation they needed. If not, charge and overwhelm. While he watched the humans prepare, he had his soldiers spray red dye on their armor and bodies a newly arrived soldier handed them.

Some preparations were even more puzzling than most. They watched as the small Kolqux brought more large squares to stack on top of the barrier end pieces, again, the whirl of electronics. This raised the height of another five feet. More were added to make the ends into a large L-shaped box. Once completed, one of the human marines stepped in to check it out. Raising his large plasma rifle over his head, he brought the butt end of his rifle down to smack the just completed section with a massive blow. The sound reverberated loudly down the halls, yet no damage to the unit was visible. The pat on the back of the Kolqux let Omaw know it had passed whatever test the marine was doing.

It was another hour before everything was complete. And just in time, Omaw could hear the power fluctuation that occurred when firing missiles and energy weapons. He was standing there looking over all the preparations the human did when the two Captains joined him.

"We have around ten minutes before the shuttles reach us, Omar. It will take a few more before they can blast their way through the hull. We must instruct your soldiers on how to fight behind the walls we built," said Zeke as he looked at the several dozen Chohish soldiers grouped behind Omaw.

"We know how to fight human. We do not need any instruction," yelled a Chohish soldier.

A growl from Omaw silenced the Chohish but did not stop the glare he gave Zeke. Chuckling, Zeke whispered to Jeanne. "That one won't last long. I give him less than fifteen minutes before he jumps the barrier and rushes into enemy fire. Wine or dinner bet?"

"That is a sucker bet. I doubt he will last more than two. Are you sure it's worth having them here? We do not have time for this if they are going to be obstinate," replied Jeanne.

"Captain Kinsley, you may not be fully aware that Chohish has excellent hearing. I could hear your entire conversation," breathed Omaw moving closer to the pair.

Dropping to the ground, Zeke tapped his plasma rifle against the barrier. A slot opened up large enough for the barrel of his rifle to poke through. "I know Omaw. I wanted you to hear it. If your soldiers want to charge into laser fire and die, please have them move in front of this wall so their bodies can absorb fire when they die."

"Maybe it would help if Omaw knew something about it. This barrier is made from the same material as the hull of our warships. Each section contains a shield generator and a small AI. It will allow us a small-time window where it will block most fire from hand-held weapons." Moving to lie down next to Zeke, Jeanne duplicated his actions to open her own rifle slot.

Stunned, Omaw swirled to face his soldiers. What he saw and heard surprised him. They were making snide remarks about the cowardice of humans. Rage filled his heart. They had seen the humans' courage and experienced humiliating defeats at their hands. However, when the same humans were fighting for them here, and now, they were degrading them.

Unable to stop a low growl from growing rage, Omaw pushed his way into the group of Chohish soldiers. Then, in a sudden grab, Omaw grabbed the throat of the Chohish, who made the snide comment and lifted him up in the air. As the Chohish warrior fought to breathe and remove the grip stopping his breathing, Omaw glared at his soldiers.

"I watched that man take down one of our best, unarmed, in a fight I arranged. But, after losing, our so-called brave warrior hit him when his back was turned. Then when two others tried to use their swords to kill him while he lay injured on the ground, his woman used her own swords to kill both in mere seconds. Ask the officers who returned with me if you do not believe me. They were there and saw the whole thing. Courage is one thing these humans do not lack. Nor lack of wisdom, which you don't seem to have."

Letting his grip relax, he dropped the gasping soldier back onto his feet. "Don't confuse wisdom for cowardice. Listen to them, and let them tell you how best to support defending our Queen, my mother."

Omaw put his hand on the gasping soldier's head before pulling him into a hug. "Gugn, you have been my friend since birth. I would hate to lose you now because of your pride. Will you follow me once more, my friend?" The return hug gave Omaw his answer.

Gathering the soldiers, he marched them to stand behind Zeke. "What do you want us to do, Captain? How do you want to deploy us?"

Glancing up at Omaw and the soldiers, Zeke rose to his feet, slinging his rifle to his back. Looking at the faces of the Chohish soldiers, he no longer saw the contempt he saw before. Nodding, he walked back down the hallway, where he would not interrupt the final actions of his people.

"First, get them into their armor and helmets. All air left will escape through the breaches when their charges go off. I have already had the hatches at each of these halls welded shut. As far as fighting, there is not enough time to integrate you all into how we fight," Zeke raised his hands high when he heard some starting to protest. "*Yoh*, hold on, I did not say you would not fight. But, since I cannot change how you fight, we will incorporate your type of battle with ours. Let me explain."

Indicating the barriers and the soldiers manning them, Zeke went on. "That is what will slow down or pause the initial attack. I expect this will be their main attack as it allows them to get to the essential parts of the ship. Once they are slowed down, you will take the battle to them with us following."

Now he had their attention. "You will position yourselves in these storerooms. Once I give the signal, you unleash hell. I will leave someone with you to tell you when since our coms won't be integrated. Jump over the barriers, which is why I kept them low, and do the charge you insist on." The contended growls he heard let Zeke know that they agreed to the plan.

Returning to his position, Jeanne asked Zeke how it went. "Depending on how the battle goes, I may win my bet yet," he replied. "They will not charge until I give them the signal. So it will be longer than the two minutes you bet on."

"I can still hear you, Captain!" growled Omaw.

"I know."

TRANSFORMATION

BADABOOM, BLAM, BARROOM, blam, bwoom, boosh, whomp, sounded down the hall in front of them. "Smart, they are coming through at multiple locations simultaneously. Think they will be surprised when they meet no resistance?" Zeke asked Jeanne. Suddenly, the air rushed out. "Oweeeoooo, they're here."

"Stop kidding around. I am sure the first out of the shuttles will be dumbfounded. I hope they all gather and have a party to celebrate. We should have left some snacks and drinks for them. You smartass!" squeaked Jeanne. Twitching, Jeanne tried to reach her back with her hand. "Damn, I have an itch that is driving me crazy."

"You know you have armor on, right?" mumbled Zeke. "Get ready, people. Looks like they are sending out scouts."

The sound of movement could be heard through their helmets, shuffling, banging of equipment, and metal boots slapping against the floors. The noise settled down until it almost disappeared. Then a helmeted head started showing around the edge of the far wall.

"Do they think we can't see them? Really?" asked Jeanne.

Suddenly, an orange-red beam shot down the hall. The helmet disappeared before a large headless body slumped forward onto

301

the floor. That triggered a swarm of Chohish soldiers in space suits who came running and yelling around the corner. Planted booby traps exploded outward, and bodies fell. Yet more came running around the corner.

They got a dozen feet when the hallway lit up again with fire and explosions from thrown grenades. Bodies parts were splashed against the walls, floors, and ceilings. More Chohish came rushing around the corner and dropped to fire at the barricade. The laser blasts slammed into the shimmering shields.

Missiles raced outward, plowing into the invaders. Death littered the hall, and bodies were stacked multiple deep, body after body on top of each other. Yet more ran around the corner in a massive wave. They climbed over their own dead and injured soldiers in their mad rush.

Fire sounded in the RGN and Kolqux helmets. Looking down the hall, Zeke knew all he had to do was press the trigger on his plasma rifle. He could not miss the hallway was so packed, so he did. He pulled the trigger again and again. His rifles AI sent targets to his helmet nonstop. Bodies blew apart, yet they still came on. Soon they were just feet from the barrier.

That was when the large rifle on the tripod that had been quiet became unquiet. Ratatatat, ratatatat, ratatatat sounded. The supercharged plasma blasts blew holes through anything they hit. One, two, or three bodies disintegrated with each explosion as the AI-controlled rifle rotated and fired until the power packs were empty. Still, more Chohish came rushing around the corner.

Clink, clink, clink sounded. "Down" a voice yelled in the helmet. Then the world turned upside down. Fire and concussion slammed down the hall and bounced off the barrier. Several sections of the wall lost their shields and toppled. Half a dozen Kolqux were thrown backward like toy dolls and bounced several times before stopping.

The invaders rushed forward, only to stop in confusion, when the cabinet at the end of the hallway exploded violently. Dozens of invaders were torn apart and thrown through the air.

"Omaw, NOW!" yelled Zeke rising to his knees to fire over the barrier.

Omaw and his soldiers came racing out from the storage rooms, firing as they ran. As they ran through the openings or over the barrier, they were joined by Kolqux soldiers. They slammed in the invaders, who were still disoriented from the explosion. Laser and plasma flared nonstop.

When Omaw reached the bulk of the Chohish invaders, he changed from using his laser rifle to his sword. He slashed one across the throat and was about to stab another when the sword thrust from Gugn beat him to it. The pair marched down the hallway, taking out invader after invader, yelling at their lungs.

Suddenly, Gugn was thrown sideways to slam against the wall by a much smaller body. Turning angrily, he saw a Kolqux slumped against the wall with a Chohish sword impaled in his right shoulder. It had gone right through his armor. The sound of a Chohish growl brought his attention back to the invader who had stabbed the Kolqux. This Chohish was pulling a second sword from a sheath on his back. Roaring his own challenge, Gugn met the Chohish sword to sword.

This was not a sword duel using finesse, as both Chohish slashed at each other in a mad fury. While the invader had more mass, Gugn was quicker. Both were ignorant of what was happening around them as they tore at each other. It went on and on, each slamming back into the other whenever one stumbled. Blood leaked out of rents in both their suits before they were automatically sealed again.

Ducking under a wild swing, Gugn brought his cross guard up to slam the helmeted head. With his opponent off balance, Gugn rushed forward to push his opponent over a crumpled body on the floor. Then, as the invaded windmilled his arms to regain his balance, Gugn removed the need. The head, still in its helmet, landed on top of the body as it fell.

The sound of screaming and laser blasts being replaced by moaning brought Gugn back to his senses. Breathing heavily, he looked around. Bodies lay everywhere. Only Omaw and one other were still nearby. The rest could be seen running down the hall.

"You, ok?" asked Omaw.

Waving his hand and shaking his head positively, he glanced back up the hall where he came from. The Kolqux that had saved his life still lay there with another Kolqux working on removing the sword. Pain flared visibly across his face even though he still wore his helmet before his eyes closed and his head slumped to his chest. Gugn watched as a patch was thrown on the suit at the sword entry area.

As a pair of Kolqux arrived with a stretcher to remove the injured Kolqux, Gugn walked forward to put his hand on the stretcher. Shaking his head no, he bent to gently pick up the wounded Kolqux. Following another stretcher crew, Gugn left carrying the Kolqux. A small one he thought useless just moments ago. Yet now, here he was, stepping over dead bodies realizing if not for the one in his arms, he would have been one of those staring up lifelessly.

Omaw watched as his friend walked away in a daze. Most of his soldiers were chasing the remainder of the invaders. Surprisingly, others mirrored Gugn's action as there were many more Kolqux wounded than available stretcher crews. The humans and most of the Kolqux were still back by the barricade.

There had been a secondary push through another hallway, but he could not worry about that one. The humans and Kolqux would have to manage that without Chohish's support. The sound of battle had stopped a few minutes ago. And from the number of dead bodies spread out here, he was not too concerned. Even though much smaller than Chohish, the humans knew how to deal with death on a large scale.

Right now, he needed to help his injured soldiers. There were not many. He would have lost a lot more if they had not followed Zeke's recommendations. Maybe all. The number of Chohish assaulters had surprised him. They must have landed dozens of shuttles on the hull in this area alone. But he needed to concentrate and see how many he could save.

It was grisly business. It would have been impossible to tell the enemy from his own if not for the red dye. Now it helped again. Now he knew who to check on first. He hated fighting in an airless environment. Hopefully, they could patch the holes in the hull soon so he could take off this suit. Sighing, he said a small benediction for another of his soldiers. Even though the wound was minor, the suit had been too compromised to repair itself. This soldier had not died of his injury but asphyxiation. When would this end? His entire life, this is all he knew, death.

As he searched for more, he was disgusted with the number of dead bodies. There were many hundreds, even though the battle had lasted a short time. Surprisingly, it disgusted him. Here he was, looking at Chohish, whom he had killed, been killed by others, all of whom he would have called brother just a short time ago. This had to stop.

The battle was over. The cruisers had destroyed a third of the twelve carriers they found, along with two destroyers escorting them. Another seven destroyers and eight carriers had escaped. Over nine hundred Chohish in shuttles had attached the battleship and, unexpectedly, the human cruiser. Many died in their shuttles, never stepping on a ship. Under a hundred were captured alive. The attack on the human cruiser had been a catastrophe for the Chohish raiders. Who would have known that there were so many soldiers stationed there? Especially since so many humans had come to defend the battleship. The battle between the fighters was a one-way affair. The human and Kolqux fighters had shown they knew how to fight.

Now was the time to regroup and say goodbye to the humans and Kolqux. His mother, the Queen, had agreed to meet with the human high command when they came through with their fleet in several weeks. Strangely, he was going to miss talking with Zeke and Jeanne. He was not used to laughing, but their humor was hard not to appreciate. What he wished he had, was to experience a closeness with a partner like these two. And he had a particular female in mind. Maybe, just maybe, if the changes his mother wanted came to pass.

But that had to wait. Omaw's mother, surrounded by her guard and the soldiers that had fought and survived, stood in the landing bay to say goodbye to the humans and Kolqux. They watched as the shuttles loaded the injured first.

It was during the loading of the Kolqux injured that the incident occurred. A Kolqux, with his shoulder bandaged and his arm in a sling, hobbling on a crutch, stumbled and fell. Several Chohish soldiers laughed at him.

The laughter had not ended when a great roar sounded, and Gugn stepped forward. "You laugh at your own peril. Laugh again, and I will personally rip your head from your shoulders. That is my war brother you laugh at."

Several of the Chohish who had laughed stepped forward to challenge Gugn. That was until they saw all the soldiers who stepped forward with Gugn to roar their challenge. Chastised, they backed away in shame.

No one missed it when the injured Kolqux, who had regained his feet, waved to Gugn. Nor the return wave.

TRUCE

"TRANSITIONING IN FIVE... four... three... two... one... transitioning." And the queasiness, headaches, and sick feeling happened once again. More groans occurred this time than expected. Zeke was not immune and was experiencing it heavily himself. He wondered if it had to do with all the transitioning they had been doing. Was it something that could have a permanent effect on the body?

But he would have to worry about that at some other time. Right now, he was more concerned with running into one of the hundreds of ships that had transitioned with them. Along with making sure he was not in the way of the ships still to emerge. The fleet was minus the Soraths and the Kolqux, short the two in his little group. The Irracans had decided to transition with the RGN fleet but had not committed to partaking in any hostile action.

Smaller than the original combined fleet, but even without the two other factions, this was a large and extensive fleet. He thought when he saw the dreadnaughts that he had seen everything. But he could not have been wrong. Present in this fleet were new RGN warships and armaments fresh out of the shipyards never seen or used before.

307

Instead of building the massive but slow dreadnaughts like the Soraths, the RGN went in a different direction. They desired missile and beam ships that could keep up with the battleships and battle cruisers. The thought of warships that could not evade missiles was against all RGN doctrine. So the RGN missile ships used an expanded carrier frame and filled it with oversized missile tubes, shields, defensive armament, and more than enough engines to keep up with all warships except cutters, corvettes, and frigates. Same setup for the beam ships. Although they did not have the extra heavy armor as a dreadnaught, they could still take a beating like a battleship.

Then there were the new platforms for deploying mines. The mines were similar to those the Irracans had acquired and used effectively in the Pandora system. But these mines were twice as large and magnitudes more effective. Once coordinates were defined, the platforms had their own propulsion so they could be sent without personnel to deploy the mines. The AI on board the platform would determine the optimum positioning for the desired impact.

Finally, there were penetrator ships residing in their own carriers. These ships were small in size, being just half the size of a cutter. Contained no armament, just loads of shields surrounding a thick metal hull with detachable engines. The concept was to fly this at a targeted vessel using standard missile engines before kicking off a solid fuel booster just before reaching the shields. The engines would detach at the last optimum moment. The penetrator would plow through the electronic protection and hull before exploding deep within the warship. The prototypes had great results, but this would be the first time in actual use.

Standing next to Zeke on board the Lucky Strike was Uv'ei and Vopengi in preparation for the arrival of Queen Ktissi and Omaw. The Queen may have agreed to meet with the Admirals, but only if they did this on the only RGN warship she trusted explicitly. Uv'ek was staying on the Carrier. Said something to the effect that the meeting was for the bigwigs, not him. He still could not accept that he was viewed as a leader, making him a favorite among his men.

After thirty minutes, Zeke yelled for someone to turn off the proximity alarm. He was tired of hearing it go off every few minutes. It was not like they would not see the visual warning. The number of transitioning ships had started tapering off in the last ten minutes. Still, the immediate area was filled with warships. He had already received word that the Admirals and support staff were on the way and should be landing in just a few minutes. The Queen's warships were expected shortly afterward.

Someone standing at the bridge entrance asked if he had the correct ship. This brought Zeke to jump out of his seat and run. As soon as he reached Lance, the two punched each other's shoulder in a friendly manner. "Damn it, Lance, good to see you. It will be nice to have friends at this meeting. Where is Wilma?"

"Begged out. Wilma is having too much fun with the crew identifying all the ships and what they do. Who else is coming?"

"We are," answered Anne and Mason, who were standing behind Lance. That brought Jeanne hopping up and running to hug her sister. "And before you ask, Meghan has a video conference link in progress with Wilma. Both bridges are packed, looking over all the warships. Those two have become great friends."

"Where is Jan? I thought he was going to be here," asked Jeanne.

"He's here somewhere, probably with Khaleesi. And no, I am not going to go get him. Those two haven't had a moment to themselves in a long time. Leave them be," demanded Anne.

It was Isolde who broke up the group. "We better head to the conference room. Our guests are starting to arrive in the landing bays. The Chohish warships are parking in their designated orbit as we speak. The estimate is the Queen, and her escort will be here in less than fifteen minutes."

309

As the group moved to the elevators, the importance of this meeting muted the exuberance they had earlier. This was potentially the beginning of the end. If all sides cannot come to an agreement, the loss of life would be incalculable. Even if they did, the Soraths and Kolqux were an unknown factor. Would they abide by the accord?

The arrival of the Admirals brought the seriousness of the situation home. As they walked in, the mood changed. It was not lost on anyone that the RGN Admirals looked at Hawke, the only Sorath present, standing with Zeke's group. The usual chatter ended with everyone taking the seats assigned.

Seeing Admiral Condon present was not a surprise to Zeke, but his companion was. Governor Titus Muldane. So, what was he doing here? Knowing Admiral Chadsey, he was here for some reason Zeke was not privy to.

There was no time for chitchat as the sound of the Chohish stomping down the hallway caused silence to descend on the room. Walking into the room first, Omaw dressed in a flowing gold-trimmed white robe over black skin-tight armor. Behind him came Gugn and another soldier dressed in heavy armor armed with large utilitarian pistols and swords buckled around their wastes. Usually, this would be a concern, but Khaleesi, with a dozen marines in full armor and weapons scattered around the room, already had everyone on edge.

Then the Queen arrived, dressed in flowing golden robes with a golden tiara covering her head with precocious jewels rimming the crown. Underneath the robe was black armor encrusted with diamonds. Like her son, she wore a pistol and sword, both showing extensive use. What came as a surprise were the two that preceded her.

That was no doubt they were Endaen, one female and one male dressed similarly in dress to the queen without weapons. Zeke was about to ask Vopengi if he knew them, but the smile on his face and the slight nod to the pair and their responding nod answered his question. "In answer to your unspoken question, Captain, I never met them in person but have talked with them many times. They were my primary communications on the status of the rebellion."

With everyone now present, Isolde asked everyone to take their seats. Oversized seats that would accommodate the Chohish physicality had been installed. On the table surrounding those seated were drinks and food representing all races present. The food sampling occurred while introductions were made, but not many were hungry. Anxiety ruled the moment.

Admiral Chadsey started off the meeting. "Queen Ktissi, the RGN appreciates you meeting with us here. Hopefully, we can come to some arrangement to end hostilities between us with the understanding it is only for the forces and planets under your control. Some type of atonement would be necessary for the loss of life and damage incurred. And measures to make sure something like this does not occur again."

Turning to address Governor Muldane, Queen Ktissi spoke with sorrow, lacing her words. "My people have done a great wrong to your people." The Queen paused to look at Hawke, "nor have we forgotten what we have done to yours. But believe me, once, very long ago, we were a proud and honorable people before we allowed the Sovereigns to change our culture."

The Queen pointed to herself, her son, and her entourage and let the rest of the room know they were trying to bring the Chohish back to their roots when they had honor. But she was not sure they could do it on their own. Even though the home planets were rebelling, the rebellion did not have the warships necessary to overthrow the Sovereigns. The Sovereigns took command away from the monarchy many millennia ago. They were not about to give it up without a fight. Unfortunately, they controlled the vast majority of the warships and manpower.

If anyone expected the Queen to beg, that was before Omaw stood to address the room. "We will fight to the last against the Sovereigns, whether alone or not." Growling and standing tall and proud. "I once believed strength and size were everything. But that was long before I got to see the horror of our arrogance. But we will not plead for help; it is just not in our blood. Help, do not help. My mother has pledged to do what the Chohish can do to correct past mistakes, regardless of what you decide." No one could not see the pride the Queen had in her son as he sat next to her. Nor the approval of the Chohish soldiers.

Nkosana stood to take a position at the head of the table. "Admiral Chadsey and Governor Muldane will work with Queen Ktissi on retribution. But that will take more time than we have right now. Forward probes indicate a fleet of an immense size that should be here within weeks. The Admiralty has determined we will enter into a temporary truce with the system of Vion. Details can be worked out later. Right now, how best to confront the approaching fleet?"

A 3D image appeared on the table showing many hundreds of warships. "This is what we can expect. We shared this with Queen Ktissi earlier. She has identified this as under the command of Sovereign Meon." Holding up his hands, Nkosana asked for quiet. "From what we understand, if we can somehow capture him, we could possibly get the fleet to surrender. They are fiercely loyal to him. And from personal experience, Omaw knows him as a coward."

Everyone looked at Omaw in amazement, who shrugged. "Meon wanted to punish one of my soldiers for no reason. I threatened him with a challenge if he touched him. Backed down like the coward he is. If not for his relations, he would not be in command."

"We are going to incorporate that into our plans. So, Isolde, if you would bring up the sequence of images I sent you, we can review the attack plan. The first image is the disposition of the RGN forces, and the next is where the Chohish will put their warships."

Asked why the Chohish forces were off to the side, Nkosana said he planned to use the Chohish fleet like Zeke had done with the soldiers. Knockout blow? Besides, the RGN does not have total confidence in the Chohish command. One traitor found. How many are unknown? That will have to be guarded against.

As for capturing Meon, a special task force would be assigned for that particular task, and there was no confusion about who would be in charge of that force. Not when the Admiral directly looked at Zeke and Jeanne while explaining that plan element. And the grins on their faces let everyone know they were excited to be part of a potential end-game plan.

The next several hours were spent reviewing general plans. Specifics would be kept to RGN command only. They may be willing to be optimistic about the Queen and her forces, but they were surely not going to trust them until proven.

After the meeting, they all went to the cafeteria for a more comfortable format. Vopengi went to meet the two Endaens that came with the Queen, while Omaw and Gugn came to stand with the usual crowd around Zeke and Jeanne. "Captain, Gugn, and I understand you will lead the group going after Meon. We would like to be part of that group."

"That would be acceptable to me, but I would have to verify with everyone else. Give me a few days to give you a reply," answered Zeke. "If I do say yes, would you be able to bring some additional soldiers? Soldiers that you can trust explicitly?"

"Give me a number, and you will have them," Omaw growled. "I was able to stop one beating, but there were others I could not. So taking him down would be an honor."

"Make sure that your soldiers would have to understand they

would be fighting with Kolqux and humans. If they have any issue with that, in the slightest, we do not want them," said Jeanne.

"There will be no problem in that regard. We will wait for your answer on how many you require," replied Omaw. Whispering to Gugn, "it is not like we will survive this crazy human's plan anyway."

Looking around to make sure no one could hear him, Gugn murmured back. "What do you mean?"

Growling in laughter, Omaw answered. "Think about how crazy these humans are. Their leader fights unarmed against a foe that outweighs him by hundreds of pounds, double the reach, and height. He could have been crushed with one good blow. His mate, more petite than himself, fights off two of our best with swords and wins. Then he risks himself and his friends on two hair-brained schemes to save the life of his enemy, my mother, from traitors. They fly through our warships with defenseless shuttles to land on our planet and then go on to fight the Queen's guard. Then instead of running when we are ambushed, he stops it against all odds. With the way he thinks, he could have us attack Meon's battleship by shooting us at it in just our spacesuits. With that nut leading, be ready to go splat!"

"Omaw, I may not have the hearing of a Chohish, but I can still hear you," said Zeke looking at him over Jeanne's head.

"I know."

UNDERSTANDING THE ENEMY

THE RGN FLEET moved slowly into the center of the system. Rear Admiral Nkosana Okeke stood on the bridge of the battleship RGN Liberator. It was fresh out of the shipyards and was the first warship modeled using the designs put forth to rebuild Lucky Strike and the Fox. The new battleship designs did not incorporate the spartan living areas as profoundly as those blueprints called for. Not everyone was ready for such a lack of privacy. Yet, they were able to reclaim space from almost all areas.

As he stood on the bridge, Nkosana admired the new design. It still had the colors he loved, but all the workstations now had improved safety features. The shell of the bridge had been heavily reinforced and moved toward the rear of the warship. With the bridge relocation and improved structure, it had been decided to remove the backup CIC altogether. Those new changes were not visible to Nkosana.

What changes he did see were the chairs he and the crew now sat in. They were much broader and taller than typical chairs in everyday use. But when in combat, they would go semi-horizontal to the floor. Each chair would enclose the occupant upon catastrophic bridge damage while supplying air. In addition, each chair would be able to communicate individually to allow for recovery.

What did bring a slight smile to his face was when he first walked into the living spaces for officers. He had waited for the officers to get settled into their new quarters when he entered to make his rounds. While some complained, he was glad to hear most favored the changes after they had seen the benefits. And that was when his smile widened.

The number of missile tubes increased by a third, and lendolium and fusion-powered lasers doubled. Defensive armament upgrades were impressive, to say the least. Putting fighters on the hull like the Lucky Strike was passed on. Instead, the integral sections of the ship were heavily reinforced, especially the engines located at the rear. Engines were the weak point in all warships. Storage rooms at the back of the battleship were moved to other areas and replaced by additional shields and defensive missiles. Overall, the battleship was made more fully into what it was always intended to be. A brutal, formidable beast to throw down the throats of an enemy.

And he had over a hundred of them. But even though the battleships were the heavy beasts of the fleet, the battlecruisers came in as a close second place. They had been toughened up in the same fashion. Same for the cruisers. Although the additional number of fighters had worked well for the Lucky Strike and the Fox, it had been decided to use those blueprints for the units built for exploring or when stationed remotely. Otherwise, they needed the brute strength these warships provided. That was what the carriers were for. And they had now doubled the number of fighters they carried. Separate escort carriers carrying bombers were now a standard part of any fleet.

Now though, he was positioning his fleet. All large fleets of this size had multiple command structures. Other Admirals had command of a smaller subset of warships that all reported to him.

The tricky part was not to break up cohesiveness when placing the pieces to fit their plan. But he had picked every Admiral here before the fleet set sail when Fleet Admiral Chadsey gave him his orders. Katinka, along with his wife, were stationed near the slipstream that they had control of with a small fleet of her own in case of his demise. She knew he tended to be in the middle of the action and may need to step in.

Looking at the plotting chart of the warships, he was satisfied they would present the picture on tracking monitors he wanted when they reached their final position. He would love to see the expression worn by the opposing commanding Chohish officer's face upon contact. Well, it looked like things were going according to plan so far. It was time to check on the final piece. "Coms, please get me, Admiral Nguyet Smithson, on the line. Make sure she is on a secure link."

As he waited, Nkosana checked on the Chohish warships. He had them positioned near their home world in three stages. One group, the largest, was facing the slipstream they expected the enemy fleet to arrive from. Another smaller group was positioned behind them a short distance. Finally, the last circled the planet. They were there just in case any warships attacked Certh.

Upon hearing Nguyet was on the line, he waited to connect until he was sitting in his command chair. Looking at the main plot chart, he "Hello, Nguyet, Nkosana here. Can you give me a status report of your sweep?"

The sound of activity in the background preceded her reply. "Hello, Nkosana. We are making progress. The laying of the new mines is progressing as expected. I do not see any reason why we cannot finish deployment on schedule. They are working as designed."

"And our special package?" Nkosana asked.

Again, he had to wait on some activity in the background

before she came back on. "Sorry, I spoke too soon earlier. We just had an issue with several of the new platforms. But it was resolved after reboots, and my engineer used the tried-and-true method. He kicked the crap out of one. What were you asking?"

"The status of our special package."

"Package is in place. Said to remind you not to forget them. Once they make their move, they expect they will become the target of the entire enemy fleet," Nguyet said with emphasis on the last sentence. "Nkosana, this is my opinion, but that assignment is a suicide mission. There is no way we can get there in time."

Crossing his arms across his chest with one hand on his chin, he replied with a heavy heart. "I have a plan in place that I hope will disprove your last comment. But even with that, the odds are against them. Just so you know, I was against the decision on this part, but after they insisted, Admiral Chadsey reluctantly agreed. Though I disagreed, I understand the Captain's reasons. So many lives will be saved. Have to run Nguyet. You take care and let me know once you finish your task and are in position."

The pieces were falling into place. Now Nkosana had to go deal with one more. But, since Bridgette was here in this system, he could do it in real-time instead of leaving a recording. Signaling that he was heading for his room, he left quietly. As he passed Captain Tory Mesa, he heard him ask to tell her he said hi. Nkosana smiled in reply.

The Captain had been with Nkosana for many years and, through him, knew his wife. Tory was familiar with his habits and understood what Nkosana was going to do. That Nkosana was going to say his goodbyes to the love of his life in case he did not survive the coming action. Bridgette had come into his life at a really rough time for him. She gave him a reason to live when he had survivor guilt and wanted to end it all.

Entering his room, Nkosana had to remember where he was.

For decades his room on a battleship was luxurious and massive. Now! This room was the size of a Captains' room on an old frigate. And he couldn't be any happier. That was one area where he failed. Too many officers loved the perk of a large room. But even he would never have thought the room would become this small. But first, he needed to clean up before he contacted Bridgette. He would have to hurry as she would be anxiously waiting. Then, a feeling of warmth spread through him as he thought about her. She was such a strong woman. Not much phased her. Yet when it came to him, she was terrified he would not come back to her. No less than he worried about her when she went off on her missions without being able to contact him.

Thirty minutes later, he walked back onto the bridge. New faces greeted him as shift change had occurred. Then, sitting, he checked his pending messages. Nguyet reported all but one platform had been deployed successfully. The one they thought was resolved by rebooting failed again. Instead, they ended up deploying the mines manually for that platform.

No other vital messages, just updates on deployment. That seemed to be going well enough. Rechecking the board, Nkosana had the ship's AI place times on each group and when they would be in place. Per the AI's estimate, the last group should be in place in a few hours.

Taking a moment, he had the AI run the simulation one more time. Nkosana must have run this thirty times, but one more wouldn't hurt. He paused the simulation so many times to check the deployments that the total time more than doubled. But it paid off. There was one group repositioning that he felt necessary, Nguyet's. Once done, he ran through the simulation one more time. It would be nice if the enemy would follow the AI's assumptions using detail from all the known battles, but he knew how that went. Somehow the enemy never did as you hoped.

One thing gnawed at him, but there was nothing he could do about it. He hated that he could not verify everything was in place due to the necessity for security. So, he waited. This gave him time to review the information they had learned last week.

The Queen had made available their history and access to other Chohish in her government that could help understand how the Chohish lived and worked. How many warships are in their fleet? How many planets made up their empire?

The RGN already knew Certh was the original Chohish home world, where the race started. But they did not have information on the other worlds they considered home. The makeup of the worlds they controlled. Just because a world counted as part of its empire, it may only have a small population, such as a mining colony.

Looking at the data supplied, he reviewed the planets Dikaronia and Vulpidor. These were considered Chohish home planets as only Chohish and Endaens lived there. They were brutal planets, wild weather, poisonous fauna, and carnivorous beasts, having never been fully terraformed. Terraformed just enough to support life. The Chohish considered the planet's brutality integral to what made them who they were and wanted to keep it that way.

Two slipstreams in the Vion system, other than the one the RGN came through, led to systems that contained these two worlds. Two other slipstreams led to empty star systems. Dikaronia was in the Sotanbula system, while Vulpidor was in the Noryn system. Dikaronia had joined with Certh against the Sovereign's rule. But Vulpidor, who had started voicing opposition, was swiftly suppressed before open rebellion.

The Noryn system was where they expected the enemy fleet to arrive from. The Sotanbula system was only accessible from this system. The problem the Chohish rebellion faced was that most of the shipbuilding was in other systems controlled by the Sovereigns. In reverse, the Sovereigns lost more than two-thirds of their personnel recruitment as Vulpidor did not have the population as on the other two planets.

From what Bridgette sent him, the Chohish empire consisted of several hundred planets. Even so, the Chohish did not live in any significant numbers on any of them. Nkosana did not understand the reasoning behind that. Power? No matter. That was something Bridgette was researching. However, he did understand the logistical nightmare of supporting the personnel for such a far-flung empire. The realm had been in decline for centuries from everything he could find. Slowly, until the current war with the RGN and Sorath sent it into high gear.

Well, if he could help it, he would end it.

ROLL THE DICE

SILENTLY DRIFTING IN the far reaches of the Vion system, Nkosana watched as Chohish warship after warship transitioned through the slipstream. Well, they knew they were coming, but seeing the numbers in person was still daunting. And there were still more to arrive. He believed the RGN military was the best that existed in the known universe, but numbers were a factor of their own. Should they retreat and wait for reinforcements? But if they did that, the enemy would recapture their home worlds and be strengthened by the warships and personnel these provided. Many more would die if they could not stop them here. Retreating was not an option he considered for long, now, if only the Chohish responded as he hoped.

Stopping an enemy from entering a system through a slipstream was usually futile. Slipstreams were so vast and extensive that determining where warships would come out was a dice roll. But he reviewed all the records of transitions supplied by the Chohish on Certh. They regularly used a glaring section as it was clear of any obstructions. Be those asteroids, meteors, dust fields, etc. Using that, he went out a reasonable distance and heavily mined it. Not in the path they would travel if they went forward but in a wide circle around that path. He did not have enough mines to be a deciding factor. All he wanted was to keep them using a predictable approach.

Signaling Captain Jacinto Cowan to join him, Nkosana leaned forward before scratching the back of his neck. "Trying to overthink it again, Admiral?"

"You know me too well, Jayce. How many times have we been through something like this? And knock off the Admiral crap, ok?"

"We have been through a lot Admiral, but nothing like this one. This time around is going to be tough." Then, walking around the table to view the deployment from all angles, Jayce stopped when next to Nkosana again. "It looks good. What is your concern?"

"Too many moving parts. We could end up in each other's way," Nkosana murmured. "And I am not surely going after their Sovereign leader is worth it."

"Still worrying about them, aren't you? They got to you, didn't they?" Jace said as he tapped the table. "You cannot protect everyone, Admiral."

"They have been through enough already in this war. It is time for others to take some of the risks." Slumping, he looked at Jayce. "Yeah, they got to me. They would have got to you too."

"From what I hear, Admiral, they asked for the assignment you put them on. No?" chided Jaye. Pointing to the emerging Chohish fleet. "How long do you think they will take to regroup?"

"Hours at max. They would have replenished everything they needed in the system next door. Delay just means more time for us to prepare. Intelligence tells us that this is their last effort to break us. They gathered everything they could. They are not having much success against the Sorath incursion. The two-pronged assault is something I do not think they ever experienced. So, if we win here, the rest may be just a mop-up," said Nkosana.

"Then, Admiral, that is why they put you in command. We all

fought with you in the past and have total confidence in you. So quit worrying about it, and let's roll the dice and see what turns up," Jayce said as he headed back to his own command chair.

"I thought I asked you to stop calling me Admiral?" asked Nkosana loudly.

"When this is over, Admiral, when this is over," said Jayce.

And Nkosana was right. It was only hours before the regrouped Chohish fleet started moving. Moving such a large fleet was not as simple as it sounds. But one thing did become apparent, they had changed how they deployed. It was expected. Per intelligence, even though Sovereign Meon was considered a coward, he was popular because he was brilliant.

The Chohish fleet came out in a pattern not seen before. Thirty-some groups lined horizontally next to each other, separated by half a mile. Another dozen groups lined up length-wise on each end. In total, it looked like a vast U shape. Anything coming in between the groups would come under fire from either group. Each group contained twenty destroyers, five at each corner, with eight cruisers and two battleships in the middle. The only odd thing was that near the slipstream were five battleships, four surrounding one. They were not following the rest of the fleet.

"Looks like they are following the path you predicted, Admiral. How did you know?" puzzled Jayce.

"Simple. They want to control Certh, and we are in the way. Once they push us back and clear out the forces around the planet, they plan to finish us off. And those five battleships in the back, we now know where he is. Omaw was right. He is a coward," responded Nkosana. "Only I don't intend to be pushed. Send out the signal to start operation '*DAM*.' Fire missiles when in range." A large section of the fleet started moving toward the enemy.

The '*DAM*' group of RGN warships heading toward the hostile fleet looked like a triangle. It was three layers of ships, with the point facing the rear. The outside ring of the triangle was made up of battlecruisers, cruisers and destroyers, battleships on the inside.

"Execute '*UMBRELLA*,'" ordered Nkosana. He watched as another group consisting of missile and beam warships escorted by destroyers and carriers started moving forward. "Captain Cowan, wait a few minutes, then I want you to follow with our group. Remember, we are the '*plug*.' Let me know of any changes with the opposing fleets heading or makeup. Buckle up, people. This is going to get rough."

Then the wait, as both fleets headed toward each other. Then as tension was at its highest on the bridge, knowing the action would happen at any moment, a single voice spoke out excitedly. "Admiral, the enemy sent several destroyers and cruisers into the asteroid field to our port."

"Steady Ensign, how many ships are you talking about?" asked Nkosana.

"Seven destroyers and five cruisers, Admiral. Appears they are trying to use the asteroid field there as cover."

"Let me know when they encounter our '*herding mechanism*.' They should get a '*blast*' out of it," implied Nkosana. "Time before missile range?"

"Just under half an hour Admiral for the missile ships. Our group will fire approximately four minutes and six seconds later, with the others depending on their position in the formation. All firing will be managed by each ship AI working in tandem together. The missiles from all groups will arrive at their designated targets at the same time," reported Jayce. "Additional salvos will continue until ordered to stop or," at which Jayce hesitated before finishing, "until we run out of missiles, or we are all dead. Hopefully, not the latter." The menacing look from Nkosana at the Captain alleviated the immediate tension. The crew was quite familiar with the playful banter between the two.

"Update on the enemy group that broke off. They came up against our mines. Several destroyers look to be damaged. One, possibly two cruisers are showing the same. No loss of speed was detected. All changed their heading back towards their fleet. Change that. One of the destroyers is heading back. Scratch one destroyer."

In six minutes, the back and sides of the V formation in the center changed direction. Several groups went up, several to both sides, while the rest headed down. Once they reached a distance away, they changed direction one more time, flying forward in a sloping manner. The Chohish made an adjustment seeing the fleet changes by the RGN. Chohish warships streamed out to intercept them.

"Makeup of the Chohish interdicting warships?" asked Nkosana.

"Mostly destroyers and cruisers, as you hoped," asked Jayce. "Why did you think they would send them?"

"Speed, they wanted to ensure they could stay with our ships. Their battleships would get left behind. The Captain was right. They are unfamiliar with battling in 3D. Otherwise, they would not have formed as if still on the ground."

"Chohish deploying fighters, Admiral. But... that is strange... I could not find any carriers. I have been looking for them since they transitioned. Still a lot of fighters, but not near what I would have expected with a fleet of this size. Could they be somewhere else? A surprise?" reported Ensign Betty Figueroa.

"Could be, but I do not think so. The Chohish never relied on carriers that much. They lost a lot of carriers, mainly in the war theatre with the Soraths. And any new ones, I am sure, are being sent there. Although I think they would be better used against us. Their pilots do not get much training, and new, barely trained pilots taking on the Soraths is near suicidal," replied Nkosana. "Hold deploying ours. I want to make sure they go where we want them to."

The Chohish fighters did not immediately head toward them. Still, they waited until they had a dozen groups of close to one hundred and fifty fighters. Only after all were formed they raced toward the RGN fleet.

Midway to the RGN fleet, suddenly, a Chohish fighter blew up. Then another. Two more. And finally, hundreds exploded in flames in a scene like it was from a movie. The closer the Chohish came, the more that exploded.

"I thought you were crazy wasting our mines where you did. But now, I see what you were doing, herding them to where you wanted them," an astonished Jayce said.

"That is why we held off on our fighters. You wanted their fighters to head directly for us. We dumped tons of small undetectable mines until you were on top of them. Short engine life with a small charge, but when you're going as fast as a fighter, quite deadly. They wouldn't have much effect against anything more significant but against a thin fighter hull, boom!"

But that did not stop the Chohish fighters. Shortly, they were through the seeded mine area, still a massive force.

Even on a ship as large as the battleship they stood on, the motion of missile firing could be felt. The missiles did not head straight for the Chohish warships as they would have had to travel through the fighters. The Admiral did not want the fighters to have a chance to take out missiles as they passed. Instead, they were set to cross over and below the fighters. Nkosana smiled when he saw the fighters make no attempt to intercept. He had counted on the Chohish not allowing independent decisions. They could have taken out thousands of missiles.

"How long before the fighters reach us?" asked Nkosana.

"They will come in a range of our forward warships in under two minutes. We will be in the range of their missiles in four, laser range twenty-seven seconds later," reported Betty.

327

"Send out the fighters. Order them to remove these fighters before they head to designated targets," ordered Nkosana. "Captain Cowen, there is nothing more I can do. Everything is in motion; everyone knows what to do, and the dice have been rolled. So, get me in the damn fight."

"Yes, Sir. You heard the Admiral helmsman, get this damn boat moving. I want to see what this new bucket of bolts can do," ordered Jayce.

As the battleship surged forward, the situation map lit up with thousands of friendly blips. Within moments, they barreled into the Chohish fighters. Although they could not see the individual action, they could see the icons representing both sides. While the icons representing the Chohish disappeared steadily, the RGN icons were not immune. Though not near the same attrition, they paid a deadly penalty. That was true until the RGN fleet slammed into the battle. The addition of their firepower was too much. Within a few moments, the enemy icons showed their remaining fighters withdrawing, A poor shadow of what they had started with. The RGN fighters flew up and away from the approaching Chohish fleet.

While the battle between the fighters had been taking place, the missile battle between the two fleets had commenced. Several volleys of RGN missiles reached the Chohish before their missiles reached the RGN. The Chohish groups sent off to chase the RGN warships had primarily been made up of destroyers, which was missed when the first missile salvos arrived. The protection radius of the remaining destroyers was greatly diminished. And, unlike the Chohish, the RGN had concentrated their fire on one group of Chohish warships for each volley. The ones with the least number of destroyers. Thousands of missiles rained down their destruction in overwhelming numbers.

Destroyers went up in massive fireballs, with cruisers and

battleships not escaping the RGN missile's wrath. Three groups were decimated before the first missile reached the RGN fleet. Although the Chohish did not group their missiles the same as the RGN, it did not mean they were ineffective. RGN warships felt it. Destroyers and cruisers destroyed many. But not all. Destroyers blew up, and others dropped back, too damaged to continue. Cruisers could absorb more damage before they succumbed, but some did.

Then the two main fleets crashed into each other. Energy blasts hit shields and armored hulls. Ships exploded, and hulls melted. Then the RGN ships descended from above and below. Chohish warships were overwhelmed. Ship after ship drifted helplessly. The Chohish warships that had chased after the RGN warships arrived with little fanfare, then they were backed up by the warships from the flanks.

It was now a battle of attrition. RGN Battleships and battlecruisers lined up against Chohish battleships slugging away at each other. Both sides were being pulverized at a distance.

Just as it looked like it was all going to come down between the weapons and tactics of the RGN against the numerical advantage of the Chohish, thousands of RGN fighters arrived. They were like a steam roller. They came in from the side and blasted through all opposition.

The sound and shock of a missile blast near the hull echoed throughout the bridge. "The Chohish cannot continue this for much longer. They are taking a beating," stated Jayce. He was about to ask the Admiral when he thought the Chohish would retreat when he had a sudden realization. "You are not going to let them retreat, are you, Admiral? We are just a distraction from now on, aren't we."

"That is why I am always on your ship, Captain. You understand me and my plans," answered a smiling Nkosana. Only to frown when the battleship was violently pushed sideways and alarms screamed. "Now, all I ask is that you keep me alive. Brigette will haunt you or your ghost to the end of time."

CAPTURE

SCREENS DISPLAYED A raging battle. "Well, it looks like it's our turn now. Will, if you would?" ordered Zeke. "I was hoping Meon would have sent the other battleships to help out, but I should have known."

"You could have asked me," commented Omaw. "I told you he was a coward. He would have had more, except it would have gone against his popularity. Four, others can understand they might be needed for his protection. More would scream coward."

A small figure next to them spoke up. "When do we get in the shuttles? I am tired of standing here doing nothing in this heavy armor."

"Uv'ei, quit the whining. Soon, we get to kill Chohish. A lot of them," a happy Hawke yelled.

"I can hear you winged one," snarled Omaw.

"I know. Don't worry. I gave my word to the Captain that I would not kill you unless you turned on us," a suddenly serious Hawke responded. "And I will be waiting as I have no doubt you will." The glare he received from Omaw only made Hawke smile back while gripping the butt of his plasma pistol.

"Enough, you two. We don't have time for your bickering.

Omaw, have your guys check their suits one more time once they are in the shuttle. Then have them pass their armor to one of Uv'ei marines. You will have to carry your own weapons, somehow. From what I have been told, your battleships' service access hatches and passageways are not made for a Chohish body. It will be tight, but you should get through. You can put your armor on after you get in the battleship. Hopefully, they will have other things grabbing their attention."

Turning to the Chohish soldiers going with him, he was surprised to see Gugn joking with a Kolqux. The Kolqux was tugging on Gugn's suit to ensure it fitted correctly with no leaks.

"Bend over. I need to check on your neck seal. And I am not about to jump up on a box for your amusement, Omaw," Uv'ek told Omaw.

It was strange to be working with Kolqux. He was told these small individuals were inferior his entire life, but his experience has exposed the lie to that. He had come to admire the Endaens and Kolqux. And he saw more and more of his fellow Chohish think the same. So, the question was, how to get that across to all Chohish?

It did not take long to settle within the shuttles as they had been preparing for this for hours. Shifting in the seat as human seats were uncomfortable, definitely not made to support Chohish. Three dozen marine shuttles were going in the initial boarding attempt. Another two dozen more would be waiting in support.

While Zeke and the regular human marine contingent would attack through the typical locations, Omar and the rest of his soldiers would take a different route through the service access hatches. These hatches were too small for armored Chohish. Still, they would follow the Kolqux in only their space suits. While the much smaller Kolqux would carry their armor, they would have to worm through the small passages carrying their weapons. This was not going to be an easy trip.

Sitting next to Zeke was Jeanne on one side, with Khaleesi on the other. In the last week or so, Omaw had heard about the Major, and at first, he took it as Kolqux hero worship full of exaggeration. Then he saw the videos. He was impressed, very much so. The more he learned of these humans, Endaens and Kolqux, he could not understand why his people held them in such low regard. His mother always treated the Endaens with respect and kindness and was harsh with anyone that didn't.

Next to him was Uv'ek on one side, with another Kolqux on the other. Gugn was next to the Kolqux that would be hauling his armor. It was the same wounded Kolqux Gugn carried after the battle on his mother's battleship. Now, what a difference in how Gugn looked at the Kolqux.

Then the notification came through that the cruiser was heading toward the battleship. Unfortunately, Omaw had no idea how this small fleet was expected to handle five battleships. But he watched with interest when Khaleesi and others stood to back into large machines. Then, in amazement, he saw the metal monster close and swallow the humans. Then, feeling someone staring at him, he saw glanced around to see Zeke looking at him.

"You know what you need to do, right?" Zeke asked sternly.

"Do not insult me, Zeke. I know what needs to be done," Omaw snarled back.

"Some, or all, of my people will die in this. All to try and get you access to the bridge. So I will ask as many times as I think I need to. Understand me, Omaw, what we are attempting has only a slight chance of success. Surprise is our only hope of success."

Dropping his head, Omaw sighed. "Please forgive me. I am still trying to get used to all the changes. My life until now has been fighting to keep my men alive. It has not been easy."

Any further talk was interrupted by the sudden shocks from missile impacts. While the safety harnesses worked well for the humans and Kolqux, the Chohish groaned as the already too-tight harness tightened even further. Omaw looked at the humans and Kolqux in envy as they rode out the sudden shifting stoically. The sound of Hawke's laughing brought the heat to his face. Still, he refused to give him the satisfaction of knowing why he was laughing by looking or responding to him.

The next twenty-three minutes went from being concerned to downright frightful. The shuttle rocked and screeched in its cradle, ready to be sent into space. Video feeds showed the ongoing battle with the five battlecruisers on the screens around the shuttle. The detail was extraordinary.

Pushing off Zeke's shoulder to get a better look at a screen, Jeanne squeezed it hard at what she saw. "Blimey! Am I seeing this correctly, my love? Those like RGN battleships and battle cruisers. Where did they come from?"

The response from Zeke was made with him grabbing her hand in reassurance. "One guess, although I think you already know, Nkosana would not have left us without additional support. He could pull it back if we did not need it, but it had to be substantial enough to make a difference if we did. Sometimes my love, you just have to trust your instincts. If I demanded or even requested it, it would make it sound like I was putting the success of our whole operation on him. Even though I am the one that suggested it."

As they watched, it soon became apparent the RGN had the edge. One by one, the Chohish battleships were subdued. Fighters came flying out of the Lucky Strike. Then, with the Lucky Strike, they flew around the battleship they believed Meon was on. Once satisfied the battleship was without power, marine shuttles were ejected. As they made their way, three bombers unloaded their unique payload into the landing bay. The EMPs shut down the emergency lighting with a pop of sparks.

The marine shuttles flew over the hull of the Chohish battleship before suddenly changing direction to enter the landing bays. As they entered, they encountered laser fire. It was not strong enough to get through the shields or armor, but the return fire from the shuttles burned through the suits worn by Chohish with ease. Bodies and weapons littered the floor before it became quiet.

The battleoids had decoupled and lined up facing the ramp even before the shuttle dropped the final feet to land with a bang. As soon as it hit, the ramp dropped violently without a sound in the airless environment. Rushing from the shuttles, battleoids took up security positions around the fighter craft that littered the area. Additional marines raced out to relieve the battleoids so the battleoids could check out the bay in its entirety.

It was not long before Zeke received the all-clear signal. Pausing to look at Omaw through his faceplate, he wished him luck before leading the rest of his group outside. Shon and Michale were waiting for him and Jeanne as soon as they stepped off. Then, as they stepped away, five Irracan marines joined them.

Moving out, the group gained in numbers from the other shuttles. Once everyone was safely away from the shuttles, the shuttles lifted off and exited the bay. Flying to the rear of the battleship, a dozen shuttles laded in a circle near the engines. Leaving the shuttles first, Kolqux came out carrying the large, heavy armor worn by Chohish, along with weapons strapped to their backs. The Kolqux, with the Chohish following, circled around a small hatch before one of the Kolqux took out a small device which he plugged into a port. To the amazement of the Chohish, the hatch opened. Several Kolqux, not carrying Chohish armor, carefully entered the hatch, and the rest followed.

Meanwhile, Zeke, surrounded by marines and battleoids, reached the main entrance. At his signal, four of the battleoids fired the missiles on their backs toward the locked massive hatch while firing their plasma rifles to hit at the same time as the missiles. The hatch blew off its hinges backward, destroying everything behind it. The four battleoids, having not stopped firing their plasma rifles, were joined by others. Fire and destruction rained down the hall as far as you could see. After twenty seconds, they stopped. Other battleoids fired their missiles that raced down the destroyed hall before soaring down the two hallways. A massive explosion rolled up from each.

Extreme heat, smoke, and floating debris hid Zeke from seeing and entering the passageway straightaway. Signaling to Khaleesi, he had the battleoids lead the way, who laid down a stream of plasma fire as they went. What awaited them was death and destruction en mass. Walking over fragments of bodies, Zeke watched as several battleoids reached the juncture ahead. Flying surveillance flew out from their shoulders to fly down the halls.

What was relayed back to him was more death and destruction. The Chohish had placed heavy weapons with dozens of soldiers to bar their way. When he reached the site, he stopped to examine one of the weapons and realized it must have been positioned here long before this battle. He recognized it as a weapon that did not belong on a warship.

Following Khaleesi's battleoid down one hall, Jeanne followed him while another battleoid led more marines down the other. Ahead of Khaleesi, marines were setting demolition charges on the hatch at the end of the hall. Within seconds, it was blasted open. The hallway beyond was too small for battleoids, so Khaleesi surrendered hers to another marine. Additional surveillance drones were deployed.

They had only progressed a short distance when a Chohish popped a weapon out of a storage room, firing non-stop. Zeke plastered himself against the wall as Shon dropped to a knee in from of him, returning fire. Jan and the Irracan marines took off running, firing their plasma weapons. The laser fire from the Chohish abruptly ended, but not before he seriously injured a marine. Indicating another marine to stay with them, Khaleesi started forward once more.

Rising, Zeke and Jeanne cautiously made their way with Shon and Michale by their side. Jan and the four other Irracan marines leading. A hand signal from Khalessi indicated stop and drop. Again, more Chohish popped out of storage rooms. Zeke fired from a kneeling position. Blasts slammed all around until one clipped his arm. Screaming in pain, he dropped to a prone position before firing again. It took a moment or two before the Chohish were eliminated. Seven Chohish lay dead, with one marine dead and two injured.

It was Jeanne applying a patch to his arm, covering the slight air leak, that Zeke remembered he had been shot. He had been so focused on firing his rifle that he had pushed the pain out of his mind. Thankfully it was not serious. But they had no time to stop. The longer they delayed, the more the Chohish would prepare. So, they needed to get to the bridge quickly.

Signaling a group of her marines to join her, Khaleesi had a short private conversation with them. Once completed, they took off running down the hall. The motor assistance of the armor made their mad dash almost seem like they were flying. As they ran, they threw grenades into storage rooms as they passed.

Barroom sssshblamm, barroom sssshblamm, barroom sssshblamm, barroom sssshblamm, barroom sssshblamm, rang out as they ran. If there were any Chohish in the rooms, it would remain unknown. Nothing could survive in a small space when one of those grenades went off. The sound warned Chohish further down the hall, who made an exit. They were quickly picked off by marines, whose only assignment was to look out for them. Their armor's AI notified them once any movement was detected by the surveillance drones. Marines swapped out as they ran out of grenades.

As they neared the closed hatch at the end of the hall, a marine following the running marines yelled, "*Down*" before launching a missile. Whomp sounded as the rocket raced to the hatch, which exploded inward with a loud *boom*.

Several marines climbed over the hatch wreckage and slipped through the smoke into the adjacent hallway. They then provided cover as the rest moved through the debris. Shortly all were in the new hallway.

As Khaleesi had her marines use the same tactic, a running Jeanne asked Zeke if he noticed no Chohish were present in this hallway. She had expected they would have met more Chohish than they had.

"They had others to concern them. Meon did not think we were the major incursion," Zeke chuckled.

His reply was puzzling until she thought it over. "Omaw! Meon would have been alerted to the service hatch access and sent forces there. Scanners would have shown him Chohish soldiers heading through the service passageways. In his mind, that had to be the greatest threat."

The nod from Zeke was all the response she got as she ran. "Does Omaw know what you did?"

"No. Omar and his soldiers needed to fight like it was. Looks like it worked."

They slowed down as they reached another hatch. Again, the same process was followed. This was followed several more times before they came upon more Chohish. These were stationed outside the bridge hatch behind barricades that glowed blue from shields. Heavy weapons were fired as soon as the marines became visible.

An Irracan marine was blown backward, screaming in pain. "Jan!" yelled both Jeanne and Khaleesi. The other Irracan marines dragged Jan back behind a corner. The damage to Jan's armor was severe, but the damage to his body was worse. An opening in his chest leaked blood, his leg was bent the wrong way, an arm was broken in two places, breathing was ragged.

Tapping Jeanne on the arm, he motioned for her to stay with Jan. Walking up to Khaleesi, he pulled her back against the wall. "Go, check on Jan. His suit needs to be sealed. There is partial air loss already. I expect it to get worse." Then, seeing her look at Jan and about to argue, he patted her armored arm. "That is an order, Major. Shon will get us onto the bridge."

Without waiting for a reply, Zeke waved Shon over. "Congrats, Corporal, you're in charge. Get me on that damn bridge. Ok?"

Yelling to the Marines, Shon held a quick meeting while he had several keep watch. The group broke up when one of the two carrying backpacks followed Shon to the end of the hall. Then stepping back a few feet, he dropped the pack onto the ground. Bending, the marine scrounged around in the pack before pulling out a medium size metal ball. A sudden recognition hit Zeke; this was one of the sappers from way back when.

Looking at the position of the heavy weapons using the video feed, the sapper paused to pull a second ball out. Smiling at Shon, he windmilled his arm like a softball player and threw the metal against the hall wall. The ball made a loud metal smacking sound before rolling down the hall.

The Chohish saw the ball and started firing at it, exploding it in a massive explosion long before it reached the Chohish. Sections of the hall were destroyed, leaving holes in the walls. Smoke and flame billowed down the hall. Smiling, the Sapper threw the second one with a lot more force. The sound of the metal ball hitting the wall let the Chohish know another was on the way. But the heat and smoke made it almost impossible to target it until it was no longer necessary. The heavy weapons platform exploded dramatically, taking the Chohish with it.

The Marines did not wait for the debris to finish settling on the ground. Instead, they ran around the corner, where they finished off several Chohish soldiers recovering from the blast. No more Chohish were seen in the immediate area.

With an arm wave from Shon at the monumental closed hatch entrance to the bridge, the two sappers started pulling all kinds of gear out of their packs. They only took a short time to place all sorts of devices around the hatch. Running back, they had everyone hide behind a wall. When it went off, it was loud but directed. The hatch sat there teetering in smoke until the sappers tapped it after waiting for all the marines to gather. The massive metal door toppled inward with a crash.

As the door fell inward, marines threw in smoke and concussion grenades. Once the door was down, the marines edged in, returning fire from the Chohish inside. Shon had another marine stand guard with the three Irracans and Michale over the two Captains while he led the rest of the marines inside.

The sound of the battle lasted for over ten minutes before Shon contacted Zeke. "You can come in now, Captain. We have a prisoner that wants to meet you."

Stumbling as he climbed over the hatch door, he almost tripped on blood that looked to be everywhere. Bodies were everywhere. Not all were Chohish; some were in RGN armor. Standing in the center of the bridge was a Sovereign. "Hope you don't mind, Captain. We put some sonic cuffs on him. We found him hiding behind his chair."

"Well, well, what do we have here? Are you Meon?" Zeke asked the large angry Chohish.

"Human, if you know what is good for you, you will let me go before my fleet arrives," yelled Meon.

"You mean the remainder of your fleet? I am not sure any will make it here in one piece," answered Zeke as he stepped up in Mean's face.

340

Surprisingly Meon started laughing.

Something wasn't right. Why was Meon laughing? "Well, I am glad you find it funny that your fleet was destroyed."

Laughing louder in Zeke's face. Meon leaned in until their faces were just inches apart. "The fleet here? It was just a probe. The actual fleet is on the way. They will wipe your forces from this system and make these rebels pay for their foolish actions."

REUNION

AFTER HEARING MEON, Zeke had a horrible feeling he knew what Meon was bragging about. Another much more extensive fleet was on its way here. Without warning, Shon pushed Zeke to the ground and stood over him. Michale did the same to Jeanne. The rest of the marines took up positions around the bridge behind anything that gave them some cover.

Asking Shon what was going on. "Movement detected of a large group headed this way. Prepare for action."

A small surveillance drone flew in to fly around the room. Shortly afterward, a squawk sounded before a Kolqux helmet peeked in. "Captain Kinsley, is that you?"

Upon acknowledging it was, Uv'ei, with his brother, led a Chohish squad into the bridge. Omaw looked at Zeke through a gore-covered helmet. In fact, all their armored suits were covered in blood and body parts. "What the hell are you doing here? We had to fight through an army. So much for your *they will never know you are coming.*"

"You ended up being the distraction," Zeke said as he walked past Omaw. "But we do not have time to go over that. We need to get back to the ship ASAP! Another fleet is on the way. Meon said this was just a probe. Shon, get our men out of here. Notify Will that all enemy ships are to be destroyed once we are out of here."

Racing out, Zeke saw Jan had been removed. Not stopping, he ran as fast as he could pump his legs. Panic was close to setting in. "Will, can you read me?" he yelled.

Static filled his helmet. "Damn it, Will, answer me?" Still nothing. There was just too much interference.

The race through the battleship felt like hours, yet it was just minutes. Arriving in the landing bay, Zeke could see the shuttles had returned. He sighed in relief. "Will, can you read me?"

"Captain, Will here. Everything alright? You sound out of breath."

"No time Will. Get the ships ready to leave as soon as we arrive. Another enemy fleet is on the way, much larger than the last. Let the Admiral know. Zeke out." All Zeke heard before the connection broke was, "*crap, not again!*"

Waving and yelling at the Marines and Chohish, he ordered all to get into the shuttles and prepare for departure. Seeing Shon leading a couple of battleoids, he saw Meon being carried by one. Meon was screaming and yelling to be let down. Zeke was tempted to shut him up, but there were some things he could not do even though he really wanted to.

Even with everyone rushing, it still took over an hour before they could lift off. Most of the time was to gather the injured and bodies of the dead. Retracing Omaw's steps showed Zeke how much of a battle they had gone through. Battle damage was evident on almost every inch of the way. It took time to transport the wounded through narrow service tunnels. Especially when choked with the bodies of Chohish dead.

But finally, the last shuttles lifted off. Resting his head back on the hull, Zeke could feel the sweat trickle down his face and neck.

343

His body felt soaked even though the armor kept it cool. "Will, can you give me a status?"

"All ships, except ours, are already headed back. You are the last shuttles we are waiting on. Once docked, we are ready to leave," Will responded.

"Have we detected anything from the slipstream yet?" asked Zeke with hope. He was sure Will would have told if they had, but he still had to know for sure.

"Nothing yet. We will let you know if we do," reported Will over the sound of frantic activity in the background.

Zeke's shuttle was just entering the Lucky Strike when alarms sounded. "Captain, Will here. Chohish warships are starting to exit the slipstream. Dozens so far, but more are coming through."

"Don't wait for me, Will. Get this ship out of here. Notify Jax we need every ounce of power he can get out of the engines," ordered Zeke.

As soon as the shuttle landed, the ramp dropped with a bang. Medical staff and others swarmed in to get the injured and remove the dead. Working his way through them, Zeke saw Jeanne waiting for him near the landing bay exit.

Without stopping, both headed to the bridge. "How is Jan?" asked Zeke as they entered an elevator.

"Jan is in medical with Khaleesi now. It does not look good; he is in pretty bad shape."

"Do you need to go there?" Zeke asked as they exited the elevator in front of the bridge.

"No, Jan would want me to make sure I get our people home."

Entering the bridge, they saw Will in a serious conversation with Isolde and Selena. Joining them, they heard the end of the conversation. Hundreds of Chohish warships had transitioned, and more were on the way. While the vast majority had slowed down and were in the process of regrouping, a dozen destroyers were chasing the Lucky Strike flat out.

"They must be redlining their engines to be able to match our speed. I do not expect they will catch us, but they must want this Meon back pretty desperately to run their engines that hard," reported Isolde.

"Where is that bastard, by the way?" asked Will.

"Omaw is taking him to the brig. I had to remind him we may still need him. He was ready to pummel him for some past wrong. We had hoped to get him to convince his fleet to surrender when he saw they could not win, but now, not sure this new fleet will care. But we cannot worry about that now," replied Zeke. "Right now, we need to ditch our pursuers."

Looking at Will first, then Zeke, Jeanne snorted before asking, "And how do you propose we do that?"

"No idea. I was hoping you two would have an idea," Zeke responded. "I am too beat to think clearly. I don't suppose I could get some coffee?"

"Well, I actually may have something," interjected Isolde. Seeing everyone looking at her, she continued. "The Jackal returned the bombers with those particular engines. They are unsafe for humans, but how about we ram the destroyers with them. Missiles will have a hard time getting through but the ...."

"Bombers have much heavier armor. Great idea, young lady, you deserve a star," exclaimed Zeke. "Will, can you get Gunner to start on that? Oh, and Isolde, have we heard back from the Admiral?"

"Selena talked with him. He said he may have to withdraw our forces depending on how many Chohish are in this fleet. He lost quite a few ships, and many more were damaged."

"I am afraid it will be much larger than what we just fought. I think Meon, looking for personal glory, brought his group of ships

345

in before he was supposed to," said Zeke. "I am afraid the Admiral will have no other choice."

It took a bit to prep the bombers, fill them with explosives, and set the AI to ram. But finally, they were ready. They only had three they could use, but it was hoped if any got through, they would break off. The destroyers had reduced the distance between them, but nothing Zeke was overly concerned about.

Watching the bombers race away was bittersweet for Roy and Camille. They helped prep the bombers but regretted it was necessary. They had grave doubts they would be given more bombers with such a powerful engine again. And it worked as they hoped. One bomber flew into the front of a destroyer, where it embedded itself before exploding. The front end of the destroyer vanished in a flash of light and fire. The rest of the destroyers slowed down before turning around.

When the Chohish destroyers turned around, Omar, Uv'ei, and Uv'ek joined them on the bridge. Hearing the news that the RGN may have to leave, Omaw was crestfallen. "I cannot blame you. You have done more than we could ever repay. But it will be all in vain. This new fleet will kill me, my mother, and all the rebel leaders."

"We could take you all with us," Zeke said, although he already knew the answer. Surprised, he realized he was starting to be able to read the facial expressions of a Chohish. Seeing Jeanne fidgeting, he whispered in her ear to go check on Jan. He would catch up with her later.

And then it happened, the engines suddenly stopped, the ship lurched violently, and all lighting went to emergency lighting. The vessel started slowing down. "What the hell is going on?" Zeke asked as he went racing to get to his captain's chair. The chair may tell him what was failing. "Someone get a hold of Jax; I need an answer now."

"Captain, we are still getting data from the probes. Those four destroyers must have seen we are experiencing trouble. They are turning around, and several more are breaking away from the fleet heading in our direction," reported Isolde.

"Jax is on the line for you," yelled Selena.

"Isolde, get me a time estimate on the Chohish. Selena, send me Jax," said Zeke. "Jax, what the hell is going on?"

"The engines themselves are ok. It is a lendolium feeder issue. A controller module needs to be replaced. It is repairable, but it will take time," Jax reported. "Best estimate, an hour."

"Damn! What is available? We got a bunch of Chohish destroyers on their way. Give me something, Jax," begged Zeke.

"One sec, checking… OK, here is what I can do. We'll have to reroute the fuel line and use a maintenance bypass feeder. But it will only give you one engine. It will take twenty minutes to set up. Once we replace the module, we will reverse the flow. That is the best we can do, Captain," said Jax.

"Make it happen, and cut any corners you can, Jax; we are out here all alone. Captain out." Zeke turned to see everyone looking at him. "Someone mark down that module needs a redundancy. Who could be so stupid?"

"Chohish will be in their missile range in forty-seven minutes, Captain," reported Isolde.

"Get me, Gunner. Looks like the fighters and bombers have one more fight we need from them," ordered Zeke. "Will, calculate how much distance we can get on one engine using Jax's estimates and add that to Isolde's calculations."

"Gunner and Librada are on the way," reported Isolde. "The second group of Chohish will intercept us in just over an hour."

Seeing Omaw looking at him like he wanted to say something, Zeke asked what was on his mind. "Have you considered that they may attempt to board to retrieve Meon once they see your engines are compromised?"

347

Shocked, Zeke turned to the ever-present Shon and Michale, where he told them to notify Khaleesi to prepare for boarding. As he asked Selena to reach out to the Jackal and the Fox and see what help they could provide, the same for the Kolqux ships, he feared they would be too late. It took time to turn around a large warship when going so fast. They would not get here in time. This was confirmed by LS1 after hearing what he had asked Selena. They would be eight minutes too late, even with the additional time one engine would give them.

When Gunner and Librada arrived, they grouped around the command chair to discuss what options were open to them. Unfortunately, there were not many.

The marines and army would do what was necessary to prevent boarders with assistance from Omaw and his Chohish soldiers. However, they did not even know if that was going to happen.

Sending out the fighters and bombers to intercept had been decided against until the enemy arrived so the cruiser could support them. Dropping missiles and firing them off as the destroyers neared was deemed not worth the effort.

So they did what they could. Pass out armor and weapons to all. Station fire and suppression repair engineers around the ship. Ensure every fighter and bomber is ready for deployment.

The cutover to one engine happened without incident in the timeframe Jax had expressed. Everyone was grateful when the lights came off emergency lighting.

And finally, after all that was done, wait.

Sitting in the command chair with armor on, a plasma pistol in a holster, and a rifle readily available nearby felt weird. Zeke rested his left hand on the helmet sitting in his lap as he looked around the bridge at similarly clad individuals.

Then it started, the sound and ship movement of missiles firing.

"Helmsman, keep us steady. Fice control, target one destroyer only. Aim for their engines when available. No need to obliterate it. Just immobilize it. Let's keep our fire concentrated. Scanners, how many do we have?"

"Captain, there are four enemy destroyers just a few clicks away. We will be in their missile range within 90 seconds. The rest are seventeen minutes behind them."

"Heard and understood. Helmsman, in sixty seconds, executes a constant ship roll. Will, you and Hawke do your thing with the secondary lasers and missiles. LS1, you have the primary. Again, the primary target is their engines. We must knock these ships out of commission before the others arrive." Zeke checked the screen for how far away the destroyers were and decided it was time. "Order all fighters and bombers to launch before our shields cannot protect them."

"Fighters deploying, Captain, bombers in the queue."

With a loud whump, the sudden warship's downward shift let them know they were now in enemy missile range.

"Redirect all available power to the shields and energy weapons. Our reduced speed is not doing us much good now. Continue the ship roll," ordered Zeke. "Brace for impact. I expect it to get rough when they are in energy range."

"*He is in his zone,*" thought Jeanne as the ship was buffeted by missiles. "*but I sure wish he would let me jump in my fighter. I am not doing any good here.*"

"Fighters away, Captain, bombers being placed in the rails."

"Damage reported, Captain, minor hull breach, no casualties, and no critical damage."

"Damage report noted. Will, can you manage without Hawke? If so, I just got a notification from Librada that another fighter is available. Hawke, take Jeanne as your wingman and get those damn destroyers off our tail before those others show up. Helman, see if you can keep the damaged section away from their energy weapons."

Both ran off the bridge as the ship rocked from missile concussions but not before Jeanne whooped joyfully. Zeke did hear Jeanne tell Hawke who would be the wingman. *"Be your wingman indeed, like that will happen!"*

"Our six remaining bombers have deployed. Captain, we have Chohish ship separations. Looks like more than a dozen shuttles heading for us. No fighters. They must have switched out their fighters for shuttles."

"This group of destroyers must have always been an attempt to rescue their Sovereign, Meon. Have the fighters and bombers concentrate on taking out the Destroyers. We must rely on our marines and army to handle any boarders. Notify Khaleesi," Zeke ordered.

Then it got serious. Energy weapons flared their shields constantly. With only one engine providing power, shields were being drained faster than usual. The only thing Zeke was grateful for at the moment was that no enemy cruisers or battleships were present. Their shields would have failed early on.

"One Chohish destroyer dropping back, engines taken out by the fighters," reported an excited Selena.

"Another destroyed by our missiles," reported Will.

The good news was overlayed with unease when the ship slowed down so suddenly that it felt like they had flown into a wall. Claxons sounded along with other alarms. Groans came from being thrust against their harnesses so hard.

"We have a significant hull breach on our port bow. Air is escaping. Engineers are on the way. Waiting on casualty report" reported Isolde through bloody lips. She had smashed her head against her console.

"Tighten that harness, Isolde," ordered Zeke.

"Harness clasp snapped, Sir, will move to a new workstation when able," acknowledged Isolde.

"Chohish boarders had entered through four different hull

sections. They are engaged with our forces," reported Will. "Khaleesi said she has it under control. And before you ask, she said to tell you to do your job. Let her do hers."

Hearing that, even as serious as things were, Zeke smiled. "*She would say that if it was just her against a dozen Chohish soldiers.*"

"A third destroyer has been knocked out of action," reported Selena. "The last one is dropping back. Bombers and fighters returning. Gunner reports they are going after the shuttles on our hull."

Smelling something burning, Zeke looked up where he saw white-gray smoke leaking from multiple vents in the ceiling. "That does not look good. Let's get someone up here to check it out."

"Do we have a casualty report yet?" asked Zeke.

"Not yet, but we have an update on the destroyers following us. The destroyers have joined and are picking up speed. I count seven total in their group. They should be in missile range any second," reported Isolde.

"But not before they are in ours. Firing missiles" reported Will. "Gunner reported the fighters and bombers are engaging the destroyers."

Listening to the missiles fire, Zeke noticed they took longer between firing cycles. But then he realized what must be happening. Power, it took energy needed by the shields to fire missiles.

"Multiple enemy missiles have been fired on us," informed Selena.

"Gunner, this is Zeke, have the fighters target the Chohish missiles. Our shields are less than a quarter of strength." He watched as the fighters changed direction.

But as good as he believed they were, the fighters could not take all of them out. Nor could the ECMs. They had no power available to take away from the shields for the defensive lasers. They watched as several missiles broke through. Then they felt it.

BAROOM BWOOM KABOOM sounded as missiles slammed into their already weakened shields. The cruiser went into a wild spin while the alarms sounded high-pitched. The smoke from the ceiling vents changed to black. The emergency lights came back on.

A deep quiet echoed through the room; they were sitting ducks.

Suddenly, massive warships appeared on their screens. Energy beams came roaring from these warships slamming into the Chohish destroyers. Several were destroyed in a burst of flames and debris. The rest turned their fire on the newcomers with little consequence. In minutes, all were floating hunks of junk.

Isolde said with surprise. "What the hell?"

Unbuckling his harness, Zeke stomped over to Isolde's workstation. But not before he grabbed his holster. Buckling it on as he looked over her shoulder, he replicated Isolde's words. "What the hell?"

Then a voice that explained everything sounded over the loudspeakers. "Captain Kinsley, Admiral Nguyet Smithson here. Can we be of assistance?"

"Admiral, I cannot say how glad we are to see you. We currently have invaders onboard and have taken severe damage. We could use all the help you can provide. But if you do not mind, where the hell did you come from?"

"Oh, come on, Captain, you should know that, Stealth Security Protocol. We had been hanging around to monitor the Chohish when we detected your ship in trouble. We got here as fast as we could. We were afraid to use missiles in case any of the destroyers were your Kolqux or Chohish friends. Once we saw them all firing on you, the rest, you know. We will send marines and engineers in support. Let me know if you require medical personnel. Meanwhile, we will put a tractor beam on you and get you headed back to the fleet. I will have one of my battlecruisers pick up the three life pods we are detecting. As far as the fighters and bombers, they will have to follow along until your power returns. We do not have enough space to house them all."

352

The ride back to the fleet took hours. They were proceeding independently when they arrived, as Jax had successfully replaced the module. The fighters and bombers were back on board. The Chohish boarders were successfully stopped. Most were killed, but Omaw had been able to get a good many to surrender.

Unfortunately, the cruiser had taken severe damage that would require a shipyard. Dozens had been killed, with many more injured.

As soon as they rejoined the fleet, Nkosana had them join a conference call with himself and Admiral Katinka Chadsey. When the video call started, it was not lost on either Admiral that both Captains were standing in Zeke's personal living quarters, still wearing dirty, blood-stained armor. Both had been helping out in the recovery aftermath of the battle and still wore their armor in case any enemy was still loose.

"Captains, our sincere condolences go out to your lost personnel. But we need to discuss the present situation that exists. The Chohish fleet has finished transitioning and is headed our way. Their numbers are staggering. Over fifteen hundred strong. We do not have the resources to defend this system," a saddened Katinka informed them. "A retreat will be necessary."

This was no surprise to Zeke or Jeanne, who had been monitoring the Chohish too. Acknowledging they did not see any other option either when the Admirals were interrupted by an excited messenger.

The look of surprise on both the Admiral's faces turned to smiles as they turned back the two Captains. "It looks like we will not have to retreat after all. The Soraths and Koqux have decided to rejoin our fleet, agreeing to our terms of allowing a surrender. And they brought another RGN fleet with them. So let's cancel this meeting until we have time to process all this."

The noise of celebration from the bridge met them when they walked in. Everyone, including Omaw, was smiling in relief.

353

Displayed on the main screens, blackened by soot, showed warship after warship transitioning into the system. They were joining the vast armada that had already completed the transition. Ships of all sizes met their gaze.

But to Zeke, the most impactful view he saw that day was Hawke and Omaw slapping each other on their backs in friendship. But, of course, Zeke did not know how long that would last.

Have you ever felt how hard a Chohish hits, even in fun? No? Neither did Hawke until then. At least Hawke could still stand after Omaw picked him up off the floor. Wobbly, but still upright, well, sorta anyway.

EPILOGUE

THE FINAL SURRENDER of the Chohish was anti-climactic. After the final tally, the combined fleet was three times the size of the Chohish. And one other fact may have assisted in their surrender.

While in stealth mode, Admiral Smithson's warships were able to get a close detailed view of the enemy fleet. Much better than their probes could. The enemy fleet wore heavy battle scars. Over half were deemed battle unworthy and, as one intelligence operative said, pieces of junk.

Details on what would happen to the Chohish were still being worked out. Had been for the last three months. But that was not a task for the military to do. That task was for the governments and diplomats of the allied forces.

Sitting in her private quarters with two guests, Admiral Chadsey sipped a rare port. Rear Admiral Nkosana Okeke and Major Bridgette Okeke were seated on the couch before her. Nkosana was also having a glass of port while Bridgette sipped red wine.

Holding his glass up to the light, Nkosana admired the precise brown Tawny Port. "Ah, you must give me a case of this port, Katinka, maybe two. I deserve it after the Chohish deal."

"Ha, you should be so lucky. That glass alone is worth a year of your salary." Katinka said as she swirled her own port in the glass. "My father sends me a few bottles when he can. This bottle is over three hundred years old. I save what he sends me for special occasions. I figure this is special."

After taking a sip with his left hand, Nkosana relaxed on the couch, leaning against his wife, who was caressing his other hand.

"Speaking of the Chohish, whatever happened to that Captain of yours, Katinka?" asked Bridgette.

"Well, you were right. I offered him an Admiralship, but he refused. He was going to resign so he and Jeanne could stay together. So, I made him another offer." She stopped to take another sip of her port, swirling it around in her mouth.

"Oh, come on, don't leave us hanging here. What did you offer him?" Bridgette asked.

"Stay on as a Captain, but with a special multiyear task," said Katinka, looking at them with a sly smile. They could tell she was enjoying this. "And he could bring whoever he wanted with him. The RGN would assign six ships to accompany him under his command."

Now it was Bridgette that caught everyone by surprise when she started laughing. "You didn't? Oh, you are one sneaky woman. You must have had that all arranged already to be able to offer it to him. You counted on his refusal."

"The RGN navy allowed you to assign six ships to a Captain for a multiyear assignment? Never heard of them being so generous," said an astonished Nkosana.

"The Navy did not allow her to assign six RGN ships, my dear," Bridgette said while smacking his shoulder. "Really, Katinka, I sometimes wonder how he can be so brilliant at war yet clueless other times."

"It is you that addles my brains, my love. I can only think of you when I am in your arms," said Nkosana.

356

"Oh please, before I barf up this excellent port. The RGN only assigned two warships. The Kolqux appointed two. The Irracans tasked one ship on loan from the planet Niflhel with the last one from Queen Ktissi," informed Katinka. "You should be familiar with the cast already."

Sitting up straight, Nkosana ran his hand through his hair. "Damn, how did you arrange that? Who did Queen Ktissi assign to go with Zeke? Oh wait, it had to be that Omaw, right?"

The nod from Katinka answered his question. "That task force is going to check on the freed planets. Some may be in desperate straits. The Soraths and the RGN will help where we can. It was agreed that sending the Chohish might not be the best idea at this time."

"What is the Captain doing now?" Bridgette asked.

"Planning his marriage. After hearing my offer, he proposed to Jeanne, who accepted as long as the wedding was done before starting her new adventure. We will be getting an invite for the six weddings."

Startled, Nkosana looked at his wife to see if she knew why. "What? Six? What the hell? Why Six?"

The laughter from Bridgette let him know she did. "You have no idea how hard it was not telling you. Katinka insisted I wait so she could see your face when you found out. It was worth it."

"And it is an order you attend all six. And the order did not come from me. It came from higher up," said Katinka. "You should be able to guess what six world locations."

"Damn, as long as you bring that port wine, it won't be all bad. What about the marine Major? Is she going to be reassigned? I would take her in a second." Then seeing the smiles on the two women, he put his head in his hands. "Now what?"

"Major Richards is getting married too, believe it or not? I think you know Sergeant de Bouff, true?" asked Katinka.

357

"Jan, yes, he is a good man. I like him. He was close with Jeanne and her family, so I assume they will be doing a double wedding between Zeke and Jeanne."

"Yes, the Kolqux are planning a month-long wedding celebration for her. They think of her as a hero saving their world."

"You know, I'm still in the dark on why the Sorath and Kolqux changed their mind? Do you know?" asked Nkosana.

Bridgette spoke up when the question was asked. "I can answer that one. Zeke sent the video of the Chohish carrying the injured Kolqux soldier to Hawke's uncle, along with the video of when they were loading the shuttles. Admiral Timeti said it opened his eyes. He said, '*Maybe it was time to move on from the past. Never forget, keep your guard up, but time to let the hate go.*'" She paused here to laugh for a minute. "And as a warning, be careful when dealing with Uv'ei, he may not look like it, but he is clever as all hell. He sent a one-sentence message to the Kolqux ruling council. '*If Major Khaleesi Richards dies because of your lack of support, I will inform our people.*' The council knew the Kolqux people would have strung them up."

Suddenly, Bridgette stopped. Sitting up straight and putting her elbows on her knees and her chin in the palms of her hands, she stared at Katinka. "In my research, I came up with some interesting facts. We knew you thought highly of Captain Kinsley. But my research says that was long before he had any real experience. Care to explain?"

Tipping her glass to Bridgette, she smiled before she answered. "How many cadets volunteer to bunk with a Sorath? I can tell you because I checked. *Zero.*"

Shrugging, she continued after looking at her wine. "Zeke was supposed to be rooming with another human. But Zeke had a relative make a change for their room and class assignments. An attendant brought it to my attention because he thought someone did it against the rules. I said to let it go. Curious, I monitored him to see how that pairing worked; it went much better than I expected. They were inseparable. We could build on that in the RGN and Sorath's future relationship since they have been on the media everywhere. And I helped where possible because I saw something rare that the RGN needed."

Standing, Katina raised her glass, and Bridgette and Nkosana stood alongside her raising their own glasses for a toast.

"To Zeke Kinsley, a true Navy Captain."

Dear Reader:

I hope you enjoyed the book. I am an independent author and publisher who relies on reviews for promotion and feedback.

I ask that you leave a review so I may know what you liked and did not like.

Any recommendations on how to improve my style would be greatly appreciated.

Thank You,
G. J. Moses

Made in the USA
Las Vegas, NV
27 November 2024

12766425R00215